THE ADVE  FUTURE

BOOK ONE

MASTERMIND'S MUTANTS

A

DAVID MICHAELS

NOVEL

Super Powers Unlimited
Burbank, CA

THE ADVENTURES OF CAPTAIN FUTURE #1:
MASTERMIND'S MUTANTS

Copyright © 2012 David Michaels

All rights reserved. Except for use in any review, the reproduction or utilization of this work in whole or in part in any form by any electronic, mechanical, or other means, known or hereafter invented, including xerography, photocopying, and recording, unauthorized digital downloading, uploading, or sharing, or in any other type of information storage or retrieval system, is forbidden without the written permission of the author. Thank you for *not* pirating this book. You're a true hero.

Sale of this book without a front cover may be unauthorized. If this book is coverless, it may have been reported to the publisher as "unsold or destroyed" and neither the author nor the publisher may have received payment for it.

This book is a work of fiction. Names, characters, places, and incidents are either the product of the author's imagination or are used fictitiously, and any resemblance to actual living or dead persons, businesses, religious institutions, government agencies, associations, any other groups or organizations of any kind, including any events (past, present, or future), and/or any cities, states, providences, countries, planets, galaxies, parallel universes, supernatural realms, or other locations are entirely coincidental and fictitious. *whew* In other words, *everything* in this book totally made up and/or used fictitiously. Got it? Great!

Thanks for reading! You're awesome!

Published in the United States by Super Powers Unlimited, a trademark and imprint of David Michaels Productions.

Paperback ISBN: 978-0-61-576053-7
eBook ISBN: 978-1-62590-552-9

For additional books, character bios, and more information, go to:

http://www.superpowersunlimited.com

Acknowledgements

Special thanks goes to Staci Dodge, Mario Velez, Terra Rose Ganem, Jett Batoon, and the many people who supported and encouraged me – and nagged me to hurry up and finish so they could read the next chapter – as I wrote this book. Especially Staci Dodge, who was without a doubt the biggest cheerleader and believer in this book, all the way from the beginning.

To my editors, already named above, thank you for catching all the typos and clearing up any confusing lines. A book this size is definitely a team effort. And thank you Laurence Walsh, for encouraging me to not hold back and really express my authentic voice, and Peg O'Keef, for teaching me about story structures, moral premises, and subjunctive verbs, all the while keeping the creative process fun, challenging, and inspired.

I'd also like to thank the many talented writers and creators of some of my favorite movies and TV shows – many of the same ones mentioned in this book – for being a source of inspiration, creativity, and memorable entertainment. It is my hope to hold a candle up to your great works, and add even more inspiration, creativity, and memorable entertainment for future generations to enjoy in the science-fiction, fantasy, and superhero genres.

Lastly, I thank you, dear reader, for purchasing this book and taking a journey through time and space with me. There's mutants, time travel, aliens, super powers, portals to other worlds, and a whole lot more ahead. And this book is just the beginning.

Thanks for being a part of it. I love connecting with fans and hearing about your favorite characters and scenes. You guys (and gals) rock! You inspire me to push my writing and creativity to an even higher level.

TABLE OF CONTENTS
Mastermind's Mutants

Chapter 1

THIS IS WHAT MAKES TIME TRAVEL POSSIBLE

It was Saturday, October 26, 1985.

Around 1:19 AM. At the Twin Pines Mall parking lot. In a little town called Hill Valley, California.

A crazy old man with eccentric Einstein-like hair held the steering controls for a radio-controlled car. A teenager, wearing a 1980s-style orange life vest and jean jacket, videotaped the whole thing.

"Watch this," said the old man. The teenager pointed the camera at the old man. "Not me! The car! The car!"

A silver DeLorean skidded into place. "If my calculations are correct," said the old man, "when this baby hits eighty-eight miles per hour... you're gonna see some serious shit!"

Luke Powers, a handsome-but-nerdy 26-year-old, sat on the edge of his couch, cramming a fist full of popcorn into his mouth. Beside him was a video projector. Connected to that video projector, a DVD player. And in that DVD player, one of the greatest movies of all time: *Back to the Future.*

If you're going to watch a big movie, you gotta see it on the big screen. Or at least, in Luke's case, projected up onto his living room wall.

The DeLorean exploded in a flash of light, leaving a trail of fire tracks in its wake. The "OUTATIME" license plate spun and fell onto the pavement.

"What did I tell you?!" screamed the old man, larger than life, filling in the entire wall. "Eighty-eight miles per hour!!!"

"Jesus Christ, Doc," said the teenager in the orange vest. "You disintegrated Einstein!"

Luke smiled. He loved this movie. One of his favorites. No, *the* favorite. There was something about this movie. Something that made it rise above all the rest. Better than any of the *Star Wars* or *Star Trek* movies. Better than *Harry Potter* or *Lord of the Rings*. Even better than Disney/Pixar's *The Incredibles.*

This was a movie about time travel.

And Luke *loved* the idea of being able to travel through time.

But who wouldn't? With time travel, you could go back and change a major regret. You could find out tomorrow's winning lottery numbers. Make a few choice stock picks. See your parents or grandparents when they were your age. Maybe even meet a historical figure or two.

Sure, sure. All that was cool. But for Luke, it was something else.

You could say, at heart, Luke was an explorer. And time travel was about "exploring" the world—the universe—in a whole new way. He loved shows like *Star Trek* and *Stargate SG-1*. Those were about exploring space and other worlds. He played his fair share of *Lara Croft: Tomb Raider*, and not just because she had big boobs. There was an adventurer living in his heart. And he longed to be one.

Unfortunately, the real world had other priorities. He had rent to pay. Credit card bills. Student loans to pay off. Sure, of course he'd rather be off on some adventure exploring through time and space – but he also needed to eat.

He had a roommate. Ray Cartwright. An African-American, business-oriented, charming, self-confident, best friend kind of guy. Luke met Ray in college in an intro-level psychology class. Luke was an art major; Ray was in finance. The only reason either of them took the psych class was because it fulfilled some general education requirement and it seemed like it'd be an easy "A". They met, hit it off, and became best friends ever since.

Now they were roommates. Ray was still in school, finishing up his MBA. Actually going somewhere with his life. Luke, on the other hand, felt like his life was somehow stuck on "pause." Everything just seemed to be perpetually on hold.

Always waiting. Always looking toward "someday" when things got better. Always hoping that somehow, magically, something would pull him out of this dull, mediocre, financially-struggling life – and help him find his real purpose, his higher calling, what he was really meant to do with his life.

In the meantime, he worked at a retail store part-time. It barely covered the bills. Just barely. If he didn't go out to eat much. Stayed home to watch a movie rather than spend $12 on a ticket at the local theater. Try not to drive his car too far or too often, to try to save money on ever-increasing gas prices.

He was definitely treading water. Always just barely getting by. Eking out a humble existence. Never making enough to break free – and experience more of what he knew, deep in his soul, life had to offer.

Maybe that's why he liked his movies and comic books so much. They were a chance to escape, a chance to go *somewhere*, do *something* meaningful, even though he never actually went anywhere, and only vicariously enjoyed the great heroics of the characters he so loved.

Luke watched the movie play on the wall, projected in front of him. How he wished he could live an adventure like Marty or Doc Brown. If only time travel were possible. If only ordinary people like him went on real-life adventures. His job sucked. He hadn't been on a date – never mind had sex – in what felt like forever.

And well, besides all that, something else was bothering him. Something he couldn't deal with. A great loss that he'd just rather not think about right now.

If he could be a super hero or time traveler, he would. No question. In a heartbeat. But this was real life. He lived in Burbank, not Hill Valley. He drove an old Camry, not a Delorean. And it was 2011, not 1985.

Come to think of it, it was almost 30 years later since that movie was made. In the sequel, Marty traveled to the year 2015. There were flying cars and hoverboards. 3-D movies and voice-activated house lights.

Some of the movie's predictions came true. 3-D movies were becoming more and more popular. But that could just be because studios were trying to give people a reason to go see movies in the theater, and not illegally download it onto their computers. Somehow the writer of *Back to the Future* failed to predict Internet piracy, cell phones, and reality TV shows.

But how could he? No one could've imagined that just a few decades later, *everyone* would have cell phones – to check their e-mail, update their status on Facebook, and play *Angry Birds* while they were at work.

If only he could time travel for real. But that would never happen. It was just a fantasy.

So he had to live his dream vicariously. Watching life-size movies projected onto his living room wall. Reading comic books. Imagining up his own stories and adventures. He wasn't much of a writer. He tried. It was kinda fun.

But his real talent was in drawing. When he was about five years old, he discovered a love and talent for it. He's been doodling, drawing, sketching, and illustrating ever since.

And what did he love drawing most? Super heroes, of course. Monsters and aliens. Killer attack robots and cyborgs. Magical creatures and fantasy dragons. Aside from being a time traveler and deep space explorer, his other – and more realistic – dream was to be a comic book artist.

But that dream had to be put on hold too. Artists were a dime a dozen. Comic books weren't as big as they used to be. Less jobs, lower pay, more competition. He made a point to attend every comic book convention within an eight-hour drive, and he always brought sample work to show exhibitors and publishers. His art was good. Just not quite good enough.

Now he worked in an independent bookstore, some local mom-and-pop shop that always seemed to be on the verge of going out of business. The owners were nice people. A husband and wife team that *loved* books – all books. They loved how books could magically transport them any where, any time, and introduce them to all kinds of memorable characters and interesting creatures. But, being a smaller store with a limited budget, it was tough to compete with the larger chain stores.

Still, they managed to stave off bankruptcy for one more month, every month so far – and although it didn't pay much, at least Luke had a job.

Yup. His life was going nowhere. Not out of apathy or laziness. He was trying. It's just that no matter what he did, he could never seem to get ahead.

He submitted resumes to better-paying jobs. Showed his artwork to publishers. Even tried self-publishing. But the more he tried to change his life, the more things stayed the same.

But little did he know that everything was about to change. While he sat alone in his apartment, watching some movie, dreaming of another life – events had already been set in motion that would forever change not only his life, but the lives of countless others.

It was a secret that had been withheld from him for too long. But soon – he'd know more than he ever dreamed he would.

"This is what makes time travel possible," continued the movie. "The flux capacitor."

Whatever that was. Technically, time travel *was* in fact possible – Luke was sort of an amateur hobby time travel theorist. There were ways to actually travel through time. If you had a fast enough space ship, you could travel near the speed of light, slowing down your own time, effectively sending you into the future. Circling really fast around a black hole (without getting sucked in, of course) was another option. You could also "somehow", in theory, create a stable wormhole that took you to another point in time and space. And a handful of other remote possibilities. But out of all the theories Luke had learned about, none of them were technologically possible. At least not yet.

Maybe, someday in the distant future, the technology would exist. And people could travel through time. And maybe, somehow, one of them would go back in time to Luke's present, and – for some reason – give him access to that time machine.

Yeah. Maybe. He wished. He dreamed.

He was always dreaming…

Then there was a knock at the door.

He looked over.

Who could that be?

Chapter 2
THE AUDITION

Burbank, if you're not familiar, is part of the greater Los Angeles area. There's a lot of movie studios there, big and small. So while Luke was at home watching his all-time favorite movie, his roommate Ray was just a few miles down the street, auditioning people for a new upcoming film.

The room was full of anxious, hopeful, aspiring actors and actresses, all waiting to be called, waiting for their chance, waiting for that big break that might someday come. Most had headshots and demo reels in hand. No one talked to each other. They were all nervous. But it was more than that. They were each other's competition.

They were all young adults, around ages 20 to 25. They were all good-looking. And at least half of them were cute blonde girls. And perhaps of those, one or two were actually natural blondes.

One of those natural blondes was a girl with a friendly face named Dawn Stein. Yep, she's Jewish, just like half the actors in this town. But she wasn't like most wannabe actress blondes in Hollywood. She was more of the girl-next-door type.

She had her own beauty that shined from the inside out. She was pretty, yes, and cute in her own way. But gentle, too. Sincere, honest, down to Earth, friendly, approachable. She seemed to have a fair degree of self-confidence. Maybe because she wasn't caught up in all this Hollywood stuff. She acted because she loved it – not for the fame or money.

She'd been involved in community theatre since she was fourteen. And appeared in a couple local commercials in recent years. And now, today, was auditioning for a "big" movie.

Well, "big" was a bit of an exaggeration. The vision was big. The story was big. The budget and crew size – very small. In fact, it wasn't even a feature-length movie. It was a 20-minute short. If they were lucky, it'd get into some film festivals. So, needless to say, it was an unpaid acting opportunity.

But Dawn didn't care. Acting was a magical experience for her. She loved the idea of being a different character, a different person, every time. The right costume, a bit of makeup, and some special effects – and she could be anybody, or anything, on camera. And ever since she was a little girl, she loved going on adventures. She'd often go camping with her dad. She went on a cross-country road trip with her best friend after their freshman year in college. Had plans to backpack across Europe when she had a little more money saved up.

Life was meant to be lived, she felt. Unfortunately, real life only had so many adventures available. That was another thing she loved about acting. She could go anywhere – fantastic journeys, other worlds, mysterious places – vicariously, yes, but it was better than nothing.

Suddenly a young college kid popped his head out the door. "Next," he said, somewhat nasally.

That meant her. It was Dawn's turn.

She gathered her headshot and resume. And just as she stood up, the previous actress left the audition room. Some Beverly Hills type girl, fake hair, fake boobs, overpriced outfit, high heels. The snotty girl gave Dawn a look of disgust as she passed by. "Good luck," she said, but she didn't mean it.

Whatever. Dawn wasn't going to let this bother her. Of course, she happened to glance back at everyone else still in the waiting room. At least a dozen other five-foot-something blondes just like her. Dawn sighed. This was not very promising. But she took a deep breath, prepared herself to give her best audition possible, and put a cheerful smile on her face as she entered the next room.

There were three guys in there: the nasal-sounding college kid that called her in, who probably still lived with his parents; the director – a slightly older, but still college-aged dude wearing an artsy hat; and Ray, Luke's roommate, sitting beside the director. Ray had some kind of official-looking schedule or budget in front of him. They were all guys in their early-to-mid-20s.

This was, in fact, a student film.

The director was in UCLA's film program, so that gave this project a little more credibility and professionalism than, say, some random guy on Craigslist. Of course Dawn dreamed of being a movie star on a *real* movie – something big budget, something with distribution, something that her cousin in Iowa would see. But those auditions were hard to come by, and even though she had managed to get in a few, no one had called her back yet.

"State your name and look into the camera, please," said the director.

They were recording.

"Hi, I'm Dawn Stein," she said, "and I'm auditioning for the part of Power Girl." She then listed her contact info and tried to smile all happy and pretty.

"Thank you," said the director.

The nasal kid handed her a script.

"Take it from the top of page two, please," said the director.

Ray leaned back in his chair and watched her.

Dawn held her script, got into character, and began reading.

"You won't get away with this, Doctor Destruction!" she said. "As soon as my powers recharge, I'll summon the archangel Michael and he'll send you back to the alternate dimension where you came from! Evil never wins."

Wow. Who wrote this? She didn't get a chance to see the script ahead of time. She just saw the open call for auditions posted on Facebook. It was a super hero movie. That's pretty much all she knew. It sounded like fun. But… wow.

The director read Doctor Destruction's lines. "Ha. Ha. Ha. You are too late, Power Girl. All I have to do is push this button and the Ragnarok bomb will explode, destroying planet Earth and turning it into a zillion pieces of astro dust!"

Dawn tried not to laugh at how bad this dialog was. She was auditioning, live, and on camera. She played along.

"But wait, aren't you forgetting something?" she read.

"And what is that?"

"My powers have already recharged. Archangel Michael, attack!!!"

"No, no! Stay away! Ahh, the light, it burns!!!"

Oh God. What *was* this movie?

"Ha-ha! See, Doctor Destruction, I *told* you evil never wins! Victory goes to my Lord and Savior Jesus Christ! Hooray!"

She somehow delivered that line with energy and enthusiasm.

"Thank you," said the director.

What had she gotten herself into?

"And now," said the director, "could you please read Power Girl's lines on page five?"

"Okay," she said. She flipped to that page. It was some kind of interior bedroom scene. The opening action line was "Power Girl moans loudly." Okay…

She tried moaning loudly, like she was in pain.

"No, no," said the director. "This is a *love* scene."

"Oh," she said. "Okay." She moaned again, this time a little more… erotic? It still sounded a little painful, but it was better.

The director decided to move on and continue with the scene.

Dawn read her first line. "Jack, you're so strong and handsome. I can't believe you're inside me right—" She stopped.

"There a problem?" asked the director.

"I'm sorry. No. Let me try that again." She moaned. "Oh Jack, you're *so* strong and handsome... I *can't believe* you're inside me right now. And with my... telepathic powers... I can tell you're only thinking about me..."

The director read, "Oh Power Girl, you're the *only* girl for me. I've loved you since I first laid eyes on you..."

"Me too," said Dawn, reading her lines. "Me too..."

"Promise me, Power Girl, promise me you'll never leave."

God this was an awful story. But Dawn was committed. At least to finishing the audition. God, she hoped she didn't get this part. "Jack, I promise! I promise I'll never leave you! Not even Doctor Destruction and his army of minion zombie robots can keep us apart for long. We're soulmates!"

"Yes, yes we are!" read the director.

Ray couldn't help but chuckle. He knew how bad this script was. And considering their budget and level of experience, this film was only going to go from bad to worse. But he needed a "real world" project management experience for one of his MBA classes. And his friend was the director. The whole thing was supposed to be filmed and finished in a single weekend. So Ray signed on as the film's production manager.

He *could've* invested some of his own money into this, if he wanted. But he wasn't going to. He actually had some extra cash set aside for the right project, business idea, or investment opportunity. He was only 27, but he was already building himself a humble fortune. It's ironic. While Luke struggled financially, Ray was on a roll.

After getting his BA in Finance, he put off grad school for a few years to start his own company. Cartwright Consulting. It was a life coaching/business consulting type thing. Lasted a few years, made some money, but ultimately he decided it wasn't for him. He started a few other part-time companies here and there. Some made a little money; some didn't. But he learned something valuable from each experience.

And one of the things he learned was to <u>never</u> put his own money into something he didn't believe in. And this student film project was one such example. He actually tried passing on it at first, but his director friend begged him. Apparently no one else would sign on. And Ray *did* need the credit for his class. This assignment was a full third of his final grade.

So he just told his director friend that all his money was tied up in other investments right now. And that was partially true. He could've sold his stocks if he really wanted to. But his friend was just grateful to have him on board helping out on production.

Anyway, apparently Ray was the only person on the team who felt it was a bad script. The director and his assistant (the nasally kid) loved it. And the actresses – well, they all at least *acted* like they loved it. Except for Dawn.

She tried to like it. She gave an honest effort to make the dialog believable. She tried to put authentic emotion into it. But the more she read, the more her cheerful face turned to one of confusion, bewilderment, and palpable distaste.

Finally, an honest actress.

Sure, she looked like just about every other girl they'd seen all day. But an honest actress, he could work with. Of course, he also knew she'd never take the part, even if they did offer it to her.

"Thank you," said the director. "That'll be all. We'll call you if we're interested."

"Thanks for your… time," she said.

She handed back the script to them. And then politely, but swiftly, bolted for the door.

Ray wasn't about to lose his opportunity. He quickly got up. "Excuse me," he said to the others. He went after her.

In the other room, where countless others still waited to read the same bad lines, he stopped her. "Dawn, wait up."

She stopped and turned around. She was almost afraid to ask. "Yeah?"

He checked over his shoulder to make sure they couldn't hear him in the other room. "Listen," he said, lowering his voice. "Don't worry, I'm not going to ask you to be in this movie."

She smiled with a sigh of relief. They laughed about it.

"What are you doing tonight?" he asked her. "I'd like to take you out to dinner. If you're not busy."

"Oh," she said, surprised. "Really?"

"Just you and me. And I promise not to talk about this film."

She smiled. "Okay."

"Great! You like Chinese?"

"Love it."

"P.J. Wang's it is," he said. "I'll call you after I'm done here. Shouldn't be more than a couple hours."

She smiled. "I'm looking forward to it."

Awkward silence. All the other hopeful auditioners stared coldly at her.

"You, um, need my number or anything?" she asked Ray.

"I got it from the audition video."

"Right!" she said. "Okay then, I guess I'll go then. Talk to you later?"

"See you tonight," he said.

And with that, she turned and left. With a pleasantly surprised smile on her face. Ray watched her as she went out the door. He checked her out from behind, too, of course. He was a nice guy. But a guy nonetheless.

At least something good came out of this film.

And then the kid with the nasal problem popped his head out the audition room door and called, "Next."

Ray couldn't wait for tonight.

Chapter 3

ENTER THE VILLAIN

Not to be confused with Bank of America, the Bank of American Savings is one of this country's largest and wealthiest banks. In fact, it's so large and wealthy that ever since the 1950s, it's exclusively catered to the world's top 15% richest.

No ordinary citizen would use this bank. If your cash assets were less than a few hundred million, you didn't have the minimum requirement to open an account here. So, as you can imagine, the bank lobby was usually pretty empty. Occasionally a super rich business man, celebrity, politician, or royalty from another country would grace this bank's halls. Its expansive, marble-floored, high-vaulted, pillar-columned, echo-y and airy halls.

The kind of place where you'd expect a butler named Jeeves to anticipate your every need before you do. The kind of place where fresh organic gourmet coffee and delicious exotic fruits were always served complimentary. The kind of place where the tellers recognized every client's face and knew every client's name.

Which is odd, because today, an unfamiliar face entered this bank.

It was the end of the day. The bank would be closing in about fifteen minutes. Rush hour had already began. It was rare for a client to come in at this time. And this man – this unfamiliar, unknown man – strolled right in with confidence and purpose as if he lived there and owned the place.

He walked right up to the teller.

She didn't recognize him, but this could be a new client, so she greeted him cheerfully and pleasantly. "Good afternoon, sir. How may I serve you today?"

He smiled.

He was tall, dark, and handsome. Just over six feet tall. Suited up in the sharpest business suit. Perfectly tied tie. Spotless, shiny shoes. Neatly groomed, clean shaven. And a confidence, a presence, about him that only the super rich – or super clever – seemed to possess.

"Yes, I'd like to make a withdrawal today."

Bank employees were required to memorize important data about every client. There was a file for each and every account holder at that bank. Photo, name, date of birth, spouse and children names, favorite hobbies, favorite foods, favorite countries to visit, favorite flavor of coffee... All to provide "legendary" customer service. Another perk of being super rich.

But this teller had *never* seen this man before. Not in person. Not on file. Not anywhere, ever. So for him to make a request for a withdrawal was ... odd. She almost didn't know how to handle it. But she was a trained professional.

"Certainly sir. I apologize, I must be having an off day. Would you please remind me of your name again, sir?"

"My name is not important," he said.

She looked him in the eyes.

And suddenly, she felt okay about that.

"No problem. I understand, sir. How much would you like to withdraw today?"

He thought about it. "Eh, let's say… A hundred… thousand."

"One hundred thousand dollars."

"In cash."

Exactly which account was she supposed to withdraw this money from? She was afraid to ask. She made eye contact. He seemed polite, gentlemanly, respectful – but quickly growing impatient.

"Now, please," he said, a little more sternly.

Right. It didn't matter *where* she got the money from. She just knew she needed to give it to him – fast.

"Right away, sir. I will need my manager to open the vault."

"Go ahead."

She left her station. The mysterious man leaned against the marble counter as he waited. He checked his nails. Looked up at the clock. Began whistling some old tune.

The teller returned with the manager – but not the money – a moment later.

"Good afternoon sir," said the manager. "I'll be happy to release your funds immediately. I just need your signature here, and your full legal name printed here…" He handed the mysterious man a standard bank withdrawal form. But it was also a discrete way to reveal the man's identity, so they could figure out which account to draw from.

The mysterious man sighed. He looked the manager right in the eyes and said, "You don't need my signature. Just hand over the money. Now."

The manager paused for a second, but only a second.

"Y-Yes sir. Gladly, right away, sir."

The teller and manager left – and returned a few minutes later with all the money in cash. The teller quickly counted the stacks of hundreds. Each bundle contained fifty one-hundred dollar bills. Each stack was $5,000. Twenty stacks equaled the $100,000 total.

The entire time, something deep inside her knew this was weird. But at the same time, she didn't care. It was almost as if she *wanted* to give this man, this total stranger, *whatever* he wanted.

The manager seemed to agree.

They pushed the bills across the counter. The mysterious man loaded them one by one into his own briefcase. After the last one, he closed the case, locked it up, looked at them, and smiled. "Thank you. You've been most compliant."

"A pleasure to serve," said the manager.

"Have a good evening, sir. Come again soon!"

"Perhaps," he said with a smile, walking out the door.

And he was gone.

The manager stopped for a second, reflecting on what just happened.

"Who was that man?" he asked.

The teller was at a loss. "I have no idea, sir."

Confusion set on his middle-aged face. "Did we just give away all that money to a complete stranger?"

"I… I believe we did… sir."

A terrible sinking feeling came over them both. What just happened? *Why* did they just do that?

They remembered everything. They willfully, gladly, unquestioningly complied with everything he asked of them. Of their own free will. At least, it sure felt that way.

They needed to figure out who that man was. And quickly.

Both the teller and manager went into the back security office, where the video feeds from all the cameras were recorded. A security officer was on duty, watching the videos the entire time.

"Pull up camera three from five minutes ago," said the manager.

The security officer did so. The camera showed the teller, by herself, waiting at her station. The mysterious man never appeared in the video.

"Try going back farther."

They watched the video in reverse. Nothing. Except, around three minutes before the man allegedly entered, there was a brief "blip" in the video. A split second when everything went black, and then seemingly returned to normal.

"Wait a second," said the teller. "Go forward again." She watched herself closely. "Look at my hair!" she exclaimed. Her hair was pulled up. But today, right now, her hair was down. "My hair was like that *yesterday*," she said.

"Oh my God," said the manager. "Someone hacked our security feed and played back tape from yesterday."

"That's impossible!" said the security officer. "We're on a closed circuit."

"Then how do you explain that?" she said, pointing at herself on the screen.

"We both saw the man," said the manager. "He's not anywhere on this footage."

"I've been watching the whole time," said the security officer. "I didn't see anybody."

"Oh, so now you're telling me we saw a ghost?" exclaimed the girl.

"No, I just—"

"It's not important," sighed the manager. "Check the security cameras from out front."

The officer pulled up that footage. Same thing. A small blip at the exact moment the mysterious man would've entered.

"Damn."

This was not good.

"Should we…" she was almost afraid to ask. "Should we call the police?"

"And tell them what?" said the manager. "That we voluntarily handed over $100,000 to a total stranger – and the only proof he was ever here is that you let your hair down?"

"You gave him what?!" shouted the security officer. He nearly spilled his coffee. "Did he hold you at gun point? Was he wearing a bomb? How come you didn't trigger the alarm?"

"No," said the teller, shaking her head. "He just asked… politely."

The manager sighed, pulling back his thinning hair. How were they going to explain the missing money? They would both be arrested for grand theft. This all sounded exactly like an inside job. And they'd never be able to get the money back. It was rush hour. He was long gone. They'd never see him again. Even if they filed a police report and gave a description of the man, how were they going to explain why they just freely *handed* over all that money?

"We have a problem."

Several miles away, the mysterious tall, dark, and handsome man strolled into one of the more luxurious hotels in Burbank. He took a seat in the lobby. The briefcase with the $100,000 casually placed at his side.

He waited.

Another man entered. By far a less attractive, wild-haired, unkempt fellow. "Eccentric-looking" some might say. "Crazy homeless guy" others might say, if not for his lab coat and apparent purpose in this luxury hotel's lobby.

The crazy-eyed, wild-haired pseudo-scientist sat down across from the tall, dark, and handsome mysterious man.

They made eye contact. But the scientist didn't speak. He began moving and flashing his hands around, quickly signing different words. He spoke in sign language.

He signed a question. *"You have it?"*

The mysterious man interpreted the words. He nodded, and began signing back, while also quietly speaking just in case the scientist could read lips.

"I do," said the mysterious man. "Is the formula ready?"

"It's in a safe location," signed the unkempt man.

The mysterious man reached for his briefcase and pulled it closer. "No formula, no payment," he signed and said.

"No payment," rapidly signed the crazy, wild-eyed scientist, *"no formula."*

He looked the mad scientist in the eyes and sighed. Fine. He had no choice. He'd have to trust him. "Alright," he spoke and signed. "Where?"

The crazy scientist reached into his lab coat pocket and pulled out a small business card. The front of it read "Dr. Albert Troyd, Freelance Geneticist" with a TTY telephone number, e-mail address, and even a Facebook page. On the back was written an address, not far from here.

"Alright," said the mysterious man. He passed over the briefcase.

The crazy mad scientist smiled with glee. He opened the case and looked inside. He saw twenty stacks of hundred dollar bills. His eyes went wild with excitement. He even let out a small little mad scientist "muwahahah" kind of laugh.

The mysterious man stomped his foot on the floor a couple times to get the mad scientist's attention. "Hey," said the man, and he signed, *"What time?"*

"Eight o'clock. Bring the test subjects."

The mysterious man nodded. And a small grin came to his face. No problem.

The mad scientist locked the briefcase, signed goodbye, and got up to leave. But then he stopped himself. He signed, *"Don't forget about the message."*

The mysterious man sized him up. *"You're really confident it'll work this time?"*

The crazy scientist nodded yes.

The mysterious man sighed. "Fine," he said aloud, holding his hand out.

The scientist reached into his lab coat pocket and pulled out his cell phone. It was one of this special cell phones for deaf people – but it worked like most smart phones too. The mysterious man grabbed it, opened the video recorder app, and pointed the camera at himself.

He recorded himself saying, "You will grant this man access to anywhere and anyone." He stopped and saved the recording. He handed the phone back to the scientist.

"Don't use it until it's time," he signed.

The scientist nodded, looked down at the briefcase, and smiled. Then he headed out the exit.

Hmm. Eight o'clock. The mysterious man pushed back his jacket sleeve to check his Rolex. He had some time to kill. And some new test subjects to find, to make sure this formula batch actually worked.

At that very moment, a young couple entered the hotel. Judging by their luggage, they had just gotten off the plane. And noticing by how happy and playful they appeared together, their shiny new wedding rings, and the fact that they were still holding hands and smiling constantly made it easy to conclude that these two were newlyweds.

Probably, he figured, vacationing in Los Angeles to do the whole Hollywood tourist thing. But he couldn't imagine why. There were many places more romantic than here.

Over twelve million people crammed into 4800 square miles. Full of crazies, drug addicts, homeless bums, and sleazy car salesmen. Full of celebrities, politicians, executive producers, and people who slept their way to the top. Aspiring actors and writers. Musicians. Religious leaders. Real estate tycoons. Average Joe Schmoes who anonymously worked like cogs in a faceless machine. And everybody else in between.

All stuck in rush hour traffic.

And there were even the occasional "mad scientist" types willing to push the boundaries of science and ethics for the right price. And in a city like this, there were also the occasional special someones – like this mysterious man – who had a few secrets of their own.

As the newlywed couple walked past, he couldn't help but get a good look at the woman. She was quite attractive. Nice long legs, soft skin, tight ass, decent size breasts. He wanted her.

And he decided he was going to have her. Tonight.

"Excuse me," he said, standing up and gently grabbing her arm as they passed by. Both the husband and wife stopped. "I need to tell you something."

This, of course, caused them to make eye contact.

He grinned and looked directly into her eyes. "You're going to sleep with me tonight. And it will be the best sex of your life."

The husband was flabbergasted and outraged. But he tried to be polite. "Excuse me, sir. This is my *wife*."

He looked directly into the husband's eyes next. "And you're going to pay for the room, and wait here in the lobby the entire time. You can have her back after I'm done with her."

Both the husband and wife stood there speechless, dumbfounded, and… strangely, willing to comply.

The woman let go of her husband's hand. She immediately, and very sensuously, placed both her hands on the mysterious man's chest. The husband dropped his luggage, without another thought, and went straight to the check-in counter.

It was so nice of the husband to pay for the honeymoon suite. The woman laid on the bed, summoning the mysterious man with a turn of her finger and a sensual bite of her lower lip.

The man opened a bottle of Champagne. He was a man of class, after all. He poured them a couple glasses. They drank. Then he leaned in. And they kissed.

He took off her dress slowly. She quickly removed his pants. They kissed some more. She loved every moment of it. In the back of her mind, an inaudible voice questioned what she was doing. She was just married to the man of her dreams. Or so she thought. But for some inexplicable reason, she *really* wanted this new man. She *had* to have him. She wanted only him – and her desire for him only grew irresistibly stronger.

Of course, it didn't help that he kept looking her deep into her eyes and frequently telling her, quite specifically, just how desperately she wanted him. And that's exactly how she felt. It was like he was controlling her mind, controlling her thoughts and desires, controlling her very body. She was a slave to passion – a passion that only intensified every time he told her it would.

Whatever he wanted, he spoke, and she willingly, gladly, enthusiastically gave it to him.

After she gladly pleasured him in a variety of ways, he told her to stop and lay on her back. She did. Immediately. He told her to spread her legs. And she did. And he told her that she wanted nothing more in the world than to have him inside her – right now. And she bit her lower lip, yearning, waiting, squirming, longing for him.

He loved being in control of others. It was a rush. And it was a mind-fuck, too. Because right now, down in the lobby, her newlywed husband was waiting quietly, knowing full well what they were doing.

Maybe he should've told the husband to read a magazine or something. Nah. It was better this way.

The mysterious man fucked her. Normally, honestly, he wouldn't have been that good. But because he *told* her it was the best sex of her life, she screamed out with escalating orgasmic passion and her body trembled with it.

He finished inside her. He wasn't wearing any form of protection.

He didn't care.

And when she went to kiss him, he pushed her aside. He was done with her.

He got up to put his clothes back on.

"Wait," she said, pulling the sheets over her naked chest. "Where are you going?"

He pulled up his pants. Put on his shirt.

She crawled to the edge of the bed. "But… but…" She wanted more. That was *amazing*.

He put on his suit jacket and tightened his tie. Then he looked himself in the mirror, inspected everything, and felt he was flawless.

He went for the door.

"Wait…" she begged.

Their eyes suddenly locked. "Listen to me. You will not follow me. You will not speak to me ever again."

She opened her mouth to say something – but couldn't.

He began to turn the door handle, but stopped, and turned to face her and said, "And every time you fuck your husband, you'll always think of me."

Her mouth hung open. She stared blankly.

And he walked out of the room.

Chapter 4
THE VISITOR

By now you should know who the villain of this story is. Hopefully that's pretty obvious. But if you really don't know, put this book down immediately and seek professional help. Otherwise, continue reading.

So anyway, earlier that same day, back in his apartment, Luke was happily watching one of his favorite movies. *Back to the Future*. And then there was a knock on the door.

Who could that be?

Luke looked at the door. His boring, plain, white apartment door. Much like the rest of his apartment – boring, plain, and white. That is, except for a few movie posters and comic book pin-ups. Had a woman lived here, of course, the apartment would've been decorated with pretty things. Maybe a few house plants. Some nice art on the walls that didn't feature spandex-wearing fictional characters. And decent furniture too. But since two single guys lived here, and one of them was back in school and the other worked at a minimum wage part-time job, the apartment only had the bare essentials…

A used couch and old recliner chair they had bought from Good Will. A movie projector from Best Buy that Luke was still paying for on his credit card. The latest video game systems including the Nintendo Wii, which of course, had all the characters and bonuses tracks unlocked in *Mario Kart*. A bean bag chair in the corner. And a small home -style movie popcorn maker machine in the living room. You know, the bare essentials.

Unfortunately, Luke had lost the remotes for both the projector *and* the DVD player, so to pause the movie, he had to actually get up from the couch, walk half way across the room, and physically manually push a button on the DVD player.

Both remotes disappeared several months ago. He searched everywhere – under the couch, between the cushions, even in the kitchen cabinets (which were mostly empty to begin with) – and they were nowhere to be found.

Of course, he could've bought one of those universal remote controllers. But those things cost like $20, $40, or more – and do you know how many comic books he could buy with that kind of money?

Anyway, the movie paused right as Marty McFly was about to travel through time for the first time. Out of all three *Back to the Future* movies, Part 2 was his favorite. That's when Doc and Marty travel to the future. If Luke ever had his own time-traveling Delorean, he'd definitely want to go to the future first. Like the distant future. With starships and teleporters and stuff from *Star Trek*. The past was boring. Too "low tech" for his tastes.

He reached for the door handle and opened it.

Two young men, barely old enough to vote, greeted him with ridiculously large smiles. They wore matching monochromatic dress shirts, ties, slacks, and clean shoes. They had name tags on. One was named "Elder White". The other, believe it or not, was "Elder Young."

Really? Mormons?

"Hello!" said Elder Young. "We're from the Church of Jesus Christ of Latter Day Saints."

"Have you heard about the *complete* gospel of Jesus Christ?" enthusiastically asked the other one.

Luke scratched the back of his head. He glanced back at his movie, frozen in time on his wall. "I'm really not looking for a new religion…" he said.

"Oh, we're not trying to convert you," said Elder White. "We're just out spreading the Good News about the gospel of our Lord and Savior Jesus Christ."

"May we come in?" asked the first one.

"Um, well…" Luke looked toward his movie again. Sure, he had seen it about a million times already. But today he'd like to watch it a million and one times. Even if he didn't, even if he had, say, *chores* to do – he'd rather do that than listen to a couple of Mormons, well intentioned as they were, try to push their religion on him. But what could he say? What could he do? He was too nice to just slam the door on them. And he was too honest to make up some lie. He couldn't pretend to be on his way out the door either, because obviously, he was at home watching the best movie of all time.

They just stood there, flashing those pearly whites at him, patiently and eagerly waiting for him to let them in.

He sighed.

"Sure, come on in…"

How long could this take, anyway? Five minutes? He'd just let them say their spiel, thank them for their time, and before he knew it he'd be on an adventure again

– vicariously, of course.

Two hours later… and the Mormons were *still* talking. And by now, somehow, Luke had already accepted a free copy of the Book of Mormon, several pamphlets and flyers, and agreed to go to church with them Sunday morning.

The video projector started to overheat long ago, so that was turned off. At least Luke was a nice host. He brought both the missionaries some non-alcoholic, non-caffeinated, family-friendly drinks.

He smiled and nodded a lot, pretending to listen. Actually, he did like learning new things. And although he still had no interest in joining the Mormon church whatsoever, he did learn a few interesting things about their religion.

But whatever. Enough was enough. He was getting hungry. It was dinnertime. And he had to get up early for work tomorrow.

"Look, guys, can we continue this another time? It's getting kinda late…"

They hadn't realized how much time had passed. They were having so much fun. "Of course," they said. "Definitely." They got up, thanked him for his time, and reminded, "We'll be by at 8 AM to pick you up Sunday morning."

"Right…" He was going to have to remember to call to cancel later.

They headed for the door. But not before reminding him to say some prayer to confirm the validity of everything they had just taught him.

Luke nodded, smiled politely, and held the door for them. They *finally* left.

He closed the door and locked it.

At last. Time to eat. And then get back to his movie.

There was *another* knock at the door.

He stopped dead in his tracks. *Now* who could that be? Jehovah's Witnesses? He was afraid to answer.

He looked through the peephole. And a big smile came to his face.

He quickly unlocked the door and opened it.

"Uncle!"

Standing there was a tall, skinny, charming older man. He was a little older than Luke's father, so that put him in his early 60s. But you wouldn't know it by looking at him. Luke's uncle was a vibrant old man, full of youth and laughter. He had a twinkle in his eye and a big grin on his face. He wore a Hawaiian "aloha" shirt, pair of jeans, and New Balance sneakers. And he carried a small box labeled "fragile" under his arm.

"Hey!" said the man. "How's my *favorite* nephew?"

Luke laughed and rolled his eyes. "Uncle, I'm your *only* nephew."

The old man smiled. "It's still true. May I come in?" He peaked his head in the door. "You have a cute girl over or something?"

"No, no, please, come in!"

"I see nothing's changed since the last time I was here," he said walking in. "What'd you do with all that money I gave you for Christmas last year?"

"Amanda."

"Oh yes. I'm sorry. I forgot. Old age and all that. How's she doing?"

"We – she decided it was best we saw other people…"

"Oh. Sorry."

"It's alright. She was pretty high maintenance anyway."

His uncle relaxed onto the old recliner chair, making that loud "ahhhh" sound old men tend to make as they settle into a comfortable spot.

"Seeing anyone new?"

Luke shrugged. "Not really."

"You'll find someone," he said. "A handsome young man such as yourself."

"Thanks." Luke sat down on the couch next to him. "Things just haven't been the same since… you know."

His uncle nodded silently. He quickly changed the subject. "So, you ever gonna decorate this place?"

"What are you talking about?" Luke remarked. He looked at his *X-Men* and *Star Trek* movie posters on the wall. "The place is totally decorated."

"Uh huh. Here, I brought you something."

"Yeah?" Luke got excited. Every time his uncle came to visit, he always brought a special gift. His uncle was a world traveler. Well, archeologist and anthropologist, really. He got paid to travel the world, learn about other cultures, study ancient history, and then lecture about it all at different universities.

He was more or less retired now. Just did an occasional project or lecture now and then for fun. He spent most of his time out traveling, exploring, and adventuring around the world on his own dime and on his own time now.

Last year he went to India and Peru. The year before that, he did a month-long "walkabout" in the Australian Outback. Earlier this year he participated in some big research project at Oxford – and did a little sight-seeing around Europe while he was there. And then he went to somewhere in India or the Middle East or somewhere. Some country Luke had never heard of. Geography wasn't exactly Luke's best subject.

"What is it?" Luke asked. Uncle – or Charlie, to most people – always found something unique from the culture he had visited. Whatever his uncle brought him this time, it was sure to be exotic and special. "Is it something from Saskatchewan?"

His uncle laughed. "Skardu. In Pakistan. Nowhere even close to Saskatchewan."

"Right, that's what I meant."

"And yes, it's something I picked up in Skardu." He held the small plain box, a seemingly ordinary cardboard box marked "fragile", in his hands. He wanted to give it to Luke. But he wasn't sure he was ready.

"You know," said his uncle, "there's a lot of Tibetan Buddhist monks in Skardu. So many, in fact, that some people call it the 'Little Tibet' of Pakistan."

"That's… great." Luke couldn't wait to find out what it was. But his uncle was also a professor, and every time, Luke always had to hear the "story" behind it first. Uncle Charlie simply loved telling stories about the places he'd been, and how he came across this gift, and what made it so special and unique.

Luke learned to patiently wait. Let the old man tell his stories. And then finally he'd get the cool thing – whatever it was.

"Lots of mountains there," his uncle continued. "Great for hiking, climbing, all sorts of things. On one of my hikes, I met and befriended a most interesting monk. He was convinced we were brothers in a past life or something – I don't know about that – but we sure had a lot of great conversations. And then he mentioned something to me… Something interesting, something that when he told me about it, I thought right away about you, Luke."

"Oh yeah?"

The old man smiled and winked. "This," he said, holding the box. He paused to study Luke. Was he ready? Was it time? He took a slow breath and nodded.

He opened and reached inside the box. He pulled out a small pink crystal. A semi-transparent rock. The light entered it, and refracted somehow, creating a faint but beautiful iridescent glow.

"Wow," said Luke. "It's pretty."

"Apparently a traveler donated it to his monastery, several years ago, as a token of thanks for their kind service and hospitality toward him. At first they thought it was some kind of precious stone, nothing more. But then one day, one of the monks did this…"

Uncle Charlie took the stone, pointed tip down, and dragged it along the arm of the chair. Where the tip traced, it left a magical sparkling trail of pink light.

Luke's eyes widened with amazement.

"Whoa."

Several seconds later, the trail of light faded away. No trace, no remains, no markings of any kind were left behind.

"The monks called it a magic writing stone. I think it's got some kind of phosphorescent chemical in it, that probably temporarily activates whenever it's rubbed against another surface. I'm guessing."

Luke's mouth hung open.

"And I thought you, being the artist of the family, might really enjoy this." He smiled. "Want to try it?"

"Do I?" Luke grabbed it, held it up to his eyes, and then immediately began to "draw" with it. He pressed the tip of the crystal to every surface around him – the couch, his arm, the wall behind him. Wherever the tip of the rock touched, a momentary trail of pink light remained. Several seconds later, the glowing residue faded away, vanishing entirely. "This is *so* cool!"

As an aspiring artist, he had worked with a variety of tools and mediums – pencils, pens, markers, acrylics, oil paints, chalk, charcoal… But *none* of them behaved like this. It was almost a supernatural experience. Like writing with light.

"Buddhists aren't big on worldly attachments, and I mentioned how much you love to draw."

Luke kept "drawing" with the crystal. Lines, waves, spirals, his name…

"So I traded him for it. Consider it an early Christmas gift."

The crystal stone never seemed to run out of "light-ink" – or whatever it was that was creating this effect. Phosphorescence. Some kind of bioluminescence, perhaps. Or some other chemical reaction. The crystal must've had some mineral in it or something that reacted this way. Luke had no idea. True, he was a bit of a nerd and geek, and science was one of his favorite classes… But they never covered anything like this. Any guess was as good as any other.

Still, it was a cool toy. Too bad the light-ink always faded away after several seconds. He could draw some really amazing pictures otherwise.

"It's awesome." Luke stopped playing for a second to give his uncle a hug.

His uncle relaxed back into the comfortable old recliner chair, and smiled. "Just take good care of it. And don't lose it."

"Oh I will," he said. "Take good care of it, I mean." He paused for a second. "Hang on, I want to try something." He got up and ran towards his room. He returned a moment later with a large artist sketch pad. He sat back down on the couch, drawing pad on his lap, and began to "doodle" with the magic writing stone.

Everywhere the tip of that crystal touched, it left behind a line of sparkling pink light.

For several seconds – and then it faded away.

"And some Buddhist monks had this all along?" he asked.

"You could say that."

"I wonder if there's other crystals out there that can do this too."

His uncle shrugged.

Luke continued to play with the crystal on his large sketch pad. Up until now, he had only drawn disconnected lines and random patterns. Now, for the first time, and entirely by accident, he drew a complete and enclosed circle. And suddenly, something very unexpected happened.

The circular line actually glowed *brighter.*

"Whoa."

His uncle smiled.

This was new.

Luke waited several seconds – the time it normally took for a random line to fade away. The circle didn't. It stayed there, still glowing, still bright.

Interesting.

A few seconds after that, he started doodling inside the circle. His uncle watched closely. But then, suddenly, *everything* faded out, instantly – including the outer circle that was, until that instant, still glowing brightly.

"Huh."

Luke tried again. He started drawing. The instant the lines connected into a complete circle, the pink light-ink grew significantly brighter. Just like last time.

"Okay," said Luke.

His uncle smiled.

Luke tried drawing something else in the center. But then suddenly, *everything* disappeared, again!

Not "faded away", like normal. More like, "instantly erased". All of it. Simultaneously.

Normally, whatever he drew first faded out first, followed by where he drew second, and so on.

If this was just some kind of normal chemical reaction, he should get the same results every time. Why did it behave differently if he drew a circle first? What difference did that make?

He quickly drew a simple straight line, left to right, horizontally across the blank paper. It remained its normal brightness. Still glowing, still pink, still sparkling. Then, a few seconds later, the left end of the line started to fade out, down along the line, all the way to the right end. Just like all the other times and patterns before.

He drew a rectangle. The *instant* the ends connected, creating an enclosed and defined space, the lines grew significantly brighter – and stayed there. He waited a few seconds. No fading.

"Alright." He was on to something. He turned to his uncle. "What do you make of this?"

His uncle had been watching closely the entire time. He smiled warmly. "You're good. Took me a lot longer. Keep going."

Luke had an quizzical look on his face, but loved a good puzzle, so he went back to it. What difference did it make if he drew a straight line or an enclosed circle? How did it know what pattern he made? There had to be a reason.

He tried drawing an open, *almost* complete circle. Left maybe a half an inch gap between the ends. Nothing happened. The pink glowing line faded normally, in order of being drawn.

"Ah hah!" Luke had no idea what he was ah-hahing about, but he knew he had figured something out.

He quickly drew *another* circle, complete and connected. The line instantly became brighter.

"Okay, there's definitely something to this." He was determined to figure it out.

His uncle just sat there and smiled. "Want a hint?"

"No, I can do this."

He drew something else in the center of the enclosed circle. Something simple. A triangle. A basic three-sided equilateral geometric shape. Nothing more.

And suddenly those lines grew brighter too – and even brighter. The outer circle matched in brightness, and suddenly – something very strange happened.

The lines didn't "fade away" or "disappear" like before. *The entire space within the drawn circle disappeared* – including the material of the sketch pad – leaving *an empty hole* in its wake.

Suddenly, where solid material used to be, there was an opening, a window, a hole of some kind – leading to and showing somewhere foreign and completely far away.

Luke looked through the hole in the center of his sketch pad. He didn't see his apartment floor. He saw a hot and dry desert. Sand everywhere. Vast and endless. Giant rolling sand dunes and wide desert plains in between.

And in this distance, was that – a pyramid?

It was no optical illusion. Or if it was, it was a damn good one. It wasn't a hologram or picture of anything. It was actual 3-D space, another world, viewed through the opening in his sketch pad.

Weird.

It was like looking through an open window – no, maybe it was a wormhole, or some kind of portal, he thought – that somehow was attached to his sketch pad. And he could feel the heat and dry air passing through from the other side, blowing onto his face.

He freaked out, threw the pad onto the floor, and jumped on top of the couch. The portal was still there, still open to that desert land with a pyramid in the distance.

The only difference was now the sketch pad was on the floor. But the view on the other side did not change.

His uncle started laughing. "Luke, it's alright. Here, come down from there. It's okay."

Luke did not want to get off that couch.

He shook his head.

Uncle Charlie laughed. "Alright." He pulled himself out his comfortable chair, picked up the pad, and showed it to Luke. "See, it's fine. Not going to hurt you. You act like you've never seen a portal before."

Luke got down from the couch, but was hardly as calm or nonchalant as his uncle seemed to be. "Portals only exist in science-fiction," Luke stated. "In reality, wormholes are too unstable to—"

His uncle laughed. "Fine then. It's not a portal. Here, let me see the crystal."

Luke hesitantly handed it to his uncle.

Charlie took the crystal, held it over the magical portal, and made a big "X" motion over it. The portal abruptly closed and disappeared. Luke's sketch pad was back to normal, completely whole and unaltered, as if nothing had ever happened to it.

The look of confusion on Luke's face was priceless.

"Have a seat," Uncle Charlie said, returning to his own.

Luke couldn't stop staring at the sketch pad. That couldn't have been real.

"It's okay," said Charlie.

Charlie eased into his comfortable recliner chair, making that loud "ahhh" relaxing sound again. "You know what I love about this chair?" he asked.

"What?" It was more of a statement of disbelief – why was he talking about that old chair and not what had just happened – than a replying question.

"This chair cost you, what, fifty dollars at Good Will? And this is the most comfortable chair I've ever been in. Better than that Ikea stuff. And certainly better than that high end stuff rich people fill their houses with."

"Uncle, what's that got to do with anything?" He looked back at his sketch pad. "How did you do that?"

"Do what?"

"That optical illusion. The desert scene." Luke looked around for a hidden movie projector or something. "It looked so real… and in 3-D too!"

His uncle chuckled.

"What?"

"That's the problem with this generation. Everything's all special effects and PhotoShop. You don't recognize anything real when you see it."

"No," Luke said, still arguing his point about unstable wormholes. "You mean to tell me… that *this* crystal just opened up a portal to some desert, here in my living room?"

"On your drawing pad."

"On my drawing pad."

"Precisely."

He shook his head. "Not possible."

"Okay, if you say so." He held out his hand. "Can I have it back then?"

Luke paused for a second. His uncle had never lied to him. Never even played a practical joke on him. And the illusion looked so real, with depth and total, real-life resolution… He could feel the heat and the breeze. The dry air coming through. Like he was actually looking through a window that somehow opened to a far away land. But… how was that possible? *Was* it even possible?

Then again, lots of things seem impossible … until they happen. Luke decided to hold onto the crystal, for now.

"You knew about this?"

Charlie nodded. "I did."

"But how... Why... I don't understand. How come I've never heard of anything like this before?"

"It's the only one."

"Still, I'd think—"

"Something like this should be kept a secret," said Charlie. He turned and looked away for a second.

This was a lot for Luke to take in.

"How did you make it disappear, anyway? The portal, I mean."

"Any time you have an open portal, you close it by marking a big 'X' over it. Works every time."

"Every time?"

"Every time."

Could this actually be real?

Luke glanced at his movie and comic book posters. And his DVD collection. And thought about all the comic books, super hero novels, and sci-fi/fantasy video games he had. Okay, sure, he knew about portals. Heck, he even played and beat a game called *Portal*.

Portals could instantly transport you across any distance, just by walking through a doorway. Only instead of walking into an adjacent room, you could walk into another room, thousands of miles away. But they didn't exist in real life, did they?

Of course, in his amateur study of time travel theories, he did come across a possible method of time travel that included wormholes. Portals and wormholes were basically the same idea. And apparently, scientists believed wormholes did exist in the universe, but were so small, random, and unstable that no technology in our lifetime could make use of them.

How – and why – did this small, unassuming little glowing pink crystal create an open *stable* wormhole?

"I know what you're thinking," said his uncle. "You're thinking, 'Golly gee, why would my sweet dear old uncle give me such a cool doo-hickey?'"

"Actually, that's not—"

"Well the truth is, my favorite nephew, I'm retiring. And I think it's time you had it."

"Uncle?"

Charlie sat up, reached over, and held his hands over Luke's hands, which still held the crystal. "This belongs to you now. Don't lose it. You wouldn't want this falling into the wrong hands."

Luke pulled his hands away. He looked at this small crystal, this semi-transparent pink rock with a beautiful iridescent glow.

Fascinating.

"The story I told you about the Buddhist monk wasn't entirely true."

"No kidding!"

"I didn't meet him on this last trip to Skardu. We had already been acquainted. I went there, this time, specifically to see him, to get this stone."

"But why?"

"He held it in safe keeping for a while."

"I don't understand."

"It belongs to me. Or rather, my grandfather, originally. But… something that valuable can draw attention—"

"Wait, what? My great grandpa used to own this?"

"Yes. And he gave it to my father, who gave this to me when I was a little younger than you are now. I think it's about time you had it now."

Charlie didn't have any children of his own. Luke was the closest thing Charlie had to a son. They were always close. He was the fun uncle who always had cool stories to tell, went on all these amazing adventures, and always brought back something interesting from his travels – although nothing like this before.

But more than that, he was Luke's trusted confidante and friend throughout his life. Even his teen years. When Luke couldn't talk to his parents about something important, he knew he could talk with his uncle about it.

Uncle Charlie even helped pay for college. Picked him up if his car broke down on the highway. Gave him good advice when it came to girls. He was more than an uncle. He was a friend, a mentor, the kind of family that everyone wished they had.

So Luke chose to remember that and trust him now.

"Okay," he said. "Thank you."

It was still hard to believe. But he saw it with his own eyes. That's kind of hard to deny. Fortunately Luke's love of science-fiction and fantasy – and secret wish that some of it could actually be real – made it a little easier for him to accept and believe. But still, he had a lot of questions.

"How does it work?" Scratch that, not important. "How on Earth did Great Gramps get his hands on something like this?"

His uncle laughed lightheartedly. "He found it on an excavation." Uncle Charlie sat up, excited. "Have you ever heard of the Babylonian Tablet of Ningishzida?"

Luke shook his head no.

"As the story goes, in 1880, a famous archeologist named Hormuzd Rassam did a major excavation on an ancient Babylonian site, in what's now modern day Iraq. They found the usual pots and artifacts you'd normally find left behind, but they also found a bunch of ancient cuneiform tablets."

"Okay."

"Among those," continued his uncle, "they found a tablet, now called the Tablet of Ningishzida, that talked about a magical stone that could be used to open passage ways to other realms. They believed it was a tool of the gods, used by the gods to travel between our realm and theirs – and possibly others as well."

Luke stared at the crystal in his hand.

His uncle continued. "Ningishzida was a guardian at the gate to the celestial palace, in ancient Babylonian mythology. Hence the name of the tablet."

"I see."

"But hundreds of miles away, years later, and on a completely different dig, my grandfather led the excavation that uncovered this crystal. He had never seen anything like it. He bargained with his sponsors to keep it as his compensation, instead of his usual cash payment. At the time they didn't think it was anything more than a precious gem, so they agreed."

"Like you said the Buddhist monks thought."

"They believed that too. Only I was the traveler who gave it to them, many years ago."

"But how… When did you, or Great Gramps, or the monks realize it could open portals?"

"The Tablet of Ningishzida told us. My grandfather thought his crystal might be the one mentioned on the tablet, and quite a number of years later, finally figured out how to use it."

Luke nodded.

"He then shared it with my father, who gave it to me, and now I'm passing it on to you. Use it well. Please, keep it safe."

He stared at the crystal carefully, almost entranced by its beauty and power. "But how's it work? I mean, how does *this* create a portal?"

His uncle shrugged. He really had no idea.

Luke paused for a second. He got a determined look in his face.

His uncle had seen that look many times before.

"What are you thinking?"

Luke got up, walked over to his blank wall – the same one where he had projected his favorite movies.

"I've got to try something."

He drew a larger circle, much larger than he could possibly fit on a small sketch pad. Large enough for, say, two people to walk through.

He completed the circle. The sparkling pink line grew brighter.

He drew a triangle in the center. The symbol instantly became significantly brighter, as did the outer circle, and suddenly a giant hole appeared in his living room wall.

It revealed the same desert location again. Hot gusts of dry air blew into his apartment. Some sand came along with it, spilling onto his living room floor. In the distance, they could see the pyramid. "I assume the portal works both ways," said Luke.

"Sorry?"

"If we step through, we can turn around and come right back, right?" asked Luke.

"Of course."

"Good. Wanna see that pyramid up close?" Luke smiled.

"Sure," said his uncle, pulling himself up from his comfortable chair. "Let's just be careful, alright?"

"Of course!" said Luke.

His uncle joined him in front of the portal. The hot wind continued to blow into his apartment. The air conditioner kicked on. "Well, ready for an adventure?" asked his uncle.

Luke couldn't help but smile. And he smiled much bigger than he had in a very long time. "I'm ready. Let's do this!"

Young Luke took a breath, prepared himself, and looked back at his uncle. The old man, dressed in an aloha shirt and sneakers, was right by his side.

They stepped through. Their feet hit the soft off-white sand. The burning sun blazed above their heads. The air was so dry. The hot wind continued to blow forcefully against them. They had walked into an oven of endless shifting desert.

Luke looked around. Behind him stood the remains of a stone wall. Old and weathered. Possibly part of a larger structure that was now possibly in ruins under the sand. He saw a few other decaying walls, pillars, and worn-down stone statues scattered about, all of different sizes, all slowly weathering away into oblivion.

The portal stayed open on the stone wall behind him. Looking through the large opening, he saw his living room, his couch, his old recliner chair, his video projector, everything.

Everything else around him, in this desert place, was nothing but sand and ruins. The air burned so hot and was so void of any moisture, it almost stung his nose. His lips and throat quickly became parched.

He quickly stepped back through the portal into his living room – where it was significantly cooler – and ran into the kitchen. He grabbed a couple of cold water bottles from the refrigerator and then jumped back through the portal into the desert.

"Smart," said his uncle.

Luke held the crystal over the top corner of the portal and went to X it out.

"Whoa, whoa, what are you doing there buddy?" His uncle grabbed his wrist and stopped him half way.

"Closing the portal."

"And do you know the symbol to get back to your apartment?"

Luke paused. "No."

"Me neither. Let's leave the portal open for now, shall we?"

"Good idea."

Luke, already starting to sweat under the sun and heat, shook his head in disbelief one last time. He couldn't believe it. Here he was, thousands of miles away, walking in the middle of an Egyptian desert. On the other side of the world.

Better start walking. He didn't want to stand here all day.

They started heading towards the pyramid.

"This is so cool," said Luke. "We just traveled to Egypt in the blink of an eye. If these things were ever mass produced, it'd put all the airlines out of business."

"They're doing a fine job of that of their own," joked his uncle.

Luke smiled. "I wonder where in Egypt we are. Like is that the pyramid at Giza, or somewhere—" He stopped abruptly.

"What?"

Luke stared at something in the sky. He pointed up at it. "Uncle, look."

The old man looked up.

They saw two moons in the sky: a larger one, colored icy blue and dark gray; the other one, smaller, reddish-black. Neither looked like Earth's moon.

"I don't think we're in Egypt..."

Chapter 5
WAS IT SOMETHING HE SAID?

At the exact same moment Luke and his uncle stepped through that portal, Ray and his beautiful date sat down at their table in P.J. Wang's China Bistro, arguably the best place to go for Chinese food in Burbank.

High quality delicious food. Exotic décor. Comfortable atmosphere. Mood lighting. And a candle lit at every table. Customer service was usually excellent, too.

A perfect place to take a date.

"Thank you," Ray said to the host who seated them.

Dawn sat down across the table from him. She looked so beautiful tonight. Beautiful, without trying too hard. Somehow she pulled it off. She did a little light makeup, teased her hair, and put on a nice dress – nothing too fancy, this was only a first date. But somehow it looked really good on her. *Really good.*

"Sorry things took so long," said Ray. "Auditions ran longer than we expected."

"No problem. I understand. " She grabbed her menu. "I hope you're hungry though," she said, "because I sure am!"

"A girl with an appetite. Nice. You continue to impress me."

She smiled playfully.

"You have no idea. It drives me crazy when I take a pretty girl to a fancy restaurant, and all she orders is a small salad and a diet Coke. I mean, come on!"

Dawn laughed. "Not me. I mean, I'm not a pig or anything, but I'm not trying to starve myself either."

"A lot of girls in LA do."

"Yeah, well, they think they need to be skin and bones to be pretty. Me, I know that beauty's on the inside. And I'm pretty damn hot if I do say so myself." Then she stuck her tongue out at him.

He laughed. "Nice." He looked at his menu. "So, let's see. What looks good here?"

"It all looks so good. Last date I was on, the guy took me to Denny's."

"Denny's?"

"I know, right?!"

"I would *never* take a girl to Denny's. Even if I was dead broke, I'd do a packed lunch and take her on a picnic somewhere."

"See, *that's* romantic. Denny's is… not."

"Mmm. The Mahi-Mahi looks good. Think I'll order that."

Dawn still couldn't make up her mind. She continued perusing her menu.

"So," Ray asked, "how long have you been acting?"

"Oh, I've done community theatre for years. Finally found an agent a few years ago. Got me into a couple local commercials in the beginning, but that's it. Hasn't done a thing for me since."

"Yeah, that happens. Until you land some blockbuster hit on your own, and then everybody wants you."

"Yeah, when you no longer need them!" she said. "What about you? Been making films long?"

"No, not really. I'm just helping a friend."

"The director or that other guy – the one who sounds kinda like Steve Urkel?"

Ray laughed. "The director."

The server came up to their table. A pretty girl, early 20s, red hair, cute freckles. Possibly another aspiring actor-waiter for all they knew. "Hi, I'm Tiffany, welcome to P.J. Wang's. Can I start you two with some drinks?" She mentioned the night's specials.

Ray ordered a beer. Dawn just wanted some water.

"Great," said Tiffany. "You guys ready to order?"

Ray was. Dawn still needed more time.

"I'll go get your drinks and be back in a minute," said the cute redheaded server.

"So," Ray asked, keeping the conversation going, "you from LA originally or did you come out here to be an actress?"

Dawn put down her menu. "Actually, my dad moved out here to be a film director. Nothing ever came of it though. He ended up working in a real estate office."

"That happens too."

"I was only 10 at the time. He still talks of 'someday' directing his own independent film. But he never seems to have the time."

"Must've been rough moving at that age. Where'd you live previously?"

"Indiana. In some small town you've probably never even heard of. Cedar Lake."

"You miss it?"

"A small town surrounded by endless corn fields? No. Not at all. People complain about LA a lot – but I love it here. There's always something going on, a million people doing a million different things. And I do love acting. And New York gets too cold for me. Yeah, LA's the place for me."

Their server returned. "Here you go," she said, placing their drinks. "Figure out what you want?"

"Oh!" exclaimed Dawn. She still hadn't figured that out. She returned to her menu. "You go first," she told Ray.

Ray knew exactly what he wanted. Unfortunately that didn't give Dawn too much time. Finally, she quickly, randomly picked one that maybe, probably sounded good.

"Alright, I'll put your orders right in."

And the server left to attend to another table.

"How about you?" asked Dawn. "You from LA?"

The restaurant was pretty busy, even on a Monday night. Of course, in a city as big as Los Angeles, most places were pretty busy all the time. So no one paid any notice to a well-dressed business man as he casually strut in the front door.

Spotless shoes. Perfectly tied tie. Luxurious business suit.

It was the mysterious man.

Hey, even super villains gotta eat.

He checked his Rolex. He figured he had about twenty minutes to sit down, order, eat, find some "volunteers" for his little project, and have enough time to drive to the designated location. Twenty minutes was not enough. He was going to have to speed things up a bit.

"How many?" asked the host, ready to put him on the waiting list.

"Just one," he said.

"You're looking at about a 30 minute wait. Is that alright?"

"No, I'm afraid it's not," he said. "I want you to give me the next table available." The mysterious man quickly surveyed the busy restaurant. The next table could still take a while. "On second thought, I'll find my own."

"Sir?"

The mysterious man locked eyes with the host. "You will not interfere in any way."

The host obeyed.

The mysterious man walked confidently into the restaurant, looked around, and found a table in the corner to his liking. Unfortunately, there was a young couple there. Who just happened to be Ray and Dawn.

Uh oh.

He walked right up to them.

Ah, young love. How… repulsive. He cleared his throat to get their attention.

They both looked up at him.

"I'm sitting here," said the mysterious man.

Ray was about to say something.

"Now!" demanded the mysterious man.

He held intense eye contact with Ray.

Something came over Ray. And although normally he'd never interrupt a date like this, he suddenly felt compelled to invite this total stranger to sit and dine with them.

"Please, join us."

"Not with you!" the mysterious man exclaimed. "Both of you, get up, leave."

Ray obediently stood up from his seat. No sense getting into an argument or a fight over this. It was just a table. They would find another one.

Dawn happened to be looking at Ray when the commands were given. So the villain's mind control had no effect on her. She couldn't believe Ray so readily complied. "Ray? What are you doing?"

The mysterious man turned and locked eye contact with her. "You too, get up, go away."

Dawn immediately felt herself compelled to stand up and obey too.

The mysterious man got a good look at her. Nice body. Young, healthy, pretty.

"On second thought," said the man, "I want you to stay with me."

"Okay," said Dawn. She was hesitant to sit down.

"Please, sit. Join me."

Ray watched as she did.

"Dawn?" His feelings were getting hurt. "What are *you* doing?"

"I want to stay with him now," she told Ray.

"What?" he remarked.

"Without you here," she said.

"But—" They were really starting to connect and hit it off. How could she just dump him like that and choose to finish *their* date with this complete stranger? Things were going so well. Was it something he said?

"Leave now," the man told Ray.

As if he wanted to stay. He was really starting to fall for Dawn. And now – he was too insulted, too hurt to stay anyway. "I'm out of here!" said Ray. And he promptly left.

Ray sat on the street curb, just outside of the restaurant. A giant dragon statue – part of the restaurant's décor and grand entrance – towered over him. Lots of people came and went, entering and leaving the restaurant, walking by to other shops and restaurants along the street, heading to wherever their busy lives were taking them.

But Ray just sat there. Head lowered, staring at the pavement beneath his feet. He had only just met Dawn earlier that day. But there was something different about her. Something special. He really liked her.

She wasn't just pretty. She was smart, self-confident, relaxed, able to be herself. They joked and smiled a lot together. They had common interests. She felt easy to talk to. Easy to be himself around. He really liked her.

But she was in there, right now, finishing their date with some rude self-absorbed man. A well-dressed man. That suit he wore looked pretty expensive. He obviously must've had a lot of money. That's probably why Dawn dumped him. Along came a better looking guy with more money.

Ray would be rich one day, some day. He was an entrepreneur, had started his own companies, and even had a little money earning interest in some investments right now. He was young, he was still learning, he was on his way. He wasn't exactly rich yet, but he was doing well – right?

Maybe he should've went into a little debt and taken her someplace nicer. Obviously she was into men with money. Maybe she thought he had more money than he actually did, because he was the producer on his friend's film. But he wasn't getting paid. This was a volunteer project, a credit for one of his graduate school classes. And when she figured that out, she lost interest.

Just then, he saw the mysterious man exit the restaurant.

Ray immediately stood up, waiting for Dawn. She was worth holding on to. Maybe if he just explained that he'd be a better financial provider in the future— No, what was he thinking? If she really was that shallow, she obviously wasn't the girl for him anyway. He didn't want to explain anything to her. No, he wanted an *apology* from her! Even if their date was going badly – which it wasn't – that's no excuse to treat him like she did!

The mysterious man walked past, not even noticing Ray standing there. Dawn followed closely behind. As did their redhead server. And the host.

All three of them trailed behind like… like lost puppies or something.

What the hell was going on here?

"Dawn!" Ray shouted.

She stopped to look at him.

"What's— You owe me— How could—?"

Maybe he should've planned what he was going to say better.

"This way, all of you, don't delay," said the mysterious man.

Dawn was about to say something, but when the mysterious man told her not to delay, she just shrugged with a loss for words, and followed the man down the street. The redhead server, and the restaurant's host, followed right behind.

"Dawn, wait," Ray called.

They kept walking.

Something was not right.

Ray needed to know what was going on. He follow them, from a distance, so not to be noticed. The mysterious man entered the nearby parking garage. The three went in with him.

Ray stuck close to corners and lurked behind cars. If anyone was racist, and saw him – a young black man – sneaking around expensive cars in a parking garage, they might've thought he was up to no good.

But Ray was a good guy. Never stole a thing in his life. Except maybe some music he pirated from the Internet. But who hasn't done that?

If anyone was up to no good, it was this guy. This mysterious, sharply-dressed, strangely persuasive man. But *what* exactly was he doing? And *why* were Dawn, the server, and the host quietly going along?

He watched as they all stopped at a black BMW. The mysterious man told them all to get in. One by one, they did. Then the man got into the driver's seat and started the engine. Now where was he taking them?

Ray had to think fast.

He quickly memorized the BMW's license plate. MASTRMIND. Ray also pulled out his cell phone and took a picture of the car. Everyone seemed to be going with him willingly, but it didn't make any sense. Things were going great on his date with Dawn. And he seriously doubted that both the server and host got off work at the same time in the middle of the dinner rush. Maybe they were secretly being coerced somehow. Blackmailed. Or something. Maybe that man had a gun that Ray didn't know about. Or... maybe they all knew him? No, that couldn't be it. Dawn would've said something, reacted differently, if she knew him.

They drove off. Ray bolted for his car, which luckily wasn't too far away – just a little ways down the row. He never ran so hard and so fast in his life. He really needed to get into better shape.

He arrived at his Ford Focus.

He looked back. The BMW headed for the exit.

He pulled out his keys so fast he almost dropped them. Shoved them into the lock, turned, and opened the door. Started up the engine, pulled out way too fast, and nearly hit an oncoming car in the process. He sped after the black BMW, nearly losing sight of him around the corner. Ray buckled up as he raced forward.

Thank God for traffic lights. He saw the black BMW stopped at one just ahead.

They were in a turn-only lane, heading right. Probably headed for the freeway. It was a single lane road with several cars in between them. Ray couldn't risk losing them. He looked ahead. No oncoming traffic. He dangerously weaved into the oncoming lane, floored the gas, and sped ahead to get in front of several cars.

The BMW turned onto the freeway. I-5 Southbound. Ray was still a few cars behind. But the freeway was good. He could catch up and follow them much more easily. And rush hour was almost over now. He turned onto the freeway, going the same direction. He made sure not to lose sight of them.

Every instinct told him something was wrong. He didn't know what. He couldn't explain it. Maybe it was some kind of kidnapping. It was the only thing that made any sense. He reached for his cell phone to call 9-1-1. But then he hesitated. They were all adults. They all appeared to go with him of their own free will. No one called for help or tried to escape. No resistance. No sign of any weapon or danger. No threats from the man they went with.

For all Ray knew, they were all going to some mansion in the Hollywood Hills for a big orgy. But Dawn didn't seem like that kind of girl. He put the phone down. He needed more proof first. He didn't know how, but he sensed she was in danger. But so far, all he could report was three consensual adults willingly catching a ride with some guy in a nice expensive car.

Hardly the crime of the century.

Damn, what was going on?

The BMW got into the fastest moving lane and sped ahead. Ray couldn't lose them. He switched on his turn signal, quickly checked his mirrors, and suddenly swerved his car into the fast lane too. He pressed down the gas.

There was just one more car between them. Ray needed to think. What could he do? Suppose she was in danger. Ray had no training, no karate skills, no self-defense classes. He had no weapon or blunt objects in his car. Unless he counted the tire iron used to loosen lug nuts when changing tires. Yeah, actually, that was an ideal blunt instrument. Okay, but still, whatever this guy was using to coerce and manipulate Dawn and the others was obviously a lot more dangerous than a tire iron.

What did he want with Dawn, the server, and the host anyway? What was their connection?

The BMW moved to an exit lane to connect to a different freeway. They were headed for the 110 Southbound. They were headed downtown.

This could be tricky. A lot of lanes, a lot of junctions, a lot of freeways all converged here. There'd be a lot of merging and exiting traffic. Ray couldn't risk getting separated. He accelerated to get closer to the BMW.

Really close.

Like *right* behind him.

Hopefully the mysterious man was unaware of him. Hopefully, Ray realized, he wasn't putting himself into unnecessary danger.

He followed the BMW south on the 110 freeway. They weaved through Downtown Los Angeles and continued on the same road. They kept going south, past the I-10 freeway, and on down towards Long Beach.

It was getting dark fast. Ray memorized the shape and brightness of the BMW's rear lights. He followed them all the way down to Long Beach, where they got off the freeway, traveled through some local roads, and eventually found themselves on some dark and scary narrow streets.

Long Beach, to non-locals, sounds like a really nice area. Like a nice, long beach. And there were nice parts, sure, but a lot of Long Beach was very industrial. And this part, where they arrived, was one of the grimiest, dirtiest, darkest, and scariest parts Ray had ever seen.

The BMW pulled into a small parking lot next to an old industrial building near the harbor. It was dark. All the street lamps here were broken or burnt out. Chain-link fences, graffiti-covered concrete walls, and an eerie, total absence of other people surrounded them.

Ray stopped a little farther back, turned off his lights, and tried to act inconspicuous. He waited in his car and watched them from that relatively safe distance.

All the industrial buildings around here looked old and abandoned. Lots of "No Trespassing" signs. Trash and litter piled up in dark corners. A few abandoned, rusting, gutted cars nearby.

Okay. He didn't care how willingly Dawn appeared to go along with the mysterious man. This was definitely not the place she wanted to be.

Ray grabbed his cell phone and scrolled through the contact list. He called the only person he could trust right now.

Luke's cell phone rang.

And rang.

And rang.

"Come on, come on. Pick up dude."

Luke's voicemail answered. "Hi, this is Luke Powers. I can't pick up the phone right now, so leave a message after the beep. Beeeeep." And then it beeped, for real.

"Luke, it's Ray! Listen, something weird's going down. I was on this date with a girl I met at auditions today, and all of the sudden, this guy shows up and tells me to leave but wants her to stay. I don't think she knew him. Twenty minutes later, they're walking out of P.J. Wang's together, without a word, and gets into his BMW – license plate MASTRMND – along with our server and the host. Something's not right, I couldn't just leave her… But, um… I'm at—" He looked for an address somewhere. Nothing. Not even a sign to tell him what street he was on. "Somewhere in Long Beach. Near a bunch of old, what looks to be abandoned industrial factories or shipping facilities or something. I can't— Wait, something's happening."

Farther up ahead, the mysterious man got out his BMW and opened the passenger doors. Dawn, the waitress, and the host all got out. They stood there, patiently, like they were awaiting further instructions.

Then they started walking towards the abandoned building.

"They're headed inside now. I think they're in some kind of danger. I need to—" The voicemail beeped, cutting him off. He got an automated message saying that he reached the voicemail's time limit.

'—call the police," he finished. He still didn't have any real evidence of a kidnapping or mugging or whatever the hell was going on. But the circumstances were suspicious enough now, he thought. He dialed 9-1-1.

Chapter 6
ALTERED

A patrol car was dispatched to investigate. The 9-1-1 operator told Ray to stay in his car and out of view. His safety was a priority. He was specifically told not to follow them inside the old, empty, run down, probably condemned industrial building.

But Ray couldn't live with himself if something happened to any of them while he waited for the cops to show up. He was just going to have to be really, really careful – and really, really quiet.

He snuck in after them.

Inside, the building was completely gutted. Construction tape blocked off some rooms and doorways – the overall structure looked particularly unstable. Plastic sheets hung from the ceiling at random spots. Muddy footprints and old fast food trash littered other parts of the rooms. Even an old, grimy sleeping bag laid in the corner. And a ratty old mattress with broken springs exposed.

Ray did not have the best feeling in the world right now.

Worse still, he lost track of them. It was a pretty large building. Tens of thousands of square feet per floor level, easily. And it was several stories high.

Where could they be? Where could they be?

Ray trusted his instincts. He went up – slowly, carefully, quietly – one of the stairs that looked sturdy enough to support human weight.

What was he thinking? This was *clearly* not where he should be. But this wasn't about his date anymore, or getting answers, or anything like that. Clearly these people were in some kind of danger, and he may be the only person able to help them right now.

Kinda put things in perspective. Suddenly his college grades, his friend's film project, his own personal businesses and investments... None of that mattered. These people were going to be raped, mugged, and probably axe-murdered in a place like this. But not if he could help it.

What, exactly, he *could* do – he hadn't figured that far ahead yet. He trusted that when the moment came, he'd know what to do. Opportunity favored the prepared, too, though. He remembered that as well. And shit. He forgot his tire iron back in the car!

Okay. He could go back for it now. But… who knows what could happen during all that time. It was too risky. So he did the next best thing – he turned on the GPS in his cell phone, just in case something went horribly wrong and he turned up missing too.

Then he heard voices. It sounded, kinda like, was that Tiffany, the waitress?

It was hard to make out. The random debris, half-torn walls, and winding corridors made it difficult to not only understand what she was saying, but make out exactly where her voice was coming from.

"Why are we here?" it sounded like she said, somewhere nearby.

"Silence," said the mysterious man's voice. That was louder and clearer. Ray followed the direction it seemed to be coming from. "Do not speak unless spoken to."

He was definitely getting close.

"W-What do you want with us?" asked the young man, the host from the restaurant.

Ray peeked around a corner. He saw them. He quickly pressed his back to the wall, on the far side of the corner, keeping himself out of sight. His heart raced. He waited a second. No one seemed to spot him. So he carefully, very very *very* slowly, angled himself to see as much as he could, without revealing his presence.

The mysterious man pushed up his sleeve to check his Rolex. "He's late. I hate waiting."

Just then, someone else entered the room from the other direction.

He wore a white lab coat, had wild eccentric hair, and a crazy look in his eyes. Mad scientist? Check. He began rapidly moving his hands around. Ray was confused at first, but quickly recognized it as sign language.

Too bad he didn't know sign language. He might be able to know what they were talking about.

The mysterious man signed back, but also spoke aloud. "These are the test subjects. Now <u>where</u> is my formula?"

Formula? Test subjects?

Okay, this was worse. Dawn and the others weren't getting rapped or mugged. They were about to become victims of illegal human experimentation!

No, wait, calm down. His imagination was getting carried away with him. A hazard of being best friends with a guy who lives and breathes comic books all the time. He was sure there was a less insane explanation.

The crazy – and apparently deaf – scientist signaled for the mysterious man to wait a moment. He walked into a nearby vacant room and retrieved a small metal case. The eccentric scientist stood before the mysterious man, unlocked and opened the case, and showed him what was inside.

Ray couldn't see. He tried to look closer.

The mad scientist spotted Ray from across the room. The guy started rapidly flashing and signing all sorts of things – probably, "Hey look, over there, some idiot-who-should've-stayed-in-the-car spying on us!"

The mysterious quickly turned to see Ray too. For a second, their eyes locked.

Ray immediately ducked and hid around the corner.

Oh shit. Oh shit. Oh shit.

He still had time to run.

But he couldn't leave Dawn and the others. No, he had to. He was no good to them dead. Save himself first, then save others.

The mysterious man placed his hand on Ray's shoulder.

Oh. Shit.

"And who the *hell* are you?" asked the mysterious man.

Ray slowly, in absolute terror, turned around to face the man.

"Care to buy a magazine subscription to keep kids like me off the streets?"

He didn't buy it.

"Walk over there and join them," he said, staring deeply into Ray's eyes. "Stand next to them and *don't move* until I say so."

Ray's fear melted away in an instant. He suddenly felt calm, relaxed, at peace. Almost serene. He gladly walked over to the others, stood next to Dawn, and stopped. It was as if his body was on auto-pilot. Thinking and moving for him. But at the same time, he *wanted* to go stand over here and wait. He felt no need or desire to resist it. He looked at Dawn, who looked back at him, and he stood in place, waiting until told otherwise.

And then that serene feeling faded away. And terror overwhelmed him as he realized where he was – and the uncertain fate that now awaited him too. But, even though every instinct told him to run, something kept his feet in place. He couldn't move.

The mysterious man sighed. "It appears we have a fourth volunteer." He signed to Doctor Troyd, the mad scientist, *"Is there enough formula for all of them?"*

The scientist replied with a nod of his fist, meaning "yes".

"Good," said the mysterious man. *"It better work this time,"* he signed.

The mysterious man walked slowly, deliberately. He examined each of his four volunteers. First in line was the host, a young college-age kid, male, average looks, nothing special. But he appeared healthy, so he would do.

Second was Tiffany, the redheaded server. She was cute. Too cute. Especially with those freckles. He definitely intended to change that.

Third was Dawn, an attractive blonde, about the same age as the others. He hated blondes.

And last, his unexpected guest volunteer, a black kid who was too smart for his own good. Didn't he see this kid at the restaurant? That's right. He was the blonde's date. Didn't he tell him to leave? Well, technically he did; he left the restaurant. But after that, the fool obviously followed them here. And no doubt reported their location to someone. They may not have much time.

"Bring in the animals," he signed to Doctor Troyd.

The mad scientist walked into the nearby room again. This time, he wheeled out a large platform truck – the kind of thing used to move heavy crates around. But this platform didn't have crates. Not exactly. It had several small cages and glass tanks with weak, starving animals inside. The cages were all about the same size – way too small for one of the larger animals. They looked sick and weakly, obviously neglected for large periods of time.

In one cage, a cat. In another, a dog. In one of the glass tanks, a snake. Another had a rather large and unfriendly-looking spider. And the last cage included a parrot who had already plucked out most of its feathers.

All four of the twenty-something kids watched uneasily and uncomfortably as those poor animals were wheeled in. But the greatest question on all of their minds – why were those poor animals here, anyway?

Those animals just laid there, lifeless and listless, having long ago given up hope of escape or survival. But they were still alive. Barely.

Whatever the mysterious man and mad scientist had planned, it couldn't be anything good.

"You," the mysterious man said to the male host. "Take off all your clothes. Everything. Your shoes, your socks, any piercings you might be wearing, *everything*."

The young host did exactly that. He disrobed, quickly and without hesitation. In that moment, he forgot all about where he was, the obvious danger he was in, those poor caged animals, the fact that these men shouldn't be trusted – all of that. All the young man thought about, all he wanted to do, was take off all his clothes, right now. He actually *wanted* to get completely naked.

"Now give me your clothes," said the mysterious man.

He handed them over.

"You won't be needing these any longer."

The other three watched and stared, both in horror and confusion. Why did that guy so shamelessly and readily go naked, especially in a place like this – and why on

Earth did the mysterious man want him to?

The well-dressed mysterious man reached into the metal case provided by the mad scientist. In it were two bottles each filled with a strange glowing green liquid inside. The case also contained a few large syringes, bigger than what most hospitals use to draw blood.

"Tell me," said the mysterious man as he loaded a syringe with the glowing green chemical. "What's your favorite animal?"

"Um," said the young man, "I guess… a zebra?"

The mysterious man glanced back at the caged animals.

"I guess you'll have to settle for a dog," he said. The syringe was fully loaded. He walked over to the young man. "Now hold still. *Stay*." He cracked a sinister grin.

The young man, stark naked, stood in place, holding as perfectly still as he could. The mysterious man grabbed his arm, found a vein, and injected the glowing green liquid directly into the young man's bloodstream.

As soon as the syringe was empty, the mysterious man stepped back. He waited, and watched, for a moment.

"Good. Last person didn't last this long. You're already doing well."

"What? What do you mean? What did you just put inside me?" The young man started to panic. The momentary euphoria of obeying the mysterious man's commands had suddenly worn off again.

Satisfied his test subject hadn't died or exploded yet, the mysterious man walked over to the cage with the cramped, listless dog. He stabbed the dog with the same syringe, drew a fair amount of blood, and then returned to the young naked man.

"W-Wh-What are you going to do with *that*?" he pleaded.

"Continue holding still. Stay… Good boy."

He injected the host with the dog's blood.

"Ow, stop it, please, ow, ow, OW – it's burns, ohmygod, *please stop*, it BURNS!!!"

All of the dog's blood had been injected into the young man. The young man, who was in so much pain, he buckled at the knees and lost all his strength. He fell to the floor, body locked as still as he could be in spite of the pain, and he screamed louder and louder in gut-wrenching pain.

He promptly vomited all over the floor.

He fell over, partially into his own vomit, and uncontrollably jerked and squirmed in what looked to be blood-boiling, unspeakable pain.

He screamed louder. Blood spewed out of his mouth. His arms and legs twitched uncontrollably even more. His hands and feet began to mutate, deform, and reshape themselves into something absolutely grotesque. He screamed even louder, snapped back, and vomited some more.

The mysterious man turned to look at Doctor Troyd.

The mad scientist shrugged.

The poor naked young man began growing fur all over his body. Still convulsing in pain. His nails grew longer, thicker, sharper. He screamed as more blood flew out of his mouth. Then they all saw his teeth lengthening and sharpening.

His blood-shot eyes filled with intense pain and horror. His scream got drowned out by blood in his throat. His body spasmed a few more times. And then, finally, at last – peace came over him.

Not peace from calming down. Not peace from the pain subsiding.

The kind of peace brought only by death.

He ceased breathing. His body stopped convulsing. The man – a mutated half animal now – was no more.

"Dammit," angrily exclaimed the mysterious man. He sighed, obviously frustrated. He rapidly signed to Doctor Troyd, *"How long has that dog been here?"*

The mad scientist had to think for a moment. *"Two weeks,"* he shrugged.

"He's OBVIOUSLY sick. Get that mutt out of here! He's no good to me anymore," he loudly spoke and signed.

"What should I do with it?" Doctor Troyd replied.

"I don't care. Dump it in the harbor!"

Dawn, Ray, and the server Tiffany stared at the gooey mess on the floor that was once a human being. Tiffany worked with him, but barely knew him. She was still fairly new herself. She only met him briefly during training. And now, in this moment, she wished she took the time to know him a little better.

Dawn and Ray didn't even know his name.

None of them could make peace with what they just saw. The hideous mutation and unbearable death that young man just experienced. Worse still, none of them could comprehend why they stayed. Part of them wanted to move, to run, to escape, to fight back, to help him, to do *something*. But, for some reason, they just stood there, in line, waiting obediently.

The mysterious man walked over to redhead Tiffany next. "What's your favorite animal?"

She began to cry.

"Stop crying!"

The tears abruptly stopped.

"Answer me."

"I love cats," she admitted. "Have two of my own at home."

"Okay," said the mysterious man, nodding. He looked back to Doctor Troyd, who was currently prepping the dog's cage to be carried out. *"Hey,"* he called and signed. *"Is this cat healthy?"*

Doctor Troyd nodded. *"Looks healthy."*

"Good."

"Don't man," said Ray. "You don't have to do this. Just let us go, we won't say anything."

"Yeah," added Dawn. "We were never here!"

"Shut up, both of you," he said, quickly making eye contact with the both of them. Their mouths shut. They did not, could not, speak another word.

The mysterious man couldn't re-use the old syringe. It was probably contaminated with whatever disease or illness that dog was carrying. So he dropped it on the floor and stepped on it, crushing and breaking it. He reached into the metal case and pulled out a second syringe. He loaded the glowing green liquid into it.

The redhead swallowed hard.

He looked her directly in the eyes. "Take off all of your clothes. Everything. Your earrings, any other piercings you might have, socks, shoes, underwear. *Everything*. Do it now."

She suddenly felt so free, so uninhibited, so wild and loose. She pulled off her shirt and unlatched her bra. Ahh, that felt so good to feel her breasts free in the open air. She pulled off her shoes, one by one, and then her socks. She slid down her pants and silky underwear. She took out her earrings.

"Now give them to me."

She did.

"Stay where you are. Hold still."

She did.

He grabbed her arm, stabbed the needle into her vein, and injected all of the glowing green chemical inside.

Dawn and Ray watched silently. They wanted to ask what that glowing liquid was, or what he was trying to do, or why… But they couldn't speak. An overwhelming compulsion told them to remain quiet and stand in place. So they just watched helplessly.

Tiffany stood completely naked, right by Dawn's side. Why couldn't Dawn move? Why wouldn't she do *anything*? It would've been so easy just to reach over and— No. She couldn't move. She didn't want to move. She wanted to… wait.

The mysterious man had told her to stand there and not move. So that's exactly what she did.

Was he using some kind of mind control on them?

The chemical fully went into Tiffany's bloodstream. The mysterious man stepped back, watched, and waited. She, too, appeared to be well – for the moment.

"Let's try this again, shall we?"

He went over to the cat, stabbed it with the same syringe, and filled it with the cat's blood. The cat meowed in painful protest. It didn't seem too happy about this. But neither was Tiffany.

The horrible man returned to Tiffany, about to inject her.

She looked at the half-furry, semi-mutated naked man – her former co-worker – lying dead next to her. This was about to be her fate. She started crying again.

"I said STOP CRYING!" he shouted, locking eye contact with her.

Tiffany's tears suddenly stopped.

Dawn noticed something.

Tiffany stopped crying, both times, the moment the mysterious man told her to. And, it seemed pretty important he made eye contact when he gave such a command. Dawn didn't understand how or why any man could have such a power, but after witnessing and experiencing all that she just did, she was willing to make a leap and draw that conclusion.

He injected Tiffany with the cat's blood.

But wait – there was another small curiosity. The mysterious man had told them all to stand in place, hold still, not move, remain silent. And they all gladly, willingly did. Even now, when certain death awaited Dawn next, she only *partially* felt the need to run. Part of her – unfortunately, the dominant part – still wanted to obey, still wanted to stay silent and stand in place.

He gave that command several minutes ago. And it still held power over them.

But Tiffany – he told her to stop crying less than a moment ago. And she was already starting to cry again. He had to tell her again. Reinforce the command. But why?

Could it be that her impending death was more real, more present, more important – and her survival instinct, the deepest and strongest instinct of them all, somehow broke through his mind control just enough?

Obviously not enough. Because a louder command and repeated eye contact made her stop crying again.

All of the cat's blood was now in her system.

The mysterious man stepped back to observe the impending transformation.

Nothing happened at first. But it had only been a few seconds.

"How do you feel?" he asked her.

"I feel… I feel… Funny," she said.

"Fascinating. Describe it."

"I feel like…" Tiffany searched for the words. "I feel like I'm stretching and growing. Everything feels loose and tingly. Almost," she giggled suddenly, "a little ticklish."

The mysterious man smiled.

She started laughing some more, a little louder and longer each time. And her hands and feet began to shift, alter, and transform. Her nails grew sharper. The palms of her hands grew pads. And a little tiny nub of a furry tail began to emerge from the her lower back, just above her butt. A soft, faint layer of hair sprouted up all over her body, from head to toe. It grew thicker, turning into a soft and smooth layer of fur. Her tail grew longer and longer, extending out several feet.

Her ears formed pointed tips, grew larger and wider, and resembled feline ears far more than human ears now. Her nose became a little smaller, turning into a cute little button nose. Long thin whiskers extended out from face.

Even her tongue became a little rougher, a bit more like sandpaper. Her tail stopped at just over three feet long. Her hands and feet were still humanoid, but were far more like paws than she cared to realize. A soft, smooth, even layer of black fur covered her entire body. All except for her hands and feet, which had white fur.

She looked over at the cat in the cage. Its fur was colored the same way.

Her teeth were now razor sharp. Her eyes reflected the light. She could hear subtle sounds she never heard before. She could feel vibrations in the air through her new sensitive whiskers. And she felt an overwhelming desire to get down on all fours and lick herself.

The mysterious man held a very satisfied and content look on his face. He crossed his arms and watched with personal fulfillment, as if he was god, as if he had just created new life.

In a way, he did.

"Now how do you feel?" he asked her.

"Scared," she admitted. She could still talk normally. She was still very humanoid in size and shape. But also very feline as well.

The new mutations seemed to have stopped. The transformation experience finally appeared to be over. She was now part human and part black cat. She felt alive, she felt healthy, she did *not* feel like she was about to vomit or roll over and die.

It was a weird sensation. As her brain adapted to its new body, she felt a new center of balance, new control over her tail, strange cat-like impulses and desires mixing with her own human thoughts and feelings.

It was odd. It was weird. But it also felt like *her* body. Her skin. Her fur. Her whiskers.

"Am I?" she asked, "Am I stuck this way?"

"Obey me and do as I command – and one day, when my plan is complete, I may free you and return you to your former self, if you've served me well."

"I…" She started to cry. "I can't *live* like this. How will I eat? Where will I live?" Even if she did as he asked – where and how would she live in the meantime? She couldn't go to work. Couldn't go out in public. Couldn't do *anything* looking like this. She was *completely* dependent on him for survival now.

"Relax."

She felt relaxed all of the sudden.

"I will feed you, I will give you shelter, but you must work for me, swear your full allegiance and eternal loyalty to me, and all will be provided for."

She nodded, sniffling back her tears.

"Do you swear it? Will you be my servant for life?"

Like she had a choice.

She nodded. "Uh huh."

"Say it."

"I will be your servant for life."

He smiled.

"You'll enjoy working for me?"

She nodded. "I'll enjoy working for you. Master."

He smiled more.

"And so it is."

What just happened? She felt different somehow.

"You are now free to move and speak as you wish," he told her. "Embrace your new life." It was the last time he needed to make eye contact with her.

Suddenly she felt herself free to stretch and move about. She held out her arms and examined her legs and body. Practiced waving and moving that new tail of hers – something she quickly found easy to sense and control. She stretched, and when she did, her claws extended from her fingers and toes, much like they do when a cat stretches. She yawned real big. Licked her lips. And smiled.

She walked around. First on two legs, then on all fours. Both felt easy and free. Both started to feel more and more effortless and natural. What had happened to her? How did this happen to her?

It didn't matter. She worked for the mysterious man now – for as long as he needed her. And when his plan – whatever it was – was finished, he'd set her free. Like he promised.

It was a little weird at first getting used to her new body, but she quickly found herself getting very comfortable in it.

For a brief moment, she thought about her old self. The human-only version of Tiffany. She had a whole life waiting for her. She was going to college, pursuing a degree. She looked forward to one day meeting the right man, falling in love, getting married, and having children of her own.

Children, not kittens.

But those dreams would have to wait for now. Her new master could return her to normal when he was done with her, if she served him well. So for now, she worked for him – gladly, willingly, faithfully – and he promised to feed and clothe her, provide shelter, give her a new home.

She worked for him now. But maybe that wasn't such a bad thing. She felt a strange acceptance, an easy embracing of her new life. And the more she thought about it, the more she felt she'd actually *enjoy* working for him. And although she never would have imagined it before, she actually *wanted* to be his faithful servant. It felt good. It felt right. It felt natural.

That's who she was. That's what she wanted. This was where she finally belonged.

Fully embracing her new cat-self, she got down on all fours, gracefully walked over to him, and sat by his side. Her tail flapped playfully.

He petted her and lightly scratched behind her ears. She actually started purring. Yeah, she thought, this was gonna be good. She was really going to enjoy this new life, as a humanoid cat girl, faithfully and obediently serving her new master.

She was sure it had *nothing* to do with the fact that he told her to think and feel that way. As far as she was concerned, she really did, all on her own.

And he seemed very pleased with her.

He walked up to Dawn.

Test subject #3.

He smirked at her. "What's *your* favorite animal?"

Dawn looked at the animals in the cages. She swallowed hard. She knew exactly what was coming. She could choose between a cat, a snake, a spider, or a parrot. None of them seemed particularly ideal for spending the rest of her life as. She didn't buy the "I'll return you to normal after I'm done with you" bit either. Nothing about this man told her she should trust him.

"Choose one," he told her.

She tried to avoid eye contact, but she instinctively glanced toward his eyes, to see if he was still looking – and he was. Her eyes immediately turned to the cages and tanks. She had to choose one.

A cat? And be like Tiffany over here? Maybe that wouldn't be so bad. Cats were friendly, cuddly, and "purrrrfect". Ha ha ha. Yeah right. No thanks. She did *not* want to suddenly find herself coughing up hairballs or using a litter box. Hmm. The snake. That was easy: no. What about the spider? Ew, yuck. Or the bird. This one had plucked out most of its feathers, but of the few that remained, it looked like a very colorful and beautiful bird. And birds can fly. So that could be cool.

"I'm waiting," he said impatiently. "Make a decision now, stupid girl."

She had better control of her reflexes this time. Her eyes remained fixed on the animals, not the mysterious man.

She wanted to choose – but, amazingly, she still hadn't. He *just* told her to make a decision "now" – and she was still delaying! Awesome! It worked. He didn't have complete power over her anymore! All she had to do was avoid eye contact at all costs! No problem … right?

"Never mind!" he shouted. "I'll choose for you."

He walked over to the metal case, grabbed a fresh syringe, and filled it with the glowing green chemical.

He came up to Dawn. And standing directly in front of her, he said, "Now take off your clothes. All of them…"

Her eyes were closed shut tight.

He stopped for a moment. She was obviously avoiding eye contact. "Open your eyes. *Now*," he demanded.

It took *all* her strength and willpower to keep them closed tight. She resisted him with every fiber in her being.

"I said, OPEN YOUR EYES NOW!" he shouted, uncontrollably losing his temper.

She turned her head away, eyes still tightly shut.

"You little bitch. You think you're *sooo* smart."

He stabbed her in the arm, injecting the chemical into her.

"Ouch! You son of a bitch!" The sudden pain and shock made her turn to look at him, even if only in anger, for a split second. It was all he needed. "Now keep your eyes open and obey me!"

Oh shit. She felt her resistance melt away. She suddenly *wanted* to keep her eyes open and obey every word he said. It made her happy, made her feel good. She *longed* to do as he willed for her.

Her eyes stayed open. He made a direct command. "Now get naked, fully. I'm going to enjoy watching you mutate."

Dawn felt all too happy and willing to get completely naked in his presence.

He sighed. "Finally."

Suddenly, a loud masculine voice called from the far end of the room. "Alright, everybody, *freeze*!"

Dawn and Ray turned to see a police officer holding a gun from across the room. It was pretty easy for him to figure out who to point the gun at, too.

The mysterious man, holding an empty syringe needle, in front of a naked girl and her fear-paralyzed friend, was the clear choice.

"Drop the needle, now!"

He faced the cop and started laughing.

"Don't look in his eyes! Cover your ears!" Dawn shouted.

"What?" he replied.

"Just do it!" shouted Ray.

"Don't listen to them," said the mysterious man.

"I said drop the needle!"

"You will obey every word I say," he said, stepping closer and closer.

The cops eyes were moving around rapidly enough that, apparently and rather luckily, they hadn't been looking into the mysterious man's eyes the two times he spoke.

This was one f'ed-up crime scene. A bloody mutilated body on the floor, a naked young woman getting injected with God-knew-what… What the *hell* was going on in here?

The mysterious man continued getting closer.

"I said drop it and put your hands up!"

"Officer, I can explain…" he said, taking another step closer.

Maybe it was instinct, maybe it was a reflex, maybe it was good training, maybe it was just luck – but the officer fired off one shot, and it hit the mysterious man, right in the shoulder.

The mysterious man fell over, landing hard on the floor, bleeding. Momentarily stunned, he looked down at his flesh wound. Blood. His own blood.

He lightly touched it. He couldn't believe it. He was shot. Someone *actually* shot him!

"Down on the ground! Hands where I can see them!" The cop moved in closer to cuff the mysterious man, holding the gun over him at all times. He looked to Ray and Dawn. "You two okay?"

"Just in the nick of time, officer," said Dawn.

"You have no idea."

But wait. Weren't they forgetting somebody?

Out of the shadows, from a high up ledge, a large black humanoid cat leaped out and pounced onto the policeman. She slashed at him with her razor sharp claws, instantly slicing bloody lines into his flesh and cutting through his uniform.

"Don't you dare!" Dawn exclaimed, charging towards Tiffany. She slammed into the cat girl, and the two tumbled off of the officer. Tiffany slashed at Dawn, slicing through her skin like butter. It stung with unimaginable pain.

Dawn had to grab Tiffany by the wrists, holding those lethal claws at bay.

Suddenly it became a strength of wills, a battle of muscle and nothing more.

Tiffany started to win.

God, Dawn would give anything for more strength right about now.

And suddenly, in less than two seconds, her arm muscles grew significantly larger and stronger. In seconds, she had the arms of a professional body builder.

"What the hell?" she asked herself.

Tiffany was equally confused.

But that question could wait for now. With her sudden new strength, she easily overpowered and pushed back Tiffany.

Meanwhile the cop quickly surveyed his wounds, determined they were non-life threatening, and continued to hold his gun over the mysterious man. "Hands over your head!" he shouted. The mysterious man, still staring at his flesh wound, slowly moved his hands to the top of his head. Handcuffs suddenly latched and locked over his wrists.

Dawn held Tiffany pinned down on the ground. The cat girl tried to squirm her way free, and almost did break free twice, but Dawn's body somehow naturally adapted and countered it. Her arm muscles remained big and strong. But for better traction and grip on the ground, her bare feet had morphed into multi-toed claws with large thick nails that dug into the concrete floor.

The cop clicked his radio. "...How you doing out there? There's some seriously freaky shit going down up here."

His partner's voice called back over the radio. "I got him. But I'm going to need an interpreter to communicate with this guy. I think he's deaf."

"Yeah. I might need some backup up here," said the first officer.

"Be right there."

Several minutes later, a few more police cars had arrived on scene. Their blue and red lights flashed in silence, reflecting off the graffiti-filled walls and rusting metal gates.

Doctor Troyd and Tiffany were placed in the back of separate cars, handcuffed and safely locked up. A crime scene investigation team had already begun canvasing the area, collecting all the evidence they needed to lock up these weirdos for a lifetime. They also called animal control to pick up and treat the caged animals. And the team collected all the samples of the strange green glowing chemical they could find.

At the same time, an officer took Dawn and Ray's statements for his report.

Dawn had her clothes back on by now, of course, and once again looked fully human and totally normal. Apparently those strange mutations appeared in the heat of a needed moment. Probably just a reaction from the glowing green chemical that had been injected into her. But once things had calmed down, Dawn's body returned to its normal size, shape, and appearance. Even her slash wounds from Tiffany's claw attack had miraculously healed up.

They told the cops everything. About the mysterious man's apparent mind control. Who Tiffany was and how the mutated guy died. The strange chemical. Everything.

The officer was skeptical about the "mind control" part. It sounded just a little too far-fetched for him. The mysterious man obviously must've threatened or coerced them somehow. Maybe "mind control" was just less embarrassing for them. Or they had seen one too many sci-fi movies. Whatever. It didn't matter. They had the deaf scientist and mysterious man on charges of kidnapping, illegal human experimentation, animal cruelty, and murder.

Under normal circumstances, the mysterious man might've been taken to a hospital under policy custody, to tend to his bullet wound, before being put in jail to await trial. But based on what the arresting officer saw, and Dawn and Ray's statements, they didn't want to take any chances with this one. Just to be safe.

So instead, they called a paramedic to come down and patch him up on site. It was a minor flesh wound. Bullet went right through. Left a lot of blood, but other than that, the man would be fine.

The mysterious man sat there, silently staring blankly, as the paramedic stitched him up. Then with his wound closed up and his arm in a sling, the medic cleared him for transport.

Ray let out a slow sigh of relief.

It was over. They were finally safe.

He held Dawn's hand. So glad he decided to trust his instincts and follow them here. He couldn't believe he almost died – or got mutated into something weird – in the process. He was going to need a lot of therapy after this.

After patching up the mysterious man, the medic checked Dawn for all her vitals. She had, after all, been exposed to the unidentified chemical. But they assured the cops it was a two-part process; Dawn never received the animal blood injection. The medic couldn't find anything wrong with Dawn, but still advised her to check in to the hospital for more thorough tests and overnight supervision.

But Dawn didn't have any health insurance. And she felt fine. She was sure she was fine.

Dawn leaned onto Ray's shoulder. He wrapped his arm around her and held her close. This was an evening they'd never forget. But somehow, terrifying as it was, it brought them much closer together.

"Hey, idea," Ray softly said to her. "Next date, how do you feel about staying in?"

"That sounds wonderful," she said.

"Okay," said the officer, finishing his report. "You two are free to go. We'll be in touch if we have any more questions."

Three of the other police cars drove off, each carrying one of the bad guys safely to prison.

"Thank you, officer," Ray said. And then, lightly squeezing Dawn's hand, he said to her, "Come on, let's go home."

Chapter 7
RETURNING HOME

Dawn was pretty quiet the whole ride back. Ray understood. It was a lot to take in. A lot to process. He could barely get a handle on it all himself.

"Where should I turn?" Ray asked.

"Sorry?" She seemed lost in another world.

"Which exit, to get you home?"

"Scott Road." She paused. "But Ray?"

"Yeah?"

"I don't want to be alone tonight."

He completely understood. He kind of felt the same way. He thought about it for a moment, still driving northbound on the freeway. "I know we just met and all, but how would you feel about—"

"Yes!" she interrupted. "Please."

He laughed. "You didn't even let me finish."

"Okay. Sorry. Please continue."

"I was just saying, I know I only met you earlier today, and we've only had one date – well, sort of. Anyway, if you're comfortable with it, if you want to – you're welcome to stay at my place, if that'll make you feel safer tonight."

She nodded. "It would."

"Okay. Cool."

She laughed softly. "You know, technically, you've already seen me naked."

"That's true."

"I'm not usually that kind of girl. Just so you know. It was his mind control."

"I know," he smiled. "I know."

"But I really do like you. And I'm just saying that, if you play your cards right, *someday*… you might see me naked again. Not tonight. But someday."

"Is that a fact?" he said, smiling.

"Maybe. We'll see. If you're lucky," she said, smiling playfully.

"Some first date, huh?"

"Tell me about it."

"You're sure you still feel fine, right? I'll cover the hospital bill. I just want to make sure you're okay."

She smiled. "I'm fine. Really. I just want to go to sleep."

He nodded.

And they turned off the exited towards Luke and Ray's apartment.

Chapter 8

THE JOURNEY BEGINS

While Ray's imagination got lost picturing himself naked in bed with Dawn, Luke and his uncle were in… well…

They had problems.

Here's what happened. Luke and his uncle stepped through the portal, out onto the sand, and saw the ancient stone ruins all around them. In the distance was a pyramid, which Uncle Charlie seemed a little confused about, and Luke soon noticed two alien moons above.

Clearly, they were on another planet.

"I don't think we're in Egypt..." said Luke.

Beloved uncle Charlie nodded. "I know," he said softly.

Luke seemed surprised. "You do?"

The old man looked around, took a long deep sigh, and drank from his water bottle. "Actually, I've been here before. Once, maybe twice, a long time ago." He thought about it. "Maybe twenty-something years now. You were just a baby back then."

Luke's mouth hung open.

"You see, the Tablet of Ningishzida had five symbols on it," he said. "A basic triangle was one of them. Apparently each symbol led to a different destination. Draw any circular or doorway shape with the crystal onto a solid surface, mark a specific symbol in the center, and a portal would open up to specific world."

"What?"

"The triangle shape you drew was one of the five symbols. Every time we opened a portal with that symbol, it always led here. My papa – your great grandfather – also came here first."

Charlie looked at the pyramid ahead.

"Although, I don't remember him mentioning seeing any pyramids. Just the ruins we saw back at the portal exit. It's why we never came here much. This place is just a whole lotta desert."

"Should we go back now?" asked Luke. His water bottle was already half empty.

"If you want. Although, to be honest, I'd like to get a closer look at that pyramid."

"Okay," said Luke. And they continued to traverse the long, burning hot desert sands.

The endless desert went on as far as the eye could see. Giant sand dunes slowly shifted across the desert floor as fierce hot winds continued to blow. The air was so dry. Luke took another drink from his water bottle.

Meanwhile, his uncle explained more about the crystal and its history.

He, himself, had been to all five locations. Well, sort of. Three led to other worlds. He had visited all of those. One was too dangerous to visit, so he never went there. And the last one, he said, actually led back to Earth.

"And you'll never guess where," he said.

"Where?" asked Luke, finishing off his water bottle.

"Stonehenge."

Stonehenge? Yeah right. Luke was never big on alien conspiracies, despite his love of science-fiction. "Whatever."

"Told you you wouldn't believe me," said Charlie, grinning. "But if you're ever lost or trapped, draw that symbol, and it'll take you back to England. Last minute international flights are a bit expensive, but at least it'll get you home."

They stopped for a second.

"Here," said Uncle Charlie, leaning down toward the sand. "Let me show it to you."

He drew a small circle, then divided it horizontally and vertically with two straight lines. Luke had actually recognized it from before. It was the astronomical symbol for Earth.

It gave him chills.

Every celestial body in the solar system had its own symbol. The sun was a circle with a dot in the middle. Venus's symbol was the same one used to represent "female"; Mars's symbol was also used for "male". Saturn's symbol looked kind of like a lowercase "h"; Neptune's symbol looked like the Roman god Neptune's trident. And Earth… a circle divided into four corners.

These symbols went back to ancient times. Was it just a coincidence Earth's symbol was the same one that opened a portal here – or was there some deeper meaning?

"Stonehenge, you say?" he was almost afraid to ask.

Charlie stood back up. He saw Luke's empty water bottle. He didn't have much left himself. He looked back. The portal was still open, in the distance. They had already walked a long way. If they were going to make it to the pyramid and back, then had better get going. Charlie knew what would happen if they waited too long.

"Come on, let's keep going. I need to see something."

Luke was a little lost in thought for a moment, staring off into space. When his uncle kept walking, Luke snapped out of it and caught up.

They hiked up a large sand dune, still headed towards the pyramid in the distance. It wasn't too far now. The pyramid looked a lot larger than Luke expected. He had never seen one in real life. They started descending down the sand dune. But sand can be deceptive. Sand can appear stable when it's not. Sand can appear solid when it's anything but.

One misstep and –

Suddenly, without warning, Luke lost his footing and began sliding uncontrollably down the shifting hillside.

"Luke!" his uncle yelled. He reached out, but missed.

It all happened so fast. Luke tumbled down the steep sand dune, pulling more and more sand along with him, triggering an unstoppable avalanche. Within seconds, the ground under Charlie's feet began shifting too.

"Wh-whoa!" he said as he fell down, sliding backwards, falling all the way down the collapsing sand dune's edge.

The two men – one a young man in his mid-twenties and the other an old man in his early sixties – tumbled, rolled, bounced, and slid farther and farther down. Their momentum built, sand flew everywhere, and Luke managed to glance ahead at where this was taking them.

In the middle of the desert, nestled between steep sand dunes, was a dark rocky pit.

A giant hole in the ground.

"Oh nooooo!!!" Luke shouted as they slid down, down, down – no way to stop or change course – tumbling over, about to fall in. Luke reached to grab at the ledge. Sand flew at his eyes. He managed to grab a stable rock. Then Charlie crashed into him, Luke's grip slipped, and they both fell in.

Suddenly free falling.

Falling.

Falling.

Falling farther down still, deep into the darkness, as sand from above continued to pour in over their heads and all around them.

"Hold on!" yelled Charlie.

"To what?!" remarked Luke.

SPLASH.

At least there was water on this planet.

But damn, was it *cold.*

They submerged deep into the icy, dark waters. It slowed their decent. Slowly, they both came to a stop at some unknown black depth, and began to rise to the surface.

Several impossibly long seconds later, they surfaced. They each gasped for air.

"Luke, Luke… are you okay?"

He coughed. "Yeah, Uncle. I think I'm fine." He coughed up some water. "You?"

"We've got to find some shore."

Easier said than done. It was all but pitch black down here. They had fallen pretty deep. They treaded water, trying to let their eyes adjust to the darkness.

The only think Luke could see was the little light that leaked in through the pit opening, *way* high above.

"I think I see something," said Charlie.

"This water is freezing!"

"I know. Try to keep warm. This way."

They swam deeper into the darkness, farther away from the little light that did reach this far down. The sand pouring in from above slowed down and finally drizzled to a stop. For a moment, there was an eerie calmness. A stillness to the light and dust.

This place was huge. Some sort of enormous underground cavern or aquifer. They could be anywhere.

"Yup, I definitely see something," said his uncle.

"How?"

"Trust this old man, would ya?"

"Okay." Luke swam after him. He glanced one last time at the dim shaft of light that reached this far. He hated to swim farther away from it. But he couldn't keep treading in this icy cold water.

Good thing he could swim. He couldn't imagine just how deep below he'd find the bottom. They crashed pretty hard. Went under pretty deep. He was going to feel all sorts of pains and bruises in the morning, he was sure.

"Ah hah! I knew it!" declared his uncle. "Look! Look!"

Luke strained to see farther ahead. "What? Where? I don't see it."

"Here!" said his uncle. "Follow my voice, it's right here!"

Luke treaded closer. He reached out into the darkness. Suddenly he felt his hand touch something solid.

Charlie climbed up onto it. Some kind of large smooth rock surface. It was nearly impossible to see. How on Earth – or wherever they were – did he see that?

He got a secure footing and reached out to help Luke up. Luke climbed up onto the ledge.

"W-Where d-d-do you th-th-ink we ar-r-re?" Luke asked.

"You're shivering. Take off your shirt. We need to get you warm."

Luke peeled off his soaking wet shirt. He and his uncle quickly rubbed his arms and torso, trying to create some friction to warm up his core vitals. It started to help.

"You okay?"

He was still shivering a bit, but getting better. He nodded as he continued to rub the sides of his arms. "Yeah. I'll b-be fine." He laughed. "Been l-living in southern C-California for too long. Not u-used to being this c-cold."

Uncle Charlie licked his finger and held it out in the air. He couldn't feel any breeze coming from any direction. "No breeze. That's good. As soon as you start to dry, you'll be fine."

He started to warm up. "This is crazy. Where are we?"

His uncle looked around. "My guess is some kind of subterranean ocean. Makes sense. Whoever built the pyramid would need access to water somewhere."

"Hello?" Luke shouted into the darkness. Several seconds later, his voice echoed back. "Hello!" Another delayed echo. "Echo! Echo! Echo!" Luke laughed. "And presenting, weighing in at 175 pounds and shivering cold, Luke Powers, champion of the underworld!"

His uncle laughed. "Glad to see you haven't lost your sense of humor."

Luke smiled. But soon the reality of the situation kicked in.

"You still have the crystal?" asked Charlie, trying to stay upbeat and positive – but with a clear worry behind his voice.

Luke quickly searched his pockets. He pulled it out.

"It's here."

It was their only source of light. It still glowed.

They both gave a sigh of relief.

"Thank God for that," said Charlie.

"So… I guess we're going to Stonehenge, huh?"

Charlie balked. "Not necessarily. You give up too easily."

"Huh?"

"Now listen carefully, Luke. I want you to always remember this. No matter how bad things get, no matter how dark the situation looks… you always have hope. There's *always* a way out. If there's one thing I've learned in all my years, it's that there's always hope, there's always a way out – or through – any problem."

"Okay. So… what do you suggest we do?"

"Got me."

At that very moment, Ray unlocked his apartment door. Like a true gentleman, he held it open and invited Dawn inside.

"And here we are. Welcome to my humble abode."

She walked in, looked around, saw the comic book and movie posters on the wall, the minimal cheap furniture… "Nice place," she said.

"Thanks. We like to keep our costs low. Luke only works part-time and I'm in grad school, so… you do the math."

"Got it. No worries." She stopped for a second. Just took a deep breath.

"You okay?" He reached his arm around her.

"Yeah, sorry. Just can't stop thinking about that poor guy, and our waitress… I can't believe that man could control us like that… It's…"

"It's okay," said Ray, trying to be strong. "I know. I was there too. It's going to take some time to—" He walked past the wall that currently still had an open portal to a desert world on it. "What – the – fuck?"

Dawn saw it at the exact same time. A giant hole in the wall, open to a huge desert on the other side. What the hell? She was dreaming, right? This whole evening – everything – was all some really weird, really messed up dream. Right?

"What the hell is that?" she asked.

"Uh…" Ray wanted to answer. If only he had one.

Sand spilled out into the living room, overflowing from the base of the portal. Hot air blew in from the other side, keeping the air conditioner on full blast. The apartment was still warm.

Ray looked deeper through the portal. He saw the vast open desert – and what looked to be a pyramid in the distance.

"Luke?" he leaned back, calling down the apartment hallway. "Luke, are you home?"

No response.

Dawn pulled herself closer to Ray, holding onto his arm.

"Luke?"

"Maybe we should've gone to my place," Dawn said, trying to be funny.

"I swear we've entered the Twilight Zone or something."

"Or something."

"Luke!" he called again. "Dammit, where is he?" He pulled out his cell phone and dialed Luke.

It went straight to his voicemail.

"Um, Luke…? Where are you? You okay, buddy?"

Dawn bravely stepped closer to the portal. She looked around the edge, seeing more of the world on the other side. She raised her finger, about to poke it through.

"What are you doing?!" exclaimed Ray.

She pushed her hand all the way through the opening. "I think it's real," she said.

"Just stay away from it."

"I think…" she said, looking back at Ray. "I think it might be a portal or something."

"A portal?"

"Yeah. I acted in this really low budget sci-fi short one time. The characters used 'transdimensional portals' to travel to other worlds half way across the galaxy. Only there was this evil alien race that wanted to use the portal technology to attack Earth and enslave the human race."

"I… see."

Dawn shrugged. "Well, you have a better idea?"

"No."

She waved her hand through the opening, feeling around.

"You think… Luke went through it?" Ray asked.

Dawn shrugged. "Only one way to find out. You feel up for another crazy adventure tonight?"

Ray laughed. Not really. But Luke was nowhere to be found; he should've been home by now. Why wasn't he answering his calls? Ray stared at the open portal. Knowing Luke, if he saw this, he couldn't resist going in and exploring it. He sighed. "Dammit, Luke."

Dawn walked over to Ray. She held both his hands, looked him in the eyes, and smiled like an excited little girl. "Just *imagine* what might be on the other side!"

"Wait," said Ray. "Just a minute ago, you were still in shock from the whole mind control guy. And now you want to go do this?"

"You don't?"

"No, that's not what I'm saying. I'm saying, I mean…" He looked at her and he looked at the portal. "How do we know it's even safe?"

"We don't."

"How do we know the portal won't close on us as soon as we walk through?"

"We don't."

"How do we know somebody *worse* than Mr. Mind Control isn't waiting on the other side?"

"We don't," she said.

"Then how can you so confidently want to just walk through and see what's on the other side?"

She nodded. He had a point. And then she placed both her hands gently on his face, looked deeply into his eyes, and kissed him. "Because," she said, "I learned a long, long time ago that when opportunity presents itself and you feel afraid – do it, do it anyway, and do it right away."

He gave her a curious look.

"Everything I've ever done worthwhile has always been scary at first."

"But, what if something goes wrong?"

"Then you live and learn. And you grow from it."

He looked at her carefully. She was serious. She meant it.

"There's always something to be afraid of, if you let it," she said. "But an opportunity to cross through a real-life portal and set foot on another world? That comes once in a lifetime. Less. I bet this is the *first* time *anyone's* had this opportunity."

"Yeah, but… where the hell did it come from? Why is it *here* in my apartment?"

She shrugged. "I don't know. But I bet the answers are on the other side…"

Ray shook his head. This was crazy. But… she was right. Luke was off work today. He didn't have much of a social life. So he probably stayed home watching movies or playing games all day. And wherever this portal came from, if Luke was here when it happened, he almost definitely would've walked through it.

He sighed.

"Alright."

She smiled with excitable enthusiasm. "Awesome!" She got up, holding his hand, leading them to the portal.

"Wait, wait. One second," he said.

"What?"

"We need to go in prepared. I'm a business man. I like to plan for contingencies. If we get stranded on the other side or find Luke dying of heat exhaustion or something, we need to come prepared."

"Right. Good thinking."

"I've got some old camping gear in my closet. We need to bring extra water, some food, a first aid kit… Maybe change our clothes into something more fitting. It might be a little loose on you, but you can borrow some of mine."

"Already trying to get me in your pants, eh?" she smiled.

"Well…"

She giggled. "Right, right. Got it. I'll help you pack."

"This way," he said, leading her to his room.

Chapter 9
MASTERMIND

The mysterious man sat in the back of a police car, hands cuffed, waiting silently and patiently for just the right moment.

There were two officers up front; one driving, obviously, and the other undoubtedly his partner. Neither were the one who shot him. He couldn't believe it. Some son of a bitch actually shot him.

Whatever. There were more important things to think about.

Doctor Troyd finally did it. The formula worked. Only took three batches, just short of a dozen "volunteers", and nearly a half a million dollars to make it work. But the crazy and morally-gray scientist finally came through.

Doctor Troyd named the formula "BioGen-X". The first batch, despite promising results from animal lab tests, proved completely ineffective. It made the volunteers sick and woozy, with some vomiting or diarrhea, and a few days later killed them with some strange kind of cancer… but beyond that, nothing. If he wanted to take over the world by making people sick, that version of the formula would've worked fine.

But that wasn't his plan.

Batch #2 was a little more effective. But the results were unstable. It caused various random and unpredictable mutations, but every single volunteer died in the process.

Up until this point, the mysterious man had selected his volunteers from society's forgotten, rejected, and abandoned. Homeless men and women from Skid Row, teenage runaways, unemployed drug addicts. That sort of thing. People no one would miss. People that had already disappeared from society's attention.

But, after the second batch of BioGen-X, he began to realize just how sensitive the formula was to the volunteer's health and biochemical state. Everyone he had picked up so far were alcoholics and drug addicts, with traces of God-knew-what still lingering in their systems. Not to mention any possible number of random diseases and illnesses they had picked up from living on the streets, eating out of dumpsters, and having unprotected sex with questionable characters.

It was a little riskier – okay, a lot riskier – taking ordinary, healthy, hygienically-pleasing people as volunteers. But it had to be done.

And it was worth it. It worked!

He smiled. It worked.

He looked down as the bullet wound in his left shoulder. It still hurt like a bitch. They were going to pay for this. All of them. With their lives.

No, better yet, with their loyalty. He would enslave them all. The arresting police officers. The blonde girl and that black kid that escaped. All of them. He'd make them his mutants, enslave them, and control them for the rest of their unnatural and inhuman lives!

Obeying his every command. Bidding to his every will. Following every order. Living only to serve him.

"Muwahahah!" he laughed out loud.

"Hey, quiet down back there!" ordered one of the officers.

Later at the police station, the mysterious man found himself at the wrong end of an interrogation table inside a locked room.

A young woman in uniform dropped several photos in front of him. Cliché, yes, but to be expected. They were crime scene photos of that kid who died. The half-mutated failure, all because the donor blood from the dog was clearly infected.

"What the hell is going on here?" she demanded. "We can't even ID this … man … because his fingers aren't even human anymore! Safe to say his dental records are going to come back negative, too."

She dropped the police file photo of Tiffany next. "Looks like *she* was more successful. What kind of sick, twisted—?"

"You really want to know?" he asked her, smirking.

"You're looking at life in prison for this shit. Kidnapping, illegal and unethical human experimentation, murder… You *sure* you don't want a lawyer?"

"I don't need a lawyer," he said calmly.

Doctor Troyd was a little less confident. He panicked. He cracked like an egg. Once they had an interpreter in the room, he told them *everything*.

"Please," he signed. *"I'll cooperate!"*

Unfortunately, he wasn't much help. He merely confirmed Ray and Dawn's story. Information they already knew. Doctor Troyd was unable to name the mysterious man. He swore he didn't know it either! And he felt *terrible* about the conditions the animals were left in, and what happened to the kidnapped victims. He couldn't control any of it. He got no special pleasure out of it. The mysterious man was powerful. And even though Doctor Troyd seemed to be immune to the mysterious man's mind control – there were other ways of getting leverage.

"My daughter," he signed. *"Please, protect my daughter."*

The scientist told them the whole story. He used to have a prestigious job doing research at a major university, until budget cuts ended his employment less than a year away from tenure. He tried to get another job at another university, but there were hiring freezes everywhere!

Desperate to survive and provide a home for his teenage daughter, he found work doing freelance research and development for various pharmaceuticals and biotech firms.

But it wasn't very steady, credit card bills stacked up, and he fell behind on his mortgage payments. He was two weeks away from getting kicked out onto the streets. Then the mysterious man somehow came across him – and offered him an irresistible deal.

If Doctor Troyd agreed to develop a mutagenic chemical that met certain requirements, the mysterious man promised more than just money. He promised something that money couldn't buy.

"And what's that?" asked the interrogator.

The translator signed it for him.

"My daughter," the scientist signed. *"She sings."*

"And he threatened to harm her if you didn't help?"

"Yes, but," signed Doctor Troyd, *"if I helped, he promised to restore my hearing."*

His wallet and other personal items were out on the table. He reached for his wallet, opened it up, and pulled out a picture of his daughter.

She was beautiful. Maybe seventeen years old.

"She won the state competition," he signed. *"She's flying to Vegas for the regionals next month."*

The interpreter translated all this for the interrogator.

"I just want to hear my baby girl sing. She's all that's left of my wife."

Meanwhile, back in the previous interrogation room, the officer was quickly losing patience.

"Dammit!" she shouted. "Tell me what you were planning to do with these kids!"

"Tell me," he grinned, and said to her, "what's *your* favorite animal?"

And speaking of animals, Tiffany was dealing with her own private interrogation.

She at least had the sense to ask for a lawyer to be present during her questioning. It was late at night, and she had no money or matching ID, so a public servant had to be called in last minute.

When he arrived, he stopped dead in his tracks, and stared at the girl in disbelief for several long seconds, before snapping himself out of it. "Okay," he said. He was a young man, well dressed in his suit and tie, carrying a briefcase. Barely old enough to have just graduated from law school. "This is…" he said, seemingly at a loss for words. Suddenly he lit up with excitement. "…going to re-write the law books! I'm going to be famous! Wahoo!" He actually jumped for joy into the air, briefcase in hand, suit and tie and all.

"Counselor," said one of the two officers present in the room.

"Yes, right, of course. I'm sorry." He eagerly sat down next to Tiffany. He leaned over to her. "We'll have your case tied up in court for *years* while the politicians, legislature, and religious interests debate over the definition of 'person'."

She gave him a strange look.

"Oh, no offense. I'm just saying – the law only applies to humans."

"Oh," she said with a smile. She started to flap her tail excitedly. She was neither human nor animal. She was something new. Something special. She liked being a cat person more and more with each passing second.

Meanwhile, elsewhere in the police station, the arresting officer worked closely with one of the detectives. They stared at a computer screen currently trying to match the finger prints.

"Still nothing? How long does this usually take?"

"No matches in the national database. I've extended the search to partnering nations. Could take a while. But if he had a criminal record in the States, we would've found something by now."

"What about his plates?" The officer checked his notepad. "Black 2011 BMW 550i sedan, license plate M-A-S-T-R-M-N-D. What's the DMV record say?"

"Blank."

"What?"

"There's a record for it, but all the fields are blank. It's like someone went in and erased everything."

The officer sighed. "Think he's some kind of hacker?"

"Sure, why not? Mind control, turning college kids into mutant monsters, computer hacker too… Might as well call him a 'super villain' and save the paperwork."

"That's not funny."

"What about his personal belongings? Any leads there?"

The officer had everything in a small box beside him. "There's not much. Car keys, cell phone, wallet with a few hundred dollars cash and no IDs or credit cards, Doctor Troyd's business card... And whatever the hell this is."

He held up a small pink crystal that gave off a faint glow.

"Precious gem of some kind?"

"Maybe."

"Alright, we'll have to go with that. There's gotta be a paper trail somewhere. Find every gem dealer in the area and see if any of them recognize this guy. I seriously doubt he picked this up at the local mall. And while we're at it, let's check any museums or exhibits that reported any thefts recently."

The mysterious man was anything but cooperative. He almost acted as if this whole scenario amused him. He was confident, he was cocky, and he couldn't care less what they said to him.

Life in prison? Doubtful.

Death row? Improbable.

Finding out his real name? Even less so.

He told them nothing. He gave them nothing. He just taunted and mocked them, every step of the way. Strangely, though, he never once used his mind control powers. He could have. He had *plenty* of opportunities. But no, for now, he just played along.

He was up to something.

He was about to make his move.

Finally frustrated with him, they threw him in a holding cell with a handful of other random criminals. Car thieves, bank robbers, drug dealers. The random scum of the day, caught by the ever-vigilant Los Angeles Police Department.

They were an intimidating and frightening crowd, to be sure. And the mysterious man, in his well-dressed expensive suit, looked dangerously out of place inside the same metal cage.

But he wasn't scared.

Nope, not one bit. Okay, maybe a *tiny* bit, but he didn't let it show. "Gentleman," he approached to the leering crowd. There were a couple females in the group too, one of which was so butch, she could've easily been mistaken as a man. "And ladies," he added, with some disgust. "I have a proposition for you..."

"Wait a second, we got something," said the detective. The computer apparently found a match in one of the international databases.

The arresting officer took a closer look.

"No, this can't be right," said the detective.

"What?"

"Look at the file photo."

It was a man – but the similarities stopped there. The person in the picture was easily 70 years old, if not older. Thinning, gray hair, he did not age well.

"You sure it's a match?"

"Prints match. And the face recognition software says there's a 92.7% match based on the eyes, nose, and facial structure. This is our guy."

"It can't be. You saw the guy I brought in. He's what – in his 30s? Maybe we're looking at his father."

"With the same finger prints?"

"Oh. Right."

"That's what I'm saying," said the detective. "There must be a mistake. This can't be our guy."

"You think he hacked this file, too? Linked his prints to some random old guy?"

"Maybe. I wouldn't put it past him," said the detective. He read the file report. "Says here this man is named William Gates."

"Bill Gates? As in Microsoft?" remarked the officer. "He's totally playing us."

"No," said the detective, reading the rest of the file. "Says here he was born in Amesbury, England in 1938. No police record until about five years ago, when he was arrested for stealing some artifact from the British Museum in London."

"Okay, so our perp found someone with similar facial features and linked his own prints to him, in case he ever got caught. We're still at square one."

"Yeah," said the detective, still reading. "This can't be the same guy. Obvious age difference aside, it says here that William Gates was legally deaf and going blind. And had a really bad limp, apparently from complications at birth."

"Definitely not our guy. So it's back to searching for leads on the gems dealer market."

"I'll keep searching the computer anyway. Maybe he missed something. No one's *that* good."

"I'm *that* good," said the mysterious man to his audience of thugs and random fellow criminals. "I can do anything."

One guy, a big black dude weighing in at over 300 pounds, crossed his arms in disbelief.

A prostitute – and clearly dressed like one – rolled her eyes while chewing bubble gum.

A tall skinny white guy, wearing a ratty white sleeveless shirt that exposed his hairy armpits and chest, seemed skeptical – and he believed UFOs abducted his aunt.

There were only two other people in the holding cell with him – a college-age kid, who judging by his colored bandana and tattoo was part of some gang; and the extremely masculine-looking woman, who lacked the foresight to realize that selling drugs to a teenager in front of a police station wasn't a very bright idea.

A bank robber, a prostitute, a car thief, an attempted (but as of yet, failed) murderer, and a drug dealer. Perfect. They'd do just fine.

"Proof?" said the mysterious man. "I understand." He looked at the five of them. Hmm. Who should he demonstrate with first? "You," he said to the big black guy. "Try to hurt me."

"What? Hell no. I'm in enough trouble already."

The mysterious man made eye contact. "Do it, now."

An irresistible compulsion came over the big guy. He was tired of all this arrogant man's ridiculous claims. "You know what?" said the black man. "You've been asking for a fight." He approached the mysterious man, ready to pummel him into the ground. And he could do it, too.

As soon as he took one step forward, the mysterious man again made eye contact and commanded, "And now, I want you to go over and kiss… 'her'." He pointed to the butch woman.

The big guy turned direction on his next step and headed straight for her.

The unattractive woman tried to back away. "What? Fuck off. Get the hell away from me."

The big guy went right up to her, grabbed her, and kissed her deeply and passionately. He seemed to enjoy it. She, on the other hand, squirmed and flailed her arms chaotically, trying to escape from his massive embrace.

The mysterious man chuckled. "Good, very good."

Everyone else was a little on edge now.

The big guy stopped. He paused for a moment, apparently a little confused. Why did he just do that?

The woman wiped her mouth with great disgust. "What the hell did you do that for?" she demanded.

He shrugged. "I dunno. I just wanted to."

The mysterious man smiled. "You," he said to the white-trash guy, the one who believed his aunt had been abducted by UFOs. "Pee in your pants right now."

"Whuh?" he replied, but before he could control himself, a wet stain appeared in the crotch of his pants. "Hey, not fair!"

Everyone stared at the wet spot. They were starting to believe. But they weren't completely convinced yet.

"And… how about you," the mysterious man said to the prostitute. What could he command her to do? Take off all her clothes? Nah. She might do that anyway. Hmm. Ah, he had it! "I want you to call over a cop right now and tell him who your 'manager' is."

Normally, she'd never reveal such a thing. But some strange compulsion came over her. It felt like a good idea. "Offic'r, hey offic'r!" she called. "Offic'r co'mere!"

"Yeah, yeah," said a nearby officer, having better things to do. "What is it?" He approached their holding cell.

She immediately told him the name of her pimp and how to find him. As soon as she did, she regretted it. If he ever found out – she'd be in so much trouble. But… something just came over her. She really *wanted* to tell the police all that information.

"Who *are* you?" she asked the mysterious man.

"Work for me, swear your loyalty and servitude – obey all that I command you – and I will give you riches and powers beyond your wildest imaginations."

"Look," said the big guy. "We ain't saying we don't believe you. But—"

Just then, Tiffany was escorted into the holding cell with them.

The other cellmates stared speechlessly.

"Oh, hi boss!" she said cheerfully to the mysterious man.

Her lawyer stood just outside the bars. "Don't worry," he told her with conviction. "They can't hold you here for long. I'll have you free by morning."

The mysterious man glanced at the lawyer. "She'll be free before then."

"She will?"

"Now go, leave us alone," he said to the lawyer, a command with eye contact.

"Yes, right. I have to go. I'll speak with you again soon," he said to Tiffany.

"*Now*," said the mysterious man, growing impatient.

The lawyer said not another word. He turned and left the room.

"They treating you okay, boss?" Tiffany asked her master.

"As well as to be expected." He lightly scratched behind her ear.

"Whoa, whoa, whoa," said the big guy. "Who—*what*—is *she*?"

"This is my first. Speaking of, we need a new name for you," he said to her. "Your old life is over. Your old name no longer suits you."

"Cat Girl? Should we call me Cat Girl?"

"I was thinking something a little less on the nose," he said.

"Ooh, how about Claws? Or Kitty? Or—"

"I like…" He thought for a moment. She was almost an entirely all-black cat, except for her white paws and feet, and the tip of her tail and ears. She'd hide well in the shadows… "Shadow. I'll call you Shadow."

She liked it.

And he turned to the others, "And you too can be one of my mutants. Gifted with superhuman form and abilities, and if you prove yourself loyal to me, powers even greater than this."

The butch woman seemed repulsed at the idea. "And why would we want to become *that*?"

Tiffany, now called Shadow, answered freely, "Boss takes care of me. He'll feed us, give us food and shelter. Protect us. He empowers us. I feel more alive, more powerful, more excited to be alive than ever before." She pranced around the cell with unexpected energy. "I know at first it looks weird, being a mutant – but let me tell you, that lawyer you just saw with me? He said that because I'm neither human nor animal, the law doesn't apply to me anymore."

The mysterious man said, "You will all be above the law. Working under my guidance, you will *be* the law. You will help me usher in a new world order, a time of world peace – under my control."

They all still seemed a little doubtful.

"It doesn't matter. You're all coming with me." He looked each one of them in the eye, one by one. "You agree to this. You want this. You will follow and obey me. You also agree. And you *definitely* want this," he said to each one of them.

They stood there, feeling a little dazed and confused, yet strangely willing to go along with him.

"What's our next move, boss?" Shadow asked him.

He smiled. "This."

Shadow got excited.

He called a police officer over. "Officer! Oh, officer!"

"What? What? Geez, you guys are the neediest group of cellmates I've ever—"

"Unlock this cell now. You're letting us go free."

All his years of training, all his police instincts – all sat aside to a suddenly overwhelming desire to unlock and open that cell, and let these people go free.

And that's exactly what the officer did.

The other cellmates, the new team of soon-to-be-mutated criminals, watched the whole thing. They were *definitely* convinced now.

"This way, follow me," he ordered them all. "Stay behind me." Then to Shadow he said, "Find Doctor Troyd. We still need him. Use whatever force necessary to retrieve him, but keep the good doctor unharmed, understood?"

"Right boss!" And she ran ahead with unnaturally fast cat-like speed and reflexes.

The others watched as she leaped over a desk, pounced on the back of a police officer, slashed the gun out of another's hands, and bolted around the corner with incredible speed and agility.

"Damn!" said the big guy.

Of course, all the present officers quickly went on alert. Most chased after Shadow, but a few saw the mysterious man and the other criminals walking free. A couple officers pulled guns on them and ordered them to stop.

The mysterious man locked eye contact with each of them, quickly one at a time, telling them each to point their gun at the other and shoot.

They fired on each other. They missed vital organs; they'd both live. But they wouldn't be interfering with his escape any longer.

The mysterious man and his recruited criminals walked fearlessly out into the main lobby.

"Shots fired! Shots fired!" an officer yelled. Two more took defensive positions and pointed their weapons at the mysterious man and small entourage of criminals.

"You," he commanded to one of the defending officers. "Fire upon all fellow officers!"

Bullets stared flying.

Another officer ran up to grab and re-arrest them. But the mysterious man locked eyes, gave an order, and the cop was irresistibly compelled to defend them, counter-attacking his fellow officers along the way.

Anyone within eye contact and earshot was given new commands. Some became voluntary human shields, escorting the mysterious man and his criminals toward the exit. Others were told to randomly start firing on each other. A few didn't need specific instructions from the mysterious man – the chaos and confusion of officers firing upon officers was enough to cause more officers to start firing at each other, if only to minimize the bloodshed.

Any detectives and other agents who weren't wearing a protective vest were among the first to go down.

The criminals, led by the mysterious man, made it out to the main room. The exit was just ahead. The mysterious man quickly mind-controlled anyone else nearby. They couldn't resist turning on each other.

More officers ran in from outside and adjacent rooms. A few stray bullets shot a couple unfortunate souls in the head before they even could grasp what was going on. Others were seriously wounded. Even those with bullet-proof vests weren't completely safe. The officers the mysterious man had enslaved had superior training and expert marksmanship.

It was officer against officer, many yelling for cease fire, but one by one the mysterious man locked eyes and commanded more and more officers to turn on and attack each other.

Bullets ripped through the air. Screaming, yelling, shouting, "officer down!" repeated a lot, "call for backup!" and more, too.

As one confused and mind-controlled officer ran past, the mysterious man grabbed his vest and tugged him closer. "You," he said, intensely locking eyes, "fetch my personal belongings."

Shadow soon returned with Doctor Troyd in tow, skillfully dodging around officers in defensive positions and ducking below flying bullets. "Found him, boss!" she shouted over the noise.

At the same time, the officer returned with the super villain's car keys, wallet, and the mysterious glowing pink crystal.

"Excellent work," he said, staring at his crystal.

Doctor Troyd looked around at the rapidly deteriorating situation – rapidly deteriorating for the "good guys" anyway. Everyone was in defensive positions. Fewer shots were now fired, because everyone was either in hiding or already shot down.

"We need more of the formula – and a variety of healthy animals." He signed to Doctor Troyd, simultaneously speaking it aloud.

"Right, yes, I know where to go," the scientist replied.

One officer, probably a new recruit, hid under his desk, shaking in terror. He had never seen one man so powerful, making fellow officers turn against each other in an instant, with nothing more than a spoken word. Wounded, dying, and already-dead officers were all around. Blood all over the walls. In the blink of an eye, everything had turned to chaos – and now, suddenly, nearly all officers were down.

He shook uncontrollably. Who was this man? What power did he possess?

What would he do next?

"You," he said to the trembling young officer, spotting him under the desk. "Come out from there."

He covered his ears, clenched in terror, burying his face between his legs.

The mysterious man sighed. "Shadow, get him out of there for me."

Shadow extended her claws, reached down, and painfully pulled him up. She stood him in front of her boss. He looked the young officer directly in the eyes.

"Listen to me. Give me the keys to one of your vans. Now."

The young officer's eyes were filled with terror. "Y-Yes, sir." He ran to another room, grabbed the keys, and immediately returned. "H-Here you are. It's the one parked right outside. Please don't kill me."

He grinned.

"Do not report it missing. You will tell no one that you saw or spoke to us." He looked around the bloodied room. It was filled with death and those on flirting on the edge of death. The few survivors hugged and hid against the walls – or lay in a pool of their own blood, waiting to enter the light, out on the open floor. He wasn't too worried about being followed. But still, prudence was always a good course of action. "Now go back to hiding under your desk and forget you ever saw us."

The young officer did that.

And the villain led his team outside.

There were a few officers outside, guns at the ready, hiding behind their cars. The mysterious man could see them through the window. It was unlikely they'd wait to shoot.

"Shadow," he said to the cat girl formerly known as Tiffany. He handed her the keys. "Bring the van around."

She took the keys in her paw-like hands. "I'm on it, boss."

He opened the door, but held himself and his five new criminal recruits to the side along the wall.

"Keep your hands up and don't move or we'll open fire!" yelled one of the officers through a megaphone outside.

Shadow leaped out into the air. Bullets started flying. She landed skillfully on her feet, bolted around a car, and slashed an officer across the face. Before anyone could react, she leaped over that car and headed for the next.

They fired at her. Being carefully not to hit each other as she moved skillfully, agilely, swiftly through their cross-fire. She was like poetry in motion, with all the grace and speed of a cat's body, and all the intelligence and anticipation of a human's brain. And as soon as she was close enough, she extended her claws and slashed someone's face, arms, or other exposed areas.

And while they focused on her, the mysterious man got a nearby officer's attention, made eye contact, and mind controlled him. And then another. And another.

And suddenly, the threat had been neutralized. Every officer was soon disabled and completely under the mysterious man's control.

Shadow went up to the van, stuck the key in the ignition, and started it. She drove the van up to the front of the station.

The villain walked confidently down the police station's steps, hesitantly followed by the other five criminals.

"Did I do good, boss?"

"Very good, Shadow."

"Wow," said the big guy. "Remind me to always stay on your good side."

The mysterious man nodded. He held open the back door, gesturing for everyone to get in.

The prostitute, gang member, butch woman, and white trash guy all got inside. Before the big guy did, though, he stopped to ask. "I gotta know," he said to the mysterious man, "who *are* you, I mean, really?"

Was he some kind of god – or maybe a demon? Perhaps an extraterrestrial with crazy psychic powers? Or maybe he was just a regular man who made some horrible deal with the devil.

"I am your new master," said the mysterious man. "From now on, you all will be working for me."

"I don't suppose we have a choice," said the big guy.

"No," said the mysterious man, "you really don't."

"I ain't gonna fight you. But, I gotta know, who are you? What do we even call you?"

"Call me Mastermind. Now get in. We haven't got much time."

Chapter 10
THE PYRAMID

Luke coughed. His clothes were still really damp. He had warmed up enough, but it still felt pretty cold down here. His uncle seemed to be handling it okay. Or at least he hid it well, for Luke's sake. But one thing was sure: they couldn't stay down here much longer.

But where could they go? It was nearly pitch black, they were God-only-knew how deep underground. In some vast cavern and deep aquifer. With absolutely no known way back up.

Luke had the pink crystal in his hand. They could've opened a new portal, back to Earth. But according to his uncle, it'd only take them to Stonehenge.

Not that he had a wallet or any money on him anyway. Even if he did, Luke was on a budget. Do you know how much it costs to fly from England to California? At the last minute?

"Oh God," said Luke.

"What?" said his uncle.

"I'm so going to lose my job."

"What?"

"I'm supposed to open the store tomorrow." He looked around the expansive total darkness. "Kind of hard to do from down here."

His uncle smiled. "Relax. We'll figure a way out."

Luke sighed. "Like what? Why don't we just go to England and get it over with?"

"You bring your passport with you?"

"No."

"Any kind of ID at all?"

"No…"

"And they'll let you back into the United States because…?"

Luke sighed.

"Don't worry. We'll think of something." He continued to look around.

"Think of something? Uncle, we're on *another planet*, at the bottom of some deep hole, with *no way out!*"

His uncle shook his head. "There's *always* a way out." He looked at his nephew funny. "Since when did you become so pessimistic, anyway? That's not the Luke I remember."

He shrugged. "Yeah, well… I dunno. I guess… I just haven't felt the same since… well, you know." He didn't really want to talk about it.

"Well," said uncle Charlie, "you and me are getting out of this, and we're not going to England. Not today, anyway."

Luke continued to rub his arms, trying to keep warm. "I'm *freezing* down here. How are you not cold?"

"Handsome old men like me don't get cold," he said, still peering through the darkness, looking for a way out. "Didn't you know? We Powers men are lovers. Our inner fire never burns out."

Luke laughed. "Okay. Whatever."

"Ah hah! I think I see something!"

"What? Where?" Luke tried to look in the same direction. He saw nothing but total darkness. A wall of endless empty black.

"Yup, definitely something there. Okay, let's go. We'll have to swim some more, but it's not far."

"What? Where? I don't see anything."

"Just stick close. Sometimes you have to go deeper into the darkness to find the light."

Okay. That was a little enigmatic. But not like he had a choice. His uncle seemed convinced something was over there. And they couldn't stay here on this rock forever. "Alright," said Luke, summoning his courage. "After you."

Meanwhile, up at the surface, Dawn and Ray had just stepped through the portal.

"Wow!" exclaimed Dawn, stepping foot on an alien world for the first time in real life. This was totally amazing. Way different than she imagined it'd feel like when acting in that low budget sci-fi film. She made a mental note of how she felt and acted as she looked around, to give a more realistic performance next time she had to do it in front of a green screen. "Would you look at this place?" she said.

"Incredible," said Ray, examining the ruins around them. "And the portal back to the apartment seems to be staying open. So that's good."

"See, I told you we had nothing to worry about."

He laughed. "Oh, I didn't say that. There's still lots to be careful for." They both wore large hiking backpacks, loaded with bottles of water, energy bars, trail mix, first aid kits, camping gear, flashlights, extra batteries, matches, and a variety of other essentials. "We have to be prepared for anything."

"Two moons!" she shouted, pointing at them.

Ray looked up. "And judging by the position of the sun… it's probably around mid-day… wait, look over there." At the edge of the horizon, the crown of another sun started to rise. The first sun still glared brightly above them.

Two suns? On a desert planet?

Not good.

"Okay," he said, thinking out loud. "Desert everywhere, no sign of water or plant life anywhere. Two suns. It's about to get *really* hot here pretty quick."

"Right. We better find your roommate and get out of here."

"Luke!" Ray called.

"Luke!" Dawn also called.

"Luke!" they called again.

No response.

Ray pulled out his cell phone. They were still close enough to the portal to get a faint signal. But it was just one bar, and barely at that. He tried dialing Luke's cell phone again. Got an error message: Unable to connect.

"He's definitely in here." Ray looked around for foot prints or any kind of tracks, but the wind was too constant. The sand constantly shifted and moved. Any trail would've been quickly erased. "Dammit Luke."

"Maybe he didn't come here," Dawn reasoned. "Maybe he's just out on a date or something?"

"You don't know my roommate," he said. "He wouldn't leave home without his cell phone. And I guarantee you if he saw this portal, he went through."

"Then I say we go check out that pyramid."

"Agreed." There was nothing else in sight. "But we better hurry. With that other sun coming up – let's just say we don't want to stick around for it."

"What are we talking? 120 degrees?"

"Feels close to 100 now, with just one sun overhead. Double that with two suns."

"Right. Let's get going."

Luke and Uncle Charlie swam through the icy cold water for a considerable distance. Luke was getting tired. He was so out of shape.

"You sure you know where we're going?" asked Luke, getting short on breath.

"Almost there. Just a few more feet."

One stroke. Two strokes. Three and… contact. Luke's hand felt something cold, smooth, and hard. Land. Another solid rock ledge. "Oh thank God!"

Charlie climbed up. "Here, let me help you up." He reached down and grabbed

Luke. "Here you go," he said, pulling him up.

"How did you—? I can't see a thing."

It was pitch black. They couldn't even see the faint light from the opening to the cavern anymore.

"Trust me. This way. There's a tunnel up ahead."

Luke held onto his hand. They began walking forward into more total darkness. Somehow, Charlie seemed to know or see where he was going. It was a fairly straight path, but there were some twists and turns too. "Have you been here before?"

Charlie laughed. "Heavens no! Like I said, I only came here once, maybe twice some twenty years ago. Walked through the portal, saw desert all around, and turned right back. No sense in exploring a wasteland."

"Then why the hell did we come here!" Luke exclaimed.

"Would anything I have said stopped you?"

"Uh, yeah. Like, 'Hey Luke, don't go in there – there's nothing to see. How about we go to a tropical paradise beach planet instead?'"

Charlie laughed. "Oh, you mean the dual wave symbol."

"The what?"

"It's one of the five symbols from the tablet. A pair of horizontal waves. Opens up a portal to an exotic ocean planet. Ninety percent of the surface is covered in water, but it's really shallow in some parts. Beaches, swamps, rivers, lakes, oceans, amazing cliffs that jut right out of the sea. An abundance of strange and fascinating plant life and animals of all sorts. What a sight. I do love that planet."

"What?!" Luke couldn't believe it.

"It's okay. We can go there another time."

"Why don't we go there *now*?" Luke pleaded.

"Same problem. The crystal only opens one portal at a time. If we open a new one, it'll close the one to your apartment, and then our only ticket back to Earth is via Stonehenge."

"How long will the one at my apartment stay open on its own?"

"Don't worry about that. The important thing is we keep moving."

"Is there a time limit or something?"

"I said don't worry. Our focus now is finding a path back to the surface."

"How do you even see where we're going?"

"Trust me."

Luke stopped. He wasn't walking blindly into the pitch blackness anymore. He pulled his hand free from his uncle's. "No. You need to explain to me what the hell's going on."

His uncle sighed. "Alright. But if I promise to tell you, will you keep walking?"

"Fine. But you better tell me everything!"

"Deal." He grabbed Luke's hand. "This way. And watch your step, there's a bump here."

Luke's foot hit it anyway. "Ow. How did you—? I can't see a damn thing!"

"This way. We're getting closer."

"To what?"

"The way out. I hope."

"Uncle…"

"Right. I made a promise." They continued walking, led by Charlie, deeper into the total darkness. "I, uh… How should I say this?"

"Just tell me, Uncle. I don't think anything can top the magic crystal you gave me."

"I have super powers."

Ray and Dawn traveled across the open desert. The second sun continued to rise. And the heat continued to escalate.

Good thing they brought plenty of water.

The pyramid looked closer than it actually was. The farther they walked, and closer they got, the bigger it appeared. This pyramid was monstrous. Huge. Several times larger than even the biggest pyramid on Earth.

To make matters worse, the path between here and there was anything but flat or straight. Shifting sand dunes made the landscape uneven, forcing them to hike up hill and descend back down more than once. Fortunately, though, they happened to walk a slightly different path than Luke and his uncle did. The route they took unknowingly avoided certain other problems.

As they descended down another steep sand hill, Dawn drank out of her water bottle. Sweat stains appeared under her arms, down her back, and across her chest. More sweat dripped down the sides of her face. And Ray was in no better condition.

"I say we walk another hour," said Ray, feeling the increasing heat as they reached the bottom of this hill, "and if we don't find anything… we're gonna have to turn back."

Dawn drank some more water.

"Try to conserve your water," Ray said.

"I'm thirsty."

"I know. I am too. But we need it to last."

"This is crazy," she said, her feet starting to drag. "All I wanted was a nice dinner with a nice guy… but *nooo*, some crazy villain had to go and control my brain, make me go to some creepy warehouse, and almost turn me into some kind of animal mutant. And then all I wanted to do was just put it all behind me, get some rest—" she swallowed some more water "—and cuddle up with that cute nice guy. But *nooo*, some freaky portal had to open up and your roommate had to go missing… and now…"

"Save your breath," said Ray. "Talking expends energy and you lose a lot of water vapor."

"Shut up," she said. "Shut the fuck up. It's hot. I'm tired. I'm soaking in my own sweat. I'm gonna damn well talk if I wanna talk!"

"Okay," said Ray, backing off.

Dawn sighed. "I'm sorry. It's this heat. I didn't mean it."

"It's alright. Look, I think we're finally getting close." He limply pointed at the enormous pyramid ahead. There appeared to be a shaded entrance at the base, too. "Shelter. I say we get some shelter."

"Yeah. And water." She finished off her water bottle. "Find some more water."

"Super powers?" asked Luke. "Like in Superman? As in, flying, super strength, x-ray vision, that sort of thing?"

"Well, yes, sort of."

Luke stopped walking and pulled his hand free again. "You're messing with me."

"Not at all," said Uncle Charlie. "My gift is enhanced sight. I can see in the dark – almost pitch black. I can also see heat, and I have a sort of zoom-magnification ability too. I can read a book up to 2 miles away!"

"What?!" Luke started laughing. "Why would you ever… Anyway, like, for real? You *really* can do all those things?"

"How else have I been able to see our way?"

"But it's pitch black down here."

"*Almost* pitch black. There's just enough trace light for me to see the basic walls and surroundings. And I can see heat too. And this tunnel is gradually getting warmer. It's hot on the surface. So I put two and two together and assumed this tunnel eventually leads up."

Luke stood there, nodding his head, processing all this.

"So you can see me now?" he asked.

"Yup," said Charlie. "Nodding your head. I can also see your overall body temperature has warmed up since we got out of the water and started moving again. I was worried for a moment. But you'll be fine now."

"How did you— why do you—?"

"Words, Luke. Use your words," his uncle joked.

"Hey, I'm an artist, not a public speaker."

"Right. To answer what I think you're asking, I got my powers— Uh oh."

"What?"

He quickly grabbed Luke's hand. "Run!"

"What?"

"RUN!"

They started running. Blindly, for Luke, nearly blind for Charlie.

"What's going on?!" Luke yelled.

"Something… coming up behind us… large snake!"

"A WHAT?!"

Charlie glanced back. "It's getting closer!"

Luke ran even faster.

And by "large snake," Charlie meant a VERY LARGE snake. Something so large, it barely fit inside this underground tunnel. For all they knew, it created this underground tunnel. And unlike most snakes, this thing had teeth. Big, shark-like teeth. And eight eyes, spread across two layers on its head.

"Is it still behind us?" Luke shouted.

Charlie glanced back.

The snake's mouth started opening. It was less than a dozen feet away from Luke – and quickly closing!

"Um, faster Luke!"

Luke's heart raced. This was *not* what he had in mind when he wanted to check out the other side of the portal! Nearly falling to his death, nearly freezing and drowning, and now being chased by a giant alien snake – no thank you!

They ran faster. Charlie navigated them around the corners, up the tunnel, racing as fast as the old man's legs would take him. If only he had super speed instead!

Luke tripped.

Still holding onto his nephew's hand, Charlie fell too.

They scrambled back to their feet.

But not fast enough.

The snake opened its mouth.

They reached the entrance to the pyramid. The base of the massive pyramid seemed to stretch a mile wide. And near one of the corners, where Ray and Dawn now stood, a small circular nook appeared to be some kind of entrance inside the pyramid.

It provided some shade and shelter from the suns. The temperature had skyrocketed beyond sizzling hot. Waves of heat distorted light everywhere they looked. It was like the entire planet was cooking. So blindingly bright, too. They leaned back against the pyramid wall, in the shade, at this little entrance cut-out.

They caught their breath. Drank what little water they had left. Looked at each other. Neither had to say anything. They both knew it was too late to make a run back for the portal now.

Ray looked around. Their shaded entrance was only a few feet wide and deep. The doorway inside was interesting. Big, round, almost metallic-looking. Like a giant vault door. He looked at the rest of the outer pyramid walls. They weren't made of sand and stone, like he'd expect. They, too, were built out of some kind of metal alloy.

This was no ordinary pyramid.

Then he noticed something else.

"What the—?" He started to get up. "Do you see that too?" Ray asked Dawn, pointing toward something.

It looked like a control panel. Three large buttons – red, green, and blue – beneath a small flat screen.

He had to be hallucinating.

"No, I see it too. What is it?"

Its proximity to the door could only mean one thing. "A doorbell?"

Ray pushed the green middle button.

Green seemed like the safest color, and it was in the middle, so… it seemed like the best choice.

Nothing happened.

"Try the red one."

Ray pushed the red button, on the left.

Still nothing.

"The blue one?" she asked.

He tried that one next.

The door made a sound. Like large, heavy deadbolts unlocking – several of them, in sequential order.

Ray and Dawn stepped back.

The door rolled to the side, spinning like a wheel.

"Whoa," said Dawn.

"You can say that again," said Ray.

"Whoa," said Dawn, again.

The inside the pyramid was dark, but a second later, tiny lights lining the edge of the walls illuminated, lighting their path.

"Whoa," said Ray.

"You can say that again," said Dawn.

"Whoa," said Ray, again.

"Okay, not as funny the second time around," said Dawn.

"Should we, um… go inside?"

"And get out of this heat? I'm thinking yes."

They walked inside.

As soon as they both were in, the door behind them rolled shut. Its deadbolts locked in place.

The air was cool inside.

"Thank God," said Dawn. She sat down on the floor and leaned against the wall. "Air conditioning."

Ray sat down to rest too. He finished off the final drops in his water bottle. "And that," he said, "is the last of our water."

"Maybe we'll find some more in here."

Ray looked around. The hallway was long. The lights lining the walls continued to illuminate farther and farther down. And there appeared to be several intersections and junctions along the way. This place was massive. And he had no idea which way to go.

"This place is incredible," said Ray.

"You think your roommate's in here?"

"Oh I hope so."

"Any idea which way to start looking?"

"Not even remotely."

Ray dug into his backpack and pulled out some nutrient bars. "Want one?"

"Please."

He tossed her one. Kept the other for himself.

"What is this place?" she wondered.

"Beats me. Whatever it is, it ain't ancient. Might be some kind of base. Or a giant alien space ship, who knows. But if Luke is in here, I bet he's having a field day! I hope he's okay."

"He seems like more than just a roommate."

"He's my best friend."

"He's got a great one."

"God, this is so insane! I still can't figure out where that portal came from in the first place."

"Yeah," said Dawn. "Sorry I got us into this."

"What?"

"I feel like it was my idea to go through that portal. I just couldn't believe my eyes, and when you see something so amazing in front of you, it's kinda hard to resist."

"No," said Ray, shaking his tired head. "I'm the one who should be apologizing. I should've gone alone. We just met. It wasn't fair to ask you to come along."

"But Ray," she said, moving closer to him. "I wouldn't miss this for the world." She leaned over and kissed him. "And I'm so glad I got to experience this with you."

He smiled. "Some first date, huh?"

"I know, right!"

"We better get moving," said Ray, summoning all his strength to stand up. "Luke's gotta be somewhere in here."

Ray helped Dawn to her feet.

"Alright," she said. "Let's pick a direction and hope we get lucky."

"Sure," said Ray. "Because we've had such great luck so far today."

"Exactly!" said Dawn. "What more could possibly go wrong?"

"You had to say that, didn't you?"

She smiled.

Chapter 11
IN THE BELLY OF THE BEAST

The giant alien snake had swallowed them whole. Its long slippery tongue wrapped around Luke's feet, pulled him in, then shove him down its slimy throat.

Luke suddenly knew what it felt like to swallow a bug – from the bug's point of view. Dark, sticky, wet, and hot. He felt enormous muscles on every side press against him and push him farther down into the beast. Within the eternity of a second, he felt himself unwilling pushed into the creature's stomach, a large spacious area filled with warm sticky goo, a tight enclosed space with only a tiny amount of air left to breathe.

His uncle suddenly got shoved next up to him.

Oh my God. He was going to die in here.

Eaten alive, swallowed whole, left to be digested in some monster's stomach in the dark depths of an underground cavern on some God-forsaken alien planet.

If that morning you had asked him how he expected to die, this would have never crossed his mind. And yet, now here he was.

It was already getting hard to breathe. The little oxygen got used up in just a few short breaths.

Twenty six years old. Never married. Never had any kids. Never had a career. Never saw the world, followed a dream, or made any difference. So young, so unexpectedly, it was all over just like that. He struggled to breathe. This was it. He was about to die.

But no. His uncle was right. He gave up too easily. There *had* to be a way out. But where? How?

This would've been a great time for his uncle to reveal some other powers – like laser vision, energy blasts, or razor-sharp claws.

"Uncle!" Luke strained to say from inside the snake's guts. He reached around inside the warm, confined, murky and sticky belly. He couldn't see a thing. The slimy lining of the beast's stomach stuck to the back of his neck and covered much of his body. Sticky warm juice – probably the beast's own digestive acid – slowly started to sting Luke's flesh.

He gasped for breath from the small air pocket along the side of his face. His lungs started to burn now too. He had precious seconds remaining before he choked to death in here.

He whispered, calling out for his uncle. He needed to conserve his breath – every breath needed to count.

His uncle didn't respond.

Maybe he was already dead? Maybe the creature chewed him a bit first. Maybe Luke was just the appetizer.

"Uncle," he whispered, more of a prayer that his uncle was still alive than a call for help now.

Still nothing.

Damn. He resisted the urge to cough, knowing instinctively it would quickly become uncontrollable.

He had to do something. And he had to do it fast.

What were his options? He had no powers, no weapons, no tools. Wait. He still had that crystal. Maybe he could use that somehow. Open up a portal inside the snake's belly? That might work. Or poke at it and make it vomit them back up? Possibly. Or…

The muscles around the stomach started to contract. They pushed against Luke, squeezing him tight.

Now he was to be crushed to death before he suffocated.

Awesome.

He reached into his pocket for the crystal.

The space in the stomach grew even tighter. He felt his uncle's body pressed up against his – and suddenly, the muscles around them convulsed violently, and uncontrollably, Luke and his uncle were launched back up through the snake's throat again—

—tossed out onto the cold hard floor.

Luke rolled several feet, crashing against a stone wall. Charlie's body slid against the floor with the same momentum.

There was light in here.

Not much. A faint red glow all around, from an unknown source down the tunnel up ahead. Luke saw the giant snake's sharply-toothed mouth open in front of them. Did it just vomit them up? Then why was it about to eat them again?

Luke quickly looked around, hoping for an exit or something he could use to defend himself. Nothing. It was a small enclosed cave. Just a narrow tunnel ahead, where the red light seemed to be coming from.

The snake's mouth opened wider as it made a hissing, rattling sound. Luke saw the inside of its mouth. It had two rows of sharp teeth. A long flailing tongue. And swelling sacks or glands of some kind on each side. Suddenly those sacks contracted, and a white substance fired out of the snake's mouth, quickly covering Luke.

The substance was sticky, like a thick spider web, that quickly hardened, trapping him where he sat. The snake angled its mouth towards his uncle's body – which was heavily bleeding – and quickly covered him too.

Some of the sticky web substance landed on Luke's face and neck, but most of it covered his arms and legs and torso, making it nearly impossible for him to move. But at least he could breathe now. For some reason, the snake wanted them alive.

Luke didn't like the idea why.

There were animals on Earth that sometimes captured or momentarily swallowed live prey – only to feed them to their young later. Or worse, maybe it was going to use them as host bodies, and implant its snake alien eggs inside their guts!

Or maybe the snake simply wasn't hungry yet, and was merely saving them for later for itself. Spiders will do that. Trap a bug in the web, save it for a later dinner.

Either way, the outcome was the same. They had bought some time, but some form of horrible death still awaited them.

Charlie moaned.

"Uncle!" Luke shouted.

Charlie moaned again.

"Uncle, wake up! Are you okay?"

"I feel… ohhhh… "

"You've lost a lot of blood. Try to conserve your strength."

"That would explain the intense pain in my side."

His uncle must've scraped against the snake's teeth when they got swallowed. Probably got caught and cut up. But, with any luck, it wouldn't be fatal. People survive shark bites all the time. This was no different.

He hoped.

Except there wasn't a hospital around for several light-years.

"Just hold on," Luke said.

His uncle tried to be strong. "Where are we? I thought we were dead."

"I don't know."

Charlie tried to move. His body was completely immobilized, but considering his severe wounds, that was probably good thing for him. He was able to move his neck a bit, though, and look around.

"Seems we're in some kind of cave. What's down there?"

Red light emitted from the tunnel. “I have no idea.”

“Lot of heat coming from there. I bet…” His pain started to overwhelm him. “I bet,” he struggled to speak, “that’s probably our way out.”

“Don’t try to move. Just relax. I’m gonna… I’m gonna figure something out.”

His uncle smiled. “That’s my boy.”

Sure. But what?

Meanwhile, the giant alien snake just sat in the corner, watching… and waiting.

Chapter 12
TEMPLE OF THE GODS

"I'm betting on alien space ship," Dawn said.

The corridors were all perfectly straight. Ceilings were fairly high. Evenly spaced lights lined the walls, illuminating their way. Not to mention, the outer walls of the pyramid seemed to be made of some kind of metal alloy. Plus a high-tech mechanical door with an electronic control panel at the entrance. It all seemed to point to one thing: this pyramid was some kind of space ship.

"I don't believe in aliens," said Ray.

"Really?" she asked, still walking.

"Flying saucers abducting cows and people, prodding them with metal sticks, and then dumping them off naked in some field somewhere… I doubt it."

"Well, I'm not saying all alien stories are true."

"It just seems too unlikely. Even if there were intelligent life on other worlds, what are the odds they'd find and come to Earth?"

"Okay," said Dawn. "Then how do you explain this? We're inside a giant pyramid on another world. Two moons, two suns. You know we're not on Earth."

"I didn't say there weren't other planets."

"But why is there a *pyramid* here; similar design to the ones found on Earth?"

"I don't know. It's an architecturally simple, stable design."

"But who built it *here*?"

"Oh, I see. Sorry, I'm a little dehydrated. Uh, I dunno. But just because it's here doesn't mean aliens exist, or they've visited Earth. In fact," he said, "we came through a portal *on Earth* to get here. Who's to say a similar portal didn't open up somewhere else, and modern humans went through and started building this place?"

"You *really* don't want to believe in aliens, do you?"

"In comic books and movies, fine. But in real life? We've got enough problems on Earth already than to add extraterrestrials to the list."

"True. Our military would probably blow any alien ship out of the sky as soon as they saw it. Ask questions later kind of thing."

They passed another junction – they could've turned left or right, but decided to keep going straight. If they started making random turns, it'd be really easy to get lost in here. Every corridor looked pretty much the same.

"But still," said Dawn. "I believe aliens, and intelligent life, are out there. And who knows, maybe some have visited us in the past."

"Well you and my roommate would get along great. He's totally into that sort of stuff."

"God, I'm so thirsty."

"Me too." He called out for his roommate again, sending his voice down the corridors. "Luke! Hello? *Anybody*?"

Nothing.

"This place gives me the creeps," he said.

"You think it's abandoned?"

"It's still running on power. If it was abandoned, it couldn't have been that long ago."

"Oh!" said Dawn, getting a little excited. "Maybe they're still on board."

"Who, Luke?"

"The aliens!"

Ray gritted his teeth. "Let's hope not. I really don't want to add that to my list of 'weird things that happened' today."

Going in a straight line paid off.

It eventually led them to a door. Same mechanics as the entrance outside. A large circular doorway with a control panel next to it on the wall. A small video screen and three buttons: red, green, and blue.

Ray tried the blue one first, the same one that opened the entrance door.

And it worked. They heard large heavy deadbolts unlocking. The door rolled to the side, opening the way inside.

What it opened to was nothing less than amazing.

They must've reached the center of the pyramid. The vaulted ceiling hung over a mile high, coming to a point at the pyramid's tip. Four angled walls surrounded them – flat, smooth, and mirror-like. Concentric circles lined the floor, illuminated, all centering around a pedestal in the middle.

The pedestal was ornately designed, carved out of some kind of stone, with detailed images and shapes on every side. The carvings represented some kind of animals or creatures. Nothing either of them recognized. Some kind of winged creature, something reptilian-looking, a humanoid figure with enlarged head, and something aquatic-looking emerged out of each of the four sides of the stone pedestal.

The illuminated concentric circles on the floor were not normal lights, like the usual ones that lit the corridor walls. No, these were actual symbols and letters – an alien language – written in light, across the floor.

And each circle was illuminated with a different color, starting with purple in the outermost ring, then blue, green, yellow, orange, red, and finally white with each concentric ring inward towards the center pedestal.

Were they warnings, instructions, or the names of the pyramid designers? Other messages entirely, perhaps? They could only guess.

"Still don't believe in aliens?" Dawn asked.

Ray remained silent.

A brilliant beam of light suddenly appeared from the center top of the massively high ceiling, shining down brightly and evenly over the pedestal like some kind of mystical spotlight.

As they cautiously walked closer, they saw their reflections mirrored in infinity on the walls. The overhead beam of light shined ever brighter over the pedestal, the closer they got. The circular alien writing on the floor also grew brighter, glowing with increasing intensity as they took each step closer.

Ray looked to Dawn. Not sure what to do. Not sure what to say. Not sure what to even think about all of this.

Dawn felt the same way. But whatever this room was, they were approaching something very significant, very special… perhaps even something religiously sacred.

A few steps closer and Ray started to see an illusion hovering inches above the pedestal. It appeared like a glass sphere, fading into view the nearer they got.

"What is that?" Dawn asked.

"I don't know."

They hesitantly stepped even closer.

Ray began to see his own reflection – but only his – within the hovering sphere.

Dawn saw her own reflection, but nothing else.

Ray stepped up to the pedestal. The spotlight shined down brightly from overhead, completely engulfing them in its brilliant white light.

The concentric circles of alien writing on the floor also illuminated ever brighter, beaming colorful energy straight up into the air. And the massive room's mirrored walls only amplified and intensified all this light and energy – filling the entire vaulted room with a flood of brilliant colors, swelling light, and an aura of magic and sacred mystery.

It was beautiful, magical, and mystifying.

And the sphere, hovering above the pedestal, was so vivid and clear it looked almost tangible now.

Ray cautiously reached out to touch it.

"What are you doing?!" Dawn shouted.

"Is it real?" Ray couldn't tell. There was an "other-worldly" essence to it. Something mysterious, magical, extra-dimensional. It looked solid and real – and at the same time, nothing more than an illusion, a hologram, or a hallucination.

Dawn looked around nervously. She was all for adventure and exploring – but this was beginning to be a bit too much. The lights, the massive room, the pyramid itself, the alien world – this pedestal was clearly an object of great significance.

Maybe mere mortals like them shouldn't be messing with it.

Ray touched the floating sphere.

His fingers went right through it. It wasn't real. It wasn't tangible.

"Huh," he said. "Guess not."

But when he tried to pull his fingers back, out of the sphere, he couldn't. They were stuck. He tried pulling harder.

"What? What?" Dawn asked.

"I'm stuck!" he exclaimed.

She helped pull his wrist. He placed one foot against the pedestal for leverage. They pulled with all their might. Nothing. Not even the tiniest budge. His fingers were stuck inside!

He stopped for a second. He needed a new plan.

But just then, some unexplained force began pulling his hand deeper into the sphere.

"Whoa!" he said, feeling its constant and gentle pull. "It's… it's pulling me in."

The sphere wasn't that big. Maybe six inches in diameter or so. There wasn't much "in" for him to be pulled into. And yet, slowly, more of his fingers did move in – followed by his hand, then his wrist, and half of his arm.

"Help!"

The pull only got stronger.

Dawn stood behind him, wrapped her arms around him, and leaned back, pulling with all her might.

The rest of Ray's arm slid inside the sphere, disappearing as soon as it entered.

Dawn pulled back harder and harder. God, she needed more strength. Suddenly, she felt her arm muscles growing again – just like before, when she wrestled with the mutant cat-girl Tiffany.

"What the hell?" she remarked, as her arms grew larger and stronger. All the muscles in her body increased in size. She suddenly had a *lot* more strength.

But it was no use. Ray's entire right arm was inside the sphere, up to his shoulder. To make matters worse, the sphere had started to enlarge.

"I'm not going to let you go!" exclaimed Dawn.

"Save yourself!"

The sphere quickly doubled, then tripled, then quadrupled in size. And it kept growing!

"Get back!" he told her.

The sphere engulfed half his torso. Dawn had let go just in time. She stepped back, away from the ever-expanding sphere. It was now almost six feet in diameter, consuming the entire pedestal, and Ray right along with it.

His face started to be absorbed by the sphere. Ray strained to look towards Dawn. "Just get out of here," he said as part of his mouth began disappearing along the edge of the sphere. "Please."

Dawn reached for him.

"No!"

Two-thirds of his face – and nearly all his body – was now inside the sphere.

"Ray!" she exclaimed.

He said something – but she couldn't hear him. His mouth was entirely inside the sphere. She watched as it continued to pull him in, inch by inch, until only the last traces of his left ear, hand, and foot could still be seen.

And then, even those were gone, completely consumed by the sphere.

"RAY!" She reached out toward the sphere.

And in an instant, it collapsed, completely disappearing.

Gone.

Just like that.

No sphere at all. And all the lights – the spotlight above, the glowing alien writing on the floor, everything – dimmed to a faint and barely visible glow.

"Oh my God!"

Dawn started to cry.

"Oh my God…"

Chapter 13
ECHOES OF TIME

Ray suddenly found himself in an unlikely place.

He was apparently back on Earth. Inside a small apartment.

There was an old plaid couch, with rips and tears along some of the edges. A recliner chair with a broken handle. An old television box – it had manual dials to change the channels, antenna rabbit ears, and brown plastic casing.

No one was in the room, but the television was on. The colors weren't very bright or vibrant. Image quality was pretty low overall. But it displayed some kind of sitcom. A brown furry puppet with a large long nose was talking, saying something about how delicious it'd be to eat a cat. The other actors in the show were all normal looking humans.

"Wait a minute," he said to himself. "I recognize this show." It was *Alf*, a family sitcom from the late '80s. It must've been a re-run or something.

Over by the window he saw a small Christmas tree. Much more similar to a "Charlie Brown" Christmas tree than anything else. It had a few ornaments and some tinsel. Not much else.

This apartment seemed really familiar.

He walked around. That old beat-up couch. That broken recliner chair. That sad little Christmas tree. This room. He recognized it.

Suddenly, all at once, he knew exactly where he was.

He lived here as a child.

"Oh my God," he said. "I don't believe it."

He thought he heard someone in the kitchen. It was a small apartment. The kitchen was just around the corner. He quietly stepped closer and peaked around the wall.

"Mom?!"

There she was – much younger – making herself a peanut butter and jelly sandwich. She had really big hair and wore a flower-pattern dress. She walked barefoot. The refrigerator next to her looked really old, like something from the

1970s. There was a small oven, but no microwave or dishwasher.

This was exactly the apartment he remembered from his early childhood. Yeah. It had to be. He lived here for three years, up until he was seven years old.

"Mom?" he said louder.

She seemed completely unaware of his presence.

"Mom. Mom, can you hear me?"

She finished making her sandwich, put it on a little plate, and carried it into the living room. She sat down at the edge of the couch and laughed at one of the jokes on the TV sitcom.

Ray followed her and stood right in front of her, between her and the television. "Mom, can you see me?"

She kept watching the show, laughing again at something else.

He looked back at the TV. And then again at the small little Christmas tree.

Wait a minute. It was the middle of the day and Mom was home. After Dad left, she had to work double shifts to make ends meet. She worked two or three jobs for most of his life.

Ray started to piece it together. The little Christmas tree. The old apartment and TV show. How young his mom looked. He didn't know how or why – but apparently, he was somewhere back in time.

He then heard the loud engine of an old car pull up to the window. This apartment was on the first floor. Parking was immediately outside. He looked out the window.

"Oh my God." A 1981 Plymouth Horizon – a boxy little yellow car – parked in front of their apartment. And the man who stepped out looked vaguely familiar. "Dad?"

He unlocked the door and came in. "Hey Liz, come check this out!"

His mom diverted her attention from the TV. "What is it?"

"Come and take a look," he said.

She went to the door. His dad returned to the car and opened the back. And he carried out a small red bicycle with training wheels.

Ray followed behind his mom, looking out the door with her. "Oh yeah!" he said. "I remember that bike!"

"What the hell is that?" his mom complained.

"It's a bike. For Raymond. For Christmas."

She sighed. "You know we can't afford that."

"I put it on our MasterCard."

"Dammit, Tom, get that out of here before he comes home and sees you. You know how bad he's been wanting a bike."

"I know, exactly," said his father. "That's why I bought it for him."

She sighed and stormed back in the house.

"Liz, wait. Liz!" He followed her inside, leaving the bike leaned against the apartment wall. "Can we talk about this?"

"Dammit, you think I don't want that for him too? You think I wouldn't *love* to see his face Christmas morning when he opened it? But Tom…" She went up to him, gently placed her hands on his face, and said more lovingly, "We're having trouble making ends meet as it is. We *really* can't afford this. We talked about this. Nothing over five dollars. You want to pay rent next month, don'tya?"

He sighed, frustrated. "Look, I'm the one working ten hours a day, five days a week. It's my money. If I wanna buy Raymond a nice gift, then I'm gonna."

"Hey!" she shouted. "I work too."

"As a waitress!"

"It's hard work, Tom. Something you don't know nothing about!"

"You think my job ain't hard too?"

They started fighting.

Ray had memories of a lot of heated arguments between them. He was little, but he still remembered.

It pained him to see them fighting again now.

Ray knew what year this was now. It was the year he got that red bike. It was also the year his dad left them.

"I'm tired of slaving away all day for an unappreciative boss just to come home to another unappreciative boss!" his dad yelled.

"It's not easy working at the diner *and* taking care of Little Ray-Ray *and* all the house!" she defended.

"You know what? That's it."

This was it. Ray was too young to remember at the time, but in later years his mom had told him the story. She and his dad fought a lot. Things weren't always this bad, but money was tight, bills got more expensive, and they never seemed to have any fun anymore. They argued all the time – and sometimes he threatened to leave, sometimes she told him to leave. They were just words – mostly. But one day, this day, he finally meant it.

"I'm outta here," he said. "I don't need this bullshit anymore!"

"That's right, you leave my house and never show your ugly face 'round here again!"

The only way they got that apartment was because Ray's mom's parents co-signed on the lease. They did that throughout most of his childhood and teenage years. And since *her* parents made it possible to live there, she always felt it was *her* place.

"I'm tired of spending all my hard-earned money on you and that boy," said his dad. "You know I didn't want him. I told you we couldn't afford no baby!"

That hurt. That was hard to hear. Ray tried to tell himself that his dad didn't really mean it. But his mom did say, when Ray was much older, that he almost was aborted. His father didn't feel ready to have kids yet. But Ray was an unexpected surprise, and she wasn't about to give him up. They made it work, for a while. But in financially stressful times like this moment, Ray's presence felt more like a financial burden than an unplanned gift.

Obviously his dad did love him. Why else would he have spent all that money to buy that red bike?

But… maybe he didn't love him enough to stick around through all the fights, nagging, and constant financial hardship. Maybe it was just easier if he didn't have to support a wife and kid.

Ray never felt so worthless in that moment.

His father slammed the door on his way out, started up the car engine, and drove away.

His mom collapsed onto the couch and cried.

Watching this, Ray doubted that his mom really believed he'd be gone for good. She probably figured he'd just blow off some steam and come home later, like always.

But not today.

Ray knelt down next to his mom. He was on the verge of tears himself. "I'm sorry, Mom."

If only she could hear him.

A slow tear escaped down the side of his face. He couldn't bear watching his mom cry like this. He couldn't bear witnessing their fight – the final moment that made his dad leave forever. And reliving all this hardship just reminded him of the years of fighting, struggle, and poverty he and his mom experienced throughout his life.

All the childhood dreams and memories he never got to experience, because they couldn't afford it.

All the times he couldn't afford to take a girl out on a date. The used clothes he wore from the Salvation Army. The excuses he'd have to make when his friends wanted to go out to eat or see a movie.

Just then, the school bus stopped nearby and unloaded several kids for the surrounding apartments.

Ray saw his younger self – around age six – get off the bus, carrying a Superman book bag loaded with homework and pencils. His younger self walked up to the apartment, saw the red bike, and got really, really excited. He rushed inside.

"Mommy! Mommy! There's a red bike outside! Is it for me?"

She tried to hide her tears. This wasn't the first time Little Ray-Ray had seen her cry. He was used to it. Still, he gave her a hug. "I love you, Mommy."

She laughed. "Aww, I love you too, baby." She hugged him back and held his hands. "Yes," she said with a forced smile. "Santa brought it a little early for you."

"Yay!!!" Little Raymond shouted, jumping up and down. He ran back outside to play with it.

Big Ray – present-day, mid-20s Ray – watched the whole thing as an invisible observer. He saw his younger self climb onto that bike and ride it around the cul-de-sac. But then, still inside, he watched his mom cry again.

He remembered that his dad left that year. But he didn't know why until now.

That stupid bike. He loved it so much. He had no idea.

But that wasn't fair. Ray realized that if it wasn't that bike, it would've been something else. They were always fighting. Sometimes they hid it from him, sometimes they did it in front of him. They weren't happy. They were always stressed and worried.

Reliving this experience was more intense than he would have expected. Even though everything he observed was just a faded memory from his distant past, being here now made it all too present and real. And vividly painful.

He shook his head. "Why am I here?"

That sphere – he touched that sphere and it pulled him in. Was this all a dream? A holographic illusion? Or had he actually traveled back in time to his early childhood, even though no one seemed to see or hear him?

Why was he here?

Dawn. Oh, that poor girl. She was back at the pyramid. Probably worried about him. He wished there was somehow a way to let her know he was okay.

Reliving a painful memory, but okay nonetheless.

This was no illusion. It was too vivid, too detailed, too real. He was actually here. Somehow. But why?

He needed to think this through logically. They were in some kind of special room, a cathedral or sanctuary of some sort. All the alien writing must've meant something important. The pedestal, the lights, the floating sphere. Clearly something significant for the pyramid builders.

But what was it?

A type of portal or wormhole, designed to transport someone back into their own past? Or was this some kind of simulation or test?

"Hello? Can *anybody* hear me?"

He waited and listened. Nothing.

His mom dried her tears and watched her son – Little Raymond – joyfully and ignorantly ride his bike outside. No one else was around.

"Why am I here? Why am I watching all this? What's the point?" Ray asked aloud, still hoping someone or something would answer. "There has to be a purpose to all this!"

Suddenly his mom disappeared, as did Little Raymond outside. The television jumped back to the earlier scene of *Alf*. He heard a noise in the kitchen. He walked over and saw his mom making herself a peanut butter and jelly sandwich.

"Huh?"

She finished making her sandwich and returned to the living room, where she sat down at the same spot on the couch. She laughed at a joke on the TV show.

"Okay…"

Then the car pulled up. It was his dad again.

Time was repeating.

"Please, I don't want to see this again," Ray said aloud.

But the whole thing repeated, exactly, in perfect detail, all over again. Right up to the very same moment it did before, before it reset and started all over again, a third time.

A time loop.

"Luke, where are you when I need you?" Luke would know what to do. Time travel and time loops were his thing.

But the same drama, the same painful loop, repeated over and over and over again…

Word for word. Action for action. Beat for beat.

His dad coming home with the bike. Their argument. Him storming out the door. Ignorant little Raymond having no idea that his daddy wasn't coming home ever again.

Ray broke down into tears – partially from experiencing this painful moment in his past over and over, partially from feeling trapped with no way out from this nightmare.

The scene repeated around him again.

Over and over again.

It was enough to break any man. After it had repeated countless, perhaps hundreds of times, Ray found himself balled up in the corner, weeping, doing all he could to keep from going insane. There was no way out of this nightmare!

"Daddy," he wept, "why couldn't you love me? Why wouldn't you stay…?"

Chapter 14
REUNITED

"How you holding up?" Luke asked his uncle.

They were still trapped beneath the quick-hardening spider-like web substance. Barely able to move at all. The cave had minimal illumination, thanks to a tunnel nearby with a glowing red light.

The giant alien snake, with all its freaky eyes and scary teeth, wandered off some time ago. When it would return was anyone's guess.

"I'm okay," said Charlie. "I think the bleeding stopped."

"How can you tell?"

He couldn't. He was lying. He just didn't want Luke to worry. Truth was, he was in bad shape. His body started shivering. His core temperature was dropping from the loss of blood. But he put on a good face and tried to stay positive. They needed to figure a way out – worrying about his rapidly dwindling life would be a distraction, not a help.

"Just trust me. I'll be fine," said his uncle.

Luke struggled to move his arm. With enough effort, he started to move it. Barely. Just a little. But it was enough. He wasn't free. Not even close. But he stretched the sticky substance enough to be able to move his hand into his pocket. It took some work, but he finally grabbed the crystal.

"Okay, I got the crystal," he said.

"Good, what's your plan?" said his uncle, trying to hide his shivering and slowly fading consciousness. It took all his strength to stay awake.

He tried using the pointed tip of the crystal to cut at the hard web-like substance. Little progress. This would take forever.

"Maybe I can somehow draw a circle around me, open up a portal beneath me."

"That'll close the portal back at your apartment."

"I know. One problem at a time," said Luke.

But it turned out to be a useless plan, anyway. He drew a very short line by his side – it was all the range of motion he could get. Even if he could open a portal on the floor beneath him, this web was thick and sticky. It might still hold him there in place, preventing him from passing through the portal anyway.

"Never mind," he said. "I'm open to ideas."

"You g-got m-me," he said, his trembling getting worse.

"You sure you're okay?"

Uncle Charlie realized he might be more than just cold and bleeding to death. For all he knew, the snake bite also poisoned him. But whatever the case, it took all his strength just to hold on. If they were going to escape, it'd be up to Luke to figure it out.

"Just c-concentrate on g-getting us out."

Alright. This was crazy. Luke had to think creatively. This was no ordinary problem. He was trapped in the web of some alien creature, in an underground cave, on another planet, with a crystal that could open up portals. The only kind of people who end up in situations like this are super heroes. And it was time he started to think like one.

What were his options?

Wait until the creature – or its babies – came back to eat them? No, too risky. Try to cut his way out with the crystal? That would take too long. Open a portal to escape? Not possible with his current limited range of motion. Hmm. Call for help?

"Help! Help! Anybody, help!"

No answer.

Charlie, weary-eyed, looked over toward Luke. This situation looked more and more hopeless.

Alright. Hmm. What would Superman do? Break free with his super strength or heat vision. But Luke didn't have either of those. Batman? He'd used some kind of gadget. Luke didn't have any of those, either. The Flash would vibrate his molecules so fast that he could phase right through the solid material. Again, not an option.

The answer had to be with the crystal. It was the closest thing to a super power Luke had.

"Uncle."

"Yes?" he whispered.

"You said there were five symbols, right? What are they, where do they all lead?"

He paused. Took a long deep breath. "F-First is Earth."

"Right, right. I know that. And there's this planet and the ocean world. What are the other two?"

"One leads to another Earth-like planet," he shivered. "And the l-last… a vacant s-starship adrift in deep s-space."

"What? Really?"

He tried to nod. Best he could in his weakened state trapped in the sticky alien webs.

Hmm. There had to be a way. His uncle told him that when they fell into the cavern. "I want you to remember this always, Luke," his uncle had said. "No matter how bad things get, no matter how dark the situation looks… always have hope. There's *always* a way out."

So what was their way out now? How could he use a portal to his advantage? He had a limited space. He couldn't make a very large portal. Not big enough for him to go through, anyway. But maybe he didn't need to. Maybe it just needed to be big enough for something else, on the other side, to come through to here.

When he opened the portal in his living room, sand and hot air blew into his apartment from this desert planet. The portal went both ways.

But would sand and hot air be any good to him right now?

No… but maybe an icy cold vacuum would.

"That abandoned starship," said Luke, "does it have life support?"

"What?"

"Space is really, really cold. Starships need life support to keep the air warm."

"No," said his uncle. "No life support. No air. If y-you open a portal there, it's a v-vacuum. We n-never open that p-portal."

"We are today!" said Luke, suddenly confident. "What's the symbol?"

"You d-don't understand," said his uncle. "It'll s-suck all our air out. It's not s-safe!"

"Trust me," said Luke.

If there was ever a time, now was it.

"Okay," wearily said his uncle. "It looks like an upside-down 'U', with a little circle on each end."

Luke drew a small circle at his side, under the ensnaring sticky web. It was only a couple inches wide, but it would have to be large enough. Then, carefully in that small circular space, he drew the symbol.

Instantly the lines of the circle and symbol shined brightly, before disappearing into a new portal opening. Pitch blackness awaited on the other side. Immediately air began draining down the hole. It quickly got really, really cold around the portal, too.

Charlie angled his head best he could to see what Luke was doing.

"Come on, come on," Luke said impatiently.

The vacuum of the portal began pulling down on the web. His arm and side began to feel freezing cold. As did everything else near the portal – including the web.

It started to ice up and become brittle. Smaller segments broke off and spun uncontrollably down into the narrow portal. As the web lost integrity, more segments began stretching and breaking, falling into the opening.

"How's it going over there?" asked his uncle.

"Almost there…"

More of the web fell in. His flesh near the portal started stinging from the icy cold vacuum. He felt a pull on his entire body towards the hole, too, but so far the majority of the web was still intact, holding him securely to the ground.

A big chunk of the web finally broke apart, spiraling into the air vortex draining into the narrow hole. Okay. This was it. Time to act now or risk getting painfully pulled in himself.

Holding very tightly onto the crystal, he held it over the opening and used all his strength to move it over, left and then right, creating an "X".

The portal closed instantly.

Luke caught his breath. The air was getting rather thin around him, but it quickly returned to normal. He might suffer from a little frost burn too, but he'd live. They'd both live. They were going to be okay.

And enough of the web had broken apart to enable him some freedom. With a little effort and wiggling, he tore himself free and crawled out from under it.

"And *that*," he said, standing up confidently, "is how it's done."

His uncle smiled proudly.

Luke looked towards the tunnel emitted the faint red light. What was down there? He turned to his uncle, just as Charlie's eyes drooped closed.

"Uncle?"

No response.

"Uncle!"

Luke rushed over to him.

"Hold on, Uncle. I'll get you out of there." Luke began tugging and pulling at the outer web layers, tearing off small pieces. "Almost there…"

He thought about creating another portal to that abandoned starship. Another icy vacuum should do the trick again. But seeing all the blood his uncle had lost, he worried the vacuum would make him worse. And it wasn't exactly easy closing the portal last time. One slip and his crystal would be sucked right through. That was one possibility he didn't want to risk a second time.

Fortunately, the web was more hard than it was sticky now. Piece by piece, segment by segment, he tore away at his uncle's entangling prison.

Damn, he wished he was stronger. He really needed to start working out.

"Come on…" he grunted, tearing at an exceptionally thick piece. "Almost…" It started to bend. And suddenly it snapped, broke free, and he felt backwards onto his butt.

"Goddammit!" he exclaimed, frustrated at it all. He was making progress tearing off his uncle's webs. The old man was almost free. But the very fact that they were in this mess was all Luke's fault!

His uncle seemed to be breathing, but clearly unconscious. He wasn't as "okay" as the old man had implied.

It wasn't fair. It wasn't right.

"Don't die on me, Uncle."

Luke was the one who wanted to go exploring through the portal. He was the one who slipped and fell down the pit. He was the one who then tripped and got caught by the snake creature. Luke was the one who wanted the fantasy adventure – to travel to other worlds, meet strange alien species, go on adventures, travel through time, be a super hero…

Yeah, right. Some adventure. In all likelihood, this cave was going to be his tomb. And his fantasy, his childhood need to be some great explorer or adventurer, was about the be the cause of his uncle's death too.

He couldn't bear the thought of being the cause of *another* family member's death.

"Don't die, Uncle. Hold on, I've almost got you…"

He broke away the final large piece. Enough to pull his uncle out and away from the web.

At last!

Wow. Half the old man's side was cut open to shreds. Blood soaked his shirt and side of his pants. Not a good sign.

"Dammit, Uncle!"

Luke looked around. For something. Anything. What could he do? The nearest hospital was some untold number of light-years away. The portal back to his apartment was closed now anyway. It closed the instant he opened the new portal.

He'd have to just open a new portal to Earth, arrive at Stonehenge, and hope somebody was nearby to call an ambulance.

Luke pulled out his crystal and faced the nearby wall. He drew a large circle.

But just then, the snake creature returned.

Its eight eyes stared at him, reflecting the dim red light from the nearby tunnel. Its mouth opened – possibly to eat him, possibly to cover him in more of that web stuff.

And it brought babies. About a dozen smaller immature versions of itself, all slithering by along its sides. They may have been small – relative to their mother –

but they were still plenty big, and already enhanced with sharp teeth.

The circle was too big. If Luke completed this portal, it'd open a wide window for these creatures to chase after and find themselves on Earth. And knowing how fast these creatures moved, they'd be dead the moment they stepped to the other side anyway. Only then, Earth would be infested with these monsters. Possibly living in the sewers. Eating small stray children. Breeding like crazy. Luke had seen one too many sci-fi alien movies to know how dangerous it was to let a lethal alien species arrive on Earth.

Couldn't do that.

And the circle was too big to open up to the derelict starship either. Luke and his uncle would be sucked right in with the rest of them. Die within seconds.

Couldn't do that either.

The snakes crept closer, circling around them.

This was it.

This was the end.

But no. Now was no time to give up. He couldn't let them die here. Not like this. Not today.

The baby snakes circled closer, going after the easier meat of his uncle. Luke stomped towards them and yelled, trying to scare them away.

It worked for a second.

The glowing pink line of the circle on the wall finally faded. This was it. Think fast or die here now.

The red-lit tunnel was behind them. The snakes approaching from the front. Maybe the portal vacuum was a good idea again – but they needed some distance to prevent from getting suck in themselves.

He nervously held the crystal. His whole body was shaking. The snakes came closer – but then stopped. They lined up in a half circle towards them, but came no closer than five feet. Why?

Don't look a gift horse in the mouth. Luke didn't care. He started drawing another, smaller circle on the floor.

The snakes crept back away from the crystal.

They each had eight eyes, so it was hard to tell exactly what they were focusing on. But the glowing pink crystal in his hands was the likely candidate. Maybe that's why they hadn't just jumped and attacked them already. Maybe they were frightened of the crystal for some reason. Or might, more likely, their eyes were super sensitive to even the faintest light, living down here in these dark caverns. The glow of the crystal might hurt their eyes – or at least, fascinate or frighten them.

Luke waved the crystal out in front of him. All the snakes backed up.

Yup. It was definitely the crystal.

Good. So as long as he held that out, they were safe – for now. Until their eyes adjusted, or they realized it was no threat, or whatever.

Holding the crystal out in one hand, he grabbed his uncle's shirt and dragged him away, towards the red-lit tunnel behind them. The snakes seemed to avoid that area, too.

The snakes followed after, keeping their safe distance from the glow of the crystal.

They got to the tunnel. Luke popped his head around the corner to see if he could see where the red light was coming from, or how far the tunnel went. It curved around, so he really had no idea. But distance was the best defense. And sooner or later these snakes would get too hungry to care about the crystal anymore. Still dragging his uncle along the floor, Luke pulled him around the corner.

And he quickly drew another circle on the floor, at the mouth of the tunnel. Something a few feet wide. And he placed the upside-down "U" symbol in the center.

Instantly the portal opened to the icy vacuum of the abandoned starship again.

Luke immediately dodged around the corner, into the tunnel, where his uncle waited unconscious. Wind gusted down the corridor against them, rushing down into the portal. He heard the high-pitch squealing shrieks as the snakes were sucked into their doom. The air got a little thin and kept blowing hard against them, but Luke dragged his uncle, and with all his adrenaline and strength, pushed forward through the tunnel.

They went around the bend. The farther from the portal they got, the easier it became to walk. But the air quickly got thinner and thinner. It became hard to breathe. Luke felt light-headed. He sure hoped all those snaked had been pulled in. But he couldn't wait any longer.

Falling to his knees from the physical exhaustion and lack of oxygen, he started to draw another small circle on the floor. He drew the triangle symbol. The other portal down the tunnel instantly closed; the new one here opened up. He saw blinding bright sunlight and sand. Intense sizzling heat poured through. He quickly X-ed out the portal, closing it. They could breathe again.

He wanted to collapse. He caught his breath and checked his uncle. Still alive. Barely.

"Hold on, Uncle."

He took a few more deep breaths. He didn't want to go through that again anytime soon.

Or like, ever.

Then he heard a faint humming ahead. Was it just his ears? No, it was real. It sounded almost… mechanical. What was that?

His uncle coughed. And then some more. He regained consciousness, but barely. He took several deep breaths himself. He still shivered. "Where am I?"

"You're awake!"

"Luke!" His tired eyes seemed to smile. "Thank God you're safe."

Luke laughed. "Me? Thank God you're alive! You had me really worried there. We need to get you to a hospital. Do they have one near Stonehenge?"

He began drawing a new portal.

"Wait," said Charlie. "There's another way."

"What?"

"The healing ch-chamber."

"What are you talking about?" Maybe he was delirious from the loss of blood.

"Trust me," weakly said the old man. "I've got a b-better chance of survival with the chamber…"

"What chamber?"

"Inside the pyramid. It… It can do miracles."

"The pyramid? On the surface?"

His uncle nodded.

"I thought you said you never saw a pyramid here before."

"I didn't," said his uncle, wincing in pain. "I saw one just like it on another p-planet."

Luke shook his head. "I dunno."

"Trust me, Luke."

"Uncle, I…"

"We must be close to the surface," his uncle said, using his power of super vision. "There's a lot of heat up ahead."

"You sure? Socialist healthcare is just a portal away…"

"Luke, no," said his uncle, very solemnly. "I could be infected with something. Can't risk bringing something back to Earth. The chamber here will heal me, I promise. I used one once before…" He struggled, with some significant pain, to get up from the ground.

Luke sighed. "Here, let me help you walk."

He lifted his uncle up and let the old man lean on him. Together, slowly, they walked up the tunnel toward the red light and growing audible hum.

Meanwhile, in the mirror room, Dawn anxiously circled around the pedestal.

"Ray! Ray!" she called out. She looked really worried. "Ray, where *are* you?"

Reunited

She sighed in frustration, stamping her foot and crossing her arms. The mysterious sphere that floated above the pedestal was gone. And nothing she said or did seemed to make it come back. Ray was gone. Just like that. Pulled into a wormhole or *something* to God only knew where. And there was nothing she could do about it.

She looked down at her arms. When she tried pulling him back, her muscles grew again. Just like before, when she was fighting Tiffany-turned-cat-mutant.

Her arms looked normal now. What caused her muscles to grow like that? Did she have "super strength" now or something? She didn't feel any stronger.

Or was it something else?

She could think of only one explanation for any of it. It had to be that green chemical that man injected into her. It was designed to mutate her into a human-animal hybrid, like Tiffany. But she never received the animal DNA. Just the raw chemical. Did it alter her genetics somehow? Make her… genetically unstable?

Her body seemed fine. Looked and felt normal. Except for moments of extreme stress and emotional need. Then her body shifted. Gave her super strength. Or morphed her feet into claws that could dig into the ground for better footing.

She thought, at first, that it was a temporary side-effect to the chemical, but had worn off shortly after.

But now… it happened again. Was it still in her system?

She wondered…

Could she do it again, on her own, by choice?

She held her arms out. She wanted to grow those big muscles again. She concentrated.

But nothing happened.

She sighed, frustrated.

What a day.

It all started with that terrible audition. But then she met Ray. He seemed like a nice guy. Cute, too. She went home, told her roommate about her date that night, got showered and changed. All in all, a pretty average and ordinary day. But then, that night, everything got weird.

The mysterious man sat down at their table. His power of persuasion was irresistible. She'd follow him to the end of the Earth if he asked her to. It wasn't until later she realized he had some kind of mind control power. Incredible. Hard to believe – but yet, now, somehow the easiest part to believe after everything else that's happened.

Seeing her waitress mutated into a cat-girl. Feeling her own body re-shape itself according to the needs of the moment. Going back to Ray's apartment and finding that portal there. Setting foot on another world. Almost dying of dehydration. Entering this giant pyramid. Losing her new boyfriend into some kind of supernatural energy sphere. And now… And now… She was tired, hungry, thirsty, and exhausted. And all she could think about was Ray – and the questions arising about the changes in her own body.

This was too much. But, here she was. Inside this magical room. Inside a massive metal pyramid that clearly was some kind of high-tech alien ship or something.

She'd hardly call herself a comic book geek, but she did enjoy watching the *X-Men* cartoons and movies. Having super powers would be cool. Who wouldn't want powers if they could? But she wondered, did *she* have powers now too?

She held her hand in front of her face and wiggled her fingers. If only she could make them do something. Catch on fire. Create an energy ball. Shape-shift into an animal paw. *Something.*

Where was Ray? She was afraid to leave this room, just in case he came back the same way he disappeared. This was clearly no accidental or fluke thing. This whole room was designed to focus around this pedestal, where the sphere appeared.

Call it women's intuition, but she just knew he'd be back. This place wasn't a prison and it wasn't a trap. Clearly, it was something special, something sacred, something magical. She had no idea where he was or what he was doing right now, but she doubted he'd be there forever. He'd be coming back.

He had to be coming back.

"Please, Ray," she said, "come back."

She sat down at the foot of the pedestal and buried her face in her hands. She started crying.

Maybe it was the exhaustion, the stress, the feeling lost and alone inside an alien spaceship on another world… All the events of the day. Everything.

Sometimes she wished she could just crawl up in a corner and hide like a turtle in its shell. She felt so vulnerable, so alone, so scared. What was she going to do?

It all caught up with her.

The trauma of watching that kid die, and then seeing Tiffany get mutated, and almost experiencing the same fate herself. Being humiliated standing naked in front of that mind-controlling freak. Losing Ray now, and feeling abandoned, all alone on this strange world.

She cried.

She curled up and wrapped her arms around her sides. She really wished she could hide inside a shell right now.

And just then, she felt her back changing, growing harder and larger. Her arms and legs simultaneously began mutating.

Was this some kind of delayed effect from the mutation chemical she was injected with?

Her body transformed, growing larger in some areas, shrinking smaller in others. But overall, as a whole, her body got smaller, thicker, and harder.

And smaller… and smaller…

She shrank inside her clothes. They collapsed around her and covered her ever-shrinking body. And she kept transforming, getting smaller still. Her back became bone hard. Her skin became rough and scaly. Her face morphed and began changing form.

Suddenly, she saw the world from a whole new perspective. She felt different. Saw different. Heard different. Smelled different. Tasted different.

She had a tail, short arms and legs, a long extending neck, and a large turtle shell on her back.

She had somehow become a turtle.

She still had all her human thoughts and awareness. But physically, she now felt and experienced the world as a small turtle. How did she do that?

She crawled forward, out from under her pile of clothes. This was so weird. Walking slowly, crawling on all fours. Steady, deliberate movements. One foot, then the next, and the next. Feeling her bone-plated belly brush against the floor. And the strong, sturdy protection of her shell on her back the whole time.

Wait. She *wanted* this. This was how she felt. She wished she could hide inside a shell.

She pulled her head, arms, and legs inside. Curled her tail in too. So this was what it felt like. Snug, contained, protected. She couldn't move. Didn't want to; didn't need to. She felt content, safe, and secure. She was a turtle.

How cool!

But she didn't *really* want to be a turtle. Not permanently, anyway. It was just a feeling, an emotional need of the moment. She wanted to return to her human form.

And just like that, her body began shifting, changing, transforming again. Her hands and feet morphed back to normal. Her arms and legs extended and became human-like again. Her neck returned to its normal size. Her face regained its familiar human appearance. Her hair grew back on her head. Soon she was standing erect and upright again. Completely human, completely normal… and completely naked.

That's twice in one day. Sheesh.

She grabbed her clothes and quickly put them back on.

"Wow," was all she could say.

This was *so cool!*

She was a shape-shifter!

She had to try something else. A dog perhaps. She focused on being a dog. Nothing happened. Darn it! Why wasn't this working?

Okay, think. What was the difference? Why did her arms and feet change the first two times? What was she thinking and feeling right before she became a turtle?

Emotion. A clear and focused emotion.

Needing strength. Needing a better footing. Needing to hide and felt sheltered like a turtle. Maybe her power was triggered by her emotions.

Okay. So now she had to try it. She thought about getting out of here – flying free, like a bird. She focused on it, pictured it clearly in her mind, and really *felt* what it would be like. And suddenly, her body began shape-shifting again.

She smiled with excitement and said, "I did it!" as feathers grew across her skin and her mouth began forming into a beak. Her arms quickly morphed into wings. Long tail feathers extended out from her lower back as she shrank and shrank into a tiny bird.

Seconds later, she was on the ground, buried under her clothes again, experiencing life as a bird.

Wow, this was incredible. Her heart beat faster than normal. She felt so light and free. She hopped out from under her clothes and looked around. Her vision was so sharp and clear. And she could see details from far away. She opened and stretched her new finely-feathered wings.

Could she do this? Was she really about to fly?

She flapped gently.

She was about to fly.

Oh God. Oh God. Oh God… Here goes…

She gave herself a little running start, held her wings out flat, began flapping as hard and as fast as her little birdy wings could, and suddenly… her feet left the ground, air supported her, and she felt herself going higher and higher.

She flew circles around the room. Saw her own reflection – a green parakeet – along the mirrored walls. Flying felt so incredible. So amazing. So freeing and – well, just totally awesome! She chirped with joy. That was a weird sound to come out of her mouth. Well, not weird for a parakeet. Just weird for a parakeet that's used to being a human.

She landed on top of the pedestal – the only raised surface in the room. Poor Ray. Here she was, flying around, having the time of her life with her newly discovered super power – and he was… she had no idea where he was.

Ray sat curled up, crying, trapped in his own unending nightmare.

It had probably played a thousand times by now. Maybe more. He lost count. It was unending.

Nothing he said, nothing he did, ever changed anything.

He was an observer, nothing more.

He couldn't stop his father from leaving.

He couldn't make him mom take back those words.

He wanted nothing more than to keep his family together. Poverty was tough – but feeling unloved and unwanted was worse. If only they stayed together. Things would've gotten better. They would've *been* better, simply because they were together.

Why'd they have to break up? Why'd he have to leave? Why didn't she go after him?

Ray watched his younger self ignorantly ride his new red bike out in the cul-de-sac. Ignorance was bliss. But that didn't stop the pain he'd feel for the rest of his life.

The scene restarted. Again. His mom was in the kitchen, making a sandwich. *Alf* was on the TV. His father came home, excited about the bike. They started arguing.

"DAMMIT!" he screamed at them. "WOULD YOU JUST STOP ALREADY!!!"

The scene continued playing around him.

He finally threw his hands up into the air and sighed. He stopped crying. There were no more tears.

Whether he liked it or not, this was his past.

This was the defining moment when everything fell apart.

And he couldn't change any of it.

But if he could… if he could change one thing… it'd be that his parents stuck together.

Money was a problem. But together they could've worked through it. Life will always have problems. Life is full of challenges. What makes it worthwhile, what makes it possible, is the relationships we have in our lives.

But his family didn't have that.

His mom had to pick up extra shifts and jobs to make ends meet. His dad was never around. Ray grew up feeling alone most of the time. Unwanted.

He shook his head, watching his parents argue with each other. Saying things they probably didn't mean. If only he could force them to stay together. Push them closer, instead of let them push each other away.

He wished.

But there was nothing he could do.

He could only watch as it happened again and again.

Would he ever escape this hell?

But strangely, he felt a little odd. Tingly, almost. All over. Like an electrical charge ran across his skin, softly tickling him, absorbing deep into his organs and bones.

This was new.

Maybe he was just finally losing his mind. He didn't know how long he had been here, watching this scene play over and over again. Maybe he had been here for days. And was finally going insane from the hunger, sleep deprivation, and dehydration.

But, strangely, he didn't feel that hungry, or sleep deprived, or thirsty right now.

He felt tingly. All over. And charged up, empowered, gifted somehow. He couldn't explain it. He couldn't explain how he knew. But somehow, he felt like he had received some kind of blessing or gift. He was still the same man, the same Ray. But he felt different. Reborn, almost.

He felt a certain power in his hands.

The scene started over, again. He sighed. Everything replayed up to the part where they were fighting again. His dad was about to quit and leave.

"That's it. I'm outta here," said Ray's dad. "I don't need this bullshit anymore."

"No," exclaimed Ray, "I don't want to see this anymore! YOU'RE STAYING HERE!"

Ray intuitively held his hands out, and with a single motion, actually moved his dad closer to his mom.

Ray froze. "Whoa." What just happened?

This was different.

The scene stopped playing. His mom and dad weren't frozen in time or anything. They still breathed. Still blinked. Still stood there, alive. But the scene had been interrupted. His dad didn't walk out the door. His mom didn't say another word.

"What the—" This was new.

Ray looked at his hands. Did he do that?

He walked closer to them. "Mom? Dad? Can either of you hear or see me?"

No response.

Ray looked down at his hands again. He started to put two and two together. He tried something. With his right hand, he swiped away – and his dad flew across the room. With his left hand, he motioned towards the couch. And his mom suddenly landed there.

"What?" He couldn't believe it. Were *his* hands doing this?

He tried something else. The lamp. He focused on the lamp, raised his hand, and the lamp lifted into the air.

He tried something bigger. The couch. With his mom still sitting on it. With both his hands – from across the room – he raised the couch into the air. His mom crawled to the edge and hung on for dear life.

"Help Tom! Get me down from here!" she cried.

Ray let the couch gently back down.

"Mom, Dad…"

They still seemed unaware of his presence.

"Mom? Dad?"

His dad went over to his mom. And suddenly, everything – his parents, the furniture, the walls, the bike – all faded to white.

Back in the mirrored room inside the pyramid, the sphere reappeared over the pedestal.

Dawn was in human form again, putting back on the last of her clothes. She looked and saw the manifesting sphere. "Ray?"

The sphere grew larger and larger, and suddenly, Ray got spit out – launching several feet away through the air. "Whoaaaaa!!!" he yelled, unintentionally flying.

"Ray!"

But right before landing hard on the floor, he held his hands out – and magically delayed his fall, allowed him to descend gently, and he landed softly on his feet.

"Wow! You got powers too!" Dawn exclaimed.

"What?"

"Look what I can do!" Dawn shouted excitedly. She closed her eyes, concentrated, and focused her emotions. Suddenly she began shape-shifting her face and appearance. She stayed human, but changed her hair color, made her breasts bigger, and shifted the overall shape and appearance of her body. Within seconds, she looked like a completely different woman. Different face. Different hair. Different everything.

"What?" Ray stared in disbelief and confusion.

"That's not all I can do," she said. "I can do animals too!"

"What?"

"You're getting repetitive, Ray. Try to keep up."

"I don't… you're saying you're a… a changeling?"

"That's right," she nodded excitedly. She shifted back into her normal form, height, weight, and appearance.

Ray smiled. "You're prettier this way."

She blushed.

"But why… how did… how come you can suddenly do this? How long was I gone?"

She shrugged. "I guess it's a side-effect of that chemical they injected me with. But forget about that – how'd you get *your* power!"

"What? Oh… I'm not sure, to be honest." He seemed a little disoriented. "To be honest, I'm not even sure I'm really here. Are you real?"

She laughed. "Yes, silly, of course I'm real!" She walked up to him and hugged him. And then kissed him.

"Definitely real," he said.

"Where'd you go? What happened to you?" she begged to know.

"I'm not sure. I saw… my parents. When I was a kid. The day they broke up and my dad left… It was… difficult."

She hugged him again.

He seemed lost in thought, still recovering, still processing his experience.

"You okay?"

"I think so. I will be. That place – wherever I went – it really messes with you."

"But it gave you a real-life super power, too! Just like in the comic books!"

He laughed. "My roommate would be *so* jealous if he was here right now."

"So what can you do, exactly?"

"Well, I didn't get an instruction manual or anything, but I seem to be able to move objects with my mind."

"You did more than that," said Dawn. "You levitated. You slowed down your fall."

"Yeah," he said, looking at the distance he traveled from the pedestal, and the floor where he now stood. "I guess I did."

She hugged him again. "This is so cool. We got powers!"

He laughed. "Keep saying it. It doesn't make it any easier to believe."

"Seriously. I was a turtle, then a bird, and a cat, and then I was a—"

"How long was I gone?"

"Oh, I dunno. Fifteen minutes? Maybe less."

"Fifteen minutes!" he exclaimed. It seemed a *lot* longer than that.

"Or less," she said.

"Whatever. It's not important. We still need to find Luke."

"This place is enormous," said Dawn.

"I know. And we're not even sure he came in here."

But Luke was a lot closer than they realized.

Helping his uncle limp along, they climbed up the narrow and twisting tunnel, around the bend, and suddenly stepped into an open room.

Unlike the cave before, this place had been carved out. The walls were perfectly flat. The room was evenly square. The humming noise was quite loud – and they now knew what was causing it.

A large metal cylinder extended from ceiling to floor, with bright glowing red lights on the outside. It gave off a lot of heat, too. It was artificial and mechanical, whatever it was. It seemed to extend higher up through the ceiling, and deeper down through the floor.

And a lone control panel with several buttons and a video screen hung on the cylinder's side.

"This is it," said his uncle, struggling to hide the pain.

"The healing chamber?"

"No. Take me to the console."

Luke helped his uncle limp up to the control panel. It had several buttons, much like a keyboard, but all marked with strange alien writing and symbols. "What is this thing?"

His uncle looked at the large cylinder. "No idea."

Suddenly its humming went quiet, like it was powering down. The red glow dimmed almost completely off. It was too dark for Luke to see anymore. But his uncle, barely, still could.

"If I remember correctly, one of these is the recall button."

"Recall button? Uncle, when you're all better, you're going to tell me *everything*, right?"

"I think it's…" Charlie pressed a button.

A circle of white light instantly appeared around their feet, lifted up into the air above them, and both they and the circle of light disappeared.

Elsewhere, the same circle of white light appeared on the floor, lifting up, causing them to appear.

There were in another room entirely. A large hexagonal room, with three circle platforms side by side along the floor. They stood in the center one.

They were inside the pyramid now, although they didn't know it right away. The same small lights lined the walls. The ceiling was high. The walls were made of the strange metal alloy. The air was cool and conditioned.

Luke took a relaxing breath.

"This way," urged his uncle.

The left that room, entering the long narrow corridors. His uncle looked left and then right. Either direction appeared pretty much the same. He leaned up against the wall. Placed his palm flat to the surface.

Suddenly a section of that wall came to life, illuminating with text, symbols, icons, menus, and more.

Luke's jaw dropped. He was in nerd heaven. A touch-based interactive computer monitor built into and hidden within the walls? Awesome!

"Healing chamber," his uncle spoke to wall.

A map of their current location suddenly displayed. Then a red dotted line appeared from their current location, showing them which way to go, turn by turn, to get to the desired room.

Charlie memorized the directions. Then he placed his hand flat on the wall a second time, and the screen menus disappeared. It looked like a completely ordinary empty metal wall again.

Luke shook his head. "You've got a lot of secrets, Uncle."

Charlie smiled. "This way."

With Luke helping him along, together they limped down the hallways, made the correct turns, and soon enough arrived at the doorway.

His uncle pressed the blue button. The door rolled open to the side. They walked in.

This room looked like a full-scale medical lab loaded with only the coolest high-tech stuff that most movies never even dreamed of. There were beds, imaging chambers, glass cylinder stasis pods, all kinds of electronics and various machines that even Luke could scarcely imagine what they were used for. A variety of alien tools, high-tech scanners, medical supplies, computer screens, and all sorts of stuff. And all very clean, white, and sterile.

"Help me onto the bed," his uncle said.

Luke helped him onto the nearest bed. His uncle laid down.

Instantly, a wide beam of light appeared from overhead, scanning Charlie from head to toe. The light color changed and then passed over him again for a second sweep. And a few more times, undoubtedly analyzing and scanning for different things.

On one hand, this was so cool for Luke. Never in his wildest dreams did he ever imagine coming to a place like this. On the other hand, his uncle was in pretty bad shape. In this better lighting, he saw just how bad the wounds were. It was amazing the man survived this long.

"I'll be fine," said Charlie, reading Luke's concerned face. "Just give it a sec."

A hologram suddenly appeared beside Charlie's bed. It was a 3-D, realistic, lifelike, fully-animated representation of an actual human doctor – lab coat and all. The doctor had a friendly, kind face. It was clearly a hologram. But it almost looked like it had substance.

And then it spoke.

"I've completed my diagnostic," he said. "Are you ready to be repaired?"

"Yes, heal me," said Charlie.

Luke just watched in awe.

The holographic doctor grabbed one of the nearby devices. It looked like some kind of spray gun, like something you might use to paint small surfaces with. He held it over Charlie's wounds and began spraying a fine mist. His uncle's skin immediately began repairing itself, and within seconds, looked good as new.

"Your external wounds have been repaired," said the holographic doctor. "Please wait for immunization. You have been infected by an unknown virus."

"Unknown?" Luke repeated. "Are they sure they can cure it?"

"Relax Luke," said Charlie, laughing for the first time in far too long. "Their medicine's a little more advanced than ours."

"No kidding!"

"Please lay still for this procedure," said the doctor.

A beam of blue-green light shined from overhead, slowly passing over every inch of Charlie's body.

"The virus has been removed," said the doctor. "You have lost some blood and need to be refilled. Please wait."

"Told you," said Charlie.

Luke shook his head in disbelief, but smiled.

"Your blood type has been replicated. Your lost blood will now be replaced."

The doctor held a small, flat, round device over Charlie's heart. He held it there for several seconds. Charlie immediately started feeling much better. A few seconds more, and then doctor removed the device.

"All repairs have been completed. Please wait for final diagnostic."

Different lights from overhead scanned Charlie again, just like before when he first laid down on the bed. A few seconds later, they stopped.

"Confirmed. No additional repairs needed. You are cleared to go." And suddenly, the holographic doctor disappeared.

"Uncle?"

Charlie sat up and looked himself over. Even the blood had been cleaned out of his clothes. He lifted his shirt and checked his wounds. All gone. No trace. Not even a scar. It was as if he had never been injured.

"That's incredible."

"You're telling me!" he laughed. "And just a tad bit better than a hospital back on Earth."

"Uh, yeah. Just a tad."

Charlie hopped down off the bed and onto his feet. He felt like a new man.

"So now what? We're gonna—?"

"Shh," said his uncle. "You hear that? Voices."

Luke listened. He did hear voices, coming from just down the hall. Shit. He suddenly realized he and his uncle were inside some kind of alien facility and just used their technology without authorization. Had these aliens even ever seen a human before? They must have – the holographic doctor looked human. Were the aliens human too? Maybe they weren't aliens at all – maybe this entire facility was from the future! Or… maybe…

No, wait, one of those voices sounded really familiar.

"Ray?" he remarked.

Luke ran out into the hall.

He saw Ray and some cute blonde girl, carrying backpacks, wandering down the hallway. "Ray!"

"Luke!"

They ran toward each other. Gave each other a big hug. And then realized how gay that probably looked, even though they were best friends. They were in the presence of a hot girl, of course, so they stopped hugging and shook hands firmly. "Good to see you."

"What the heck are you doing here?" Luke exclaimed.s

"Well, I… we…"

"The portal! Doh!" Luke slapped his forehead. "I left that open at the apartment. You came home and saw it, didn't you?"

"You could say that. Anyway," said Ray, "this is Dawn, the date I told you about."

"Oh," said Luke. He shook her hand. "Nice to meet you."

"I've heard so much about you," she said.

"Ray and I go way back," Luke said.

"Yeah. All the way back to college," Ray added.

Dawn smiled. "I'm glad you're safe."

Charlie leaned against the doorway. "So, you going to introduce me anytime soon?"

"Of course!" said Luke. "Ray, you already know my uncle. Dawn, this is my uncle, Charlie."

"Nice to meet you," she said, shaking his hand.

"Oh my gosh, you'll *never* guess what just happened!" exclaimed Luke. "This hologram just healed Uncle Charlie with some kind of spray gun after we used this teleporter to get inside and when he pressed his hand to the wall a computer screen appeared and there was this giant snake with eight eyes and it almost ate us but trapped us in this web instead, and I have this crystal that opens portals and stuff, and we fell down a giant pit in the desert and almost drowned!"

Ray and Dawn just stared at him like deer in headlights, trying to keep up. "What?" they both said.

Charlie placed his hand on Luke's shoulder. "That's my favorite nephew. Always up for an adventure."

Ray said, "I'm glad we found you. We were getting pretty worried. We weren't even sure if we should be looking for you here."

"Good thing we did, huh?" said Dawn, proudly. It was, after all, her idea.

"How did," said Ray, "I mean, *why* is there a portal back in our living room? Do you know how it got there?"

"Well…" said Luke. "That's a long story."

"One for another time," said Charlie.

"So do you also have powers?" asked Dawn.

"What? No. It's this crystal. It creates the portals," said Luke. "Wait. What do you mean, 'also'?"

Ray chuckled. He wasn't sure how to tell his friend this. "Well buddy, there was this… well, yeah, you could call him a super villain, and he injected Dawn with some chemical… and now she can shape-shift."

"WHAT?!"

"And," enthusiastically added Dawn, "Ray disappeared into this alternate dimension or something, and when he came back, he can move objects with his mind!"

"Wait, wait, wait," said Luke, looking at his uncle and the two of them. "Do you mean to tell me that I'm the *only* one here without any powers?"

"What? Charlie's got powers too?" asked Ray.

"How is *that* fair?" said Luke.

Chapter 15
BORN AGAIN

A zillion light-years away back on Earth, in the city that doesn't sleep… No wait, that's New York City. Los Angeles is the City of Angels. Land of the fruits and nuts. Home of the LA Lakers, the famous Hollywood sign, and the Walt Disney Concert Hall. A city with countless millions of people, most of them good and decent hard-working Americans… or unemployed aspiring actors and writers, but we love them too.

But tonight, right now, none of those other people mattered. They could've all been robbing banks, stealing cars, and speeding through every red light in town. Right now, every police officer was on alert and in hot pursuit of just one man.

Mastermind.

Of course, they didn't know him by that name. Not yet. He was just a "John Doe" they picked up – who then made an embarrassment and mockery out of some of their finest uniformed men and women. Too many good cops lost their lives that night. The claim that he had some kind of "mind control" power no longer seemed so silly. A grave mistake they would never repeat again.

This asshole was going down.

After he mind-controlled several officers at the station and turned them against each other in an open fire fight, he freed his accomplices plus five other arrested perps – and they all escaped in an armored police van.

But that was his mistake. Because every one of their vehicles had GPS tracking. They knew exactly where he was and where he was going.

Interstate 5. Northbound. Cruising along at a nice and steady 72 miles per hour.

It was the middle of the night, so there wasn't much traffic. The highway onramps and exits had all been blocked off. Six police cars chased up from the rear. Another four joined in farther up ahead. And six more came from ahead, traveling south on the northbound side, preparing to trap and block him in.

They had him. They controlled all the exits. They raced ahead in every direction, ready to box him in and take him down.

Two police helicopters flew overhead, beaming a pair of spotlights down on the fleeing police van.

And it wasn't long before the news media was swarming the area with their own helicopters. Reporters pointed their cameras down at the freeway, filming it all as it happened. Of course, most people wouldn't see any of this until the morning news as they sipped their cups of coffee. But the few people who were awake right now and watching TV – they'd get to watch it all gone down, live, and on camera.

"I'm Alex Alvarado reporting for NBS News. You are looking at live footage of the Golden State Freeway. The black police van moving right on your screen was stolen less than fifteen minutes ago from an unidentified criminal who was arrested earlier this evening. He escaped from police custody and is considered armed and extremely dangerous. The LAPD has blocked off all exits and onramps to the I-5 Northbound freeway in an attempt to box in this fugitive and prevent further casualties. He's wanted for the murder of over twelve LAPD officers and attempted murder of several more. We believe the fugitive is driving with seven other recently arrested persons – all arrested for various crimes from drug dealing to illegal human experimentation. The fugitive's connection to these individuals is unknown at this time, but they appear to be headed into Santa Clarita or beyond."

The police cars from both ahead of the escaping van and from behind quickly closed in. Several boxed in the van on all sides, slowly forcing the van toward the shoulder of the highway.

"And you can now see them forcing him over to the side of the freeway, where they will apprehend and take all the fugitives back into custody. Again, let me remind you, that man we believe to be driving this stolen police van is considered armed and extremely dangerous. He is wanted for murdering and seriously injuring several highly trained and well-armed police officers. The LAPD is not taking this arrest lightly. They have assistance from the California Highway Patrol, state marshals, and it is believed even the FBI is involved. My source tells me that all officers and agents involved have been informed of the danger and taken extra precautions. There may be an exchange of firearms, but the police will do everything they can to keep nearby civilians safe, including blocking off access to the freeway until this man and the other fugitives have been safely taken into custody."

Several more patrol cars pulled up alongside the others. They forced the stolen van over another lane. At the same time, they slowed him down. They blocked him on every side: front, rear, left, and right. More police cars surrounded from a safer but nearby distance. FBI and SWAT vans joined in as well. More police helicopters hovered overhead, with both snipers and spotlights trained on the stolen van.

"The main fugitive who appears to be the leader of the others was arrested earlier tonight for four counts of adult kidnapping, one count of murder, at least three counts of animal cruelty, and two counts of illegal human experimentation. We still don't have a confirmed identity for this man, but you should be seeing the police photo of the man in question on your screen now. If you have *any* information regarding this man's identity, home address, place of work, or any other information at all, please call the Los Angeles Police Department at the number on your screen."

The cops coordinated their efforts flawlessly. The stolen van came to a complete stop along the empty shoulder of the closed off freeway.

This was it. The moment of truth. No one acted hastily. Caution, strategy, careful calculated moves. That's what they needed for such a dangerous and powerful man.

Dawn's testimony claimed that his mind control seemed to require direct eye contact. Every officer and agent on site was told to take the "mind control" claim with extreme credibility. The surveillance footage back at the station confirmed everything. With nothing more than eye contact and a few carefully chosen words, he made fellow officers see each other as lethal enemies. They opened fire on each other without hesitation or delay. The surviving officers, after the mysterious man had left, were confused beyond all reason. They remembered everything. They *knew* the officers they were shooting at were friends and co-workers. But something overpowered them. Something made them *want* to shoot at each other. *Need* to shoot at each other. As if their own lives depended on it.

And after the first few bullets started flying, all their lives actually did depend on it…

But the crisis was over now. All the officers and detectives at the scene were either dead, rushed to the hospital, or disarmed and put under strict surveillance. These new officers and agents, now on scene on the highway, were nervous and frightened, sure – but they were also focused, determined, "a little" angry, and a lot better prepared.

This would not be a repeat of the police station massacre.

If the mysterious man didn't come quietly and peacefully, snipers high above in helicopters – safe from his mind control's influence – were authorized to shoot to kill, if necessary. Every officer and agent there wanted to personally blow his brains out – you mess with one of their own, you mess with them all. But they were not above the law. If possible – and that was a big "if" – he had to be taken in alive, for due process, appear before a judge, and get the death sentence through the justice system. Not even the best lawyer in the world could save him now.

The van door opened – on the driver's side.

Police officers ducked behind their car doors, guns aimed forward, shouting, "Down on the ground, get down on the ground! Keep your hands up, face away, lay flat on the ground!"

No chances. Everyone avoided direct eye contact. They kept a safe distance away. Countless guns all aimed at that one spot right now. Other nearby officers watched their partners, ready to disarm them with a second's notice, just in case the mysterious man somehow controlled them again.

A man stepped out of the stolen police van, hands in the air. "Don't shoot! Don't shoot!" He got down on his knees and then laid flat on the pavement.

The man… was short, had curly red hair, and wore pair of jeans, faded t-shirt, and an LA Dodgers cap.

"I'm sorry!" he shouted. "Please don't shoot!"

It wasn't their man.

Some members of the SWAT team approached the side of the van and cautiously – but quickly – opened the door and looked inside. Empty. No other fugitives.

"It's empty!"

Other officers arrested, handcuffed, and took the red-haired Dodgers fan aside. Meanwhile the SWAT team searched the van for explosives or other threats.

"Please," said the Dodgers fan to the arresting officer. "I don't know what came over me. I was just getting a Slurpee from the 7-Eleven and this guy in a suit came up to me and told me to take the van outside and drive it to Bakersfield. Then he and his buddies took my SUV – *and* he took my Slurpee!"

The officers sighed. "Alright," said one of them. "We're gonna need a description of your vehicle and its tag plate number."

Mastermind slurped up the last of his Slurpee as he casually drove *south* on that same freeway. In the front passenger seat beside him was Shadow, who at this moment, was inspecting her razor-sharp nails.

In the back, Doctor Troyd sat with the other five criminals.

"So, uh, where we going, exactly?" asked the big black guy.

Doctor Troyd didn't respond.

At first the big guy just thought he was being ignored. But then he noticed Doctor Troyd seemed unaware he even said anything. "Hey," said the big guy again. "Hey, I'm talking to you!"

Doctor Troyd noticed him talking. He started signing something. Pointed to his ear.

"I think he's deaf," said the ugly butch woman. "That's what happens when you make a deal with the devil."

"Say what?"

"How else you explain that man's powers?" she snorted.

"I dunno. Magic?" shrugged the big guy.

"It's witchcraft, I tell ya!" said the white trash guy.

"Whatever it is," said the gang member, "we're way in over our heads now."

"You think he wants ta kill us?" asked the prostitute.

"Shh!" said the big guy. "He can hear you!"

"He doesn't want to kill you," Shadow chimed in from the front seat. "He's gonna make you reborn… like me."

"Say what?" said the big guy.

Shadow turned around and smiled. Her cat-like eyes practically glowing at them. Her whiskers, pointed-tip cat ears, the smooth even layer of black fur all over her body. Her paw-like hands. She held her long tail across her chest. "You're gonna *love* it."

Somewhere in Orange County, they pulled into an empty parking lot outside a large office building.

It was the middle of the night. Cold, quiet, all alone. The parking lot lights illuminated the scene. And on the six story office building, in shining letters, glowed the sign "BioGen Industries".

Mastermind parked their stolen SUV near the building's entrance. He looked back at the others and told them all to stay here. Then he looked to Doctor Troyd and motioned for them to continue.

The scientist and the super villain stepped outside onto the quiet pavement. They approached the door. It required a keycard swipe to gain access.

"You're sure your card still works?" Mastermind signed to Doctor Troyd.

"Yes," he replied. *"It worked earlier this morning when I picked up the solution."*

Doctor Troyd pulled out his wallet and retrieved the keycard. BioGen Industries had hired him numerous times for consulting and research. The company worked on a variety of unique and interesting projects – and his, shall we say, "gray zone ethics" were perfect for the job. So he had a temporary, but long-term access card.

He had come up with the formula for the BioGen-X solution. But it was this company that actually manufactured it. The company authorized the manufacturing of this "product" – provided they could keep and use it for themselves.

Mastermind had no association with the company. What they planned to do with it, if anything, was a bit of a mystery. But it didn't matter. Mastermind's plan would be done long before they could do anything about it.

Doctor Troyd swiped his card. The door buzzed and opened.

Mastermind and Doctor Troyd went inside.

Past the lobby, up the elevator, and down the hall – and they arrived at Doctor Troyd's part-time lab. Several more liters of the glowing green chemical waited for them there in the dark.

Troyd switched on the lights.

Mastermind walked in, looking around at all the machines and chemical components in the lab. Fascinating. He grabbed a glass container of the glowing green chemical and held it in his hand. He stared deeply into the thick green goo inside. This was his answer. This was his tool. This was how he planned to take over the world.

"Beautiful." He turned to Doctor Troyd and signed, *"You over-nighted a sample of this to New York like I told you, right?"*

Doctor Troyd nodded his head yes, rolling his eyes. He wasn't an idiot. He didn't forget the plan.

"Excellent," signed Mastermind. *"And tonight's subjects?"*

"Over here," Doctor Troyd replied. He went over to a large refrigerator nearby. But this was no ordinary refrigerator. It wasn't used for holding snacks or drinks. He opened it.

Blood samples.

Dozens of small vials, each containing individual blood samples of various animals from around the world. Kept cold and preserved in this special refrigerator.

Mastermind walked over. He looked at his options – nearly fifty unique vials to choose from. He hand-picked one, and then another, and then another. He searched through them and found another he liked. Considered a few, moved on, picked a different vial from among them.

He finished with ten vials. Doctor Troyd grabbed a padded case to hold and carry them. Mastermind carefully placed the samples inside the case, closed it up, and carried it out.

The glass cylinder of green chemical in one hand – and the metal case containing nearly a dozen different blood samples in the other.

A moment later, they were back outside in the empty parking lot. Mastermind summoned everyone out of the van – and told them to line up in front of him.

He looked back at the building behind him. Security cameras were positioned above the door. He made sure he, and his new recruits, were being recorded.

"Shadow," he said, "hold this." He handed her the case with the ten blood samples. Doctor Troyd stood at Mastermind's other side, holding the BioGen-X solution and handful of syringes.

Standing before them were the five criminals Mastermind had selected for his own purposes. "You," he said to all of them, "are about to be made new. You will embrace your new lives, all of you, and swear loyalty and life-long service to me. You will worship me as your master. You will obey every command. You will be extensions of my will. And in return, I will give you power. Power like you've never known or dreamed of. Power that, under my command, will be used to reshape the face of the world."

"An' why should we serve *you*?" demanded the prostitute.

He stepped closer to her. Their eyes locked intensely. "Take off all your clothes, right now."

She did. The other four watched and stared in both horror and amazement. They had seen the incredible power he had over the police officers at the station. They all came along willingly – at least, it felt that way – but they all started to have a nervous gut feeling.

"Pleasure me," he told her.

She unzipped his pants and gently reached inside.

The suddenly others felt awkward and uncomfortable. Well, most of them. The young gang member thought it was hot. But no one moved. They didn't say a word. Of course – only a moment ago, he had told them to line up and wait in place. Maybe they were too terrified to speak. This woman, a young and somewhat beautiful prostitute, asked a simple and justified question. And now he demonstrated his power over her.

The same power he probably had over all of them.

She began sucking on his dick. As an experienced hooker, she was quite skilled at this. Normally she'd only do this for money, but for some reason, right now, she felt this irresistible urge to give him one for free. She *wanted* to serve him. She *desired* to pleasure him right now, even with all the others watching.

But he had had enough. He pulled on the back of her hair and tossed her away. "That's enough," he said. He quickly zipped up his pants. "I haven't decided if you're worthy to do that to me yet."

She sat naked on the pavement, confused and hurt.

"Stand up," he told her. They were still making eye contact. She obeyed. "For you… hmm…" He tried imagining what new form he wanted for her. He walked over to Shadow who held the case of specimen samples. He looked at the ten vials, all labeled, and made a decision. He picked it out and held it in his hand.

"Yes," he said. "I think this will be fitting."

Doctor Troyd opened the glass cylinder, exposing the green chemical to the open air. He seemed nervous. He clearly did not want any of it to accidentally spill on him.

Mastermind took a fresh syringe and filled it with the BioGen-X. As soon as he did, Doctor Troyd sealed up the cylinder again.

Mastermind stepped up to the naked prostitute. He held her arm.

"W-What're ya doing ta me? Stop. Don't!"

He injected her.

"What was that?" she demanded.

"Your destiny," he said.

Then he reloaded the syringe with the vial sample he had selected. It didn't look like normal blood. It was… thicker, gooier, slimier… A brownish-yellow color. Not quite normal.

"Now hold still," he told her. She couldn't resist him. He injected the strange substance into her blood. It started tingling immediately.

She looked at him, searching for mercy or pity in his eyes. She found none. "What was that?" she pleaded.

"A combination of a few different species. A little cocktail mix I had ordered up for fun, a little experiment."

She looked at him with disbelief.

"Mostly *Arion subfuscus*, *Tandonia budapestensis*, *Ariolimax columbianus*, and a few others."

"What?"

"Slugs, my dear. A beautiful variety of slimy, sticky, disgusting slugs. Just like you."

Her mouth fell open in shock. She had never been so insulted – and she had heard a lot of insults. People judged her and criticized her because of her "work" – but she didn't choose this life! She fell on hard times, it was just supposed to be temporary, but it was a hard business to get out of. People looked at what she did for a living and judged her as if that's all she ever was or ever would be. But she was more than that. She was a person. Her own life. Her own dreams. Her own fears.

And now… what was happening to her?

She looked at Shadow. A human-cat girl. Shadow said they'd all be reborn, like her. Mastermind said they'd all be made new. She felt a tingling sensation expand throughout her body. What was happening? She felt… strange. Different inside. Like her guts and internal organs were all shifting around.

"Slugs?" her voice broke.

"BioGen-X is still an experimental solution," he said, almost as if he enjoyed that fact. "We're still learning exactly how far the mutations go. When Shadow here was injected, I really wasn't sure what it'd do to her. It might've turned her completely into a cat – or it might've simply made her a little hairier. But, as you can see, I'm quite proud of my work."

The prostitute's skin started to look really moist and slick. And it began turning into a brownish-yellow color.

"Honestly," said Mastermind, "you may not be able to stand, or even have legs, in a moment or two. Slugs are invertebrates. No skeletons. No arms or legs, either."

"You son of a bitch!"

"NO!" shouted Mastermind. "*You* are the scum here, the slimy betrayer! You use men for your own pleasure and gain. You are worthless!"

Unfortunately they were making eye contact when he said that. He was clearly angry. It wasn't a command. More of a statement. But she took it as a command. She lowered her head. She began to feel very worthless. More than she ever had in her entire life.

Then a slick layer of green slime spread across her body. It started in spots, but soon circulated all over, eventually covering every inch of exposed flesh. At the same time, all of her body hair, include on her head, retreated into her skin and disappeared entirely. Her entire body became smoother, softer, rounder… Still humanoid, but slightly less defined.

Her legs grew weak.

Gravity suddenly felt so hard.

Her body started to lose form. She began melting into a puddle of slimy ooze at her feet. At least, where her feet used to be. She was now just a blob at her base. A green, slimy blob with brown spots. And she sank lower and lower into it.

And as she sank, she looked up at her master, and said, "Fuck you."

A second later, her entire body collapsed into a pile of slime. A morphing, formless mass of goo and stickiness, dripping in slime, neither human nor slug.

"Interesting," was all he said.

But then, the blob began to shift and move. It moved to the left a little, and then to the right, and suddenly, it began to rise up again. It re-formed into a humanoid shape. She took form again. She stood up again.

She was completely made of slime – and other gooey, mushy, sticky, slime-like material too, no doubt. But she was humanoid. Two arms. Two legs. A face.

"Very interesting," he said.

And she could talk. "What have you done to me?"

"An unexpected result." He looked her up and down. "But promising, nonetheless." He looked her in her eyes – her yellow, slime-coated eyes – and commanded her, "From now on, you will only and always obey me. I am your master, you are my slave. You will always do as I wish and command. You are my faithful servant for life. You are my creation. I am your god. You belong to me. Now call me master."

"Yes, master," she said. It just erupted out of her, uncontrollably. She agreed. She accepted. She obeyed. Her mind, her will, her body belonged to him now.

"Good. My second mutant. I shall call you…" He examined her shifting, dripping, slime-filled form. "Slimer."

Not the most creative name, but it was late and he was tired. It would do.

"Now join Shadow and wait over there."

"Yes, master." She slid – moving her legs back and forth, sliding on her feet – over to Shadow and stood by her side. The two mutants stared at and examined each other.

"Who's next?" Mastermind asked. He looked at the remaining four. Fear filled their eyes. "You," he said, pointing to the big black guy. "Take off all your clothes."

One by one, he changed them all.

The big guy found himself in a new body – part human, part rhinoceros. A large spiked horn on the front of his deformed face, tough thick gray skin, powerful muscles in his arms and legs, and even a little tail that didn't seem to do much.

The gang member was transformed into a humanoid spider. He grew extra arms and legs – eight in total – and they were more spider-like than human-like. He also benefited from extra eyes across his face and forehead. A benefit, he found, because it allowed him to see and notice a lot more things at once without needing to move his head much. He also developed small fangs, that mostly hid inside his mouth. His body bloated into a rounder shape with a red diamond marking on his back. He had yet to test this – but he felt lethally venomous.

The white trash guy got a cocktail mix of squid, octopus, and jellyfish specimens. The resulting transformation was hideous. He still stood on two legs, but had six long tentacles for arms, each with powerful gripping suction cups and stinging tips. His head had sunk into body. He looked headless from a distance, but up close, his eyes and inhuman mouth sat center in his chest.

And lastly, the ugly woman became even uglier – turning into a humanoid snake. Dark green scaly skin, extended razor sharp fangs in her mouth, piercing eyes, a flattened face, and a long narrow snake-like body that could twist, turn, and bend in any direction she so desired. Her bite, too, was no doubt highly toxic.

And there they all stood – Shadow, Slimer, Rhino-Man, Arachnus, Kraken, and Venom, as he named them – his six first mutants. The first of many.

Mastermind eyed Doctor Troyd. For a moment, he considered transforming the scientist too. But no. He still needed the doctor in human form for a while yet.

"Mutants," he said to all of them. "Your transformation is not yet complete."

They were all his loyal servants. And all fully mutated. He was very satisfied with the results. But one last critical detail remained: he had yet to give them their powers.

Mastermind walked over to the building. He faced the wall and glass window. And then he reached into his pocket and pulled out a small glowing pink crystal.

"Your destiny awaits." He drew a large circle. The pink lines sparkled and glowed on the building's surface. And then he marked a triangle shape in the middle.

Instantly, a portal opened to a vast, hot, dry desert world. A strange world with two blaring suns – and, of course, a mysterious pyramid waiting in the distance beyond the sand dunes.

The mutants – and Doctor Troyd – all marveled at this man's incredible power. What magic was this? Where did he come from? What other powers did he have? Who was this man – and was he even human?

He stepped through the portal, one foot on each side.

"Come, follow me," he said.

Chapter 16
THE PAST THAT CAN'T BE CHANGED

"Is anyone injured? Everyone alright?" asked Charlie.

"Yeah, we're fine," said Ray. "Why?"

"Just making sure. There's a medical lab here."

"Yeah!" interrupted Luke. "It was AMAZING! It totally healed him, and there was this hologram, and—!"

Luke was clearly excited.

And why wouldn't he be? He was living his ultimate fantasy. Super powers, alien planets, portals, future technology… All the sci-fi and fantasy goodness that any comic book geek like him would love. An adventure beyond anything he watched in a movie or read in a book – because it was real. He was really here, standing on an alien world, inside a mysterious alien high-tech pyramid, surrounded by friends with super powers!

The only think that would make it better was if he, too, had his own super power.

He looked to his uncle. "Do you think, I mean, is it possible I can get a super power too?"

His uncle smiled. "Why do you think I gave you that crystal?"

"Because…" Luke paused. "Wait, why *did* you give me this? You knew what it could do all along. And you said some Buddhist monk in Singapore was holding it for safe keeping… Was that a lie?"

"Skardu. And no, I wasn't lying. He really did hold onto it for a while. James didn't want it falling into the wrong hands again."

"Wait, what?" asked Luke. "What's my dad have to do with any of this?" Suddenly Luke had a realization. The magic crystal had been in their family, passed on father to son, for several generations. If Charlie knew about it, if Charlie got the crystal, maybe Charlie's brother – Luke's dad – did too.

Charlie peeked his head down the long hallway. "Come on, I want to show you something." Charlie placed his hand flat on the nearby wall.

Instantly part of the wall came to life, illuminating with symbols, icons, and menus, just like before. None of the writing was in English.

"Temple chamber," Charlie said.

The interactive wall displayed a map of their current location, and displayed directions with a red dotted line. Charlie then placed his hand flat against the wall again, and everything disappeared. It looked like a completely normal and blank wall again.

"Whoa!!!" said Ray.

"Awesome!" exclaimed Dawn.

"This way," led Charlie.

It wasn't far from their current location. They returned to the very same room Dawn and Ray had just left.

"We were just here," said Ray.

"This is where you got your powers, isn't it?" said Charlie.

"Yeah, how'd you know?"

"There's a *lot* he apparently knows," said Luke.

Charlie pressed the blue button and the circular door rolled open, allowing them inside.

"A lot," Luke reiterated.

They walked into the massive inner chamber – the very center of the enormous pyramid. High vaulted ceiling, mirrored walls all around, and strange alien writing faintly glowing along the floor. Everything circled and centered around the pedestal.

"This," said Charlie, "is the Temple of the Gods." He pointed at the pedestal in the middle, illuminated from a shining spotlight above. "And that," he said, "is the Altar of Destiny."

"How do you know all this?" asked Ray.

"This isn't my first time here."

"No kidding!" exclaimed Luke. "I think we're in deep enough. It's time you told us everything."

The old man nodded. "You're right. It is."

Luke, Dawn, and Ray gathered around him.

Finally, some answers…

"I came here – well, not *here*, I didn't know there was a temple on this planet. I really don't remember ever seeing one."

"Hard to miss, don't ya think?" asked Ray.

"Agreed. The pyramid we're in has to be new. Within the last couple decades. Anyway, that's beside the point. When I was seventeen, my father showed me a crystal."

Luke held the glowing pink crystal in his hand. It had a magical, almost mystical presence to it. But any glowing crystal probably would.

Charlie picked it out of Luke's hand. "Mind if I borrow this?" He knelt down to get closer to the floor. "He showed me how to use it." He drew a circle. "First, define the boundaries. It can be any shape or size. Then, inside the boundary, you have to mark the appropriate symbol. We know of five… well, technically, six… symbols."

"Six?" remarked Luke.

"I'll get to that." Charlie continued. He marked a pair of horizontal wavy lines. Instantly a new portal opened. Everyone leaned in to look. Through the portal, on the other side, they saw a beach – crystal-clear sparkling water, dense lush green jungle, a clear blue sky, scattered white clouds… They could hear the gentle, relaxing sounds of the ocean waves. A symphony of tropical birds chirped, squawked, and sang endlessly. Some kind of fish jumped out of the water in the distance. It was amazing. An absolutely gorgeous, tropical paradise.

Hawaii. Fiji. Costa Rica. That kind of place.

Why didn't they come here first?

"Each symbol opens a portal to a different location. This is the planet Aquaria. As far as we've explored, it pretty much looks like this all over. A lot of diverse vegetation and animal life – but no sign of humans or other intelligent life. No technology. No pollution. No remains of any civilizations, as far as we know. Just pure, untouched natural beauty as far as you can go."

"Wow," said Dawn. "I know where I'm taking my next vacation!"

Charlie smiled. "To close the portal, mark a big 'X' over it." He did. The portal instantly closed. "Opening a new portal will close the previous one, too."

"And you said you know of six symbols?"

"Yes," said Charlie. "Five were found on the Tablet of Ningishzida. We dated the tablet to around 3,500 to 4,000 years ago. Possibly older, but archeological clues place it in the Babylonian dynasty. These are the five symbols engraved on the tablet."

He drew a circle divided horizontally and vertically into four equal sections. "This takes us to Earth. Stonehenge, specifically. The portal appears on the ground, in the center of Stonehenge. So keep that in mind when drawing your portal on this end. It can get a little disorienting sometimes. If you draw a portal vertically on the wall and step through, you'd suddenly find yourself horizontal on Earth with your feet in the air. It's best to jump through at an angle, or just place the portal on the floor or ceiling and climb through."

Next he drew the triangle symbol. "This takes us here. To this desert planet. Like

I said, it used to be empty. I went a long time ago. Never came back. This pyramid is new."

Then he drew the third symbol. The upside-down "U" shape with a tiny circle on each end. "This," he said, "leads to an empty spaceship drifting somewhere in deep space. Do *not* open a portal here. There's no air on the other side. My grandfather told me a story of how his friend got sucked in and died one time. So be very, very careful with this one. I'm showing it to you so you don't draw it on accident or go in blindly."

He drew another symbol. It looked kind of like a pair of "P" symbols, but the left one was reversed and faced the opposite direction. "And this last symbol," he said, "is one I think Luke will be especially interested in."

"Yeah? Why's that?" he said, getting excited.

"It leads to the future."

Luke's mouth hung open.

Ray looked to him. He knew Luke's favorite movie was *Back to the Future* – or anything with time travel in it, for that matter. He had always wanted to travel through time. Especially to the future. He wanted his own hoverboard, flying car, and other cool yet-to-be-thought-of future technology.

Luke asked, "Is this… this pyramid we're in… Is it from the future?" He looked around the mysterious mirrored room. "I mean. This whole facility, is it extraterrestrial or human? I didn't recognize any of the writing or symbols, but that doctor hologram looked human, and the interactive wall consoles seem to respond to English words…"

"That's true," said Uncle Charlie. "Well, I've only once ever seen another pyramid like this. At this last symbol location, in the future. Earth looks really nice. They finally cleaned up all the pollution, people seemed to live in peace, no medical problems… Your father and I went there once and were greeted with a warm welcome."

"How far in the future is it?" Ray asked. "Any stock tips, any companies I should be investing in now?"

Charlie chuckled. "Anyway, they asked if we came for the temple. Not knowing what it was, we said yes. They took us to a pyramid just like this one. Once inside, we learned its purpose."

Luke, Dawn, and Ray listened closely.

"This chamber, this sacred room, is what they call the Temple of the Gods. It's designed, in so many words, to turn ordinary humans into, well, gods."

"What?" remarked Dawn.

"Not in the immortal, all-powerful sense. More in the ancient Greek and Roman sense. It gives people super powers. Makes them more than human."

"Yeah, but weren't those gods immortal?" asked Luke.

"You saw their medical lab here. To an ancient civilization, something like that would certainly make you seem immortal."

"So wait," said Luke, "you saying people from our future gave themselves powers and then visited our distant past, pretended to be gods, and that's where all our myths and legends came from?"

"Seems that way."

"But why?"

"I don't know."

"And why would they give you and Dad powers too? I mean, you're not even from their time!"

"Again, I don't know. But right now," said Uncle Charlie, "there's a more pressing issue."

"What's that?" asked Luke.

Uncle Charlie sighed. Something troubled him. He handed the crystal back, placing it in Luke's hand. "It's the reason why your father never wanted you to have this."

Never? Why would his dad intentionally withhold this from him? His own son. After this crystal had been passed down for generations. And it was *Luke* – he only ever *dreamed* of having super powers, traveling to alien worlds… How could his dad just keep this from him?

Luke felt hurt, almost heartbroken.

Meanwhile, a portal opened on the ancient, sand-covered ruins on the surface of this desert planet.

Mastermind, his six mutants, and Doctor Troyd all stepped through. One by one.

Slimer, the slimy, gooey humanoid blob of a girl, stepped out into the burning sand and immediately began to sizzle. "Ow, ow, ow!" she screamed, doing a little dance. "It's burning my feet!"

"Rhino-Man," Mastermind said to the big, bulky, muscular part-rhinoceros, part-human mutant. "Carry her. And Kraken too."

Rhino-Man scooped up Slimer with one arm, throwing her oozing body over his right shoulder. Then he grabbed and tossed the multi-tentacled, headless sea-monster over the other.

"The rest of you can walk," said Mastermind. The sand was scorching hot. But Shadow the cat-girl, Venom the lizard-woman, and Rhino-Man the, um, rhino-man could tolerate it for now. A beneficial side effect of being mutants. High tolerance for pain. Arachnus, the spider-guy, felt no pain at all.

The air was still blazing hot and bone dry. Two glaring suns cooked them from overhead. They'd all suffer a little sunburn and heat exhaustion. Maybe even some burn blisters on the bottoms of their feet. But Mastermind knew of the healing chamber here. He'd restore everyone to good as new – and hopefully lock in their genetic changes, just in case the mutations were still unstable. And then… he'd give them all their powers, one by one.

The first of many monstrous humans, built to serve him, to usher in a new beginning, a new age for humankind.

They traveled across the hot desert sand. Some of the sand dunes shifted and slid beneath their feet. Arachnus, the spider-guy, found it extremely easy to walk up and down the sliding dunes. Of course, having extra spider-like arms and legs were well-suited for an environment like this. Venom, the snake-woman, wasn't so lucky.

At one point – the same spot where Luke and his uncle fell down and slid into the pit – Venom also lost her footing. She nearly fell to the same fate. But Shadow's quick cat-like reflexes grabbed her – digging her claws into Venom's scaly skin to hold her – and pulled her back onto more solid ground.

"Ow!" screamed Venom. "That hurtsss."

"You're welcome."

"Your father and I got powers," said Charlie. "Your mother too."

"What?" Luke was nearly in tears. How could they hide this from him? *Why* did they hide this from him? Didn't they trust him? And why – why wouldn't they let Luke get a power too?

"But James made me promise to keep you out of this."

"Why?" begged Luke.

"They loved you too much. They didn't want to see you get hurt. It's dangerous, Luke, but that wasn't the real reason."

"Then what?"

"They were going to give it to you, when you were older. But then… then…" Charlie lowered his head. "It was my fault, really. I was careless. This crystal was just too amazing. You see, I thought it'd be safe to share with my colleagues. A few fellow archeologists. And maybe some of the other professors. I was still pretty new at the university at the time. I had to show it to give credibility to my story." He sighed. "Or maybe I just wanted to show off. Anyway, I guess word got around, and someone else found out who shouldn't have – and next thing I know, someone had broken into my office and stole it."

"Oh my God," said Luke.

"Anyway, he was pretty smart and figured out how to use it. At some point, he must've encountered a pyramid like this, found this room, and touched the Altar of Destiny. He became a changed man…"

Ray asked, "How do you know all this?"

"We eventually learned who stole the crystal. He was a custodian at the university. Some old guy, um… Gates, I believe his last name was. He was hard of hearing, going blind. Had a lot of health problems, really. We honestly didn't think he'd overhear us talking about the crystal. He was nearby, emptying the trash one day, in the other room. We didn't think anything of it." He sighed with tears filling his eyes. "It was a mistake I'll never make again."

"What happened?" Luke asked.

He cleared his throat. "Well, the Altar fundamentally changes you. James and I had already gone through it. Helen did shortly after. It's how we got our powers. Just like you, Ray. But it doesn't just randomly give you any power. It takes you through significant emotional experience, some defining moment in your past. And it plays that scene over and over—"

"And over," said Ray.

"—until it finally pushes you to reach inside and manifest some power to change what happened. It gives you a power based on what you need, what you most want or wish you could've done, in that emotionally intense moment."

Dawn looked to Ray. She had a better understanding now of what he just went through. She pulled herself closer to him.

"For me," said Charlie, "it took me back to when I was a child. It was summer camp. I went out exploring in the woods. Wandered too far, got lost. The sun went down. Couldn't see for the life of me. It was so terrifying. I was so scared. I thought I'd never find my way back. I thought I'd never see my parents or friends again. It was so dark. Like being blind. I remember that night. Completely overcast. No moon, no stars. And that's when it happened for me. Suddenly I had the power to see in the dark, and a variety of other vision-based super powers. Suddenly, I could see everything, perfectly, clear as day – and I found my way back to the cabin where I felt safe again."

"For me," said Ray, "it took me back to the moment my parents split up. I wanted nothing more than to force them back together."

"And now your power?"

"I can move things by thought."

"Fascinating. It's different for everybody. It's not always the power you might expect. But it's always significant, something emotionally driven in the moment."

Luke paused for a moment. "…What power did my parents have?"

"James had super speed. Helen could read minds."

Dawn was missing something. "Why do you keep talking in the past tense? Did they lose their powers or something?"

Luke's head lowered.

"No," said Charlie, choking up. "They died."

Mastermind and crew drew nearer to the enormous pyramid.

"That thing is *HUGE!*" exclaimed Shadow.

Far bigger than any pyramid on Earth. Several times over. But they still had a ways to go.

"What's inssside there?" asked Venom.

"Your destinies."

Dawn felt like shit.

"Sorry. I didn't know," she said.

Ray put his arm around her.

Luke turned away. "And I killed them."

"That's not true, Luke," said his uncle, going over to comfort him.

"Yeah man," said Ray. "You can't blame yourself for what happened."

"It's all my fault," he said, refusing to let anyone touch him. "If it wasn't for me… and my *stupid* decision, they'd still be here today."

Dawn so wanted to ask what happened. But she was afraid to. Maybe, if she waited, someone would say something. Poor Luke. She barely knew the guy. He looked so hurt. So sad.

"Luke, it's *not* your fault," his uncle Charlie reassured him. "Really, I promise. Have you been blaming yourself this entire time?"

Luke faced away, silently.

"Luke…"

He crossed his arms. "Forget it."

"Luke, look at me," said his uncle.

"I killed them." Tears poured out. "It's all my fault," he whispered

"Please, it's okay," said Charlie. "No one blames you. Luke, listen to me, it *wasn't* your fault."

Luke turned around, red puffy eyes, tears streaming down his face. "You weren't there! You don't know!"

"Luke, think about it. Your parents were super heroes. You think *that* could actually kill them?"

He sniffed. He started to think about it. Maybe… not.

"Luke, the real reason why your father didn't want you getting caught up in all this… is because people like Mastermind are out there. And he—and your mom—wanted you as far away from him as possible."

"Mastermind?" remarked Dawn.

"Who?" asked Ray.

"My guess," said Charlie, "the same guy who kidnapped you earlier today and injected that chemical into you."

"What?" asked Luke, wiping off his tears.

"The janitor who stole the crystal. He got a power too, you understand. Mind control. And he didn't use it for the greater good."

"What happened?" asked Dawn.

"Well, like I said, at some point he must've found a pyramid, discovered this room, and touched the Altar of Destiny. Your mom, dad, and I were out doing our little super hero thing – anonymously and secretly helping others with our powers. Then one day we ran into him, and as soon as we realized he had powers too, we thought, 'Great, another ally! Let's invite him to join us!' So that's what we did."

"Mastermind used to be a hero?" Luke remarked.

"Not really," said Charlie. "Not for long. He seemed more interested in some twisted form of revenge. Getting back at people who looked at him the wrong way. Making himself superior to everyone else. He even started manipulating women to, well… he showed little sign he cared for others."

Ray looked to Dawn.

"We tried reasoning with him. Tried to stop him. But he said he was above the law, above morals and ethics, above everyone and everything. Called himself 'Mastermind', and warned us not to interfere with his plan."

"His plan?" asked Luke.

"Yeah. Like something out of one of your comic books. Said he alone had the vision for true world peace. Said he was going to recreate the world in his own image."

"Freaky," said Ray.

"He actually told us, rather brazenly, that he used to be my janitor at the university until he swiped my crystal, came across a pyramid, and not only gave himself powers – but used the medical lab to heal his body. And I'm not just talking his failing eyes and ears. He actually made himself about thirty years *younger*! We couldn't believe it. And then he says that he's truly a god now, immortal and super powered, and nothing we could say or do could stop him now."

"Oh my God," said Luke.

Ray was speechless.

"It gets worse," said Charlie. "He used his mind control against us and escaped. We tried tracking him down, but we were always two steps behind him. Then one day we got lucky. Or he got sloppy. We learned that he was up to something in Hawaii."

Luke looked up in anticipation. He listened very carefully to every word his uncle said.

"And that trip, Luke… it wasn't some last-minute vacation your parents decided to go on. James and Helen were trying to catch Mastermind. And it was him – not you – for why they're not here today."

"What?" Luke cried. What was he saying?

"Mastermind killed them, Luke. Not you."

Ray couldn't believe it. It hit him suddenly. "Oh my God!" he exclaimed. "You son of a *bitch*!"

This was all Charlie's fault. All of it.

He flashed his hand and threw Charlie half way across the room, slamming him into the mirror wall. "*You're* the reason why that madman is on the loose! *You're* the reason Dawn was mind controlled and kidnapped, and almost turned into a monster! *You're* the reason our waitress got mutated and the other guy is now dead!" Ray flicked his wrist and launched Charlie high into the air. "And all along Luke's been feeling guilty about his parents – and you *knew* the real reason!"

Charlie went slamming into the ground. Ray stepped closer. Charlie launched into the air again. Ray sent him flying to the other side of the room. Charlie smashed into that wall, and then painfully and forcefully dropped to the floor. "I can't believe you—"

Dawn gently held Ray's arm. She looked at him with her soft eyes. "Ray, please…"

He took a deep breath and started to calm down.

"I'm sorry. I just can't believe…"

Across the room, Charlie got up and dusted himself off. Nothing felt broken. Amazingly.

Ray used his power to pull Charlie – gently – back to them.

"Sorry," he said. "I just… so much has happened… and to find out this mind-controlling super villain is on the loose because you carelessly bragged about your damn little crystal…"

"I know," said Charlie, softly. "I know. You're right. That's my guilt. That's on my conscience. That's something I'll have to live with for the rest of my life. And it's no excuse, but I only hid all this from Luke because they made me promise to keep him completely out of this. They never wanted him to know. They honestly felt he'd be safest that way."

"Then why now?" Luke asked, holding back tears of mixed emotions.

"Because," said Uncle Charlie, "I found out Mastermind was in Los Angeles. You were in danger now whether you knew or not. Remember, Mastermind was our friend at first. For a short time. He knew James and Helen had a son. I feared the worst – that he wouldn't be satisfied with just them. You were involved now whether you liked it or not. I couldn't leave you defenseless. I had to show you the crystal. I had to tell you the truth."

No words can describe what Luke felt in that moment. It was a long, slow, silent moment. No one said a word. They all watched Luke.

And finally, eventually, he lifted his head.

"Okay," he whispered.

"I'm so sorry, Luke," said Charlie. "Can you find it in your heart to forgive me?"

Part of him wanted to go up and hug his beloved uncle. They shared so much history. So many good memories. They were family. Of course he loved him. Of course he forgave him.

On the other hand, this was all a little too much to take in at once. He just found out his parents had super powers and were secretly doing the super hero thing his whole life. And because of his uncle's carelessness, a powerful super villain was now on the loose – a super villain who had already gotten a little too close to home.

"It really wasn't my fault?" Luke finally asked.

Charlie shook his head. "Not at all. I'm sorry. I had no idea you'd been blaming yourself all this time. I thought you were just depressed, understandably so, after such a loss. I tried to be cheery and supportive. But maybe that's not what you needed…"

"That day changed me," he said. "I haven't felt the same since."

Charlie looked compassionately upon him. He didn't know how to say this. Or even if now was the right time. But here they were, inside the Temple of the Gods, in the presence of the Altar of Destiny. Luke deserved to know.

"Luke," he said, clearing his throat. "You need to know… if you use the Altar to get a power, it's going to take you back to an emotionally-significant moment in your life. There's a really high chance, if you do, it's going to take you back to that day."

Luke sighed deeply. "Wow." Here was his chance to have a super power. But it meant reliving the most painful and life-changing day of his life.

The day he lost both his parents.

The thought of having a super power was tempting. Very tempting. But he just didn't know if he had the emotional strength to go through that day again.

It was no easy decision.

But… maybe it really wasn't his fault. Maybe he'd get to see a different side of the story. The whole story. Maybe, as difficult and painful as it would be to go through this – maybe it was exactly what he needed. Not just for the power. But for his own closure and healing, too.

"Okay. I'll do it," he said.

"You're sure?" asked his uncle.

He checked within himself to be sure. He nodded again, gaining confidence with each nod. "Yeah. As ready as I'm going to be."

"Okay," said his uncle. "None of us can go in there with you. This is a journey ever man and woman must take alone. Remember, the same events will play over and over again – until you experience your breakthrough. Choose wisely. For your new power will come out of your greatest desire."

"Alright," said Luke, pretending to understand better than he probably did. "What do I have to do?"

Charlie motioned toward the carved stone pedestal. "Step closer, and when the orb appears, touch it – and enter. We'll be here waiting for when you get back."

Chapter 17
IT'S ABOUT TIME

Luke stood on top of his living room couch.

And immediately, he saw his younger self – not that much younger, only by about eight months, but younger just the same. His eight-month-younger self sat on the floor, eating a bowl of popcorn, staring up at a movie projected onto the wall.

It was a familiar scene.

Doc Brown, the wily-haired lovable scientist, hung from a giant clock tower. The time was 10:03. Less than a minute before that famous bolt of lightning would strike.

But a fallen tree branch had disconnected the high voltage cable wires. Marty and his time machine accelerated up the street. Lightning flashed above the clock tower. Doc had to act fast. He looped the cable around the minute hand and ziplined down to the ground. He quickly freed the branch.

Damn, he watched this movie a lot.

It's not like he couldn't quote the whole movie line by line, without missing a beat. Sure, it was a great movie. But… "I need to get a life," present-day Luke said to himself.

The movie continued. Eight-month-younger Luke was completely unaware of present-day Luke's presence.

Present-day Luke stepped down from the couch. Waved his hand in front of his younger self's face. No reaction.

"Alright," said present-day Luke. "Which day is this? When did the sphere send me back to?"

Younger Luke's cell phone rang. He checked the caller ID. It read: "Dad".

He picked it up. "Hey Dad," he said, only slightly lowering the volume on the movie. This was before he lost his remote, obviously. Maybe present-day Luke could use the power of the time-traveling sphere to help him find wherever he lost that remote.

"What? No way!" younger Luke exclaimed. "You're going to Maui?"

Right. Present-day Luke remembered. He knew *exactly* what day it was. It was the day his dad called to say they, meaning just his dad and mom, would be making a little weekend getaway trip to Hawaii.

"Can I come too? Pleeeeeeease?" younger Luke begged.

Luke originally wasn't going to go with them. His dad, on the phone, made some story about how he and his wife needed a romantic getaway. But Luke didn't care. It was Hawaii. He *so* wanted to go. Even if it was only for three days.

"I can get someone to cover my shift!" he exclaimed. "Please, please, please!"

Present-day Luke rolled his eyes. If only his eight-month-younger self knew that, in about eight months from now, he'd be using a magic crystal to travel to other *worlds*. Enter high-tech pyramids with holographic healing doctors and a glowing orb that could send a person back into their own past just by touching it!

Younger Luke had *no idea* his parents or uncle had super powers. Or that anyone in the real world did. He secretly wished there were real-life super heroes. And he really, really wanted to be one, too.

He was so close. He had no idea.

His dad finally agreed to let Luke tag along.

"This is going to be so great! Wait 'till I tell Ray!"

Where was Ray right now? School? Work? What was he doing eight months ago?

Present-day Luke started to get nervous. He just watched himself convince his dad to let them take him along. If Luke hadn't gone to Maui with them… they might still be alive today.

Suddenly the scene changed. They were no longer in Luke and Ray's apartment. They were aboard an airplane, flying over the Pacific Ocean. It was only about a five hour flight from Los Angeles to Maui. But Luke was pretty restless. He hadn't been to Hawaii since he was five years old, the last time they took a family trip there.

His mom got up to go to the bathroom. She returned a few minutes later. No conversation or significant events here, as far as present-day Luke could tell.

The scene changed again. Suddenly Luke found himself on Maui, somewhere off the beaten path. He cringed. He knew exactly where they were. This was the last time he saw his parents alive.

"Luke, wait up," said his dad.

They were all out hiking along the rocky-edge high cliff shores. A spectacular sight. They could see out into the clear blue ocean for miles and miles. Strong, warm winds blew in their faces and kept them cool under the hot tropical sun. Down below was the ocean, with over a hundred foot drop. The white crested waves crashed into the rocks below.

"Amazing to think this was all created by lava!" younger Luke said. "Did you know that the island of Maui was formed over five million years ago!"

His dad hiked up the uneven rocky path. "No, I didn't know that," he said.

"Luke, be careful," said his mom, seeing him step a little closer to the ledge. "You don't want to slip and fall."

Present-day Luke lowered his head.

"Spectacular view," said his dad, arriving next to Luke. Together, father and son, they looked out over the vast ocean. "I'm glad you came along," he said.

Younger Luke gently bumped his shoulder into his dad's side. "Me too."

His mom finally caught up. "Wow, that's beautiful!" she said, seeing the ocean far below and expanding out as far and wide as the eye could see. Sparkling, gently waving, constantly moving vast ocean. A rich deep blue color – very different than the somewhat polluted waters near Los Angeles.

His dad leaned over and whispered something into his mom's ear. She shook her head no.

"Well," said Luke's dad after taking a deep, relaxing breath, "let's get moving, shall we?"

"One more minute," said younger Luke.

Present-day Luke began to tremble silently.

"Alright," said his dad. "One more minute."

Present-day Luke shook his head. "No," he muttered. "Don't. Don't do it." He watched as his younger self stepped down to a rocky ledge a little closer to the edge. "Don't do it."

"I think I see a cave, I mean a lava tube, down there."

"Careful, Luke," urged his mom.

"Watch that ledge. Hey Luke, get back here."

"I'm good," said younger Luke. "Really, see. It's really solid." He stomped hard three times onto the rocky edge. On the third stomp, something broke loose, and suddenly a huge chunk of rock slipped forward and fell down.

Younger Luke lost his balance and fell down with it.

"Wh-whoaaaa!!!"

"LUKE!" his mom screamed, reaching after him.

She missed.

He dropped out of their sight instantly.

"LUKE!" shouted his dad.

His parents carefully crawled up to the edge, testing the stability of the ground with each inch closer. Got down on their bellies and laid flat to stretch out their weight. "Luke!" they both called again.

They feared the worst. Waves crashed into large jagged rocks far below.

"I'm okay!" said Luke, calling up. The sound of the ocean and his precarious position made it hard for him to hear them. He held on tightly to a small stoop on the side of the cliff. "Throw me a rope or something!"

Up top, his dad called back, "We don't have any rope!"

"Hold on!" pleaded his mother. Her worst nightmare was coming true. She felt so helpless, so powerless. What could she do? "Just hold on, Luke! We're coming!"

The wind hit against the cliff fiercely. Strong gusts coming off a long travel across the ocean. Luke held on to his little ledge very tightly. He didn't have much wiggle room, but for the moment, he appeared relatively safe.

"Hurry up!" he called back.

"Can you climb back up at all?" asked his dad.

Luke looked around. Maybe. But he didn't want to risk it. "No!" he said.

"Okay," said his dad to his mom, back at the top of the ledge. "You think you can reach him if I hold onto you?"

Present-day Luke couldn't bear to watch this. This was the moment. They died trying to save him.

"Stop it, please!" present-day Luke shouted out loud. "Can anybody hear me? I don't want to watch this!"

In a few seconds, still clinging to the cliff's side, younger Luke would see his mom fall over the edge – free fall right in front of his eyes, and plummet to her death in the rocky ocean below.

A second after that, his dad would slip and fall after her.

That day – and seeing their faces as they fell helplessly through the air to their watery graves – would haunt his dreams and riddle him with guilt for the rest of his life.

It was all his fault.

Present-day Luke was crying.

Through his blurry tears, he saw his mom crawl closer to the edge. His dad anchored himself and held tight onto her ankles. She inched closer. "I can see him!" she said.

Present-day Luke shook his head. "I'm so sorry, Mommy."

She reached out. "Almost there. Just a little bit more!" Her arms and hands stretching out as far as they could go.

Too bad her super power wasn't super stretching, like Mr. Fantastic. Or Plastic Man, DC Comics' hero with a similar power. What good was reading minds to her now? Or super speed for his dad? He wasn't fast enough to catch Luke before he fell. And… not strong enough to hold on…

Any second now. She'd fall.

Present-day Luke turned away. He couldn't watch. But in turning away, he faced behind them. And he saw an unfamiliar man.

"Lose something?" the mysterious man said to them.

"Mastermind!" shouted Luke's dad, after turning to see the owner of the voice. He still held onto his wife's ankles as she dangled over the ledge.

"Release your grip," said Mastermind, eyes locked.

It happened so fast.

Luke's dad couldn't resist the mind control. Without even thinking, before he could even realize what would happen, his hands let go.

Luke's mom fell over the edge.

She screamed. Younger Luke saw. She met her maker.

Luke's dad moved to the edge in a flash. He literally moved like a blur. Super speed. He reached out. But he was too late. He just wasn't fast enough.

He saw her just as her body hit the rocks below – and the ocean waves dragged her under. His mouth hung open. A silent scream that was felt throughout eternity. The loss of his beloved. Tears swelled in his eyes.

In a flash, he was back on his feet and faced Mastermind – but Mastermind was ready. The *instant* Luke's dad stood still, and it was only for a split second, but it was just long enough – Mastermind pushed Luke's dad hard to the edge. Luke's dad lost his balance. Mastermind gave a second, final push – knocking him over too.

Mastermind watched the man fall. He waved. "Bye-bye."

Luke's dad hit the rocky death below too, and joined his wife in the afterlife.

Mastermind brushed off his hands and walked away. "Good riddens to you both."

Luke – that is, present-day Luke – saw the whole thing! He couldn't believe it – as evidenced by his speechlessness and dropped jaw.

"Oh my God!" present-day Luke exclaimed. He leaped after Mastermind, reached to grab and tackle him, but passed and stumbled right through him.

Luke swung and punched at Mastermind nevertheless. Each pass went straight through him. Mastermind felt nothing, saw nothing, was aware of nothing.

It was as if present-day Luke wasn't really there. Just an unseen, unfelt, unheard observer.

"DAMN YOU!!!" shouted Luke. "DAMN YOU STRAIGHT TO HELL!" he shouted some more, through a flood of tears.

He couldn't believe it!

Mastermind actually killed both his parents!

It wasn't Luke's fault after all.

Present-day Luke stopped and watched as Mastermind walked away. "Oh my

God," he said, wiping his face. "You are going to pay for this."

Several minutes later, after younger Luke regained some temporary composure, he started to carefully and very slowly climb back up that cliff. It wasn't easy. It took him nearly twenty minutes. His arm and leg muscles were spent after it. But no pain could compare to watching both his parents fall over a cliff, in an attempt to rescue him.

Young Luke walked several miles back to where he finally found cell reception again. He called for help. But it was too late.

Present-day Luke shook his head. "Wow."

And then the scene reset.

He found himself standing on his couch again. His eight-month-younger self sat on the floor, eating popcorn, watching *Back to the Future* for the giga-zillionth time.

His cell phone rang. It was his dad.

Present-day Luke sighed. "Here we go again."

The whole story played out again, exactly as before. Luke could do nothing to stop it or change it.

He watched Mastermind kill his parents and walk away again.

And the story reset to the beginning again.

Luke sighed. This might take a while.

What did his uncle say? He had to dig deep. Find an emotion, a need, a strong desire that would somehow manifest into a super power. How, exactly, was he supposed to do that?

Meanwhile, back inside the mirror-walled, high-vaulted temple chamber, Dawn, Ray, and Uncle Charlie stood around waiting in awkward silence.

"So," said Dawn. "You're Luke's uncle?"

"That's right."

"He and Luke are pretty close," explained Ray. "Much closer than I am to any of my aunts or uncles."

"I come from a fairly large family," Dawn said. "My mom's been pressuring me to meet and marry a nice Jewish boy. Start a family of my own. I think she just wants grandkids."

Ray laughed nervously.

"But I'm not looking for any of that. At least not right now. I want a career. I'm going to be an A-list actress someday. Have an agent at William-Morris or CAA or something. Star in all the big blockbusters. And some indies. Gotta remember your roots. Even when I'm a big star, I wanna do some no or low budget films, to give back and inspire the next generation of actors, ya know?"

"Cool," said Ray.

"How do you figure your powers fit into all that?" Uncle Charlie asked.

"What do you mean?" asked Dawn.

"Well, you both have powers now, right?"

They both nodded.

"That changes things."

Dawn suddenly lit up. "That's right! I can be *anything* now! They want a blonde? No problem? Prefer a brunette or redhead? I can do that too! Too tall? Too short? No problem, I got this! Oh yeah, I totally got this!"

Ray smiled. "I suppose shape-shifting is a great talent for an actress."

"What about you?" Charlie asked Ray.

"Me? I dunno. I'm not even sure what I want to do yet. Have my own business, sure, but doing what? Beats me. Not that I see how, whatchamacallit…"

"Telekinesis," said Charlie.

"Yeah, that one. Not sure how that really makes a difference. Unless I became a magician and did stage shows." He laughed. "Not in a million years."

"What? Magicians are cool!" remarked Dawn.

"I'm more of a behind-the-scenes kind of guy. I can run the show, market it, make it profitable. But be on stage… in front of all those people… I don't know how you do it."

"I love it!" exclaimed Dawn.

"Well, I can tell ya enhanced eyesight made finding archeological dig sites a little easier for me," said Uncle Charlie. "After a while, people started calling me Lucky Charlie. They had no clue I could—"

Just then, the door to their chamber rolled open.

They all turned and looked.

Uh-oh. It was Doctor Troyd, Shadow and the other mutants, and last but not least – the man himself, Mastermind.

Doctor Troyd tugged on Mastermind's sleeve and pointed at Ray, Dawn, and Charlie. As if Mastermind didn't see them standing there in the middle of the room anyway.

"Yes," said Mastermind, shrugging off the scientist. "I see them." He paused, staring at Charlie. He chuckled. "Could that be my dear old friend, the infamous 'look what I can see' Charlie?" And he recognized the other two, too. "And you," he said a little less pleasantly, "what the hell are you two doing here?"

Definitely uh-oh.

"Mastermind! How did— Where did—?" Charlie couldn't even finish his sentence. There was no explaining Mastermind being here. There was only one crystal. And Luke had it. The only way to access this planet and this pyramid was with a crystal. There was no way he could be here!

And yet here he was.

"You mean this?" Mastermind cockily said, holding up his own pink glowing crystal.

"There's two of them?" Charlie remarked in disbelief.

"Give up, Chuck. You can't stop me now."

Charlie hardly considered himself a super hero by any means, but he wasn't about to let a madman like Mastermind continue on running loose in the world.

Dawn and Ray hid behind Charlie.

Mastermind laughed. "This is too precious. I'll turn all three of you into my mutant slaves." He turned to his mutants. "Get them!"

Shadow leaped into the air with cat-like agility. Slimer slid across the floor straight at them. Arachnus crawled up the wall, higher and higher. Rhino-Man charged forward, big pointed horn ready to deal some massive pain. Kraken chaotically and wildly flapped his tentacle arms all around, racing toward them. Venom exposed her fangs, hissed, and moved in to strike.

Doctor Troyd hid behind Mastermind.

"Ray…" said Charlie. "Now would be a good time."

Right. This was it. Now or never. Time to put this new power to the test. He took one step forward, placed both hands forward, and suddenly all the mutants were blasted back by some invisible force.

Ray smiled. That felt good.

"Yeah!" cheered Dawn.

Mastermind looked genuinely surprised. "Interesting."

The mutants rose to their feet, a little dazed and confused, but quickly returned to action. They charged in to surround Ray, Dawn, and Charlie.

"Here comes round two!" shouted Charlie.

"I got this," said Dawn.

She stepped back and focused hard. She was still new at this. She needed an emotion. Needed to *feel* what she was to become. And she needed to become something big, strong, and intimidating. Like a 600-pound gorilla.

Her arms immediately grew hairy. The black furry hair rapidly spread across the rest of her body, as her muscles and size grew. It tore through her clothes. Her face and jaw transformed into the terrifying form of a ferocious gorilla. She bared her dominating teeth. Pounded and beat on her chest, giving out a loud gorilla-roar.

It stopped the other mutants in the tracks.

She charged after them. Picked up Shadow and tossed her half way across the room, screaming like a cat would in such a circumstance. Then Dawn sucker punched Venom, showing no fear against the snake-woman's venomous fangs.

Rhino-Man pounded Dawn from the side, which only made the massive gorilla girl more angry. In an instant, they were in a hand-to-hand brawl, raw muscle power against raw muscle power, struggling for dominance over the other.

Arachnus, that sneaky spider-guy, dropped down from above, about to trap and bite Dawn. But Ray was alert. And he reflexively blasted the mutant spider across the room, where it crashed into the mirrored wall and fell dizzy to the floor.

Doctor Troyd quietly stepped back and tip-toed away. Seeing Arachnus hit the ground like that was his cue to leave. The scientist ducked out the door.

Mastermind stood there, arms crossed, watching everything. This was his mutants' first true test. And how very, very interesting and intriguing. It seemed good old Charlie had given these two would-be slave mutants some powers of their own. Perhaps Charlie was recruiting new heroes to try – key word "try" – to stop him.

They were too late. Soon the world would belong to Mastermind. And he would exact his revenge.

Dawn finally overpowered and knocked Rhino-Man to the side and down onto the floor. She pounded and beat him a few more times.

Ray telekinetically pushed Shadow back whenever the cat-girl leaped with extended claws toward the fray. Then he quickly turned and pushed Venom against the wall, where she could do no harm. Arachnus crawled after Ray, spitting a sticky web in his direction.

Dawn raised her gorilla fist into the air, about to pound on Rhino-Man one more time, but a long slimy tentacle wrapped around her arm and pulled it back. More tentacles wrapped and twisted around her arms and legs, completely disabling her. Kraken snickered, which sounded more like a gargling sound.

Ray pushed back Arachnus, but the sticky web covered him. Totally gross. And while he was distracted by that, for only a second, Slimer flung a massive wad of slimy goo out of her hands, covering Ray in the mucus.

Dawn couldn't break free. So she shape-shifted her way out of Kraken's tentacle hold. Her arms and legs shrank and disappeared into her body. Her body became long and narrow – and green and scaly. She quickly shrank into a long boa constrictor snake. She traveled up his tentacles, slipping through his wobbling grasp as he tried to hold her – and wrapped herself around *his* body, tightening with each turn.

Arachnus and Slimer worked together to cover and trap Ray in a thick layer of slime and web. He struggled to break free – but it was no use. It was too thick, too strong, too heavy. He couldn't move!

Venom approached the entangled man, lethal fangs exposed, thirsting for blood. A single bite would end any further interference from him. And then she'd bite Dawn next. Venom wasn't too pleased the shape-shifter stole her animal type.

Rhino-Man suddenly grabbed the boa constrictor and squeezed her tight. He was crushing Dawn! She loosened her grip around Kraken.

Shadow brushed herself off, barely dazed from all the being tossed around. Noticing Ray in caught in a slimy web and Dawn squirming for life in Rhino-Man's grip, Shadow leaped toward Charlie with her dangerous claws extended.

Luke had re-lived this scene maybe a dozen times already. Maybe more. But he wasn't counting.

He was thinking.

Thinking about how badly he wanted revenge on Mastermind. No, revenge was the wrong word. Vengeance. He would avenge his parents' deaths. And yeah, he was human, there was a little revenge in there too.

Mastermind's heartless act cost more than just their lives. It wasn't just Luke's parents that this evil, evil man had killed. It was Luke's life too. The future Luke would never have. The memories, the Christmases, the birthdays, the family time they'd never enjoy together again.

A part of Luke died that day. Not just his future. Not just his lost time with his mom and dad. Something inside him died too. Seeing his parents fall. Thinking it was all his fault. Not knowing what really happened.

Even now, knowing the truth, it still didn't make anything better. He still hurt. He still mourned their loss. He still regretted begging his dad to take him with them to Maui. He still regretted being too curious and stepping too close to that ledge. He still regretted not having the courage to try to climb up on his own first, and instead made them try to reach down to him.

In a way, it still was his fault.

Sure, Mastermind pushed them over the edge. But they were only on that edge because Luke drew them there.

Maybe he couldn't forgive himself after all.

Watching this story play over and over again didn't help. It didn't make anything better. It didn't give him the closure he needed. It didn't make him understand and forgive himself. It was still his fault. He was still to blame.

Oh, God, how he *wished* he could go back in time and stop it all from happening…

There were so many opportunities to change history.

He could've stayed home. Not begged his dad to go with them.

Suddenly, everything around Luke shifted to a red hue and blurred into a stream of light. The next instant, he was back in his apartment, watching his younger self eat popcorn.

But wait. It wasn't time for the story to reset yet. Just a second ago, he was watching his younger self look out over the ocean with his dad. A beautiful heart-to-heart moment.

Part of the story was skipped. His younger self hadn't slipped yet. His parents didn't try to rescue him yet. Mastermind hadn't sent them over the edge yet. Luke hadn't climbed back up yet.

Why did they skip all that? Why was he here now, back at the *beginning* of the series of events?

Younger Luke's cell phone rang. It was his dad.

He picked it up. "Hey Dad," his younger self said. "What? No way! You're going to Maui?"

Present-day Luke sighed. If he could go back in time, this would be an opportunity for change. He simply wouldn't ask to go.

"Alright," said younger Luke. "Bring me back a souvenir. Have fun. See you when you get back." He then said "love you" and hung up.

What? That didn't happen before.

The scene changed, returning to the airplane flying over the Pacific. Now, Luke's dad and mom sat alone. Younger Luke was not present. Weird. History had changed.

The scene changed again, to an abandoned warehouse somewhere on the island. It was pitch black out. Luke could see all the stars above. No lights or signs of civilization anywhere around. Just this single old abandoned building in the middle of a large sugar cane field.

This was different. Why was he seeing this now?

Just then, a super speed blur arrived on the scene. His dad had appeared out of nowhere, carrying his mom. They must have been running like that from some considerable distance away. Nothing else was around.

"You sure he said the chemicals were being stored here?" Luke's dad asked his mom.

"He said the shipment from Singapore was stashed here, waiting for Mastermind to pick it up."

Chemicals? Shipment? What were they talking about? Was Mastermind importing some illegal chemical into the United States? For what purpose?

"Still no idea who the anonymous tip came from?" he asked.

She shrugged. "You saw the same e-mail I did."

They entered the abandoned warehouse. Three seconds later, an explosion came from inside.

"What?" Luke exclaimed. "No!"

Was it booby-trapped? Were the chemicals too volatile? What happened?

"Mom? Dad?"

Luke waited. He watched helplessly. They never came out.

"No…" He began crying again.

This can't be right! They died anyway, even if Luke didn't come along? No! There had to be another way! Maybe Luke still needed to come along, just not stand too close to that ledge. Yeah. That was it. If they just waited a minute longer, but Luke didn't fall down, they'd all be on sturdy ground and not distracted when Mastermind showed up.

That was where history needed to be changed.

Suddenly everything around Luke shifted to a bluish color and streamed into a blur of light. The next instant, he found himself observing the three of them – younger Luke, his dad, and his mom – standing near, but not at, the ledge, gazing out over the vast and beautiful ocean.

"Well," said Luke's dad after taking a deep, relaxing breath, "let's get moving, shall we?"

"One more minute," younger Luke said.

"Alright," smiled his dad. "One more minute."

Why was he jumping around out of order? Up until now, the entire scenario repeated over and over again, flawlessly and precisely, in chronological order. But now… Luke was zipping around to wherever, and whenever, he felt he needed to change something.

Had history changed here now?

Young Luke did *not* step too close to the ledge.

"Hey look," pointed younger Luke. "I think I see a cave or a lava tube or something."

"Cool," said his dead.

Present-day Luke watched and waited. Was something going to happen?

"Wanna see what's up ahead?" asked his mom.

They continued on their hike.

No one died.

The scene changed again. They were back at the abandoned warehouse in the middle of the sugar cane field. His dad super-sped onto the scene, carrying Luke's mom again. Where was younger Luke? He wasn't with them.

"You sure he said the chemicals were being stored here?" asked Luke's dad.

No! No! No! It was happening again!

Where was Luke now?

Probably back asleep at the hotel. Completely ignorant of everything. He'd wake up and his parents would be missing. Then what?

No, no, no! It's not fair!

Okay, there had to be another way to stop this. What else could he change? Maybe he could tell his parents not to go at all.

Everything shifted to a red hue and blurred into a stream of light. Present-day Luke suddenly found himself back at the beginning, watching his eight-month-younger self talk on the phone to his dad.

"I dunno, dad," said younger Luke. "I have a really bad feeling. Don't go."

His dad said they needed to.

"Please," said younger Luke. "What if something bad happens to you guys?"

His dad reassured him that nothing bad would happen.

They went – and died – anyway.

Dammit!

Could *nothing* be changed?

Nothing meaningful, anyway. Sure, the story changed a little bit each time. But the outcome was always the same.

Okay. No holding back. There was definitely one way to prevent this tragedy.

The scene shifted to red and blurred into a stream of light. Suddenly Luke was back in the same scene, at his apartment, watching his younger self answer the phone.

"Hey Dad." This was it. Would this work? "What? No way! You're going to Maui?"

Come on, come on. Work.

"Actually, Dad," said younger Luke, "there's something I need to tell you. I know you and mom have super powers, and I know because I do too. I can time travel. And I know about Mastermind. If you go to Maui, no matter what we do to change history, you both end up dead. Please, dad, I need you to believe me."

It worked.

His parents didn't go.

The scene changed to the airplane. Their seats were empty. The scene then changed to show the cliff. No one stood there. And then the abandoned warehouse. No explosion.

Luke had finally done it.

He changed history!

Wow. He couldn't help but smile. He felt great. And wait – did his younger self say he had the *power* to time travel? As in, that was his super power now? Was that it?

Was this the emotional push Luke needed to manifest a power and escape this infinite loop?

The answer was yes.

Suddenly he found himself spit out of the sphere – and into the middle of a battle. He crashed into Venom, right before she was about to bite Ray, who was still trapped in the slime-covered web.

"Luke, perfect timing!" said Ray.

Luke sat on top of Venom several feet away. He looked around. He was really confused. Who were all these mutants? And not cool mutants, like the X-Men. Ugly, part-animal, comic book reject type mutants.

Venom wiggled out from underneath him.

"Luke, look out!" shouted Charlie.

She snapped at him. Her fangs barely missed his neck.

"Guess what!" said Luke to his uncle. "I can time travel!"

Shadow pounced on Charlie, knocking him to the floor. Crawling on top of him, she went to slash his face. He grabbed her arms and did all he could to keep those claws away from him.

"That's great, Luke," said his uncle, a little distracted at the moment.

"Help Dawn!" Ray shouted.

Luke looked around. "Where?"

"She's the snake! The snake!"

Luke pointed curiously at Venom.

"No, not *her!*" Ray exclaimed. "That one!" He motioned towards the boa constrictor currently being squeezed into oblivion. Oh. Sure. Obviously *that* snake needed help. Well, duh.

And… he should do exactly what now? Rhino-Man was massive. Kraken was not someone Luke wanted to mess with either. But Luke had a super power now.

Yeah. Time to use *that*.

He had to think fast. Dawn, still mostly a boa constrictor, started shape-shifting randomly and uncontrollably. Either she was dying or… yeah, she was probably dying.

Time to save the day!

Luke needed to go back in time. Before this entourage of monster movie rejects showed up. Luke could warn the others the mutants were coming – and they could all escape before it was too late!

Suddenly, everything around him turned red and blurred into a stream of light. The next instant, he found himself standing in the exact same spot, but none of the mutants were around.

"So," said Dawn. "You're Luke's uncle?"

Ray happened to be facing in Luke's direction. "Luke?" he remarked. "You're back already?"

"Yes!" he said excitedly. "I've come back… from the future! It's my new power. Cool, right? Anyway, Mastermind and a bunch of monster baddies are about to show up and we don't exactly win the fight."

"What?" asked Charlie. "Mastermind, here? That's impossible!"

"I'm telling you what I saw."

"But he'd need a crystal to—"

"Look, trust me. Ray gets covered in slime and wrapped up in a giant web. Dawn turns into a snake and gets squeezed to death by Rhino Dude. I almost get bit by this crazy snake lady! And you, uncle, there's this cat girl clawing at you!"

"Sounds like our waitress," said Ray. "You mean he turned more people into… into mutants?"

Dawn looked to Ray. This was not good news.

"I guess," said Luke.

"This is not good," said Charlie. "Mastermind often talked about building an army of monsters. Said he wanted to turn the whole world into 'the monsters they truly were'."

"What'd he mean by that?" asked Luke.

Charlie sighed. "If you really did just come from the future, then it means you got your power and survived the sphere. Not everyone does."

"What? What do you mean? I could've died in there?"

"No, no, no. Not that I know of, anyway," said Charlie. "What I mean is, sometimes, people change. And I don't just mean by getting their powers."

"Then what?" asked Dawn.

"Look, all I know is, some girl really screwed over Mastermind a long time ago. And she didn't just break his heart – she and a bunch of peers went out of their way to publicly humiliate him. He wouldn't tell us the details. But I can say, after he came out of the sphere, he was a different man. Colder, harder, angrier. He truly despised people – and had an exceptional hatred toward women. I don't know what happened in there… but whatever it was, it made things worse. Much worse."

"That's terrible," said Dawn.

"I know. He wasn't exactly an upstanding guy to begin with, either. And now," said Charlie, "it seems he's found a way to carry out his plan."

"Well," said Luke, checking his watch, "if we don't hurry—"

Just then the chamber door rolled open.

The villains entered.

Doctor Troyd tugged on Mastermind's sleeve, pointing at Ray, Dawn, Charlie, and Luke

"Yes," said Mastermind, shrugging off the annoying scientist. "I see them." He spotted Charlie, smiled, and chuckled. "Could that be—"

Luke interrupted, "Dammit! Now we took too long!"

"Mastermind!" shouted Charlie.

The sinister villain recognized Dawn and Ray. "What are you two doing here?" He turned to Luke. "You seem familiar too. Where do I know you from?"

"Don't look in his eyes!" Dawn quickly shouted.

He smirked deviously. "Smart girl."

"Okay Luke," said Charlie. "Now's a good time for your plan."

"What plan?" Luke remarked.

"The plan—" Charlie interrupted himself. "Never mind. Just get us out of here!"

"Right!" said Luke, reaching into his pocket for the crystal.

Mastermind laughed. "Give up, Chuck. You can't stop me."

Luke drew a large circle on the ground.

"Oh, this is too precious," laughed Mastermind. "I'll turn all four of you into my mutant slaves." He turned to his mutants. "Get them! Before they escape!"

Luke drew the first symbol that came to mind.

A triangle!

The portal instantly opened. It revealed the open windy desert. Still hot and sunny. "Everybody in!" Luke waved.

"Don't have to tell me twice!" said Dawn, jumping into the hole.

"Right behind ya!" said Ray, after using a quick blast of telekinesis to push back the mutants, to buy them a little more time.

"After you, Luke," said Charlie.

"No, you first," said Luke.

"We don't have time to argue!" Charlie pushed Luke in. And the old man immediately jumped after.

On the other side of the portal, they suddenly found themselves parallel above the ground. A second later, gravity took over and they all fell on their backs.

As soon as Charlie was through, Luke scurried up to the stone wall where the portal remained open. He quickly X-ed it out just as Venom and Shadow came into view.

The portal vanished. They were safe.

"That was fun," said Ray, dusting off the sand.

"Um, Luke," said Charlie, "you do realize we're still on the same planet.

Mastermind and his mutants are just over there in that pyramid."

"I know," defended Luke. "I meant to do that."

Dawn and Ray weren't so sure.

"Anyway," said Luke, "where should we go now? Back to Earth?" He started drawing a new portal on the blank stone wall.

"Actually," said Charlie. "I have a better idea. Remember that last symbol I taught you, the one that goes into the future?"

"Yeah," said Luke. Suddenly his face lit up. "Yeah!"

Chapter 18
THE OTHER CRYSTAL

"Okay," said Uncle Charlie. "Draw the symbol."

Luke drew two parallel vertical lines. Then he made a half circle at the top of the right line, and drew another half circle at the top of the left line. Just like his uncle taught him. It worked.

The portal suddenly opened.

"Wow!" said Dawn, looking through. "It's so beautiful!"

Indeed it was. Clear blue skies. Lush green trees. A beautiful park landscape. Spectacular water fountains. Exotic birds chirping and singing. An exotic array of stunning multi-colored flowers. Endless green grassy fields littered with vibrant trees.

"Come on, let's go," said Charlie with some urgency.

They stepped through. And entered—

"The future," Luke whispered in awe.

Abundant nature surrounded them. Peaceful. Beautiful. Alive. Thriving. In a word: amazing.

And in the distance, toward the horizon, they saw a magnificent white city that towered so high, some of the buildings actually touched the clouds. These buildings appeared to be made out of a pure white material. Some buildings were layered with gardens and waterfalls, trickling down from the clouds above. Others structures magnificently spiraled upwards toward the sky. Domes, towers, architectural wonders, arching bridges, flowing gardens, floating platforms between the interconnected structures. A city of the future.

Luke smiled when he saw, all the way in the distance, what must be flying cars. Finally, after all these years, they finally did it. Maybe not as early as 2015, like in *Back to the Future*, but just knowing that someday people would be cruising around in their own flying vehicles made Luke very happy.

What other marvels of technology did the future hold? Teleporters? Holographic simulation rooms, like the "holodeck" on *Star Trek*? The cure for the common cold? Maybe even contact with an intelligent alien race?

"Don't forget to close the portal," reminded Uncle Charlie.

Luke snapped out of it and closed the portal. "You think we're safe here?" he asked his uncle.

His uncle hesitated to answer. "We will be."

Ray quickly grew concerned. "Can Mastermind follow us here?"

"I don't know," said Charlie. "He knows the symbol. If he's got a working crystal too…"

Dawn leaned over to smell some of the multi-colored flowers. "It's so beautiful here," she said. Took a deep breath. "And the air is so clean. Not like in LA."

Not like LA at all. Ray watched the breeze gently rustle through the leaves of the trees. The trees almost looked familiar. Almost. But different, somehow.

Just then, someone appeared. A short man, a little over five feet tall, wearing a white robe with silver and blue lining. "Welcome!" he cheerfully greeted them. "Welcome to Eden. I'm Ethos, Visitor Liaison. What brings you here today?"

He seem very friendly.

"Um, where did he come from?" asked Dawn.

Ray shrugged.

The man just "appeared" in front of them. Out of thin air. Luke smiled. Teleportation technology? Check.

Uncle Charlie said, "Uh, yes, we're here to see Simeon. He's a historian. Tell him it's Chuck."

"Certainly," said the friendly man called Ethos.

The friendly man stared blankly into the distance for a second.

Dawn looked at Ray, who in turn looked to Luke. Luke shrugged. What was going on?

"Match found," said Ethos. "Connecting."

Dawn whispered, "Is he some kind of robot?"

Luke shrugged again.

"Hey Simeon!" Ethos suddenly said aloud. The others looked around for another person to mysteriously appear. But no one did. Ethos continued talking. "A visitor named 'Chuck' just came in through the Ningishzida Gateway. He'd like to see you."

Who was he talking to? No one was around.

Luke leaned closer. He didn't see any Bluetooth piece or cell phone type device anywhere. It looked like he was just talking out into the air.

"Thank you," said Ethos. Then the short man returned his focus to Uncle Charlie. "He'll be with you momentarily. Is there anything else I can do for you?"

"No, thank you," said Charlie.

"Very well. We'll continue to monitor you during your stay. Should you need my assistance, just call for me." He bowed respectfully and then – instantly – disappeared.

"Whoa!" exclaimed Dawn.

Luke shook his head. "Incredible."

Ray asked, "What was that all about? Who was he talking to?"

And just as Charlie opened his mouth to answer, the man they came to see suddenly appeared before them. He was a middle-age man, good-looking, dark hair. He wore a white and blue form-fitting one-piece suit.

"Chuck?" said the newly arrived man. He seemed happily surprised. "Good to see you again! It's been a while!" They embraced with a warm hug and several pats on the back.

"Simeon," said Uncle Charlie, "this is my nephew Luke, and his friends Ray and Dawn."

"Hello, hello, hello," he said to each of them, gently nodding each time. Then he asked, "So what brings you here?"

Charlie looked back at the giant marble stone wall behind them – the place where their portal had appeared. It was blank now, except for some engraved writings along the edges – similar symbols and writings to the ones they saw inside the Temple of the Gods chamber at the center of the massive pyramid.

"Do you still have your Astaria crystal?"

Simeon stared off blankly for a second. "Yes, it's still registered in inventory. Why?"

"I think someone else has one too."

"Wait, Astaria?" asked Luke. He reached into his pocket and pulled out his glowing pink crystal. "Is that what this is called?"

Charlie nodded.

"My research has been pointing to the existence of more crystals," Simeon said. "Where was the other one found?"

"I'm not sure. I thought he might've stolen it from you."

"Doubtful. But we can check." Simeon glanced at the four of them. "Permission to port you all?"

"Granted," said Charlie.

"Wait, what'd he just ask—?" said Dawn.

Instantly, they found themselves inside a large room. The garden landscape around them had vanished in the blink of an eye. Now they were inside some kind of museum – tall pillars, glass-encased exhibits, enormous statues of strange creatures and heroically-posed figures, and wall-to-wall video screens providing education, information, and virtual tours all around them. Some exhibits looked like interactive holograms. But a lot of the artifacts, tablets, bones, and other remains here appeared authentic.

Simeon led them toward a particular display against one of the walls. Along the way, the others looked at the various artifacts and items in the museum. Luke stopped to stare at something strange. It was a semi-metallic full-body suit of some kind, like something Iron Man might wear, or Master Chief from the *Halo* video game series. A really advanced space suit – or some kind of high battle suit. He wasn't sure.

"This way," said Simeon, making sure Luke didn't fall behind. They walked up to a display case along the wall. And there they saw a dark pink crystal, similar to the one Luke had. But not exactly the same. It was dark – and it wasn't glowing.

Beside it rested a stone tablet with ancient writings. Above it, in the video screen that ran along the wall, text and pictures explained the history and importance of the items in this display. Detecting their proximity, the educational video started.

"Legends tell of a sacred crystal—"

Simeon interrupted it. "Pause guide," he quickly said to the screen. It immediately stopped. "See," he said, pointing at the crystal in the display. "Still here."

Charlie leaned in closer. "And no one's used it?"

Simeon laughed. "That thing hasn't worked for nearly four thousand years. Yours is the only one that still has any power in it, as far as I know."

"Wait, hold on," said Luke. He looked at the glowing pink crystal in his hand. "You mean to tell me this thing runs on batteries or something?"

Charlie shook his head. Simeon said, "If it were that simple, we would've found a way to recharge or replace it." He sighed. "No, whatever its power source may be, we can't find it."

Luke stared at the crystal. What exactly was this thing?

Charlie sighed. He was clearly troubled. "I think Mastermind somehow found another one."

"Who?" asked Simeon.

"Long story."

"Oh, he definitely does," said Luke. "He showed it to me. I mean, on the original timeline. Before I went back in time to save you."

"Yeah, about that," said Dawn. "I'm confused about something."

"What?" asked Luke.

"You went into the sphere, got your power, and then went back several minutes in time."

"Right."

"And then we escaped… before you—the other you, the original you—came back out of the sphere."

Luke gasped. "You're right. The other me is still inside that sphere!"

"That's what I'm confused about. Is he?" asked Dawn. "Does that mean there's now two of you?"

Luke quickly thought it over. "Oh my gosh, you're so right. Normally, I should've returned to the moment I left, without affecting my original timeline. But now that we've changed history…"

"Wait, wait, wait," said Ray. "You mean to tell me, that *right now*, there's a second you … and he's about to exit the sphere with Mastermind and all his mutants there?"

"If he hasn't already," said Luke, suddenly horrified.

And that's exactly what happened.

Back on the desert planet, in the center of the massive high-tech pyramid, in the room known as the Temple of the Gods – Mastermind and his band of mutants stood around the center pedestal.

"Why won't this damn thing activate!" exclaimed Mastermind, frustrated. "Unless…"

Just then, Luke spit out of the sphere, flying several feet across the room. He crashed into Shadow, who made a shrieking cat noise when he did. Her fur raised and she hissed at him.

On the ground, confused, Luke looked up and saw himself surrounded by a bunch of humanoid monsters. And his uncle, Ray, and Dawn were nowhere to be seen.

He immediately feared the worst.

"Grab him!" shouted Mastermind. He was a little confused by the whole situation, though. Only moments ago, he saw this exact same kid escape through a portal with the others. What was he doing here now? Thrown out of the sphere.

The sphere. Where people get their powers. Two Lukes? Could it be? It didn't make any sense. Unless the boy's super power was self-duplication – no, that couldn't be it. Only one of him would've been ejected from the sphere. He'd only be able to duplicate himself outside the sphere. It couldn't be any illusion or other trick, either, for the same reason.

Mastermind's eyes suddenly lit up. He cracked the most sinister grin.

"Let me go! Let me go!" squirmed Luke, held by several of the mutants.

Mastermind chuckled deviously. He walked over to Luke. "Look into my eyes."

"Should we go back for him?" Dawn asked.

"You saw those guys!" said Ray. "You really think we could take them?"

Luke shook his head. "Obviously not. When I left the sphere, you guys were goners. The only way to save you was to go back in time."

"That's it!" exclaimed Dawn.

"What?"

"Go back in time. Even farther back. Warn us before you even go into the sphere. We can be ready for them. Or lock the door, or something!"

Uncle Charlie seemed uneasy. "I dunno, Luke. Think this one through carefully. Using time travel already created one big problem."

"He's right," said Luke. "We gotta be smart about this. Okay, let me think. If I went back in time before I even went into the sphere, that still wouldn't stop Mastermind from coming. It's not like I could've gotten into the sphere any earlier, either, giving us enough time to leave before Mastermind shows up.

If I go even farther back, I could maybe prevent us from falling down into that pit. But you guys," he said towards Ray and Dawn, "would be coming later anyway."

He thought about. "I suppose, technically, I could go even farther back… warn you about Mastermind before you went on your date, Ray… you guys could avoid getting kidnapped in the first place."

Of course, that also meant Dawn would never get her super power. And who knew how else that might change history. If their date continued uninterrupted, they might've stayed out later, and by the time Ray got back home, the portal might've been closed in their living room. Which meant Ray wouldn't wander into the pyramid and get his super power either.

Technically, Luke could go *way* back in time and warn his uncle about Mastermind long before anything happened – warn him not to talk about the crystal around the janitor. Which would mean Luke's parents would still be alive to this day too.

"I know what to do," he said.

"What's the plan, Luke?" asked Uncle Charlie.

"I'm going to save Mom and Dad."

"What?" exclaimed Ray. "You can do that?"

"Whoa, wait Luke," said his uncle, very concerned. "Look, I want them back just as much as you. But you do realize, if you do that – none of this will happen. I see where you're going. Prevent Mastermind from overhearing anything. Prevent *my* mistake. But you realize… if you do that… you won't have this power anymore. None of you will."

"Major paradox," said Ray.

"Does that mean," asked Dawn, "if he no longer has this power, then he won't be able to go back in time and stop it, and since he didn't go back to stop it, everything happened as normal like the first time, and then he gets the power to time travel again, and goes back to... Ahhh!!!" She laughed, holding her head. "Headache."

"The grandfather paradox," said Luke. "I see what you mean. But... I dunno. Time travel was just a theory until now. Who knows how it actually works!"

"Luke, just be careful," said Charlie, gently laying his hand on Luke's shoulder. "Tampering with your own timeline..."

"...can be very dangerous, I know," said Luke.

They all looked at him. If he was successful – and didn't cause the universe to explode or something – they might all suddenly find themselves back at home, with no memory of *any* of this, living normal lives – completely unaware of anything ever being any different.

No Mastermind. No mutants. No crystals. No powers.

Just ordinary lives.

But safe lives. Safe from powerful evil villains like Mastermind.

Charlie saw the look of determination in Luke's eyes. The old man nodded with some hesitation. "Good luck, Luke. Be careful." He cleared his throat. "I was working at the university at the time. I was giving a class on ancient Sumerian civilization. Meet me after class, and show me your crystal. Tell me everything. I'll believe you. You've always been honest with me your whole life. And when I see your crystal, it'll remove all questions. I'll have to lock up my crystal and hide it forever. To make sure something like this *never* happens again."

Luke nodded slowly, fully realizing the consequences of his actions if he were successful. "Okay," he said with a sigh. "Anything else?"

"Just be aware of who might be around in earshot, eh?"

"Right," said Luke.

It was a plan. The best one he could think of. If it worked, he'd stop Mastermind from becoming Mastermind. He'd save his parents. He'd never see the crystal. Never get this power. But at least his parents would be alive. And evil men like Mastermind would never rise to power. No mutants. No super powers. Just ordinary ignorant lives.

He'd miss having this super power. His dream power. Especially after only having it for a brief few minutes. It wasn't fair. But at least they'd all be safe. They'd all be safe and sound.

He took a deep breath.

"Okay." He looked at his friends, perhaps for the last time. He didn't tell them this, but there was a chance he'd be stuck in the past. In re-writing history, and preventing himself from acquiring this power, one of several possibilities existed.

One, he might simply pop out of existence. The other him would continue to exist. Living a normal life with his parents still alive. Stuck at a dead-end job and watching movies, reading comic books, playing video games. Completely unaware he ever had the chance to be something much, much more.

But that'd be okay. There was another possibility, though. Changing his past like this could create a paradox. He wasn't exactly sure what that meant, or what would happen. Maybe nothing. Maybe the universe would self-destruct. Maybe some unknown force would prevent him from changing his own past, thus protecting the universe from any paradoxes ever existing.

Three, he might successfully change history but still continue to exist. He may or may not get to keep his time travel power. But even if he could somehow still travel through time, he'd return to a totally foreign present day. The last eight months he remembered would've been totally different. Maybe he'd still be dating Amanda for all he knew.

Time travel was a delicate thing. Suddenly now that he had this power – it seemed like too much for one person to possess. What gave *him* the right to change his or anyone else's past? It just… didn't seem right.

What if, unintentionally and completely accidentally, he bumped into someone in the past, made them a few seconds later to their destination than they did originally, which caused them to not meet the person they were going to marry. And whatever kids they'd have would never be born. And what if one of those kids would've gone on to cure cancer… or what if one of those kids was the great-great-great-etcetera grandfather of Simeon here?

It was called "the butterfly effect"; a small change in the past can trigger another minor change in something else, which affected something else slightly differently, on and on, until some major cataclysmic change happened that never existed in the original history.

It could start with anything. Holding a door open for someone. Or standing in their way. A single word. Or a single glance. Most of the time, probably, these things made no meaningful difference. But any one of them *could* create a chain-reaction the fundamentally and dramatically alters the future of the world.

Somehow real-world time travel felt a little different than Luke always imagined. For him, it was about adventure and exploration. It was just a really, really cool thing he always wanted to do. But now as he stood, prepared to go back in time to intentionally change history – a small part of him worried that he might make things much worse, even though his intentions were noble and good.

He took a deep breath. He had no choice. For even though there was great risk – and in all likelihood, if he was successful, he might cease to exist – he had to do it.

Because a greater evil, a worse threat, was already in motion.

"Here I go." He closed his eyes to focus.

Luke activated his super power. He felt himself travel through time.

And then he opened his eyes.

Dawn, Ray, Charlie, and Simeon were still there, staring at him. He was still in the museum in the future.

Huh. Odd. He tried again.

This time with his eyes open.

Nothing happened. He focused. He concentrated. He willed himself all the way into the past.

But nothing. Nothing worked. He never left.

"Luke?" asked Ray, not sure what was going on.

"I can't— I can't— It's not working!" he exclaimed.

"Calm down, take it easy," said Charlie gently. "Are you doing *exactly* what you did before?"

"Yes!" he shouted.

"Could it be because of the other you?" Dawn asked. "Maybe the power jumped from you to him, or something?" She shrugged.

That would suck. Luke didn't like the sound of that.

At all.

"Hmm," said Ray. He looked around their immediate area. He spotted a nearby artifact. Some small stone carving of a pregnant woman with big breasts. Probably a fertility goddess or something. Whatever. He waved his hand at it, and the stone artifact lifted into the air.

"Be careful with that!" exclaimed Simeon. "That's priceless!"

"Sorry," said Ray. "Just testing to see if I still had my power."

"The powers don't go away," said Charlie. "Not as far as I know. Could it maybe be a limited range thing? Maybe you can only go so far back in time?"

"I'll try that," said Luke, desperate to try anything, afraid he might've lost his power before he even got a chance to enjoy it. He wanted to go back in time one minute. Just one single minute. He could still do that, right?

Everything around him shifted into a red blur and suddenly he was back exactly one minute ago. He stood beside his one-minute-younger self.

"What the—?" remarked his younger self.

"Just testing! Bye!" Luke quickly said. Everything shifted to a blue blur and Luke returned to the present moment. He saw his friends – and no second self – there waiting for him.

"Dude, it looked like you flickered!" said Ray.

"Yeah, like for a split second, you weren't there," explained Dawn.

"It worked," said Luke. "I went back one minute, and immediately returned to the second I left."

"There is a way," said Simeon, "to test all their powers."

"I know," said Charlie. "I know…"

"What?" asked Luke.

"It's one of the reasons I brought you here," Charlie said. "They have this simulation training room type thing. Kind of like the holodeck on *Star Trek*. When James and I got our powers, we practiced in there."

"It's designed to test your limits," said Simeon, "in a safe and controlled environment. It's designed to help you discover your power's potential, its limits, and help you master control."

"Really?" asked Luke. "Like the Danger Room?"

"Danger Room?" asked Simeon, completely lost.

"Comic book thing," explained Ray. "It's not a bad idea. Ever since I discovered I had a power, I've been itching to really play with it and push it to the limit. Like, I wonder, can I lift a car? A truck? Mount Rushmore?"

Dawn laughed. "Actually, I did that a little while I was waiting on you. I tried transforming into a variety of animals."

"But that still doesn't solve the problem of Mastermind, or the second Luke," said Uncle Charlie.

"We have to do something," said Luke. "If my powers have limitations, I need to know exactly what they are."

"Yeah, me too," said Dawn.

"It would help to know our powers better," said Ray, "if we ever do have to face Mastermind and his mutants again."

"True that!" said Dawn.

Luke said, "Besides, I'm sure the other me would've time traveled out of there right away. He's probably actually back at the apartment right now."

Ray nodded. "You're not exactly one to stick around and fight," he joked.

"Hey, what's that supposed to mean?" asked Luke.

"Nothing. I'm just saying, you're a lover, not a fighter."

"Guys, can we focus here?" said Dawn.

"Right," said Luke. "Anyway, we can figure out later what to do about the other me. He's probably not even aware of my existence yet, come to think of it."

"Now there's an interesting question for the philosophers," said Charlie. "Which one's the real you?"

"I am, of course," said Luke.

Ray chuckled. "I'm sure that's what the other Luke would say too."

"The good news is," said Charlie, "apparently Mastermind never succeeded in taking over the world."

"How can you be so sure?" asked Dawn.

Luke nodded. He understood. "Because we're in the future and there's no trace of him around. No mutants. No evil world dictator. Nothing. Just a bunch of normal humans going about their business. Right, Simeon?"

Simeon nodded. "I've never heard of any Mastermind. And I'm a historian."

"So we're successful in stopping him," said Ray.

"Yeah," said Luke, scratching his head. "I guess so."

"But we haven't done that yet," said Dawn.

Luke smiled. "You're not thinking fourth dimensionally. We *will* defeat him, and that's why the future is safe."

"I don't know… Sounds like we're putting the carriage before the horse," said Dawn.

"Trust me," said Luke. "I know time travel."

"Then," said Ray, "we better make sure we're prepared. Looks like we're gonna have to face him after all."

"Right," said Luke. "We have to act like we don't know we're already going to win, so we don't get lazy or make any foolish mistakes. We still, after all, actually have to defeat him. Uncle, where's this Danger Room you talked about? I'm ready to become a super hero!"

"I'll prep a shuttle," said Simeon.

Chapter 19
STRANGE SKY

Mastermind waited restlessly inside the mirror-walled chamber. He faced the pedestal – the Altar of Destiny – and impatiently checked his watch.

He sighed. "How long is this going to take, I mean, really?"

He hated waiting.

Shadow shrugged her black furry shoulders.

Venom and Kraken sat on the floor by the wall, talking amongst themselves. Rhino-Man paced in circles. Doctor Troyd and the other Luke were not present. Neither was the spider-guy Arachnus.

Mastermind stared at the pedestal. "I don't have all day."

"What's the rush, boss?" asked Shadow.

"Nothing. Never mind. It's none of your business."

She lowered her head. "Yes, master."

Meanwhile, back in the future…

Their shuttle lifted off the ground effortlessly and almost silently. It didn't look anything like modern day space shuttles, or even the shuttles in science-fiction TV shows. This was more like a large white cube, with rounded corners. And in each corner were blinking lights. It had an almost plastic-like look, but was much sturdier and stronger.

They launched straight up into the air, quickly, but felt no unusual g-forces inside. It was an extremely soft, gentle ride.

Inside the large cube-like shuttle were several comfortable seats, display screens on every wall, and a control panel at one end. Simeon sat at the controls. Large windows lined each of the four walls, plus one on the ceiling and another at the floor. Luke looked through the bottom window as the ground rapidly moved away out from under them.

He saw their launch pad shrink away – along with the other cube shuttles and various other space craft and vehicles parked there. He saw entire buildings, entire blocks, entire sectors, the entire city itself get smaller and smaller as they flew higher and higher up into the atmosphere.

He saw the lush park they arrived in from the portal. The entire surrounding landscape. Mountains in the distance. And… a giant pyramid. Equally as large as the one on the desert planet. Just a dozen miles away from the city.

"Uncle, Uncle, look! They have a pyramid too!" said Luke.

"I know," said the old man, leaning towards a side window to get a better look. "It's where we – your parents and I – got our powers, remember?"

"Oh right," said Luke. "You said the other pyramid wasn't there before. I forgot."

Simeon turned away from the controls for a second. The thing was probably on auto-pilot anyway. "You found another one?" he asked them. Their shuttle rose through the clouds and entered the upper atmosphere.

"Yeah. Was one reason why I thought maybe your crystal was still working," said Uncle Charlie.

"Why do you say that?" asked Simeon.

"Well, you guys built the first pyramid. I figured you built a second one on Sekhmet for some reason, too."

"Sekhmet?" asked Ray.

"The name of the desert planet. According to the Tablet of Ningishzida."

"The Tablet of Whuh?"

"We didn't build the pyramid," said Simeon.

Uncle Charlie looked confused. "You didn't?"

"No," said Simeon. "It's been here as far back as recorded history. Several thousand years. If not longer."

"But…" Charlie was really confused. "You guys know all about it. You taught us about the Temple of the Gods, the Altar of Destiny, how it all works… You knew your way around inside like the back of your hand…"

"Well, sure," said Simeon. "We used it for millennia. It's a part of our heritage, our culture, our way of life." Their shuttle left the atmosphere and entered into the vast openness of space. The glowing blue-green planet waited below. White clouds. Endless blue oceans. Luke, Ray, and Dawn stared through different windows to take it all in.

There was really no experience like it. Seeing Earth from this point of view. Everything appeared so united. No borders. No boundaries. Just one planet. All sharing the same water, the same air, the same life.

Except, now that they were higher up, the three of them all got a funny look on their faces. "Uh, Uncle," said Luke, "Just how far into the future are we?"

"Not sure," said the old man. But… "Why?"

"The continents are all different," said Luke. "I mean, that kinda looks like Africa, a little. But where's South America? Is that large island mass supposed to be Australia? Nothing looks right."

"I thought plate tectonics took millions of years," said Ray.

"They do," confirmed Luke.

"Wow," said Dawn. "We must be *really* far into the future."

Luke looked out the side window. He analyzed the stars. "No way. This can't be right."

"What is it?" asked Uncle Charlie.

"I don't recognize any of these constellations. There's no way we're a few hundred, a few thousand, or even a few million years into the future. We can't be."

Ray and Dawn peered out the window too. Space. An infinite star field, reaching as far as the eye could see – and so very far beyond. It was beautiful. Magnificent. Awe-inspiring and vastly humbling all at the same time. But also absolutely unfamiliar.

"What do you mean?" asked Charlie, looking out the window at the stars too. He saw the planet's moon out his side. It was highly colonized – lights, buildings, roadways, large bubble structures with water and lush plant life underneath. It was too developed. He couldn't tell if it was Earth's moon – or just some other moon, about the same size.

"Uncle," said Luke, turning to face him. "We're on another planet."

"So this isn't the future?" asked Dawn.

"Apparently not," said Ray.

"Then where are we?" she asked.

"Eden," said Simeon. "Didn't the Visitor Liaison welcome you?"

"Well, sure," said Charlie. "I thought Eden was just the name of the city."

Simeon laughed. "No, no, no. Eden's the name of our world. The city near the Ningishzida Gateway is called Babbalonna. It means 'Beautiful Garden' in the ancient language."

Charlie was only now realizing he had it wrong all this time. He saw humans and advanced civilization – and *assumed* he was in the future. But something didn't add up. *Why* were there humans, this advanced, on another planet? Why did they speak English? And if they didn't build the pyramid – who did?

"Wait a second," said Luke, realizing something. "If this isn't our future, then that means… we still don't know what happens to Earth."

Dawn gasped.

Ray got an uncomfortable deep sinking feeling.

"Mastermind," said Charlie.

"He might still have been successful – I mean, he might still succeed if we don't stop him."

No one wanted to say it. But they all had a terrible gut feeling inside. Even if they did try to stop him, even if they gave it their best, he might *still* succeed no matter what. There were no guarantees. No assurances. No better future to look forward to.

"What can you tell us?" asked Luke. "What do you know about Mastermind's plans?"

Charlie shrugged. "Not much. He just sometimes talked about how the world would be a better place if he was in control, and how people—all people—were really just monsters inside, and he was going to find a way to make the world see them for who they really were. He hates women. Wants to enslave them. Says they're only good for sex and menial labor. But he doesn't think much better of most men, either. He really… His worldview… With his power… I don't want to even think what he might do."

"We have to stop him," said Dawn. "I saw him. How he looked at us, when we were lined up, waiting to be mutated. We weren't people in his eyes. I don't even know if cattle is the right word. We were just… just…"

Ray put his arm around her. "It's okay. We know."

"He killed my parents," said Luke. "He almost killed all of us. He's mutating and mind controlling innocent people. And he's bent on world domination. If he's not a super villain, I don't know what is." He took a deep breath. He looked at each of them individually. "The question is… are we willing to do what it takes? We're the only ones who have any chance of stopping him. Are we," he said, "willing to be heroes?"

Ray lowered his head. He never dreamed of being a super hero. Well, not since he was like 10 years old. Every kid dreams of being a super hero. But he was an adult now. He just wanted to get a good internship at some large company. Or start his own company. He wanted to live a good life. Have a family some day. Work hard to give them a better life than he ever had.

And that's why he realized he needed to do this. For his future family. For all the families in the world. Mastermind was a dangerous threat to them all. And Luke was right -- they were probably the only people on Earth who had any chance of stopping him. "Okay," he said, nodding. "I'm in."

"Me too!" said Dawn, more confidently. This actually sounded exciting. This sounded fun. Dangerous? Probably. Full of the unknown? Most likely. Worth doing? Absolutely. Who else in the world gets a chance like this? To have an incredible super power. To use that power for the greater good. To make a difference. To be a hero. It was the role of a lifetime. She thought about it. And she smiled. This was the ultimate way to give her life real meaning. "Definitely."

Luke smiled. "Me too." In a way, he felt like he was born to do this. Maybe he was.

All those comic books, all those movies, all that dreaming and fantasizing and wishful thinking – it was all because his soul longed for this. He wasn't put on Earth to hold some random job. He wasn't put on Earth to be some anonymous cog in the system.

No, he had a purpose. He could sense it. He always knew he had some higher purpose – even if, for the longest time, he didn't know exactly what that purpose was. But today, now, he knew. With every fiber in his body and soul, he knew.

Charlie smiled. A small tear escaped the corner of his eye. "I was hoping you'd say that. I couldn't ask you – any of you – to do this, to risk your lives for friends and strangers alike… But the world needs you. I need you. James and Helen are gone. You're the only hope left for stopping Mastermind and his mutants."

The shuttle docked. "We're here!" said Simeon.

"Ready for your training?" asked Uncle Charlie.

Ray inhaled deeply, summoning his strength and courage. "Yeah, I'm ready, let's do this."

"Let's make sure Mastermind never harms or mind controls another person again!" declared Dawn.

Luke cheered, "Aw right! Super friends, assemble!"

Chapter 20
STOP TAMPERING WITH THE TIMELINE!

"We're aboard a real-life space station?" Ray asked, full of simultaneous disbelief and wonder-filled awe. "But there's gravity," he said, stamping his foot on the floor.

The space station itself was fairly large. Bigger than an average big-city mall back on Earth. And like a big mall, it had all sorts of departments, sections, retail stores, places to eat, and plenty more – people lived here full-time. Housing quarters, recreational areas, daycare centers, plenty of shopping, and a scientific deep space research center.

Everything was enclosed, obviously; any windows had an open view of space or overlooked the planet below. But it was quite populated. Very busy. And not just with people who lived and worked here full-time. There were plenty of casual tourists and shoppers too, here just to grab some lunch, pick up a few items, or meet a significant other on a date.

This civilization had pretty advanced space travel. The shuttle ride up was a clear indication. Flying to this station was, to them, no different than most people back on Earth driving to a neighboring city for work or pleasure.

And this space station, clearly, had artificial gravity, as Ray was so quick to point out. And if this station was so quick and convenient for so many people to go to, Luke wondered where else they could go. Had these people colonized other planets? They already built up and colonized their own moon. Did they have interplanetary starships? Able to quickly and easily visit other worlds within their own star system?

Were they already beyond that? Interstellar, perhaps? Luke imagined the possibilities. Traveling all the way to other stars, seeing other worlds, setting up outposts on those distant planets. Maybe even more than outposts. Maybe whole civilizations.

Then he had a thought. What if these people originally colonized Earth? Simeon said their planet's name was Eden. And when they arrived through the portal, they were surrounded by this beautiful garden-like landscape. Could *this* be the Garden of Eden? Is that where the myth came from?

"The training room's this way," said Simeon, leading them through the main corridor. Shops, restaurants, and entertainment centers surrounded them on every side. Lots of signs gave visitors directions on where to find everything. Residential quarters were one way; the sports arena was another. Lover Lounges – whatever that was – was in another direction. As were more shops, places to eat, and other things to see and do. Even a small museum exhibit and high school were among the list of places to go.

"Uncle, where did these crystals come from?" asked Luke as they walked through the station.

Charlie shrugged. "Don't know. Simeon, any idea?"

"On the crystals' origin? We haven't figured that out. But we do know their network is extensive."

"Network?" asked Ray.

"He means all the places it can go," said Charlie.

"Yeah," said Luke. "You mentioned there was a sixth symbol?"

Charlie said, "We only knew of the five, the ones marked on the Tablet of Ningishzida. But when James and I met with Simeon all those years ago… He taught us a little secret."

"The crystals are programmable," Simeon said, almost nonchalantly. Like it was no big deal.

"Programmable?" Luke remarked.

"We figured that out eons ago. We used our crystal to create gateways to many different worlds. Once we figured out how the crystal worked, we used it to open supply lines all over the galaxy. That is, until the crystal stopped working. Apparently its power was more limited than we realized."

"That's incredible!" said Ray. "And there's a different symbol for each planet?"

"Each site, yes," said Simeon. "You can have more than one gateway per planet, of course. And it's not limited to planets, either."

"Right," said Luke. "Like that derelict starship."

"The what?" asked Simeon.

"The abandoned starship. That lost all its atmosphere," said Luke. "The portal that creates a vacuum every time you open it."

"Ohh, that one, yes," said Simeon. "That's not one of ours."

"What do you mean?" asked Dawn.

"That's not one of our ships."

Ray was almost afraid to ask. "Well, whose is it?"

Simeon paused for a second, staring blankly. Then he returned to normal. "We don't know. Perhaps the crystal creators. Perhaps someone else.

"Okay, I gotta ask," said Luke. "Are there other alien lifeforms – other intelligent life – out there?"

"You mean not from Eden or your world?" Simeon asked.

"Yeah. And speaking of – if you're not from Earth, how come you're human? And how come you speak English?"

They turned down a corridor into a less populated area of the station, still on their way to the simulator room.

"We speak most languages," clarified Simeon. "Any time someone visits Eden, we quickly scan them to identify their culture, native language and dialect, species, and so on. My comlink updates and I can speak fluently and easily in your native tongue."

"Comlink?" asked Ray.

Charlie explained, "It's how they communicate with each other. I think it's also connected to their version of the Internet or some super computer, too. Some implant in their brains, I think."

"As to why we're both human but come from different worlds, that I don't know," said Simeon. "Our crystal hasn't worked for nearly four millennia. We may have visited your world in the past. I don't know. We traveled to many worlds."

"Wow," said Luke. "You could be our distant ancestors. Or maybe we're yours."

"Possible," said Simeon. "This way," he lead them down another hallway.

This place was huge.

"So how many symbols are there? How many places could your people visit before the crystal died?"

"Hundreds," said Simeon. "Possibly more. Like I said, they're programmable."

"But you didn't make the portal to that derelict starship?" asked Luke.

"I don't believe so. The ship's not similar to any of our designs. And we liked to build gateways between more stationary locations, like planets, moons, stars, and outposts."

"Oh my God," said Luke, getting excited. "So it's a real alien ship!"

"Seems so," said Simeon, again, like it was no big deal.

Ray shook his head. "Aliens? Big gray heads, probes, and all that?"

"Relax," said Dawn. "I'm sure they won't want to probe you."

"And why not?" asked Ray. "I'm not good enough for their little alien experiments?"

They laughed together.

Luke was intrigued. "We gotta find a way onto that ship. You have any space suits or anything I can borrow?"

"Now Luke," said Uncle Charlie, "we can worry about all that another time. Let's not lose focus why we're here."

"Yeah. After we defeat Mastermind, I'm coming back to check out that space ship."

"We're gonna need a good plan," said Ray. "Mastermind… He's… got this power over people… makes you do things, obey him, whatever he wants – and you can't help it. You *want* to do as he asks."

Dawn nodded solemnly.

"Yeah, we've got powers now. That gives us a fighting chance. But none of us are exactly trained for this sort of thing either," said Ray. "Even if we do defeat him – then what? Do we lock him up in some sort of super prison for super villains? He obvious escaped jail at least once already."

"We'll think of something," said Luke.

"We can't kill him," said Dawn. "He's an evil, evil man. But I'm not about to play God."

Ray nodded. "She's right. If we're going to try to be heroes, we gotta stick to a moral code. Otherwise we're no different than the monsters we're trying to stop."

"I know, I know. You guys are right. Maybe we can trick him into killing himself. It happens all the time in the comics and movies."

"But Luke," said Charlie, "this isn't a comic book or movie. Mastermind won't capture you and monologue about his master plan while he gives you time to escape. And he's smart. I don't think you're going to make him fall into his own trap."

"Exactly why we need a solid plan," said Ray.

"Yeah," said Dawn. "I don't want to end up his mindless slave… or a mutant."

Luke turned to his uncle.

"Don't look at me," said the old man. "I'll help any way I can, but 'night vision' isn't exactly the most useful power for these sort of things."

"Do we even have time to master our new powers?" asked Ray. "I mean, right now, Mastermind and his mutants… what are they doing in that pyramid, anyway?"

"Getting powers," Dawn said.

Luke's eyes went wide. "You're right. That has to be it. He brought them all to that room, with the sphere. Oh my God. He's building an army of super-powered mutants!"

Dawn sighed. "Not good."

Ray shook his head. "Not good at all. We're already out-numbered. How are we supposed to do this? *Can* we even do this?"

Luke thought about it. They were surely in over their heads. Five mutants, all with their own individual super powers, plus Mastermind himself. Verses a time-traveler, a shape-shifter, and a telekinetic. It appeared Luke's ability to travel through time was fairly limited. So that ruled out the option of preventing any of this from ever happening. Ray could keep several of them at bay at once with his telekinesis, and Dawn could transform into something big and powerful – but six against three?

Sure, Charlie could join in too. But do what, exactly? What a useless power. Well, not useless when they had to find their way through the dark underground caverns. But pretty useless in battle.

They needed more people on their side. But there was no time. Right now, as they walked through this giant space station, Mastermind's mutants were gaining super powers. And then what? Return to Earth, take it over, rule the world? Or was Mastermind recruiting even *more* mutant monster slaves into his army?

They had to do something.

"Look," he said, "I know the odds are against us. But we have to do something. We have to try."

"But will we be enough?" asked Ray.

"We'll have to be," said Luke. "Look, do I think it's cool we all got powers? Absolutely. Am I loving the idea of being a super hero? You bet. But at the same time, you think I don't realize what I'm getting into? I mean, we're putting our lives on the line. We're all new at this. I'm all too aware of that. None of us are trained in fighting. None of us know the full extent or potential of any of our powers. We've never had to face off against a super villain – or any kind of dangerous criminal – before. And none of us are prepared for what might come next. But you know what?"

"What?" Dawn and Ray asked together.

"None of that even matters. Life is always full of danger. Life is always full of the unknown. Life often throws you into circumstances and problems that you don't feel ready for, that you've never faced before, that you have no idea how to solve. But that's okay. Because we always find a way. We always figure things out. We always come out ahead. We don't give up and we don't quit. Because there's something way more important than our fears, doubts, or limitations – the lives of others. Maybe even the whole world. If we don't do something – who will? Who can?"

Dawn applauded. Ray smiled and nodded.

"You're right man. You're absolutely right," he said.

Uncle Charlie smiled proudly. "Good to see the old Luke back and alive again."

Luke looked at him strangely.

"I agree," said Ray. "Ever since your parents… you haven't quite been the same. You just sorta gave up on everything. Your art, your girlfriend… everything."

They were right. Luke didn't want to admit it, but they were right. After his parents died, he closed up inside. Gave up on his art, stopped trying, detached and distanced himself from his girlfriend… Buried himself even more in movies and books.

Maybe he was just grieving. Maybe he was just withdrawn. But he wasn't. He couldn't grieve. Because until earlier today, he blamed himself for their deaths. He felt guilt, not grief. He felt shame, not sadness.

But now, suddenly, everything had changed. His parents' deaths were not his fault. Not really. Even if he hadn't gone to that cliff – or gone with them on vacation at all – they'd still be dead at Mastermind's hand.

Luke didn't have time for feeling sadness or grief now, though. He jumped straight into anger. Straight at Mastermind. Sure, he claimed this was all about doing the right thing, being a super hero, and all that – but no, the truth was, Mastermind had to pay. Luke wasn't violent or aggressive. Usually he was a pretty nice guy. But deep down, he knew, Mastermind had to be stopped, one way or another – to prevent any more future victims, and to avenge all the past victims.

Especially Luke's mom and dad.

That's where he found his strength. That's where he found his courage. This wasn't solely about being a hero. Sure, that was totally cool and fun. He did like that aspect too. But really, this was about righting a deeply painful wrong – about hand-delivering justice to a most evil man.

Dawn and Ray were right. They shouldn't become killers. Heroes had to follow a strict moral code. Otherwise he'd be no better than the villains he fought. Okay, they'd still be "better" – especially against someone like Mastermind. But it was a slippery slope. With great power came great responsibility, to quote a famous line from *Spider-Man.* They had to use their powers for good – without crossing over the line between justice and revenge.

Luke wanted revenge. But he couldn't allow himself to cross that line. Not today. Not ever.

They'd have to find some other way to defeat him.

"And here we are," finally said Simeon, stopping at a red door marked "Simulation Training Center". They were at the far end of the station, away from all the commerce and living quarters. Luke still thought "Danger Room" sounded better. But maybe that would've been a trademark infringement with Marvel Comics or something.

Simeon placed his hand against the door. It unlocked and opened. He let them in.

Mastermind checked his watch, tapping his foot impatiently. He was still in the mirrored chamber, still waiting at the pedestal.

"Come on already!" he exclaimed. "You stupid bug." He sighed with unimaginable frustration. "His power better be worth it."

"Mine was," said Shadow with a cat-like grin. And then she disappeared, turning invisible, right before his eyes.

"Yes, yes," sighed Mastermind. "Go check on the doctor and our new recruit, would you?"

"Sure thing, boss," said Shadow's feline voice in the empty air. Her cat-like body and reflexes already allowed her to move somewhat stealthily. Now her newfound power made her all the more sneaky and dangerous.

Mastermind definitely had plans for her.

"Can I go first?" asked Luke.

"I don't see why not," said Simeon, checking with Charlie.

"Awesome!" said Luke.

They stood in a small room. Very small. Practically a closet. But this was just the control center, obviously. There were all kinds of buttons – a whole table full of them – all marked with different colors and labels. A flat wall faced them. Luke assumed a video display or window would appear there. The real simulation room had to be on the other side of that blank wall.

"We'll start at Level 1. Try and use your powers. The simulator will collect data on everything you're doing. Reaction time, energy output, change in temperature, biometrics, everything. At any time you need to stop, just yell 'stop'."

"Right, got it," said Luke. "So where do I go? What do I do?"

Simeon said, "The test begins now."

Suddenly, the space between Luke and the others rapidly expanded, warping and stretching space, putting what felt like miles between them in mere seconds.

Luke stood all alone in a completely white space, void of any defining boundaries of any kind. A second later, grass sprung up around his feet and spread outward. Flowers, trees, and other plants sprouted up from the ground, as if growing in hyper real-time. The sun and sky appeared overhead, as if suddenly painted onto some massive canvas high above. Birds appeared and populated the trees. Butterflies fluttered around the flowers. Bees buzzed nearby. And then…

One of the bees stung him.

"Ow! That hurt!"

He really felt that. This was a *simulation*? Sure felt real! Damn. He rubbed his arm where the bee had stung him. It was sore. It was painful. But he'd live.

Wait. Maybe this was part of the test. His super power was time travel. Alright. Maybe he can go back in time and stop himself from getting stung.

He closed his eyes, concentrated, and suddenly everything around him shifted into a red blur of light. He went back in time several seconds. Seven, to be exact. He opened his eyes. Saw himself standing there.

His seven-seconds-younger self stood there, saw him, and looked surprised. "Um, hi," he said to his suddenly-appearing self.

"Hi," said Luke from seven seconds in the future.

"What's going on?" asked slightly-younger Luke.

"Look out! There's a bee on your arm," said the marginally-older Luke. He quickly flicked it off. The bee flew away.

"Thanks," said the younger Luke, noticing the bee sting still on the other Luke's arm.

"You're welcome," said the other Luke. He checked his arm. The bee sting remained. It still hurt. But he looked at his other self's arm. No big sting. He changed the past.

So why was he still stung?

"Okay, *stop*," yelled out the still-stung Luke.

The scene vanished. The room rapidly contracted and compressed. Everything rushed closer back together. Within seconds, he was back in the tiny room with the others. Simeon stood over the controls.

Both Lukes remained.

"What the hell happened?" asked older Luke.

Uncle Charlie looked uneasy. "Um, everyone else sees two of them, right?"

Dawn and Ray stared and nodded.

"This is fascinating," said Simeon. "Somehow, you've prevented your own causality loop."

Everyone – except the two Lukes – looked to Simeon in total loss.

"Say whuh?" asked Ray.

"Causality loop," said the first, younger Luke.

"A paradox," said the second, slightly older Luke.

The first Luke sighed and began to explain. "It's like the classic grandfather paradox. Say a time traveler goes back in time and kills his own grandfather before his grandfather had any children. Since the grandfather had no children, the time traveler's parents were never born, therefore the time traveler was never born – and since he never existed, how could he go back in time to kill his own grandfather?"

The second Luke looked at his younger duplicate. "But apparently the loop is broken. I changed his history. See. He didn't get stung. But look. I still have the bee sting."

"So you can't change your own past?" asked Ray.

Both Lukes shook their heads.

"No," said the first Luke.

The second Luke said, "Because his past has been changed."

"And now there's two of you," said Simeon.

Dawn said, "I guess that confirms we left behind another Luke back in the sphere, too."

Ray shook his head. "This is getting too crazy for me."

"The only way to avoid duplicating myself," said the second Luke, "is to not change my own history in any way that prevents me from traveling back onto my original timeline."

"Argghhh!" Ray exclaimed.

The first Luke explained, "He means, he can't change what caused him to travel back in time in the first place. So like in this example, if he allowed the bee to still sting me, he could've returned to his own time and everything would be fine. There'd only be one of us."

"I see," said Dawn, figuring it all out. "Because the first one never got stung, he'd never leave the present moment. Which means, he'd stay here – and when the second one returned from the past, the first one would still be there, and –"

"Okay, just stop. Seriously. This is giving me a headache," said Ray.

Charlie laughed, sympathizing with Ray. "Personally, I like the past where it is. I'd rather learn about it in the present, through archeology and research. More fun that way. Like solving a mystery."

Both Lukes shook their heads. "No way," one said. "Yeah, traveling through time is better," said the other.

"Even if it means creating two of you?" asked Simeon.

"Three," corrected Dawn.

Ray shook his head. "Any minute now I'm going to wake up and find this was all a dream."

"Maybe we can fix this," said Simeon. "Luke – one of you – try to go back in time and stop yourself from going back in time to prevent the bee sting. Let's see if that fixes our problem."

The two Lukes looked at each other. They both instantly knew there was only one fair way to decide who got to go.

They both counted out loud, "One, two, three, go!"

One Luke held out a fist. The other held out a flat hand.

"Paper covers rock," said the second one. "I win."

"Best two out of three?"

"We haven't got all day," said Simeon. "Simulator use is charged by the hour…"

"Right. Sorry." The winning Luke closed his eyes, focused, and traveled back in time. Several minutes.

Everything became a red blur, suddenly shifting back to the scene where his first self was rubbing his bee sting.

"Ow! That hurt!" he said.

"WAIT!" shouted the newly-arriving Luke.

"Um… hi. Future self?" asked the recently-stung Luke.

"Don't go back in time to prevent yourself from getting stung. It won't work. Well, sorta. *He* won't get stung, but it won't change you, and then there'll be two of us."

"Oh," said the first Luke.

"Yeah. I'm gonna go now before I create any more paradox duplicates." He suddenly remembered. "Oh! And in a few minutes, go back in time to now, and repeat everything I just said, okay?"

"O…kay."

"That should prevent us from doubling."

"Are you sure?"

The other Luke shrugged. "That's why this is a simulation. To figure this stuff out! Okay… well, good luck!" And he focused on returning to the present moment. Everything, for him, shifted into a blue blur – and he returned to his own present.

Now, dear reader, if you don't think all that's confusing, guess what happened next. Luke returned to his own time, but found his other self *still* there. Well, sort of. This time, his other self still had a bee sting. So it was his other-other self. They got rid of the first duplicate and created a new one.

Both Lukes sighed. This was going to be a problem.

"And there he is!" said Uncle Charlie.

"Why didn't it work?" one asked.

"We're still interfering with our own timeline," said the other Luke. "We're still changing our own past."

"But… I told you to—"

"I know! And I did. I waited a few minutes, went back in time – and saw me *and* you there! I left as fast as I could. So I called stop. And then we waited to see if you'd show up. And here you are."

The other Luke sighed.

"Oy vey," said Dawn.

"Tell me about it," said Ray.

"Is there any way out of this?" asked one of the Lukes.

Simeon shrugged with a completely baffled look on his face. "You could try preventing yourself from ever stepping into the simulator? Maybe?"

It was worth a try.

"Wait, who gets to go," said the other Luke.

"I do."

"Why you?"

"Because I'm the original."

"No you're not," said the other Luke.

"Yes I am."

"No you're not. I've been here the whole time. *You're* the one who suddenly appeared from another timeline. I should be the one to go."

"No, I was the one who started this whole mess. I'm the original Luke. You wouldn't be here if it wasn't for me."

"I'm getting a headache again," said Ray.

"Fine. There's only one way to settle this."

The other Luke nodded.

"One, two, three, go!"

One Luke held out a fist. The other used "paper" again.

"Aw man!" said the first.

"Yeah, you picked rock last time, too."

The winning Luke closed his eyes, focused himself farther into the past and – nothing. He tried again. Still nothing.

"Come on, come on."

"I think we found your limit," said Simeon. "Seems you can travel back a few minutes without any problems. How far back were trying to go now?"

"Ten minutes," he said.

"Try less."

He concentrated. "Come on, you can do this," he told himself. Still nothing. He finally gave up and sighed. "That was nine minutes. Let's try for eight."

Still nothing.

"Seven."

Dammit! Still nothing.

"Okay, six," he said.

Almost… but no.

"Five?"

Everything turned red and blurred out. He appeared five minutes in the past. The good news: he only saw one of himself. They were still waiting to see if another Luke would show up.

"And there he is!" said Uncle Charlie.

"Nope, wrong me. Sorry. Bye!" Luke quickly returned back to five minutes in the future, immediately after he just left.

Everything was still normal. Well, relatively speaking. Still just one other Luke, also with a bee sting. But at least there wasn't a third now. This proved their theory. They only create duplicates when they interfered with their own timeline, preventing the original Luke from continuing his original-timeline actions.

"This may be how the universe prevents paradoxes," said Simeon. "It creates new timelines layered on top of old timelines. And as soon as a time traveler creates a new timeline, he can't go back to his old one. He can only travel along this new line."

"Interesting," said the other Luke, "so if you went back in time to kill your grandfather, you'd change history – your dad would've never been born, and as far as the rest of the world knew, you were never born either. But you, from the previous timeline, would still exist – and would then be trapped on this new timeline you created, in a world where nobody's ever heard of you."

"Fascinating," said Simeon. "I wonder what else we can do."

"Uh, just a thought," said Charlie, "how about we let Dawn and Ray go ahead for a bit. Let's not risk creating any more time duplicates."

"Agreed," both Lukes said. They practiced rock-paper-scissors in the corner, trying to out-smart the other.

"Mind if I go first?" Dawn asked Ray.

"Go right ahead," he said.

She stepped forward. "Okay, I'm a shape-shifter, so—"

Simeon tapped a button. Suddenly the room rapidly stretched apart, swiftly sending her away from the others. She stood in the middle of empty white space.

"Yeah, I was totally ready by the way, thanks." She looked around the blank white space in every direction. She couldn't see the others from her perspective. She couldn't see anything but white. "Okay, so now what?"

A cute little furry alien creature – something resembling a koala with a large bushy tail with a black tip – emerged from the void. He crawled towards her, making a cute little cooing noise.

"Aww, how cute," said Dawn, kneeling down to pet it. It started purring. She laughed.

But then she realized the purpose of this simulation wasn't for her to pet small furry animals. It was to test her shape-changing abilities. How did she do it before? Clear mental image, strong associated emotion. Got it. Now let's see if she can turn into this cute little creature.

She had the clear picture. She was looking at it. Now she just needed to feel…

what? Cute and cuddly? Soft and furry? Maybe she just needed to feel like "it" – whatever this creature was. Could she do that? Just imagine what it'd feel like to be the animal she wanted to become?

Sure enough, it worked. Her body began shrinking rapidly. Matching gray fur sprouted up all over her body. A large bushy tail appeared, growing out from her lower backside. Her hands and feet became cute little furry paws. Her ears enlarged out the sides of her furry little creature head.

And suddenly, within just a few short seconds, she was another one of these creatures, crawling on the floor, making that cute little cooing sound. Unfortunately, her clothes didn't transform with her. In her animal form, she didn't mind – didn't even notice – that she was naked.

In her animal form, she still had all of her human thoughts. She tried speaking, but only made that cooing noise again. So she couldn't talk. She was limited by her animal form. Somehow her consciousness, her brain, survived intact though. That was good. The realization that she might turn herself into an animal – and then forget she was human – terrified her.

She was an actress. She loved playing different roles. Shape-shifting into other creatures was really no different. In this moment, right now, she was this koala-type thingy. And she enjoyed the part. Everything felt natural in this form. She could wiggle her tail with nothing more than a fleeting intention to. Her body's new size and shape had its own unique center of balance – but it took her no time to adjust to it.

But as fun as this was, she needed to return to her human form. So she concentrated on that. Looking, being, and feeling normal. A person. Blonde girl. Early 20s. The same face in the mirror she saw when she got up that morning.

And quickly, her body morphed and transformed back into her familiar self. Buck naked. Yikes. She quickly grabbed her clothes and covered herself. "Sorry," she said, knowing the others could see her from the control room. She re-dressed herself. "Let me see if I can get them to change with me."

She concentrated really hard. Focused on something simple. A hamster. She had a pet hamster when she was a little girl. She loved and played with that thing all the time. So it was easy for her to remember. Easy for her to visualize.

That wasn't the real test. She wanted to morph her clothes with her.

Her body began to change. She quickly grew smaller and smaller, and more and more hamster-like.

Unfortunately, the clothes did not change with her, hard as she might try. She immediately returned to human form and put her clothes back on, again. "Well that didn't work." She thought about something else to try. "I wonder if I can do other human appearances, too."

All it took was a clear thought and the intention to change. Almost instantly, her physical features shifted. She made herself look older – much older. Like 90 years old. A wrinkly old, gray-haired grandma. Since her body was approximately the same size, she remained fully clothed. Then she tried making herself younger. Much younger.

Her age rapidly reversed. 50s. Mid 30s. Early 20s. Teens.

She stopped around 14 years old. She even had a few zits. She was a cute teenager, sure, but also kinda gangly and awkward too. She was much more beautiful as an adult. Satisfied that she could change her appearance at will fairly easily, she immediately returned to her normal age and appearance.

"One last thing, real quick," she said.

She changed her hair color from blonde to brown to red to green to blue to pink and back to blonde.

"Awesome. Yeah, okay, I'm good now. You can stop the simulation."

The room suddenly rushed back together, rejoining her with the others.

"Very impressive," said Simeon. "According to the data we collected, your powers are unlike anything I've ever seen! It's linked to your DNA. It actually rearranged itself according to your thoughts and emotions, simultaneously activating all of your cells to reboot and update, so to say, rapidly transforming you into the desired outcome. And it seems the less significant the change, the faster and easier the transformation."

"Yeah, I noticed that too," she said.

"And even more fascinating, you maintained your same mass the entire time, regardless of your size. Even when you were a small animal, you had the same weight you do now. Your molecules were just more tightly packed together. I expect the reverse will be true for going large. You can probably make yourself a towering giant, but you'll still have the same weight. I'd be careful doing that. Since your molecules will be farther apart, you're more vulnerable to getting hurt."

"Interesting. Okay, got it," she said. "Anything else?"

"I've never seen anything like you. Did you get your powers through the Altar of Destiny?"

"Huh? Oh, no. I got it after Mastermind injected some chemical into me."

Uncle Charlie became uneasy. "That means he has the formula for creating as many shape-shifters as he wants." He looked at Dawn. "The question is, does he know it yet?"

"I'm guessing not," said Ray. "Otherwise we wouldn't have seen a bunch of new mutants back at the pyramid. Just regular-looking people with shape-shifting powers."

"I hope you're right," said Charlie.

"There's just one thing I don't get," said one of the Lukes.

"Yes?" asked Simeon.

"When I was in the sphere, I was able to travel in time more than 5 minutes."

"Yeah!" said the other Luke.

"I don't know," said Simeon. "Perhaps something's blocking you."

Ray laughed. "Perhaps the universe is trying to prevent you from messing up your timeline any further!"

"Hah, hah. Very funny," said one of the Lukes.

"Maybe I should go back in time and try again," said the other Luke.

"No!" collectively shouted all the others.

"Alright, Ray, you're next," said Simeon. "Ready to test your powers?"

"Ready as I'll ever be."

The simulation started for Ray. From some unknown distance, the others watched and observed. Simeon, at the control panel, quickly entered several commands. Objects appeared near Ray. Large ones, small ones, heavy ones, light ones. Ray moved them all with his mind.

"He's getting pretty good at this," said Dawn, observing.

"No kidding," said Luke. "Hey, you think we should come up with alternate names now that we're super heroes? I was thinking of Time-Man or The Paradox."

Dawn didn't seem to like either of those very much. "What else ya got?"

"Um, well, I was also thinking of maybe Quantum Boy," said the other Luke.

She shook her head.

"What about you? Any ideas for your new name?"

"Actually," she said smiling, "when I was a little girl, I always wanted to be a super hero. But all us girls really had was Wonder Woman. You ever notice that? There's *so many* cool guy super heroes. But not that many female ones, ya know?"

"That's not true," said one of the Lukes. "What about Supergirl, Starfire, Batgirl…"

The other Luke continued, "Ms. Marvel, Rogue, The Invisible Woman…"

"I guess so. But they're not as famous as like Batman or Superman, Spider-Man or that big green muscular guy."

"The Incredible Hulk," they both said.

"Yeah, him. Anyway, to answer your question, I have no idea." She started to think of a suitable name. Something that alluded to her power, but was still catchy and sexy. "Hmm. Maybe The Changeling. Or Shifter. Or Chameleon Girl. Hmm. I dunno. Oh, I know! Mysterious Girl – 'cause you never know what I might be disguised as, who I could be…"

"Nah, sounds too close to Mystique, a character from the X-Men cannon."

"I dunno. I'll think of something later. Why do we need a fake name, anyway?"

"Because it's cool!" said one Luke. "That, and it protects our identities, and our loved ones. But mostly because it's cool."

"We never used secret identities," said Uncle Charlie.

"Exactly!" the other Luke said. "If they had… If… Maybe Mom and Dad would still be here if they did."

Charlie slowly nodded. "And Mastermind might not have come after you. Either of you." He shook his head.

This two-Lukes thing would have to get fixed soon. But one problem at a time.

"Not that we knew he'd go insane and turn evil at first," Charlie continued. He lowered his voice. "But maybe you're right. Maybe there's a reason every super hero has a secret identity…"

"Well, not *every* super hero," corrected one Luke.

"Yeah," said the other. "Iron Man told the world. But I think that was a stupid move."

Ray continued practicing his super power. All the while, the simulator measured exactly how big, how heavy, and how far away he could telekinetically move things. And how long he could hold things up in the air against gravity.

"Fascinating," said Simeon, reading the simulator results. "What power did you say he had?"

"Telekinesis," said Dawn.

"No," said Simeon, shaking his head. "That's not right. He's actually manipulating and bending gravitational forces."

"No way!" exclaimed one Luke. "You think he can use that to make himself fly, too?" The other Luke wandered over to the control panel by Simeon. He looked over all the buttons and active measurements and statistics.

Simeon shrugged. "Only one way to find out." He held down a different button and spoke aloud. "Mr. Cartwright, try levitating yourself up into the air."

They all watched Ray on the large video screen wall. He tried lifting himself up, like he was a random object. But it didn't work. So then he tried pushing against the ground.

Instantly he levitated, floating right off the ground. "Whoa!" he said. He started tumbling uncontrollably, struggling to find his center of balance. Finally he got the hang of it. And before they knew it, he was comfortably floating several feet off the ground, stable and effortlessly. "Yeah," he said. "I think I got it!"

Simeon ended the simulation. The room seemed to shrink and snap back together. They were again in the small enclosed space. At least it appeared small. Who knew how big this place actually was. Clearly the technology was far more advanced than anything Luke (either one) or any of the others could understand.

"That was kinda fun," said Ray. "But um, can we get something to eat? I'm starving." It occurred to him that they never really had dinner.

"Me too," said Dawn. "I feel like I haven't eaten all day."

"All night, you mean," said Uncle Charlie.

"Shit," said Ray, pulling out his cell phone. The battery was almost dead. It had been searching for a signal this whole time. "He's right. Look at the time. It's almost morning."

Dawn checked her own cell phone. "That can't be right." She was feeling a bit tired. But they were all pretty much running on adrenaline right now.

"I'm not tired," said one Luke.

Charlie chuckled. "That's because the healing chamber back at the pyramid revitalized you. It did for me too. But poor Ray and Dawn here just pulled an all-nighter."

"You guys have a revitalizer-doohickey here too?" Ray asked Simeon.

"Something similar, yes," he said. "But you know you're welcome to use the healing chamber in our temple, too. Their technology is still better than ours. We've reverse engineered a lot of what's in that temple, but we haven't mastered it all."

"So," Luke asked, "does that mean aliens really did build these pyramids? Or could it still be man-made, but from the distant future?"

Simeon shrugged. "No other races have claimed it."

"Races?" asked Ray. "As in, other *alien* races?"

Simeon nodded.

"So you weren't kidding earlier. It's not just us out there in the universe? There really are… aliens."

Simeon laughed. "A few."

Ray shook his head. "And to think this morning I was worried about finding enough financing for my friend's indie film. Really puts things in perspective."

Dawn was excited. "So what are they like? The other alien races."

Charlie interrupted, "There'll be plenty of time for that later. We do have a more pressing issue to deal with right now."

"Right," said one Luke. "Mastermind."

Ray nodded. "We can't afford to be weak or tired when we face him. I say we all get a quick rejuvenation boost from their healing chamber and then immediately head back to Earth. We know Mastermind's going back there sooner or later."

"And where his portal will have to open," added Charlie.

"Exactly!" said Ray. "Maybe we can get the jump on him or something." He turned to Simeon. "Which way to the healing chamber?"

"Back on Eden. I'll notify them we're coming."

"I wish we were better prepared," worried Luke.

"We'll figure out a plan on the way," said Ray. "I just hope we're not already too late."

Maybe they were.

Back in the Temple of the Gods, Mastermind checked his watch again. The sphere reappeared – and Arachnus launched out.

"It's about time! What'd you get?" he demanded.

Arachnus smiled, revealing his spider-like fangs.

All the other mutants gathered around. Rhino-Man, Kraken, Slimer, Venom… They had all been through the sphere. All endured some tragic life experience over and over again – and all gotten a unique power to cope with it. All that remained was Arachnus.

"It's a good one, boss," he said, stretching his multiple spider arms and legs. "I can steal anyone else's powers…"

Mastermind grinned. "Perfect." He turned to the slime-based, goo-oozing girl. "Slimer," he said, "go check on the doctor and our new friend."

Chapter 21

CALLING LONG DISTANCE

Doctor Troyd laid across the medical lab table. Different colored lights scanned his body. A holographic medical doctor appeared.

"I've completed my diagnostic," he said. "Are you ready to be repaired?"

Luke stood by Doctor Troyd's side. "Yes," said the young man. "Please heal him."

The holographic doctor grabbed a nearby medical tool. It was an oval-shaped device with spinning multi-colored lights. He placed it over Doctor Troyd's right ear. The lights spun around faster and faster, then blinked three times. The hologram did the same thing again on Doctor Troyd's left ear.

"Your internal wounds have been repaired."

Doctor Troyd's eyes went wide. "What?" he said.

"Your internal wounds have been repaired."

He laid there speechless, silent. And then, slowly, a smile crept onto his face. "I–I can hear again?" he exclaimed. He started laughing. "I can hear! I can hear! Quick," he said, turning to Luke. "Say something!"

"Um, hi," said Luke.

"All repairs have been completed," said the hologram. "Please wait for final diagnostic."

New lights scanned Doctor Troyd from overhead. A few seconds later, they stopped.

"Confirmed. No additional repairs needed," said the holographic doctor. "You are cleared to go." He vanished.

Doctor Troyd jumped off the medical table. He grabbed Luke by both shoulders and shook him. "My hearing's back! I can actually hear again!" He hugged Luke tightly. "Mastermind kept his word. He gave me back my hearing…"

The crazy-eyed scientist looked like he was about to cry.

Just then, Slimer entered the room. "'Ey," she said. "Boss is waitin' fer you guys."

Doctor Troyd ran over to her – and even though she was made entirely of all sorts of gooey disgustingness, he hugged her anyway too.

He sighed with inexpressible happiness and gratitude.

"We'll be right there," he said, overjoyed.

Meanwhile, Mastermind and the other mutants waited in the mirrored room. And Mastermind pulled out his pink glowing crystal.

He knelt down to the floor and drew a large circle. Then in the center, he drew a smaller circle, with lines dividing down the top and across the middle: the symbol for Earth.

"Um boss," said Rhino-Man, "we leaving already? The others aren't back yet."

Mastermind ignored him. He didn't have to explain every little thing he did. They needed to learn to trust him. He wasn't about to abandon Doctor Troyd, Slimer, or Luke on this planet. He still had use for all of them.

The portal opened.

They saw blue skies. A few white clouds. The mutants looked down at the floor, through the portal, and saw upward into the sky. Weird. If they adjusted their angle, they could see the remains of Stonehenge on the other side.

Mastermind pulled out his cell phone. He made a *very* long-distance phone call. Probably the first interplanetary phone call ever made. Okay, not probably. Definitely the first interplanetary cell phone connection ever. Can you imagine how much his cell phone bill would've cost, if not for the help of a little portal?

Anyway, it rang.

And rang.

Rhino-Man and the others watched. Who was he calling?

Someone picked up. "I was wondering when I'd hear from you again," said the voice on the other end. It was a male voice. An unfamiliar one.

Except to Mastermind, of course.

"Were you able to hack into BioGen's security cameras?" Mastermind asked him.

"Sure did."

The man had a mostly-American accent. But Stonehenge was in the United Kingdom. Who was Mastermind talking to?

"And have you sent any copies out yet?"

"Not yet," said the man on the phone. "Was waiting on your call."

"Go ahead. We're almost ready here. Remember, I want all the major news networks to see this. Everybody. The UK, the United States, and every other country with cable TV. Got it?"

"Right, got it. Just like we planned."

"I planned," corrected Mastermind.

"Right, sorry. Just like *you* planned." The male voice sighed, probably rolling his eyes too.

"You're just the hired help. Don't forget your place," reminded Mastermind.

"Whatever."

Mastermind tightened his jaw, but kept himself calm.

"Anyway," said the male voice. "When can I expect final payment?"

"As soon as my videos go out," said Mastermind, gnashing through his teeth. "It'll be waiting in the usual account."

"It better be," said the man. "Don't screw me over."

"Just do your job," said Mastermind.

Silence on the other end.

"Fine," he finally said. "Uploading now."

More silence while they waited.

The other mutants watched Mastermind carefully. What was their master up to now?

"It's done," said the voice on the phone.

"Good."

"Now where's my money?"

Mastermind rolled his eyes. Were people really this easy to manipulate, even without mind control? He switched to a financial app on his cell phone. Entered in a total of one million dollars. United States currency. This was the final price for an unknown hacker to betray his nation and world. Mastermind pressed the big button marked "transfer."

One million dollars. Transaction completed.

"It's done," said the super villain.

A second of silence. Probably verifying the amount. "Thank you," said the man on the phone. "Pleasure doing business. Let me know if you ever need my services again in the future."

"Perhaps we can meet face to face for once?" Mastermind grinned.

"Not likely," he said, and hung up.

Mastermind stared at his disconnected phone. "Idiot."

"Who was that, boss?" asked Rhino-Man.

"No one." He X-ed over the portal, closing it. "Now where's that slimy girl and the others?"

"Right here, master," said Slimer, entering the mirrored chamber with Doctor Troyd and Luke.

Mastermind looked to Troyd. "Well?"

Doctor Troyd smiled. "Better than the day I was born."

"So what's our next move, master?" asked Luke. "I know my uncle and friends will come looking for me."

Mastermind walked over to the mind-controlled Luke. The poor fool had unwittingly popped out of the sphere and right into their hands. This was clearly an unexpected advantage and bonus in his plan. One Mastermind would definitely use.

But it also bothered Mastermind to see *another*, different Luke, seemingly identical in every way, with Chuck and the others. Could they be clones? Twins? Something else?

So earlier, while the other mutants were taking turns going inside the sphere to get their own powers, Mastermind asked his mind-controlled copy of Luke a series of questions. And under Mastermind's irresistible control, Luke told him everything.

Everything.

Like, how Uncle Charlie had given him a crystal, how they wandered onto this planet and fell down into a dark pit, almost met an untimely demise by some alien snake monster… and eventually, made their way up into the pyramid, where they met up with Ray and Dawn. And, this Luke told Mastermind, they *all* had powers.

Including the power of time travel.

So that explained it. The other Luke that Mastermind saw must've been from an alternate timeline. It was the only logical conclusion. Which meant his Luke was exactly identical to the other Luke – with one significant difference: this Luke had become Mastermind's loyal and faithful servant.

A loyal and faithful time-traveling servant. A definite advantage, indeed. Had he known, in advance, he'd have an asset like this, he might've structured his plan very differently. But oh well. No matter. They had a schedule to keep. Things were already in motion.

After all, a good plan today was better than a perfect plan tomorrow. His plan would still succeed, no matter what. No one could stop him now. Not even a handful of unexpected new wannabe "super heroes" under Chuck's pathetic tutelage.

Still, just in case, having a time traveler on his side was a little extra insurance that made Mastermind all the more confident.

Now, the only question that remained was where Chuck and the others went. A moment ago, they had escaped through a portal, back to the entrance point on this planet. But Mastermind doubted they'd stay there long. Knowing Chuck, they probably went back to Earth – or maybe one of the old man's other favorite planets.

They, too, would become useful assets to his team, Mastermind thought. The only thing better than one time traveler under his control – was *two* time travelers under his control.

The very idea of it tickled him with excitement.

Chuck, on the other hand, was pretty useless – who cared about a night vision super power? The girl – she was supposed to be one of his new mutants anyway. But she'd be more useful in her current form, as a shape-shifter. How did she get that power anyway? According to his Luke, she never went into the sphere. Was there some other way to gain powers that he didn't know about?

And then there was Ray. That kid kept showing up everywhere he didn't belong. More of a nuisance than a threat, in Mastermind's opinion. But his telekinetic powers would come in handy too. Not as useful as some of the other powers his other mutants already had. But one more super-powered mind-controlled mutant on the team couldn't hurt.

Mastermind didn't really need any of them. They were just bonus additions. But more importantly, he didn't like having uncontrolled people potentially interfering with his plan. He and his mutants needed to be the *only* ones with powers. He couldn't risk these would-be "heroes" getting in the way, causing frustrating complications, at some critical moment.

"Any chance they'll come back here?" Mastermind asked his enslaved Luke.

The young man shrugged. "Maybe, but I doubt it. If it were me, I'd wanna regroup and get some training. Master our new powers. Form a plan. Try to do the whole super hero bit."

Mastermind nodded. "Just like your parents."

Luke had a sudden mix of emotions. He wanted to serve and obey his new master – but another part of him *hated* Mastermind for murdering his parents. Especially after just witnessing it, over and over again, inside the sphere.

He clenched his fists.

Mastermind noticed. "Relax," he said, looking deep into Luke's eyes.

Luke's fists relaxed.

"Where would they go?" asked the mind-controller.

Luke really didn't know.

"Alright." Mastermind preferred to add them to his little team, but time was running out. He really didn't want to risk them interfering in some unexpected way. Best to kill this loose end now. "You still have your crystal?" he asked Luke.

Luke reached into his pocket. He did. It was with him when he entered the sphere. It came out with him when he left.

Of course, that meant the *other* Luke still had an identical crystal too. But that wouldn't matter.

"Doctor Troyd," he said, looking to the unkempt scientist. "Continue as planned. You know what to do. Take the boy with you," he said, shoving Luke towards the scientist. "Go without me. We'll find you later."

"Oh. Okay," said Doctor Troyd.

"Open a portal back to Earth," Mastermind said to Luke. "But I have a special symbol I want you to use."

"But…" Luke said, confused.

"Do as I say, now!" He pointed across the room. "Over there."

Luke obeyed. He walked to the other side of the room and began drawing a large circle on the floor.

Mastermind grabbed the doctor's arm and whispered into the scientist's newly-working ear, "And make sure the boy gets a new form. Your choice."

Doctor Troyd looked at Mastermind. He was serious.

"Okay," softly nodded the doctor.

Luke had completed the circle. He looked back. "What's the symbol, master?"

"M5," said Mastermind.

"What?" asked Luke.

Annoyed, Mastermind clenched his teeth. "It's the letter *'M'* followed by the number *'5'*."

"That's a symbol?" remarked Luke.

"Use it!" Mastermind shouted.

Okay. No problem. Geez. Luke started drawing this new, unknown symbol.

"You still have that video we recorded earlier?" Mastermind turned to Doctor Troyd.

The eccentric scientist reached into his lab coat pocket. He grabbed onto his cell phone. The same one they had recorded a quick video message of Mastermind saying "you will grant this man access to anywhere and anyone" on earlier, back at the hotel lobby, back in California. Doctor Troyd nodded.

"Good. It's almost time to start using it," said Mastermind.

Doctor Troyd would need it to gain access to someone very important very soon.

The portal opened back to Earth. "It worked!" exclaimed Luke. He saw what looked like the baggage claim area at a busy airport. Where was this? His uncle didn't tell him about this place.

The portal on the other end opened along a wall. People rushed by, carrying luggage, meeting up with loved ones, looking exhausted from their long flights. But some stopped to stare into the portal, confused and a little afraid.

From their perspective, they saw mostly darkness. Luke opened his side of the portal along the floor. So onlookers from the other side could only see up towards the mirrored ceiling of the pyramid chamber room.

More people stopped around the portal. A small crowd quickly gathered. Luke leaned over the portal. To their perspective, he seemed to be walking on and clinging to the other side of the wall. "Um, Master…" said Luke.

Doctor Troyd and Mastermind walked over to the portal. Troyd stepped up to the edge and leaned over. This was going to be a little awkward. Maybe if he climbed in at an angle… or maybe… hmm. Perpendicular floors were not his thing. He wasn't feeling too sure about this.

Mastermind sighed and shook his head. He pushed them both through. They rolled and fell through, landed hard on the floor on the other side, and the crowd gasped and murmured. One lady screamed.

Mastermind looked through from the other side. "Close the portal." Then he looked to Doctor Troyd. "You know what to do."

Luke moved the crystal across the open space. Swiped from the left and then the right. The portal instantly vanished.

The onlookers couldn't believe their eyes.

"What the fuck?" remarked one witness.

Luke smiled awkwardly. "Hi guys."

Security started approaching.

Doctor Troyd grabbed Luke's arm. "Come on, let's go."

Chapter 22
POWER FAILURE

Meanwhile, elsewhere in the galaxy… They thought they had more time.

Time to learn their new powers. Time for a quick rest before an inevitable conflict. Time to get prepared.

They were wrong.

Mastermind was already several steps ahead of them. Time was rapidly running out.

Of course, they didn't know that. Yet.

If only they'd gone to Earth immediately after running into Mastermind and his mutants on the desert planet. This little detour, well-intentioned as it may have been, was going to cost them a lot more than they realized.

But all that would be revealed in due time.

Simeon guided them into the entrance of the planet's pyramid. On Eden, they didn't call it a pyramid. Everyone knew it as "The Temple" or "The Temple of the Ancients".

Who, exactly, those Ancients were was still an unsolved mystery. But this pyramid, this temple, had been around for as far back as their recorded history.

"Welcome to the Temple of the Ancients," Simeon said, standing before the large circular door entrance. Two uniformed men, probably guards of some kind, stood watch at the entrance. Simeon had already called ahead. The guards were expecting them.

Simeon pressed the blue button, opening the front door. Standing behind him, both Lukes stared at the outer pyramid with awe and amazement. The pyramid itself was nestled between two magnificent mountains and a dense forest. What a beautiful planet. What an amazing alien pyramid. What an incredible adventure they were all on.

Dawn and Ray followed right behind. The entrance to this pyramid looked pretty much the same as the entrance to the last pyramid, on the desert world. This wasn't *quite* as exciting for them as it was for the two Lukes, but it was still pretty awesome.

Uncle Charlie, of course, had already been here a few times before. But he never lost his sense of awe and wonder.

That was the key to youth, Charlie felt. Always seeing the world for the first time. And he had lived a very long life. And seen many, many different places – both on Earth, and other worlds.

They stepped inside.

Normally, someone would have to place their hand flat on the wall, load up the computer interface, and get directions. But Simeon had been inside this pyramid several times himself, and knew his way around pretty well.

"This way," he said, leading them.

"And you have no idea who built this?" one of the Lukes asked.

"Well, we have *some* idea," said Simeon, guiding them forward. "In the Temple of the Gods, the pedestal has some strange carvings. There appears to be a winged creature, some kind of reptilian being, a humanoid figure with an enlarged head and eyes, and another creature resembling something that might live in the ocean. We believe they represent four different races who may have worked together to build this temple."

"Great," said Ray, rolling his eyes. It was weird enough that *one* alien race might have built this place. But four working together? He was almost afraid to ask. "Have you met any... aliens… who look like any of them?"

Simeon shook his head. "Not precisely. One of the builders appears very humanoid, but clearly isn't human. The others represent animals found on Eden and other planets. But again, still aren't the same. They may have used their own DNA to help seed our worlds. But we really don't know."

"It's a mystery," said Uncle Charlie. "And not all mysteries like to be solved." He smiled.

"What's that supposed to mean?" asked one Luke.

"Yeah. Is there anything *else* you've been keeping a secret from us, Uncle?" asked the other Luke.

Ray shook his head. "I still can't get used to there being two of him."

Dawn giggled.

"Luke," Charlie said to one. "And Luke," he said to the other. "I'm an old man. There's lots of things I know. But I'm not purposefully trying to keep secrets from you."

One Luke asked, "But is there anything else, right now, that you might want to share?" The other Luke agreed. "Yeah," he said.

Charlie thought about it. He started nodding. "Actually, yes, there is something you should know. I'm a little bit worried about that other crystal Mastermind has. I can't figure where he might've gotten it."

Dawn said, "Well, obviously there's more than one. They have one here on Eden."

"An inactive one," Simeon clarified. "Stopped working several millennia ago."

"Right," said Charlie. "I thought I had the only working one. If Mastermind's had another one all along – then that might explain how he kept disappearing every so often. But I'm concerned where he might've gone. He may already be a lot more powerful than we realize."

"Perfect," said Ray.

"Well, we can't worry about that now," said one Luke. "We gotta focus on the mission at hand. And speaking of, how are we supposed to get back home from England, anyway? I doubt anyone brought their passports."

Dawn suddenly stopped to lean against the wall. She looked very tired. "You okay?" Ray asked her.

She shook her head. She looked really uncomfortable. Like she was about to throw up.

"Dawn?" Ray asked again. Everyone stopped and turned toward her. She looked really, really sick.

Her face started changing. The position of her eyes, nose, mouth, and ears started to droop and shift out of place. Then they slowly moved back, and she looked normal again.

"I don't feel so good," Dawn said.

Charlie checked her pulse. "Your body temperature seems to be running a little high," he said. He counted her heartbeat against his watch. "Heart rate's a little fast, too."

"Exhaustion from pulling an all-nighter, and all the stress of everything, maybe?" the other Luke suggested.

"Maybe," said Charlie.

"If anything's wrong with her," said Simeon, "the healing chamber will repair her."

"Right! Good thinking. Let's get you to the healing chamber," Ray urged.

Dawn seemed to gain her balance. She stood on her own two feet. "I'm fine. I'm feeling better now. Probably just too much sun and excitement today. Not enough sleep or food, is all."

"Well, still," said Ray.

"I'm fine, really." She seemed to be getting better. "See?" she said, smiling, being strong and brave. "No big deal."

Ray didn't believe her. "Well, we need the quick recharge anyway. Might as well have you all checked out while we're there. Just to be sure."

"Yeah," said one Luke. "It healed Uncle Charlie from that snake bite."

"If you can call that a snake," Charlie laughed.

"Here," said Ray, helping her lean on him. "Let's go." Ray supported her the rest of the way.

A few minutes later, they were at the entrance to the healing chamber. It looked just like the medical lab back in the other pyramid. Almost perfectly identical, even down to the various medical tools and alien devices.

They laid Dawn down on the table first. The beams of light scanned her. But then it made a strange noise. The kind of beep a computer normally makes when an error has occurred.

The light beams tried scanning her again. A second later, it made the same error sound.

"That's weird," said Simeon. "Never heard it do that before."

It tried scanning her a third time. Same noise.

A disembodied voice came from above. It spoke in an unfamiliar language. Then it repeated in a second language, and a third, then with a bunch of clicking and crackling sounds – probably a fourth alien language – and a fifth language, filled with high pitch squeals and screeches. It was really loud. Everyone had to cover their ears. Then a sixth alien language, which fortunately, sounded an awful lot like English.

It said, "Error. Cannot identify genome."

Then it continued the same error message in French, Spanish, Latin, Gaelic, Hindi...

"Can you shut that thing off?" asked Charlie.

Simeon shook his head, shrugging. "Uh, thank you, cease message. Message received."

It finally stopped.

A Luke sighed. "Much better."

"What's a genome?" asked Ray.

"A person's genetic profile," said the other Luke.

"It should've recognized her," said Charlie. "Could it be broken? The other chamber had no problem scanning me or Luke."

Simeon shook his head. "Should be working properly."

"What's wrong?" asked Dawn.

Simeon looked really confused. "The scanners can't identify your species," he said. "Since it doesn't know what your optimal biological state should look like, it can't fix or repair anything."

"Could it have something to do with her power?" one of the Lukes asked.

"Shape-shifting?" Simeon responded. "It shouldn't. We've had several shape-shifters before. The Temple never had a problem with it."

"Yeah, but," reasoned Luke, "all those shape-shifters got their power from the sphere, right? From the, what was it called?"

"Altar of Destiny," Charlie said.

"Right. That."

Simeon looked confused again. "She got her power another way?"

"Mastermind injected me with some weird chemical," she said, sitting up. "It was supposed to turn me into a mutant."

"But you never got the animal blood," said Ray. "You never got the new DNA to mix with yours."

"Let's test something," said Simeon. "Someone else try getting scanned."

Ray volunteered. He hopped right onto the table. Lights from overhead began scanning him. The process continued without error. The holographic doctor appeared.

"Definitely not broken," said Simeon.

"I've completed my diagnostic. Are you ready to be repaired?" asked the holographic doctor.

Ray got up and off the table. The holographic doctor disappeared. Ray was more concerned for Dawn right now. "Are you sure you're still feeling okay?"

"I'm fine. I swear. Just got a little woozy for a minute back there. It's nothing. I'm all better now."

"Promise?" he asked her.

"I'm positive."

"Can't you just tell the computer she's human?" asked Charlie. "Let it scan her based on that?"

Simeon shrugged. "This has never happened before. But we can try."

"Okay," said Dawn. She got back onto the table and laid down.

The lights started scanning her again. The error message – in every known language throughout the galaxy – began again.

"Thank you!" Simeon shouted toward the ceiling. "She's human. Just like the rest of us here. Please use that genome for your diagnostics."

It tried scanning her again. And it still made the same error noise. "Unable. Genome incompatible," the computer voice said.

"Override," said Simeon. "Ignore genome."

It made that error noise again. "Unable. Genome required for protocol. Unable to identify genome. Specified genome incompatible. Error. Subject not in database.

Unable to continue."

Simeon muttered under his breath. "Useless alien technology…"

Dawn sat back up. "So what? It's fine. So I don't get an artificial super nap. Big deal. I'm fine. We're wasting time. Mastermind's out there and we're in here arguing with a—"

Ray helped her down.

"I'm fine, really," she said. "Just get me some food and I'll be back to normal. Probably was just low blood sugar or something."

"Alright," said Ray. "If you're sure. But if you feel sick or dizzy again—"

"Stop worrying about me," she said, smiling, almost laughing. "I'll be fine. But thank you. You're really sweet." She gave him a quick kiss. "Now get on there, get all recharged, and let's keep moving."

Ray sat on the table. Somehow this didn't feel right. But they had come all this way. And they needed every edge they could get against Mastermind. Poor judgment, slow reaction time, and tired muscles from a lack of sleep would all spell disaster in the heat of battle.

Wow. Battle. They were actually going to fight. Probably. Not that he wanted to. Not that any of them wanted to. But they had to.

He laid down on the table.

After scanning him, the holographic doctor appeared, and offered to "repair" Ray. It healed and strengthened him from the inside out. Rejuvenated and revitalized all his cells and organs. He felt like a new man. Like he just had the best night's sleep of his life. Almost like his entire body got a tune-up and cleansing. He felt *great*!

"Wow," he said. "This is really cool."

"Does this mean you'll be leaving Eden now?" asked Simeon.

Charlie nodded. "Seems so. Wish us luck."

"I regret that I cannot join you. But you know our laws."

"I understand," said Charlie. He looked to the four of them – Luke, the other Luke, Ray, and Dawn. "Ready?"

They all were in agreement. They didn't like it. But they knew what they had to do. They all wished they had more time. To better know how to use their powers. Maybe work out a better plan that didn't require them fighting a mind-controlling madman and his mutant henchmen.

God, they felt so unprepared.

They just wished they were ready enough. They hoped they'd come out ahead. And not end up dead – or worse, mutated slaves of Mastermind.

But that's exactly why they had to fight him. So there would be no more mutant slaves. So they could prevent whatever evil he had planned.

"You know, this reminds me of a quote I once heard," one of the Lukes said. "All evil needs to triumph in this world is for good people to do nothing."

"Edmund Burke," said the other Luke, crediting the person who first said it.

Charlie looked at both Lukes. His nephew had a lot of heart. A lot of courage. A strong sense of justice and heroism. Just like his parents. They really wanted to keep Luke sheltered from this life. Charlie wished he could've honored that request.

"I can't ask any of you to do this," said Charlie. "Mastermind was my fault."

"We're all involved now," said Ray. "The minute Mastermind came to our restaurant table and started mind-controlling us, we got involved."

Ray and Dawn had a lot of heart and courage, too.

"Don't worry about it, Charlie," said Dawn. "I have a feeling we're gonna win." She smiled.

That feeling was about to be tested.

And at that very moment, a portal opened at the garden of Eden. Mastermind stepped through, followed by his five mutant slaves: Rhino-Man, Kraken, Venom, Slimer, and Arachnus.

"What makes you so sure they're here, boss?" asked Rhino-Man.

"Call it a hunch." Mastermind stepped forward. Beautiful nature all around. Butterflies. Flowers. Prettiness everywhere. Now, where was…

Ethos suddenly appeared. "Welcome!" he said. "Welcome to Eden. I'm Ethos, Visitor Liaison. What brings you here today?"

And there he was.

"Venom," Mastermind said. "Kill him."

She struck with unfathomable speed and suddenness. The mutant snake woman dug her long fangs deep into his neck, instantly releasing black poison into his blood.

It all happened so fast.

It was as if she came out of nowhere.

The man's eyes were filled with both sudden horror and unspeakable pain. "But… why?" were his last words.

Ethos fell dead to the ground.

"That ought to get their attention," said Mastermind.

Back inside the healing chamber, Simeon suddenly stared off blankly into space. Like he was on pause.

Everyone looked at him.

"That weirds me out every time he does that," Ray said.

"Yeah," agreed Dawn.

He returned his focus to them. The look on his face was inexpressible. Shocked. Terrified. Stunned. "Someone just entered through the gateway – and killed the Visitor Liaison."

Ray, Luke, Dawn, the other Luke, and Charlie all looked at each other. They knew exactly who it was.

"I really wish we had a better plan," said Ray.

The two Lukes faced each other. "We do have *one* element of surprise…" one of them said.

"I've got it!" said the first Luke. "I'll go back in time – up to five minutes, right? – and warn us Mastermind's about to come through the portal. Simeon, you can warn the Visitor Liaison from here, right?"

Simeon nodded.

"Good. Meanwhile, the rest of us will rush toward the portal. Get the jump on him. Push him back. Or something. Uncle, if we open our own portal on that exact same spot, will it prevent him from re-opening his portal to here?"

"I… I suppose so," said the old man. "I've never tried it."

"Well we're about to find out!" said that Luke. He closed his eyes, preparing to move through time.

"Wait!" said Dawn. "Won't changing your own history create *another* duplicate?"

"Um… Maybe?" said that Luke. "It's a chance we'll have to take. Every second we wait is one less second we'll have…"

"Go!" said Charlie. "Good luck."

Luke closed his eyes again. He concentrated. Five minutes. That's all he could do. But it would have to work. Five minutes. Come on… just five freaking minutes into the past.

He opened his eyes.

They were all still there, watching, waiting.

"Did it work?"

Charlie sighed and looked down. Ray shook his head.

"What? I thought I could still do five minutes!"

"Let me try," said the other Luke. He closed his eyes. Focused on going as far back in time as he possibly could. It worked – sort of.

Everything around him shifted into a red blur. Suddenly he found himself in the past… but not quite five minutes in the past.

"I've got it!" said the first Luke. "I'll go back in time – up to five minutes, right? – and warn us Mastermind's about to come through the portal. Simeon, you can warn the Visitor Liaison from here, right?"

Everyone turned to see a *third* Luke suddenly in their presence.

"Uh oh," said that future, third Luke. He closed his eyes and immediately went back to the future. It took a *lot* of effort. But he made it – barely.

He reappeared a half a second *before* his previous self time-traveled backwards. Normally he'd try to arrive the second after he left, to make it like he was never gone.

Instead, he saw himself disappear the instant he arrived. Talk about a weird experience.

"Not good," he told the others.

"What happened?" asked Dawn. "You were the third Luke we saw just a couple minutes ago, weren't you?"

He nodded. He still only saw one other of him. "Looks like I didn't create any paradox duplicates, though. That's a relief."

"Yeah," said the first Luke. "We figured something was going on, but didn't know what. So we decided to act like we never saw you – let the timeline play out normally, best as possible. Guess it worked."

"Might've thrown events off by a few seconds, though. I shouldn't have seen myself leaving. I got back a second too early."

"But when we saw you… that wasn't five minutes ago. That was like, what, a minute, maybe two?" said Dawn.

Luke – the one who just time traveled – shook his head. "My range is decreasing."

"Hey, I can't even time travel at all anymore!" exclaimed the first Luke.

"You time traveled more recently than I did," said the other. "Right? Maybe it's not a range limit thing – maybe it's an energy limit thing."

"Come again?" said Ray.

The first Luke lit up. "Yeah. Like maybe we just need to recharge first. Maybe we can only do so much time traveling before the power gets all used up."

They both looked to Simeon for an answer.

"Just a minute," he said. He stared blankly ahead again.

"Why does he keep doing that?" Dawn asked.

Simeon returned. "There was one other case of someone who received a temporal manipulation power from the Altar of Destiny. After extensive tests, we discovered that use of her power diminished over time, but yes, after a period of rest, she could use her power fully again."

"Ah-hah!" said one Luke.

"So that's it!" said the other.

"Yes, well, that's all good," said Charlie. "But that doesn't help us against Mastermind right now."

Ray and Dawn turned to each other. "Looks like it's up to us," Ray said. "What are we going to do?"

"Fight him?" said Dawn.

"I really wish we didn't have to. Sure we can't try to negotiate with him or something?" Ray asked.

"Be my guest," she said.

"I know," he sighed. "I'm just not exactly trained for this sort of thing, ya know?"

"Me neither," said Dawn.

If anyone in that room believed this could be resolved peacefully – they would have done it by now.

Mastermind was on a mission. And nothing would stop him – except, just maybe, a couple of young adults with new super powers.

"You ready?" asked Ray.

Dawn shook her head. "No. But let's do this."

Chapter 23

THE SECRET OF EDEN

Mastermind waited impatiently with his arms crossed, foot tapping the ground. It had been several minutes. Where were they? These people had teleportation technology. It shouldn't take them this long. Geez, even in the future things took forever to happen.

Assuming this even was the future. Chuck seemed to believe it was. Mastermind wasn't so sure. Mainly because there was no evidence of his eventual and inevitable rise to power and rule over Planet Earth. And to his knowledge, all other portal destinations were other *planets*, not other time periods.

Ethos, the Visitor Liaison, laid dead on the ground. His veins turned black and swollen around the bite wound. Venom wiped her mouth clean. She actually enjoyed that.

Rhino-Man looked around. What were they waiting on? Who were they waiting for? He was ready and willing to obey his master – whatever that might mean – but he hoped it wouldn't come to a fight. Yeah, sure, he was big and strong and tough – and had a huge rhinoceros horn on his face – but beneath that tough exterior was, believe it or not, a decent guy.

At least he used to be. Before Mastermind gave him this new body and life. He liked serving Mastermind. Or maybe feared disobeying him. He wasn't sure. And now that he was a mutant, where else could he go? What else would he do?

Hard to imagine that just earlier that day, he was robbing a local bank. Yeah, it wasn't the smartest thing he ever did. He had robbed a couple convenience stores, gas stations, and places like that before. No one ever got hurt. They lost some money. Big deal. They had plenty of it. He, on the other hand, was struggling to get by. Times were tough. He didn't choose to be a criminal. He just got desperate and sort of fell into it.

Maybe he got a little too ambitious hitting that bank. That's how he ended up in jail with the others – and then Mastermind. And in a dizzying blur of confusion and chaos, he suddenly found himself with a new body and a new purpose. A rhinoceros-man, serving his master, working towards some greater purpose. What, exactly, that purpose was, he still didn't know. None of his fellow mutants knew.

He was along for the ride. He belonged to Mastermind now. But he was no killer. After watching the snake-lady Venom strike and kill that innocent guy in the blink of an eye – it unnerved him a little.

Would Mastermind turn them all into killers?

Charlie and the others hid safely behind some trees and large rocks elsewhere in the garden. They were a fair distance away, safe from being spotted or heard by Mastermind, but still close enough to attack as soon as they figured out their strategy.

"Okay," said Charlie, using his super vision to get a close look on their opponents. "It looks like it's just Mastermind and his five mutants. Luke, I don't see another one of you there, so either there's no other copy or he escaped."

"That's good," both Lukes sighed with relief.

"What about that mad scientist?" asked Dawn.

"Don't see him either."

"Does he have any glowing green chemicals with him?" Ray asked.

"Not that I can see," said Charlie.

"I hope our power doesn't take too long to recharge," said one Luke.

"Yeah," said the other. "What good is time travel if you can't use it?"

"Mastermind's saying something," interrupted Charlie.

"What's he saying?" asked Dawn.

"I don't know," Charlie said to her. "I have super vision, not super hearing."

"We need a plan," said Ray.

"Looks like he's ordering his mutants to spread out," Charlie said.

"Ray," one Luke said, "can you levitate Mastermind up into the air, keep him suspended and facing away, so he can't make eye contact with anyone?"

"That's a good idea," he said.

"Maybe we can dump him in a portal," said Dawn. "Drop him off on some uninhabited world and leave him stranded there."

"We'll have to steal his crystal first," said the other Luke.

"I see it," said Charlie. "Astaria crystals give off a unique energy. It's in his right pocket."

"Alright, I've got it," said Dawn. "Ray, you hold him up in the air. I'll shape-shift to stretch my arms up, reach into his pocket, and pull it out. Luke, you open a portal somewhere where he can't harm anybody – ever."

"Sounds great," said Luke. "But what about the mutants?"

"Leave that to me," said the other Luke. "I'll create a diversion. Distract them. Make them chase after me."

"That's suicide!" said Charlie.

"Maybe my power will be recharged enough for me to make a quick escape in time. I hope."

"No," Charlie shook his head. "Too risky."

"Maybe we can push them into the same portal with Mastermind," reasoned Dawn.

"Simeon," Luke said, turning to him, "don't you guys have some technology we can use? Can't you just teleport them all away, lock them in a stasis field, or something?"

Simeon shook his head. "We can't get involved."

"What do you mean?" Ray asked.

"It's against our laws."

"Well your laws are stupid," said Dawn. "He just killed one of your people! How come no one's trying to arrest him? Is he *that* dangerous, even to you, with all your super technology?"

"It's not that," said Simeon.

"He can't get involved," said Charlie. "Not without risking much worse."

"What do you mean?" asked one of the Lukes.

"I don't understand," said Dawn.

Simeon sighed. "Believe me, I wish we could. But that would break the peace treaty."

"Peace treaty?" asked Ray.

Charlie kept an eye on all the mutants. So far, they were all still just waiting around.

Simeon nodded. "Eden hasn't always enjoyed the peace and prosperity you see today. Centuries ago, our people used the Altar of Destiny quite extensively. Nearly every man, woman, and child on this planet had at least one super power. Which, as you can imagine, led to a lot of conflicts and civil wars. A lot of chaos, destruction on all sides, and constant civil unrest. Our economy nearly collapsed. Our world, a once great and mighty civilization, was in ruins. But it got worse than that."

"Damn," said Ray. "How do you get much worse than that?"

"We were the only planet with a temple," Simeon explained. "We soon became a planet of gods – and some of the more ambitious gods wanted to expand our empire, or extract resources for their wars, from other worlds. The people we attacked didn't stand a chance. We decimated other worlds for our own gain and selfish reasons, and made many enemies in the process."

"Um," Ray said, wanting to clarify, "when you say 'people', you mean other alien races, right?"

Simeon nodded. "That's correct."

"Got it," said Ray. "Just double checking."

"Over a matter of several decades, we became the galaxy's greatest threat. *Every* other race wanted us destroyed. They collectively banded together and sent wave after wave of attacks against us for several decades. We had powers and the temple – but their sheer numbers and powerful weapons eventually destroyed us. Eden was nearly wiped out. And finally, the remaining survivors surrendered, and a peace treaty was formed."

"Oh my God," said a Luke.

Charlie still watched Mastermind and the mutants. The ugly squid monster guy wandered into a small pond. The snake lady hid behind a few trees. But Charlie's super vision made it super easy to track them all.

Simeon continued explaining, "The only peaceful solution was to forbid all future generations from using the Altar of Destiny. No one from Eden was allowed to have powers ever again. And all other races – all visitors, regardless of race or planet of origin – would be allowed to use the temple at will, no exceptions.

"We feared this would make Eden even more vulnerable to attack, so it was also written into the treaty that Eden would become a political neutral zone, a planet of perpetual peace, protected by all the other races. This ensured that the temple would remain neutral and available to all.

"Since then, there have been a few attacks or attempts to take exclusive control over the temple – but all the other races quickly came to our defense and protection, secured the pyramid, and pushed back the intruders.

"That's why the people of Eden are caretakers of the temple – but cannot engage in any conflicts or give ourselves any powers. In the event any trouble comes to us, as it has again today, we are to wait for our extraterrestrial protectors to come and save us."

"That's terrible," said the other Luke.

"You guys are defenseless victims," said Ray.

Simeon shook his head. "We are extremely well protected."

"Yeah," said Ray, "by some Big Brother in the sky!"

"We deserve it," said Simeon. "Our people proved to the galaxy that we cannot be trusted with such power. That peace treaty was the best thing that ever happened to Eden. Since then, our economy has stabilized, we've rebuilt our civilization, and have enjoyed centuries of peace and prosperity. We rarely suffer any threats for long. The others keep us safe. We are a peaceful, open, neutral place for all races. Including yours."

"Then why haven't we seen any of these other races yet?" asked Ray. "Where are they? If this really was some interplanetary utopian society, where are all the other aliens?"

"An amendment to the peace treaty," Simeon added. "Any race may visit and use our temple – but only Edenites may live here. It was a way to keep this planet as our own."

Charlie kept an eye on Mastermind. The villain still stood waiting by the portal entrance, in the garden. None of the mutants wandered too far either. And their attempts to hide where no match for Charlie's heat vision.

"So what about Mastermind now?" asked Dawn.

"You are aliens," said Simeon. "You may take care of him. If you don't, or if you fail, others will come and protect Eden."

"Yeah, but," said Ray, "what if Mastermind kills a bunch of more people, or mutates everybody, while you're waiting?"

Simeon shook his head. "That is the price we pay for the terror we once spread across the galaxy centuries ago."

"Don't worry," said Dawn. "We're not going to let that happen."

"Yeah," said one Luke.

"We're super heroes," said the other.

"Think you can time travel again yet?" Ray asked them both. "Which one volunteered to be the diversion again?"

"I did," one Luke raised his hand.

The other Luke put his hand on the first Luke's shoulder. "Good luck, man."

"Thanks man."

Dawn mentioned, "We do have the element of surprise. I say we send that mind-controlling monster somewhere he can't hurt anyone ever again! Okay, so we all know what we're doing? Everybody ready?"

Ray nodded. "Good luck to us all."

Mastermind checked his watch. Come on, what was taking so long? They just killed an innocent guy for Pete's sake! Where were the law authorities? Where was Chuck and those annoying kids?

Arachnus had climbed up into a tree and hid there. Venom lurked behind some trees with large leaves – her scaly green skin blended in nicely. Rhino-Man stood guard, in place, with his arms crossed. Slimer also waited out in the open. She was no fighter – but perhaps if she saw someone coming, she could slow them down and bury them under a pile of her sticky bodily goo.

The garden and surrounding landscape was beautiful. A nature paradise. But no one was coming. Surely these people had scanners and detectors everywhere. They had some kind of artificial telepathic communication too. Did no one notice or care that – what was his name again, Ethos? – was gone?

Maybe he was wrong. Maybe Chuck and the others didn't come here after all.

But then… just as he reached for the crystal in his pocket to go home, he spotted Luke approaching in the distance. "Ahh, at last," said Mastermind. "Please tell me they sent more than just you."

Luke knees were trembling. He was so nervous. He tightened his fists. He must not be afraid. He could do this. This was what being a hero was all about. Facing one's fears, doing what's right, risking your own well-being for the safety of others. Being a hero wasn't about cool powers and flashy costumes. No. It was about standing up to powerful demons – even if that demon was a mind-controlling madman who killed your own parents.

Mastermind must die.

The plan was just to banish Mastermind and his mutants to some isolated planet where they couldn't harm anyone ever again. But maybe, a sizeable part of Luke hoped, something would happen that would "accidentally" kill this man.

Luke walked closer.

At least, that was how it always happened in the comic books. Heroes weren't supposed to kill. But they didn't have to save the villain either. Maybe one of his mutants will accidentally kill him somehow. That'd be poetic justice.

"I know about your little 'power'," Mastermind said.

That stopped Luke dead in his tracks. "You do?"

Only way he could know that was if another Luke did appear out of the sphere earlier. Made sense. There was always a copy whenever he changed his own timeline. Hmm. Hopefully that Luke escaped, though. Maybe he's back on Earth already.

Wait. If that Luke did escape – and of course he did – to Mastermind's perspective, it would've just looked like Luke simply disappeared. Did that mean Mastermind assumed Luke had the power to teleport or turn invisible – but had no idea he could actually time travel?

"Your parents would've been proud," the madman mocked.

Luke tightened his fists.

Mastermind smirked. "But if you were going to change history, you would have by now. The mere fact that you stand before me now says either you can't – or you've already failed."

Damn. He knew everything.

Alright. It's okay. Just keep him talking. Keep him distracted. Luke still kept a safe distance away, but felt a little too close for comfort. He tried to keep an eye on the nearby mutants. The rhino guy and slime girl were there. Uncle Charlie said the spider one was up in a tree a little ways over to the side. The snake lady hid on the opposite side behind some trees.

Knowing their location – thanks to Uncle Charlie's super sight – allowed Luke to watch his step, keeping himself relatively safe. Relatively. He still sensed the very real danger. If he were Spider-Man, his spider senses would've been tingling like crazy right now. But what was he worried about? He was better than Spider-Man! He could time travel. Hopefully, if his power had recharged enough by now.

Then again, maybe the ability to sling a web and escape quickly would've been better after all…

As for Ray and Dawn – their plan required a little more precision and planning – and a lot more risk.

"Maybe I just wanted to talk to you first," Luke said to Mastermind. "Try to reason with you. Surely we can come to some sort of peaceful arrangement."

Mastermind laughed, crossing his arms. Clearly this boy was up to something. Chuck would've never sent his nephew in alone or unprotected. "Oh Chuck? Chucky-boy, old pal? Where are you, old man?"

Uncle Charlie was still back at their original hiding spot, with the other Luke and Simeon, watching everything carefully.

"Why are you mutating people?" Luke asked.

Mastermind raised an eyebrow. "Where's your uncle, kid?"

"If you know I can time travel, you know I have the power to go back in time and stop you – before you even know what's happening. I can stop you from mutating anyone. I can stop you from killing my parents." He stood bravely. "I can even prevent you from being born."

Mastermind laughed. "Then why haven't you?"

"Because I'm one of the good guys," said Luke. "And we don't use our powers for evil. I'm giving you a chance. Give up. Surrender. Let's end this peacefully, now."

"Oh, there will be peace, my friend," he said.

"You're surrendering?"

Mastermind laughed out loud. "Surrender? No, my boy. Not today. Not tomorrow. Not even after the final star burns out and the entire universe goes dark. I am Mastermind. Lord of all creation. Master of all living things. God above gods. And before this day is over, I'll have recreated the entire world as I see fit!"

Oh. So they were on a deadline. Good to know. "You're no god," said Luke.

"Oh, but I am."

Luke glanced up at the sky.

"There's only one God I know of – and you're not him."

Mastermind noticed Luke's brief glance skyward. What was he up to? Mastermind quickly turned around and looked up.

A giant eagle – no, more like a fearsome gryphon – swooped down upon him. The gryphon's wings flapped and swatted, overwhelming Mastermind, knocking him backwards onto the ground. "What the hell? Stupid bird! Get the hell off me!" he shouted.

The giant gryphon stood on top of him, talons extended, gripping and holding down each arm. The feathery beast let out a victorious ear-piercing screech.

Rhino-Man, standing nearby, didn't know what to do. His master was in trouble. Only one thing a rhinoceros-man could do – *charge!*

His horn pounded the gryphon's side with punishing impact, sending the giant mythical eagle-like creature tumbling away. The gryphon quickly flapped its wings, regained control, and flew back towards them.

"Slimer, cover the wings!" Mastermind ordered.

Slimer slid across the ground, racing closer, hands extended. Her slimy, sticky goo shot out, splashing through the air, colliding with the gryphon's feathers.

Mastermind chuckled. The beastly bird crashed into the ground, unable to fly another inch farther. "How's it feel to—" He stopped himself abruptly. Something pink was floating right in front of his face. "What the?"

His Astaria crystal had somehow levitated right out of his pocket and up into the air. He reached for it, but the crystal moved away, rising even higher. Mastermind jumped to grab it a second time – he missed, and his floating crystal dodged up higher and escaped farther away into the sky!

Mastermind looked around. "Who's doing that?" Who had a levitation power? It must be that black kid again. He had some kind of telekinetic ability. "Show yourself!"

He didn't have to. The crystal revealed Ray's whereabouts. Mastermind watched it float towards one of the trees. That's where he spotted Ray. The kid sat on a branch, hand extended, drawing the crystal ever closer to him.

"That's *mine*!" Mastermind declared.

The gryphon shape-shifted back into Dawn's natural form – minus her clothes, unfortunately. She really wished she could transform her clothes along with her body. But it didn't matter. She immediately shook off as much of the goo as she could, and began assuming her next form.

"Oh no you don't!" Slimer exclaimed. She doused Dawn with more sticky slime and goo.

But Dawn was one step ahead of her. Being covered in slime wasn't a problem –

if she was made of slime too! Dawn shape-shifted her molecules to be very similar to Slimer's body. Now there stood two slime girls – and Slimer could cover Dawn with as much slime and goo as she wanted. It wouldn't slow Dawn down now.

"Hey, no fair! That's my power!" exclaimed Slimer.

Ray reached out and snatched Mastermind's crystal out of the air. Got it. Perfect. This plan was going flawlessly. "I got it!" he shouted to Dawn.

What he didn't see was Arachnus, the spider mutant, leaping from treetop to treetop, quickly coming down upon him, until suddenly – *pounce* – he ensnared Ray with all of his spider-like legs and the two tumbled down and rolled out of the tree.

Ray accidentally dropped the crystal. Arachnus exposed his giant spider fangs and went down to bite Ray. But reflexively – maybe from seeing those fangs, maybe just because a giant spider was on top of him – Ray used his power to throw Arachnus off him and several feet away. The flying spider caught a nearby tree branch, swung around, and jumped back into the action.

Rhino-Man swung his massive gray fist at Dawn, who skillfully swerved out of the way. This slime-based body was extremely agile and flexible. She could bend in all sorts of ways now. Rhino-Man threw another punch. She dodged. He charged forward, rhino horn first, but she gracefully slid out of the way and flicked a little goo on him just for fun.

Luke saw Mastermind's crystal on the ground. Ray and Arachnus fought constantly – Ray pushed the spider mutant away, he leaped back; Ray levitated himself up into the air to get away, the spider mutant shot him with a web and lassoed him back down. "I'm *really* beginning to hate spiders!" Ray exclaimed. Arachnus tackled him. Ray levitated a nearby rock and flung it at the mutant's head.

Luke ran towards the crystal.

So did Mastermind.

Suddenly Luke crashed into something and fell onto his butt – but nothing was there. Did he just collide into solid air?

A cat-like humanoid form emerged in front of him. Shadow smiled, twirling her tail, becoming completely visible. "You didn't forget about me, did you?"

Luke scurried backwards. She could turn invisible? Great. It was only safe to assume *all* the mutants had powers now.

Rhino-Man swung at Dawn again. She dodged again, laughing at him. "I can do this all day!" she said.

He huffed and he puffed. "Stop that! Play fair!" he demanded. He snorted through his large rhino nostrils. He swung again – and missed! Dawn giggled with delight.

Rhino-Man growled loudly and then stomped his foot *hard* into the ground. It created a small earthquake. The vibrations sent shockwaves through the ground. And Dawn's semi-liquid state reverberated with it, and she temporarily dissolved into a gooey puddle – as did Slimer, unfortunately.

Rhino-Man stomped the ground again. Another earthquake. Dawn couldn't rematerialize. Her goo-like body just rippled and vibrated uncontrollably in the powerful tremors. She couldn't stabilize herself into a solid form. Rhino-Man stomped again. Another earthquake. Slimer didn't appreciate this at all either, but at least they had disabled Dawn.

Dawn had no choice but to return to human form. She began shape-shifting back. And just as her human flesh returned to normal, Rhino-Man grabbed both her arms and held her in an inescapable grip. He lifted her up off the ground. Her feet dangled, kicking and squirming. Now Rhino-Man was the one laughing.

Shadow slashed at Luke with her cat claws. He jumped back to avoid the first lash. The crystal was just over there. So close. He glanced at Shadow. She made another swing. He ducked, rolled, and dashed over toward the crystal.

Did he *actually* just do that awesome move? Watching all those action movies finally paid off! He ran so hard and fast towards the crystal he nearly tripped over himself.

Maybe he was just lucky. Didn't want to feel those claws slice into his skin.

He stumbled forward. So close. He reached out for the crystal. Just inches away.

Mastermind stepped back.

Luke grabbed the crystal.

"I got it!" he exclaimed.

And Venom sprung out from behind the plants, fangs exposed, and struck – deep and hard.

"OWWW!!!" Her teeth sank into Luke's back, through his clothes, releasing her black poison deep into his body.

The intense pain shot like lightning throughout his entire body. His muscles tightened and convulsed. He lost all feeling in his legs. He fell down. Luke gasped for air. He couldn't breathe. His grip weakened. The crystal fell out of his hand.

It rolled away from him.

The last thing Luke saw was Mastermind's foot stopping the crystal. The madman leaned down to pick it up, giving Luke a sinister smile.

Everything went black.

Luke lost his final breath.

"Good work, Venom."

A safe distance away, Charlie saw the whole thing. "LUKE!!!" the old man screamed. Tears swelled in his eyes. He couldn't breathe. "Luke…" he whispered.

"What?" asked the other Luke, still standing nearby.

Charlie was speechless. Tears streamed down his face. He shook his head.

"What happened?" demanded the other Luke.

Charlie turned to him. "You… You're… dead."

"I'm what?!"

"That snake lady, she just – oh my God, he's dead."

Luke's face went numb. "I…" He had no idea what to think. He, of course, believed he was the *original* Luke. But so did the other one. Was he really the original Luke? What if *he* was the paradox duplicate?

Such a weird metaphysical experience.

Luke was dead – but this other Luke, from a slightly different timeline, was still alive. He swallowed hard. What if the paradox-preventing laws of time travel worked so that if *one* of them died, all the others would too?

Uncle Charlie immediately hugged the Luke next to him.

Luke's heart raced. Was he feeling okay? He felt a little dizzy. Oh my God. Oh my God. Oh my God. He was about to die too. He could feel it. Some timeline-fixing law of the universe. He felt tingly. He felt sick.

…

Eh, well, then again, maybe not. He was still alive. Still breathing. No part of his body was starting to fade away or anything. Actually, he felt fine. Aside from freaking himself out.

"I'm so sorry, Luke. This is all my fault," said Charlie. "I'm so sorry…"

Luke's heart started to calm down. He was still breathing. Still fine. Apparently he was safe. The timelines weren't connected. One version of him was dead – but, it seemed, this version of him was safe. At least for now. "Uncle…" he said.

"What have I done?" Charlie muttered.

"I don't want to die," said Luke.

"I know," Charlie sniffled. "No one does."

"I – the other me – is he really... gone?"

Charlie nodded. "I'm so sorry."

Luke didn't know what to think.

"But I'm still here," he finally said.

"I know," smiled Charlie, holding Luke closer. "I know…"

Did his power recharge enough yet to go back in time and save… himself?

Dawn started shape-shifting again to escape Rhino-Man's death grip. If she could turn into an amorphous slime-based person, maybe she could turn completely into organic, living water. Sure, it sounded good. It was worth a try.

It worked. She ran through his fingers like… well… water. She splashed onto the ground, reformed herself into a human-like shape, and started running – more like sliding – away. The grass left a wet trail in her wake. Slimer flung some goo at her, but it splashed right through her, and Dawn continued to flee towards Ray.

Mastermind held the crystal in his hand. "Venom, Shadow, take care of the other two."

The two female mutants headed to the nearest one: Ray. He and Arachnus seemed to be locked in an equally-matched struggle. Neither could get away, or get the upper hand, for long.

Rhino-Man and Slimer chased after the water-based Dawn. She glided so freely across the ground. Moving swiftly, flowing effortlessly, she was like one with the… one with the… uh oh.

Something didn't feel right.

Dawn's body randomly started shape-shifting. One foot turned into a talon; the other into a goat's leg and hoof. Her left arm had lots of fur; her right arm was long and loose like a string of spaghetti. Her insides felt like they were turning inside out. She felt really sick all of the sudden.

She felt dizzy, in pain – and collapsed forward onto the ground.

Rhino-Man grabbed her hoof-foot and picked her up, upside down. She hung in the air, still shape-shifting uncontrollably. Horns grew out of her head, then disappeared; wings appeared on her back, then a tail appeared, then her entire body became like melting silly putty. She stretched and oozed toward the ground, slipping right out of his grip.

Dawn, a deformed mess of random mutations on the ground, could not regain control herself.

Slimer laughed. "Not so hot now, are ya?"

"P-Please… help…" Dawn cried.

Ray heard her voice. He turned to look. Just then Arachnus had the upper hand he'd been waiting for. He bit Ray. "Ahhhh!!!!" Ray exclaimed. Right in the shoulder. Son of a bitch!

He felt suddenly dizzy, and weak.

"We need to go now," said Charlie, urgently.

"What? What's going on? Now what? Did they get the crystal?" Luke asked.

Charlie grabbed Luke's shirt and pulled him closer. "Simeon, teleport us close to Dawn and Ray, *now*!"

"But you'll be—"

"I KNOW!" exclaimed Charlie. "DO IT!"

Simeon nodded. Charlie and Luke vanished in the blink of an eye.

Charlie held onto Luke. He reached over to grab Ray. "Luke, get your crystal ready!" he said urgently.

Venom and Shadow stopped dead in their tracks. *Another* Luke? Arachnus exposed his fangs again, simultaneously extending all his spider-like arms and legs, preparing to attack.

Luke reached into his pocket as quickly as he could and pulled out his crystal.

"And run!" Charlie exclaimed.

"Where?" Luke shouted, already running.

Arachnus launched forward, trying to bite Charlie. But the old man ducked and narrowly dodged out of the way. Venom hissed, exposing her lethal fangs. No time to stick around. Charlie grabbed Ray's body, threw the boy over his shoulder, and started running as fast as he could. "To Dawn!" he shouted.

Ray moaned, struggling to hold onto consciousness.

"Hang on," the old man said. "Don't die on me!"

They bolted toward the chaotic mutating mess of Dawn's uncontrolled shape-shifting. Slimer was still laughing. Rhino-Man looked up to see the others approaching.

Rhino-Man got a secure footing, lifted one foot up, and moved to stomp hard.

"Everybody hold on!" Charlie shouted.

Rhino-Man's foot crashed into the ground, sending a powerful earthquake out in all directions. Luke and Charlie fell to the ground. Ray tumbled over. They quickly got back up, Charlie grabbed Ray again, and they ran up to Dawn.

"Dawn?" Ray struggled to speak.

Rhino-Man stomped the ground again. Another tremor. Everyone fell down again. But they were close enough to Dawn. Charlie looked over to Luke. "Now! Get us out of here!"

Luke nodded. He quickly traced a large circle on the ground with his crystal. The trail of sparkling pink light marked his path.

Ray looked up, through blurry vision, and saw Rhino-Man and the others getting close. With one hand on his spider bite wound, he held out his other hand, and used whatever strength he had left to blast them away.

The circle was complete. "Where should we go?" panicked Luke.

Charlie quickly looked at Dawn and Ray – a jumbled mess of random mutations and a man growing weaker by the second. He knew just the place. "Here, gimme," he said, holding out his hand.

Luke tossed him the crystal.

Ray used his power to weakly push back the mutants again. He wasn't able to push them back as far this time.

Charlie quickly drew a new symbol – something Luke actually recognized from somewhere else. It was the same symbol used in astrology for the constellation Virgo. Was this the sixth symbol he mentioned? Would this portal take them to a planet somewhere in Virgo?

The portal opened.

Total blackness inside.

"Come on," said Charlie.

"Don't let them get away!" ordered Mastermind.

Ray saw them getting closer. Vision getting blurrier. He felt so weak. So tired. He just wanted to give up and fall asleep. He was in so much pain. Everything was slowly going dark.

But he flicked his wrist one more time. Rhino-Man went flying backwards, crashing into Mastermind in the process. That took all his effort. Just the one mutant. Slimer got too close. Did he have the strength to do it again? He tried. God, he tried. He pulled all his strength, focused his power, and knocked her backwards several feet.

Everything got darker. He felt a hundred times weaker.

Charlie pushed Luke down into the portal. The old man looked behind. He grabbed a solid-looking part of Dawn and tossed her down too. Venom appeared out of nowhere. Ray pushed her back a few feet. That was the last of his strength. He collapsed. Charlie grabbed him, dragged him into the portal, and jumped in after.

Slimer stood over the open portal. She peered over to look inside. Total darkness. Where'd they go? The other mutants came up right behind her.

Charlie's glowing crystal emerged from the darkness on the other side, quickly moving across both directions, X-ing it out. The portal closed instantly. The mutants saw only the grass-covered ground now.

Mastermind stood up, dusting himself off. "Dammit! Did anyone see what symbol he used?"

All the mutants all shrugged.

He sighed. Wait. He counted them. Shadow, Venom, Arachnus, Rhino-Man, Slimer… "Someone's missing. Where's Kraken?"

They looked at each other. The squid guy – where was he the whole time? Mastermind suddenly remembered. He went over to the small pond, where Kraken had submerged himself earlier.

He reached in, grabbed one of the tentacle arms, and pulled the sea monster up. "What the hell were you doing?!" Mastermind demanded.

"Sorry boss," he garbled. "That desert planet really dried me out." His multi-toothed mouth, positioned in the center of his chest, grinned. "But I'm all better now."

Mastermind started fuming. He looked Kraken deep in the eyes. Those black, bottomless sea creature eyes. "If you ever betray me again," he said, "you'll wish I left you stranded on that desert planet. Do you understand me?"

Mastermind turned to face the others.

"That goes for all of you. If anyone *ever* betrays me – there's no place safe in this universe you can hide from me!" He sighed, frustrated. "And *no one* saw where they went?"

"Sorry boss," said Shadow.

He sighed again, calming himself down. He checked his Rolex watch. They didn't have any more time to waste. Loose end or not. Whatever. It wouldn't matter now. Chuck and the others may have gotten away – but by now, Mastermind's message should have reached all the major news networks – and it'd be too late to stop him.

He looked back at the deceased Luke on the ground. At least this battle wasn't a total loss. One of them died. And Ray would soon follow. The shape-shifter appeared to have lost control of her power too.

This little encounter didn't exactly go as he had planned, but it was a victory nonetheless.

"Come on," he said, calmly. "Let's go. Destiny awaits."

Chapter 24
END OF DAYS

Silence. Absolute darkness. Perfect stillness.

They might as well be dead.

"Uncle, where are we?"

"Give it a second," said the old man.

Small lights appeared along the floor and walls. Just like the ones in the corridor when Ray and Dawn first entered the pyramid on the desert world.

But they were far, far from there.

These lights weren't quite as bright as the ones in the other pyramid, either. But it was enough light to see what they were doing. Luke looked down at Dawn. Parts of her body still shape-shifted randomly and uncontrollably, although it seemed to be slowing down. Charlie knelt down next to Ray, lightly tapping his face. No response. Charlie checked for a pulse.

"He's still alive. Barely. His temperature's dropping quickly." The old man leaned down to pick up Luke's dying friend. "Help her," he said, looking at Dawn. "This way."

Luke knelt down next to Dawn. He wasn't sure how to help her. She looked up at him. Her eyes kept shifting into different colors. Her face was still slightly deformed. As were other parts of her body. But the mutations were definitely slowing down. "Can you walk?" he asked her.

She nodded her head, slowly, bravely. "I think so," she said. Luke helped her up. She seemed unsteady on her feet. Luke let her lean on him. They walked together. Slowly. One step at a time. But she seemed to be getting better. The random mutations were definitely settling down. Her body started to normalize.

Charlie carried Ray farther down the corridor. Luke and Dawn dragged behind. "Where are we taking them?"

"Not far," said Uncle Charlie. "Just ahead." He said to Ray, "We're almost there. Hold on just a little bit longer."

Luke tried to be brave. He tried to hide how he felt – scared, alone, worried, horribly defeated. He couldn't believe it. The other Luke had died – and they just left him there! Dawn, a girl he barely knew, wasn't doing so great, either.

And Ray – his best friend, his roommate, practically a brother to him – was he even going to make it?

How did this all go so terribly wrong?

Their plan was perfect. Get in, steal the crystal, banish Mastermind and the mutants, and get out. The had powers. They had the element of surprise. They had a plan.

How did they fail?

Maybe they weren't cut out to be super heroes. Maybe the reality of being a hero was a little different than the comic books. But maybe this wasn't over. Maybe it didn't have to end like this. Maybe he could still go back in time, and change all this. Somehow.

If his power had even recharged enough.

But how far back could he go? Would he be able to go back far enough to warn them their plan to steal Mastermind's crystal wouldn't work? Could he go farther back and stop Mastermind from ever arriving on Eden and killing that visitor liaison guy? He wondered… could he go even far enough back, and stop his uncle from even giving him that damn crystal?

The powers… getting to explore other worlds… it wasn't worth losing his best friend. It wasn't worth the life of an innocent girl he barely knew.

Of course, if he did go back in time and stop all this from happening, it still wouldn't prevent Mastermind from completing his evil plan. Mastermind would still have his little army of mutants. Only – without Luke and the others – there'd literally be no one to stop them.

No, they had to pull through this. Somehow. They had to make it. Ray couldn't die. Dawn couldn't die.

They had to survive.

Luke wasn't much of a religious man. But in this moment, he prayed. Please God, he said in the silence of his own heart, get them through this somehow. Keep them alive. Help them find a way to save the world. They're the only ones who even have a *chance* of stopping Mastermind now.

And right now, it looked like it was a very, very slim chance.

Mastermind was already far too powerful for them. But if they somehow got through this, if they found a way to survive this, Luke would take it as a sign they were meant to do this. Their destiny. To stop Mastermind and his mutants. To be heroes. To save the world from other powerful, dangerous super villains like him.

It was amazing how some things didn't matter anymore. Twenty-four hours ago, he would've worried about losing his stupid part-time minimum wage job. Funny how watching your best friend flirt with death put things into perspective. Or being nice to pushy door salesmen and religious missionaries. He really didn't want to talk to them. He should've just said no. They were probably used to rejection anyway. And speaking of rejection, he loved being an artist. He dreamed of drawing comic books. But he never put himself out there. Not really. Because he was afraid of rejection.

For too long, Luke had allowed himself to be too passive and just "let" things happen to him. Always waiting for things to get better someday. But they never did. He never submitted his artwork to any publishers. Never applied to any jobs at production studios around town either. He lived in Los Angeles. How much more opportunity could he have? He never approached any girls he was attracted to – he was just afraid of failing, of losing them, of things not working out.

So he ended up stuck in a dead-end, low-paying job with no girlfriend and a fantasy world of comic books and sci-fi/fantasy movies. Which was fine. He guessed. But he wanted more. Deep down, he knew he was meant for more.

Walking down this lonely corridor on some unknown planet, probably thousands of lightyears from Earth, helping Dawn limp along as they watched his best friend slowly die in his uncle's arms… Luke vowed to change himself that moment.

If they made it out of this alive, he was going to start living his life differently. He'd start living it, period.

He was determined to be a new man. Stop listening to his fears. Stop believing his self-doubts. It was time to grow up. Time to become something more. Time to become… the hero he always knew he could be, always wanted to be, inside.

Sure, he was a little afraid. But whenever someone is faced with fear, they have two choices: run and hide, or stand up and grow as a person. And Luke decided to choose the latter. He couldn't let his friends die. He couldn't let Mastermind win. He wouldn't let this story end badly.

He was determined to become the hero he needed to be.

If they could only find a way to survive their current problems.

"Here we are," said Charlie, leaning Ray down against the wall. A circular door rolled open to the side. Luke looked inside. It was another healing chamber.

Charlie looked down at Ray, limply and lifelessly slouching to the floor. Charlie could see Ray's body temperature – what was left of it. They didn't have much time. The old man picked up Ray, carried him inside, and laid him across the table.

Lights began scanning from overhead. Dawn watched from the side. Exhausted herself, she leaned against the wall, and slowly sank down to the floor. Her eyes stayed fixed on Ray.

The holographic doctor appeared. "Beginning repairs."

Charlie stayed back, watching anxiously in silence.

Luke waited by Ray's side.

The doctor began working. Used some kind of alien device. Something that made a high pitch noise and flashed different colored lights over Ray's weak body.

The hologram moved quickly. Focusing on one area, then another, and another. The doctor kept working.

And working.

This took a lot longer than before.

Luke shook his head. Both he and his uncle healed much faster than this.

"Come on, Ray…" Luke said.

Dawn's random mutations seemed to have stopped completely, at last. Her body finally calmed down. She took a long, deep, slow breath. Naked, she sat on the cold hard floor, arms wrapped around her legs, bundling herself up tightly. She looked up at the medical table, eyes fixed on Ray.

The holographic doctor used a variety of unfamiliar, high-tech alien tools. He injected something into Ray. Probably an antidote of some kind. He used a hand-held device over the bite wound too, healing that up. More lights and energy beams scanned and strobed from above.

Ray should've been better by now. What was taking so long? It couldn't be too late to save him.

No, not like this. They couldn't be too late.

Uncle Charlie's eyes looked red, about to cry.

"Come on, Ray," Luke said, still at his side. "Pull through. I need you, man. You can't die. You're my best friend." He forced a smile – so he wouldn't cry. "Ray, wake up. Wake up. This isn't your time. It's not supposed to end like this."

"Luke…" Charlie whispered.

"No, not like this."

The hologram continued working on Ray's body.

"He can't be dead," said Luke.

Different colored lights focused on different areas of Ray's body. Over different vital organs. Including his lungs. Ray didn't appear to be breathing. When did that stop? How long had Ray not been breathing?

The lights shut off. The holographic doctor looked up at them. "All possible repairs have been completed. Please wait for final diagnostic."

A final scan of Ray's body.

Luke shook his head. Ray should be better by now. Ray should be breathing.

"Confirmed," said the doctor. "No additional repairs possible. Operation terminated."

The hologram disappeared.

Still no life.

"Ray?" Luke's voice trembled.

Still no response.

"Ray?" Luke asked again, starting to cry.

He can't be dead.

No, not like this. Not like this. Please, God, not like this.

Charlie took a step back into the shadows, his hand covering his mouth.

"Ray?" Luke asked one last time.

Charlie shook his head. The old man was speechless – riddled with guilt, filled with horror, consumed by shame, shocked with disbelief. He couldn't believe it. He wouldn't believe it. Then he looked around. His face changed to one of concern. "Where's Dawn?"

Luke looked at the wall where she had been resting. She wasn't there.

Where'd she go?

"Dawn?" Luke asked, not seeing her anywhere. He ran out into the corridor. "Dawn?"

He looked down, at the floor.

"Uncle, come quick!"

Charlie glanced at Ray's lifeless body lying across the medical table. And he ran out into the hallway.

He saw Luke kneeling over Dawn.

Or what was left of her.

There was definitely some blonde hair. And human skin. A few random bones too. And lots of blood. Lots of red blood, pooled around the gooey mess of her remains. And a glowing green substance mixed in. Something a janitor would have to mop up – not anything resembling what used to be a human being.

"Can we get her on the table?" Luke pleaded.

Charlie stared at the pile of bloody goo. How? With what?

He opened his mouth to speak, but made no sound. It took him a few seconds to respond. He slowly shook his head.

Even if there was a way to scoop "her" up… and somehow carry her onto the table… the scanners wouldn't be able to identify her genome. It didn't work last time. No way it'd happen this time.

"I'm sorry," Charlie whispered, lips trembling. He shook his head. He wanted to say something – a word of encouragement, a word of hope, a word of something. But he couldn't. No words came out.

Luke really needed some guidance. What were they supposed to do? What *could* they do?

Charlie still shook his head. He couldn't bear to look at her any longer. He turned away. "Luke," he said, his back to him, "I'm sorry… I'm sorry."

The old man's face showed a guilt like no other.

It was his fault Mastermind existed. His fault his brother and sister-in-law were dead. And now two young innocents were dead too. How many? How many more would suffer and die – because of *his* mistake?

"I…"

"Uncle?"

The old man shook his head. "I can't," he whispered. "I just can't." The long dark corridor was in front of him. He started to run.

"Uncle?"

He didn't stop.

Luke stood up. "Uncle!" he shouted down the corridor.

His uncle disappeared into the darkness.

"Uncle!" he called again, louder.

Now Luke was completely alone.

Chapter 25
THE CURE

Doctor Troyd and Luke – the mind-controlled one – stepped outside from the baggage claim area. That's when Luke saw the name of the airport. LaGuardia. They were in New York City.

How did they get here? His uncle said the only portal back to Earth ended up in Stonehenge. They were nowhere near there.

"Follow me," said the doctor.

"Where we going?" asked Luke.

"We have an appointment with the President of the United States," said Doctor Troyd. "But first, I need to pick something up."

"The President? Nice…"

"Just following the plan," Doctor Troyd said.

He stepped up to the curb and hailed a taxi. They had no luggage, which the driver thought was a little odd, but he didn't care. Doctor Troyd told the driver to take them to the Bank of American Savings, New York City Branch.

It was across town, and in the middle of rush hour, but New York taxi drivers were known for their – well, somewhat "fearless" – driving skills.

They weaved in and out of traffic, raced ahead, slammed on the brakes at the last possible second, dodged pedestrians, clipped cars and bike messengers … and made it in half the time it would've taken any non-New Yorker.

Troyd paid the man, including tip, and they stepped outside.

The bank was as impressive as the one in Los Angeles. Massive columns. Marble steps. Enormous grand entrance doors. "This way," said Doctor Troyd. They went inside.

Luke had never stepped foot in such a place. He was used to the regular average-joe type of banks on every street corner. The ones that offered "free checking", provided you had direct deposit or a minimum daily balance – neither of which he ever enjoyed.

The eccentric scientist stepped up to one of the tellers. "I'm here to pick up an item from safety deposit box number 88332."

Luke waited in the main lobby hall. Snacked on some fruit left out on a fancy tray. There were a few widescreen televisions there, showing the local news, stock reports, GNN Headlines, and the like.

Something caught his eye on one of the TVs. Something – or more specifically, some*one* familiar.

It was breaking news.

Luke stepped closer to watch and listen.

"This footage was taken from a security camera at a private biotech research and development firm in Orange County, California late last night," said the news anchor.

Mastermind appeared on the TV screen, standing in front of five petty criminals. He held a syringe loaded with a glowing green chemical. Shadow, the cat girl, stood by his side with a small case of various blood samples. And Doctor Troyd was there too.

The five criminals lined up in front of the security camera.

Mastermind injected the first one. A girl.

She mutated into Slimer – right on camera, right for the whole world to see.

Luke's jaw dropped. He had seen the end result – the mutants – but he hadn't seen their transformation. Until now. On TV.

The reporter continued, "The man you see here has been identified under the alias of 'Mastermind', a bio-terrorist who escaped from LAPD custody a couple hours earlier."

The video continued, showing each criminal, one after another, get mutated into their current forms. Slimer was first. Then Rhino-Man. And Arachnus, the spider mutant. Kraken, the sea monster. And finally Venom, the all-too-lethal snake lady. With Shadow, who'd already been transformed, they made a total of six mutants. Mastermind's mutants.

"The authenticity of these disturbing images have been confirmed and verified," the reporter's voice continued. "The identity of the victims are known, but their names are being withheld out of respect for their families. Mastermind, the terrorist responsible for this horrific crime against humanity, has released a video with his demands."

"Hey Doc," Luke said, calling over toward Doctor Troyd. "You gotta see this."

"Here now is the footage we received with Mastermind's demands." The news switched to a different pre-recorded video. Mastermind's face – clear, in focus, and in high-definition – filled television screens simultaneously across America and the world.

"I am Mastermind," he said, smiling. "Your new god. Bow down and worship me." He was serious. "I am creating a new world with a new image. Humanity is a disgusting plague on this planet. You are all monsters. Cruel, selfish, bitter, angry, repulsive, worthless bags of puss and shit. You talk of peace – and yet you demand wars. You speak of equality – and then you shun those different than you. You pray for forgiveness – but seldom offer it whenever you've been wronged. Humanity's day is ending. A new world is coming to pass. I, Mastermind, your new god, am re-creating you now – transforming you, mutating you, changing all of you – into the monsters you really are."

Wow, this guy was intense. Luke was kinda glad he was working for – and not against – his lord Mastermind.

"But do not be afraid. I have come not to kill you. I, as your god, am re-creating you. You are being reborn, my children. Soon, you will be adopting your new forms. Beginning your new lives. Some of you will be animals. Creatures and monsters of all kinds. Others will not be so lucky. The mutations, I'm afraid, are somewhat random and unpredictable. But rest assured, my slaves, you have *all* been infected. By the time this video has been released, all the world's major water supplies have been contaminated with my BioGen X, the chemical I created, that has already begun transforming you from the inside out. While you sleep. While you eat. While you work. While you make love. It's happening even now, as you watch this. It's too late for all of you. There's no escaping your fate. You are mine. Bow down. Worship me. Honor me as your god. Follow me. Obey me." His eyes grew more intense, staring directly into the camera. "OBEY ME! OBEY ME NOW! OBEY ME ALWAYS! I AM YOUR NEW AND ONLY GOD – YOU WILL DO WHATEVER I COMMAND." He smiled. And then added: "Share this video with everyone you know."

Luke's eyes didn't blink. He was already under Mastermind's mind control from before. But now – his resolve, his loyalty, felt a thousand times deeper and stronger.

He *wanted* to worship Mastermind as his creator and God.

Doctor Troyd returned with a vial of the glowing green chemical. He hadn't seen the news yet. Didn't plan to, either. "Come," he said, pulling Luke away from the television. "The President will want this."

Mastermind was still on Eden, but not for long.

He pulled out his pink crystal. "Amazing piece of technology, don't you think?" he said, examining it.

His six mutants gathered around him.

"Simple, small, portable. And programmable."

He drew a large circle on the ground. The crystal left a trail of sparkling pink light wherever it touched. Then in the middle of that circle, Mastermind drew a unique symbol.

He made an "M" shape, followed by the number "1".

The portal opened.

The mutants leaned in to look through. They saw the Taj Mahal on the other side, in the distance, in the middle of the night. The portal had opened into India.

Mastermind looked at his mutants. He picked one. "You," he said to Venom. "Go through, start killing random people. Make sure you're seen doing it. Wake everyone up. Get their attention. Be as public as you can. Your job is to spread fear and chaos. Got it?"

Venom nodded.

"Now go!" Mastermind commanded.

Venom jumped into the portal – and landed in India. Everyone was asleep in their beds. But not for long…

She revealed her fangs.

Mastermind X-ed out the portal, closing it. He began drawing another circle on the ground. This time, he marked the symbol "M2" in the center. Another portal opened, this time to Tokyo, Japan.

A very densely populated city. Full of lights, advertisements, crowded buildings, and a growing crowd of curious on-lookers. It was early morning there. People were just getting up for work. Mastermind looked to Shadow. "You're up next. They think cat girls are cute? Show them your true nature."

Shadow smiled. "Okay boss." And she jumped in.

Mastermind closed that portal. Opened another one, this one with symbol "M3". Saint Petersburg, Russia. Middle of the night. It was dark. Hmm. Who next? Mastermind turned to Arachnus, a black spider mutant. A true terror of the night. "Do your worst," he said. The spider guy nodded and jumped in.

The fourth portal, "M4", opened to the City of Angeles. Middle of the day. Smoggy, but the sun got through. The famous Hollywood sign in the distance. Endless traffic. Air pollution so thick you could cut it with a knife. Mastermind turned to Rhino-Man. "Give Los Angeles some earthquakes they'll never forget. And make sure you get on camera."

Rhino-Man nodded.

"Now," Mastermind ordered.

Rhino-Man jumped into the portal.

Only two remained: Slimer and Kraken. The sticky girl of gross goop and the hideous sea monster of horrific disgustingness.

Mastermind opened the next portal. He drew the symbol "M6". The "M5" symbol went to LaGuardia Airport in New York City, where Doctor Troyd and Luke went. But Mastermind had another destination in mind. "M6" opened up to the beautiful and historic remains of the ancient Parthenon – in Athens, Greece.

Lots of beautiful stars filled the night sky. The same stars and constellations that were studied by the ancient Greeks and Romans centuries ago. The origin of many of the world's ancient mythologies.

Hmm. Mythology…

Mastermind turned to Kraken. "I want you to make the monsters from their ancient myths feel like cozy domesticated pets." He smiled. "And have fun."

Kraken dove into the portal.

Mastermind closed it. "And last but not least," he said to Slimer as he drew the perimeter of the final portal, "use your power to make them believe it's the End of Days."

The "M7" portal opened to a densely-populated desert city. It was the middle of the night, but in the distance, she could see a temple with a gold dome top. Better known as the Dome of the Rock. The famous Muslim shrine in Old Jerusalem.

"The desert?" she complained. "I hate the desert."

"Take it out on them, honey." Mastermind looked at her, giving her an order. "Now go. And do your worst."

She sighed and jumped through.

Mastermind closed that portal too. He took one last good look at Eden. Took a nice deep breath of their fresh, clean air. Then opened a portal for himself.

He marked the triangle symbol.

He was going back to the desert planet again.

Doctor Troyd and the mind-controlled Luke once again found themselves in the back seat of a fearless taxi driver. And this driver clearly didn't speak much English, either.

Luke held tightly onto the seat as they took another hazardous turn just a little too fast around the corner.

Finally they pulled up to the front of a very famous building, coming to an abrupt stop. The building was tall and slender, rising high into the air. Countless flags from nearly every country in the world lined up side by side, each waving proudly in the wind.

"The United Nations?" Luke asked, recognizing it.

"We have our appointment here."

"Is the president expecting us?"

"He should be," said Doctor Troyd, looking out the window. But he didn't sound so sure. "If that hacker Mastermind hired did his job, he will be."

"The hacker?" asked Luke.

"Let's go."

Inside the United Nations lobby, Doctor Troyd checked in with the security guard at the main desk.

Doctor Troyd asked to see the President of the United States.

The guard sized him up. Doctor Troyd was wild-eyed, eccentric-looking, and clearly at least somewhat insane. Not the typical class of people to the enter these hallowed halls. And definitely not the type to have an appointment with the president.

But sure enough, there it was in the computer. An appointment with Doctor Troyd right around this time.

"He should be expecting me," the doctor said.

Appointment or not, the security guard trusted his instincts over anything the computer said. Something was up with this guy.

"And what's your business here, sir?"

"I have the cure," he said.

"The cure?"

"That's right. The cure. You've heard about Mastermind's contamination of the water supply. His 'dangerous' chemical that's going to mutate us all?"

"I heard about that. It's real?"

Doctor Troyd nodded. Luke watched curiously.

"I'm going to need to see some ID," said the guard.

Doctor Troyd nodded. "Very well." He reached into his lab coat pocket and pulled out his cell phone. He loaded up the pre-recorded message – one Mastermind had recorded for him previously in the hotel lobby.

"Your ID, sir?"

"It's right here," he said. He showed him the cell phone and pressed play.

Mastermind's face appeared, intensely staring into the camera. "You will grant this man access to anywhere and anyone."

It was a small screen. But it was enough. The guard had looked into Mastermind's eyes, and heard his voice, and suddenly felt compelled to allow Doctor Troyd access anywhere, and to anyone.

"Oh, right. Of course. Sorry to delay you." He swiped a special access key card, handed it to Doctor Troyd, and gave him directions to the proper room and floor.

Doctor Troyd smiled.

Doctor Troyd walked in to the meeting room. He stood in front of the President of the United States. The scientist never thought this day would come. But Mastermind had the vision. Mastermind had seen all this through, long before it came to pass.

It all started months ago, when he approached Doctor Troyd to hire him for a "special project". Several test batches later, and BioGen X had been perfected. Phase 1, complete.

Then he recruited his team of mutants. Phase 2, complete.

Gave them all super powers. Phase 3, complete.

"Tell me, Mr. President," asked Doctor Troyd, "have you seen the news?"

"I have," said the president. It was hard to miss.

Also present in this meeting room were several top military advisors, leading scientists, secret service agents, and a few others neither Luke nor Doctor Troyd could identify. They had *all* seen the news. They had *all* seen and heard Mastermind's public message.

"What do you think of Mastermind?" asked Doctor Troyd.

"I will obey," the president chanted, without giving it a second thought.

Doctor Troyd smiled, wild-eyed. Perfect.

This was going to be really easy.

"Good." Doctor Troyd pulled out the vial of glowing green chemical. "Mastermind wants this mass produced and given to everyone in the world. You're to give the formula to political leaders in every nation. Those that can mass produce it, will. Those that can't, will receive shipments from those that can."

"What is it?"

"BioGen X," Doctor Troyd said. "The thing that's going to turn everyone into Mastermind's mutant. But you're going to tell them it's actually the cure."

"What about the water supply?"

"A lie," said Doctor Troyd. "To scare the people into taking this."

"I see. This is Mastermind's command?"

"It is."

The president held the green glowing vial in his hand.

Phase 4, complete.

Chapter 26
THE PLAN

Luke – the one *not* under Mastermind's control -- stood silently over Ray's dead body.

He shook his head. No good. All this advanced alien technology – and they still couldn't save either of them. Dawn was dead. Ray was dead. This wasn't fair. This wasn't right.

How did this happen?

"Computer," Luke called aloud, "try again."

Nothing happened.

"Medical doctor. Please. Save him."

Still nothing. Still dark.

No noise. No lights. Nothing.

Luke lowered his head. "I'm sorry man." He looked at Ray. It looked like his friend was sleeping. Not dead. Just sleeping. A very, very deep and long sleep. Without any breathing.

Who was he kidding? Ray was gone. And it was all his fault. Luke opened up that portal to the desert planet. Luke left it open. Ray never would've come here if it wasn't for him.

Luke was responsible for Ray's death.

Dawn's too.

"Computer, can you do *anything*? He can't be dead. Not like this. There's gotta be *something* you can do. Can you… Can you maybe…"

Turn back time?

The medical technology couldn't do that. But he could.

Luke was a time traveler now.

Sure, he always dreamed of being able to do it one day. For fun, for adventure, to explore time and space… ancient cultures and future civilizations. Travel the galaxy in a faster-than-light starship.

And maybe, well, go back in time, and change some things.

Save his family.

Right some wrongs.

Make a better tomorrow.

But he couldn't go back that far. His power was too damn limited. But he could go back a little ways. And fix some things.

Like Ray. Like Dawn.

He could change history – and save them.

But what should he do, exactly? What event needed to change? Should he stop them from trying to confront Mastermind back on Eden? But even if *that* event was changed, they might still try to fight him later, at a different time and place – with the same results. Maybe they'd be better off without any powers. He could go back in time and prevent them from entering the pyramid on Sekhmet, the desert world.

No, that'd be no good. Then who would stop Mastermind?

Maybe… Luke wondered… could he go back far enough, and stop his uncle from blabbing about the crystal, or prevent Mastermind from stealing it?

No, he couldn't do that. It was way too far back in time. He had minutes or days – not months or years.

Luke kicked a machine along the wall.

Damn technology.

This was supposed to be the so-called "Temple of the Gods". A place where people could be made immortal. Given powers. Heal fatal wounds. Given a second chance.

Hardly worked for Ray or Dawn.

Maybe he needed to let history play out almost as it did the first time, but get Ray and Dawn here, to this temple, sooner. Maybe if they just had more time, they could both be saved.

Playing with timelines – and people's fates – made Luke feel a little bit like a god. His decisions would determine if his friends lived or died.

Was he ready for that kind of power? Either way, he had it now, and he was going to use it, as best he could.

He wondered… the ancient gods from Greek and Roman mythology… maybe even the gods even older than that… were they really just humans, like him, who had access to the pyramid?

Did they get powers from the Altar of Destiny? Did they prolong their lives in the healing chamber? Was that how they became to be gods?

Perhaps the pyramids in Egypt and other places around the world were built to imitate the alien temples. Did the ancient pharaohs want immortality and supernatural powers too, thinking that if they built their own pyramids, they too would become gods?

What difference did it make?

Clearly, those gods were not truly immortal. Otherwise they'd still be around today. And these alien pyramids weren't all-powerful. They still couldn't save Ray or Dawn.

Even advanced alien technology had its limits.

"I've got to do something," he said to himself.

There had to be *something* he could do.

He just had to think. Maybe enough time had passed. Maybe his power had recharged some by now.

Time travel was the answer.

But when? Where? What should he change?

Where was his uncle? He really needed some guidance right about now.

He stepped back out into the hall. He looked down one way, then the other. Endless corridors. This pyramid was massive.

He placed his hand flat on the wall.

"Let's see if this works."

The interactive video screen appeared on the wall. Text, symbols, icons, and other options illuminated.

"Where's my uncle? Show me Charles Powers."

A map appeared. A green dot showed Luke's current location. A blue dot identified, what Luke assumed, was his uncle's position. A considerable distance away. Apparently near the edge of the pyramid base, at the exit. Then a red dotted line appeared, guiding Luke with directions from here to there.

"Thank you," said Luke. He placed his hand flat against the wall a second time, and the interactive menu screen disappeared.

Several minutes later, he saw his uncle.

The pyramid must've been low on power. The corridors would light up – dimly – while Luke walked through, but after he left, the lights behind him faded out.

His uncle used a sixth symbol to get here.

They were inside a massive pyramid. Apparently a third one – not on the desert world, not on Eden. Where were they, exactly?

His uncle faced the exit. The door was still closed.

"Uncle?" Luke hesitated to ask.

The old man turned his head when he heard Luke's voice.

"Have a seat," was all he said.

Luke sat down next to him, both facing the closed door.

A moment of silence.

"So," finally Luke asked, "how ya doing?"

His uncle lightly chuckled. "Super, and you?"

"Yeah," said Luke. "Super duper."

"I'm so sorry Luke," his uncle said.

"You didn't know any of this was going to happen."

"I should have," he said.

"Don't worry. I'm going to change it."

He looked at Luke. "Time travel?"

Luke nodded.

"You think you still can?"

"I hope I can," he said.

"It doesn't matter," said Charlie. "Even if you change history, Mastermind will find some other way to win. He always wins." Charlie slammed his fist into the floor. "Why are some men so evil?"

Luke shrugged. "I dunno. But we can't let him win. We'll find a way. I'm going to save Ray and Dawn. We're going to stop Mastermind. We're going to save the world."

"Like your parents?" Charlie said. "They thought that too. 'There's two of us,' your father told me, 'and only one of him.' Your mother could read minds, you know. She knew what he was planning before he even made his first move. And he *still* found a way… to, well…" He couldn't say it. "I'll never forgive him for what he did to them." He sighed. "And now to your friends too."

Luke shook his head. "There's gotta be a way."

"Luke," Charlie said, "we need to quit while we still can. He already killed the other timeline copy of you. He killed your parents. Dawn and Ray too. If we go up against him now… I just… I couldn't bear the thought of losing you, too."

Luke was surprised. "You saying we should give up?"

Charlie lowered his head.

Luke couldn't believe it. "Wasn't it you who told me, that no matter how bad things get, no matter how dark the situation looks, you always have hope? That the one thing you've learned in all your life experience was that there was always hope, there was *always* a way out – or through – any problem? You told me that. You told me to remember that."

Charlie looked back up at Luke. He paused. "You're… right. I did say that."

"Then there's still hope. We can't give up. We *have* to find a way. We can't quit now. We're just about to win – as soon as I figure out a way to take him down once and for all!"

Charlie smiled.

"God I wish I had a more offensive power," said Luke.

"I'm sorry?"

"My power. Time travel's cool. But it's not much good in battle. It's not like super strength or laser vision or force fields or anything. I can't blast energy beams or freeze someone in place. Time travel's more of a… strategy-based power, I guess. You use it for gaining information and insight, for making specific adjustments to key events… but not fighting. Not defending. It's a planning-type power."

"True," said the old man. "Too bad you can't just go to the future and borrow some high-tech weapons and force fields instead, huh?"

Luke perked up. "Yeah, why not? I mean, that's the one thing Mastermind can't plan for – things that haven't been invented yet!"

Charlie smiled. "So what's the plan?"

"Well, I think I need to go to the future, get myself a battle suit or something – like the one I saw at the history museum, back on Eden. I need some kind of armored exo-skeleton, for protection and defense. Shield me from attacks. And then have built-in weapons and lasers or something, that I can attack with. Yeah! It'll be perfect. Like something Iron Man would wear, with cool gadgets Batman might use, only made entirely out of future technology!"

"Iron Man?"

"A comic book character. You mean to tell me you've never heard of Iron Man?"

"Um, hello. Been traveling to alien worlds all this time. I *live* the comic books."

"You've at least heard of Batman, right? Superman? Spider-Man?"

"They have any female super heroes in these comic books of yours?"

"Yeah, well, sure. Anyway, that's not the point. I just need to get back to Earth, travel to… I dunno, a hundred years into the future or so, and get my hands on whatever cool weapons and gear they've got then. Hmm. Maybe two or three hundred years. Just to be safe."

"One question though," Charlie asked, confused about something. "If you go to Earth's future… will that be the future with or without Mastermind?"

"Good question. Probably with Mastermind. The instant I leave the present moment, time will continue on without me, until I reappear in the future. There'll be no one here to stop him. He'll go unchecked, undefeated."

"Just be careful, Luke. You sure you don't want to go to Eden's future instead?"

"Maybe that's a better idea. For all I know, two hundred years from now, Earth may be entirely populated with mutant slaves, and all technology and progress has ceased. Won't be any good weapons for me to take back with me." Luke paused. "And that's assuming I can even travel that far into the future. Even with my power fully charged, can I go that far? I really don't know the actual limits to my power yet." He thought about it. "But what about here? What planet are we on now?" Maybe this world already had advanced technology he could use.

"Planet?" Charlie asked.

"Yeah. We're inside another pyramid, right?"

Charlie nodded.

"Does this planet have advanced technology like Eden? Maybe I don't have to go anywhere. The less time-traveling I have to do now, the more charged my power will be for whenever I do need it."

"We're not on any planet," said Charlie.

"But," said Luke, looking around.

Charlie reached up for the control panel by the exit door. He pressed the blue button. The door rolled open to the side. And that's when Luke saw exactly where they were.

Stars.

Countless stars, in every direction, for millions of lightyears, all around, perfectly clear, and absolutely silent.

All slowly, and very gradually, moving sideways.

Well, the stars probably weren't moving. Most likely the pyramid was moving. Through space.

"Oh my God," said Luke.

"We found this symbol by accident. Your mom wanted to try some astrology symbols for fun. One ended up here."

"What's keeping all the air in?" Luke seemed a little uneasy. "There should be a major vacuum into space right now."

"Some kind of force field," Charlie shrugged. "Here, see?" He got up and pressed against an invisible wall, just beyond where the door used to be. "Can't move through it. I suppose that's a good thing."

"Does Mastermind know about this symbol?"

"Doubtful. We didn't share everything with him. And I don't think Simeon knows about it. As far as he knows, Eden's got the only pyramid. Until the one showed up on Sekhmet."

"The desert world. That pyramid wasn't there before."

"Right."

"So are there aliens flying this thing right now?" Luke stared at the drifting stars. They had to be moving. And someone had to be piloting this giant ship.

"As far as I can tell," said Charlie. "there's no other life-forms anywhere inside. Your father and I explored this pyramid pretty well. It appears to have been abandoned a long time ago."

Luke turned to his uncle. "It's a big ship. There could be sections you didn't know about," he said.

"It's possible."

"How many of these pyramids are there, anyway?"

He shrugged. "I don't know. Why?"

"Well, Simeon believed his planet had the only one. Then another one mysterious shows up on Sekhmet. And then it turns out you knew about *this* one all along. Look, don't take this the wrong way or anything, but I'm really getting tired of all your secrets. How many other ships are there? Where else can the crystal go?"

Charlie smiled. "We only knew the six symbols, I promise. The five from the tablet, plus this one. Simeon mentioned hundreds of others, but they keep that kind of information a secret from outsiders."

"That's right. He said the crystals could be programmed. How do they do that?"

"No idea. But what are you going to do about saving your friends?"

"Well, Earth's out of the question. Mastermind will be expecting anything Earth has to throw at him. And there may not be a future worth going to there, either. The desert world and tropical beach planet don't seem to have any civilization or technology. That abandoned space ship might have some good stuff, but I'd die instantly in the cold vacuum of space. What about this place? Did you and Dad ever find any weapons or anything while exploring this pyramid?"

Charlie shook his head. "Just a lot of empty rooms."

"Then that leaves Eden. I'll have to see what they've got to offer. Simeon said they were at war for a long time. They're bound to have *something* I can use."

"Makes sense."

"I'll find us some powerful weapons, or some kind of technological advantage, and then use my power to save Ray and Dawn before anyone dies."

"Sounds good. And then Earth?"

"Yeah. And then we save Earth."

"We can't let this be a repeat of last time."

Luke was determined. "It won't be."

Mastermind didn't like taking chances. That was why, at this very moment, he walked across the scorching, unforgiving desert on planet Sekhmet.

The massive pyramid was just ahead.

It was so damn hot. But Mastermind needed a little extra insurance. Chuck and the others were probably gone for good. But he wouldn't risk it. And even though his mutants were permanently under his mind control, and by now half the world was under his spell too, he couldn't afford anything to go wrong now.

Not right when he was so close.

He needed more power.

He arrived at the entrance to the pyramid. Pushed the blue button. The circular door rolled open. He entered inside – and headed directly for the innermost chamber.

Mind control wasn't enough.

A portal opened at the garden on Eden. Luke peered his head through, looking around.

"Is it safe?" his uncle asked.

"Seems so. Looks like Mastermind's been gone for a while now." His timeline-duplicate was missing too. "I don't even see the other me."

Luke and Charlie stepped through the portal.

"Oh, the Edenites would've taken care of the body by now," he said.

"Am I buried here?"

Charlie shook his head. "I don't believe they bury anybody here. They probably ejected him into space."

"Oh," said Luke. He wasn't sure how he felt about that. This whole other-self-being-dead thing was really messing with his head.

Was he dead? Alive? Both? One version of him lived; the other, not so fortunate. He wondered, secretly, if he should even try to save his other self. On one hand, it was cool having two of him around. On the other hand, it was starting to get really annoying too. Besides, maybe drifting through space was a fitting end for an alternate timeline copy of him. He loved *Star Trek* and other sci-fi shows. Knowing that some version of him was laid to rest flying among the stars – it was a good ending for him.

Still, the moral questions arising from time travel were becoming a bit too much for him. What right did he have to choose who should live and who should die? The power to change history and define another's fate – should any mortal man or woman possess that kind of power?

Either way, he had the power. He had to make sure he used it for good. As best he knew how.

A second later, a different visitor liaison appeared. "Welcome to Eden," she said. A pretty dark-haired girl. "I'm Tristina, Visitor Liaison. What brings you gentlemen here today?"

"Uh, we're here for the museum," said Uncle Charlie. "Is Simeon still available?"

The three of them – Simeon, Charlie, and Luke – teleported into the history museum. The same one as before, with Eden's inactive Astaria crystal.

"It's this way," said Simeon, leading them.

They walked past the tall pillars, ancient artifacts, enclosed exhibits, enormous alien statues and heroic figures of the past, video information walls, and other curious things on display. Finally, they arrived at it.

"This the one you mean?" asked Simeon, stopping at the battle suit on display.

Luke stepped up to it, staring at it with awe. This looked like it had potential. A fully-enclosed mechanical battle suit. Probably from the era of Eden's civil or interplanetary wars. It had a helmet, opaque visor, and face shield – with what looked like a filtered air breathing apparatus. The rest of the "suit" had armored plating, especially across the torso and down the sides of the arms and legs. Sturdy mechanical metal boots and gloves. A large power pack on the back. And, no doubt, a bunch of various weapons and defensive technologies hidden and integrated into the whole thing.

Maybe it was a little overkill for Luke's purposes, but when dealing with someone like Mastermind and his mutants, being over-powered was the way to go.

"Yeah. That's the one I saw. What all can it do?" Luke continued admiring the high-tech battle suit the Edenites had created.

The video screen behind it instantly activated. A pre-recorded voice began talking. "One thousand years ago," the video announced, "citizens of Eden began exploring the stars. But as you know, space is a very dangerous place. The icy cold vacuum, deadly solar radiation, tiny meteoroids traveling at over 200,000 miles per hour, and countless other hazards both known and unknown. So early explorers wore suits like this to protect themselves and explore other worlds both safely and effectively."

Wait. What?

This wasn't a battle suit at all. It was just a really cool-looking space suit.

"Explorers never knew what they'd encounter in the depths of deep space or across the uncharted territory of new worlds," continued the educational video, "so these suits were fitted with several tools, defensive technologies, and scanning equipment for negotiating all possible environments."

Defensive technologies? Hmm. Maybe it'd still be useful after all.

"For example," said the video, showing an animated graphic as it explained, "suits like these were designed to withstand a direct head-on collision of a large meteor impact. Ouch, that's gotta hurt! But hopefully the explorer would use the defensive cutting laser to break apart a meteor like that long before then."

Ooh. Cutting lasers. That sounded good.

"Later models were also equipped with protective energy fields that not only deflected projectiles, but also shielded explorers from dangerous radiation, toxic gases, and even deadly wild alien creature attacks."

Force fields? Heck yes!

"The built-in heads up display, or 'HUD' for short, allowed explorers to view the entire electromagnetic spectrum and range of bio-signs from within the comfort and safety of their suits, helping them to avoid dangerous radiation while finding rare precious metals and food sources. Life was tough on the frontier, but these special suits made earlier explorer's jobs much, much easier."

Okay, Luke had heard enough. Not exactly the battle suit he was expecting, but it would still do the job. Cutting lasers, force fields, and an electromagnetic/bio-sign scanner... He could spot mutants in hiding, much like his uncle could with his heat vision. He'd protect himself and his friends with the force fields. And then counter-attack with the cutting lasers.

It would work.

"Simeon, can I borrow this?"

"You want that?" he asked, surprised. "It's really old."

"Does it still work?"

"As long as it has power, yes."

"What's it run on? Double-As?" He laughed to himself.

Simeon had no idea what AA batteries were.

But he checked the display info. "Looks like this model uses hybrid technology. Runs on both solar and heavy radioactive elements."

"Wait," said Luke, realizing what that meant. "You mean this thing can be nuclear powered?"

"Fission, yes," said Simeon. "By the time portable cold fusion technology became available, we stopped using these things."

Luke couldn't believe it. "You have cold fusion? And it's portable?!"

"Doesn't your world?"

"Um, no."

"Oh."

"Anyway, can I borrow it?"

Simeon paused. "You're going to defeat the man who killed Ethos?"

Luke nodded. "That's the plan."

"You can keep it."

Chapter 27
RISING

"Alex Alvarado reporting live from NBS News. Reports are now coming from all over – mutants have begun appearing in Japan, India, Russia, Greece, and the Middle East. I'm reporting live from downtown Los Angeles, where another mutant – some kind of human-rhinoceros is terrorizing citizens."

The camera pointed toward Rhino-Man, right as he slammed his foot onto the ground, sending another earthquake shockwave in all directions. Then Rhino-Man pounded his fist into the wall of a towering skyscraper – and it began crumbling down.

"Local buildings are being evacuated. All freeways have been re-routed to direct traffic out of the downtown Los Angeles area. Police are urging citizens to stay inside and off the roads."

In the background, behind Alex Alvarado, Rhino-Man charged across the screen. The camera immediately turned to follow. Several police officers opened fire. Bullets pierced the gray thick-skinned mutant. It slowed him down a little. But then Rhino-Man stomped his foot again, sending another earthquake out. Everyone – including the news reporter and cameraman – fell down. The camera laid on its side, watching as Rhino-Man pounded his fist into a nearby officer's chest. Powerful tremors tore the officer's body apart.

And that was just Los Angeles.

Mastermind's mutants were all over the planet, drawing lots of media attention to themselves.

Simeon helped take the ancient space suit down from its display. He handed Luke the helmet, chest piece, and armored gloves.

"So how do I activate this thing?" Luke asked. "Does it read my thoughts? Voice-activated commands? What?"

"Yes," said Simeon, removing the leg casing and armored boots from the display.

"Yes?" Luke asked.

"Any of those will work. Just give it a few minutes to sync with our database, to learn your language."

"Wow. Cool." Luke looked at the helmet and other gear in his arms. "How long will the batteries last? I don't want this thing running out of power on me in the middle of a fight."

"That all depends on your usage," Simeon said. "Shields drain faster while taking impact, but in standby mode, they can be sustained for a very long time. The cutter lasers will vary based on the yield you need. But basic life support can last for days, if nothing else is draining the power."

The entire suit was off the display, in several pieces. All Luke needed to do now was put them on.

He got a funny look in his face. "Hey, I don't understand something."

"Yes?" Simeon inquired.

"How come my power – my super power, my ability to travel through time – how come it runs out of power so quickly?"

"It takes a lot of power," said Simeon.

"Right. But, Ray's powers never seemed to weaken or run out. Mastermind's powers seem unlimited. Uncle Charlie never gets tired and needs to recharge his super power. Why mine?"

"Different powers require different energy."

"Right, but I'm not tired," explained Luke. "What 'energy' is it drawing from?"

"The Temple's," said Simeon. "All powers get their energy from the Temple."

"That sphere thingy I went into?"

"Yes. We believe so," said Simeon, helping Luke to put on the torso part of the space suit. "As far as we understand it, the Temples draw their power from deep within the planet, convert that energy into some kind of alternative quantum state, and use that to activate the special abilities it gives people. Your time traveling ability is a massive energy drain on the Temple. It takes time to recharge its reserves."

"Wait…" said Luke. "Does that mean, if I drain all the pyramid's energy, *no one* will be able to use their powers?"

Simeon shook his head. "No. Don't be ridiculous. The Temple is far more advanced than that. Every user is independently allocated. Your energy usage has no effect on anyone else's."

Luke nodded. "I see." He was still thinking about it. "But what if, hypothetically, the pyramid was destroyed, or something? What if the temple couldn't draw any power from a planet?"

Simeon wasn't sure. "I suppose," he said, figuring it out for the first time just now, "everyone who received a power from that temple would suddenly… be powerless."

Luke smiled.

Uncle Charlie noticed. "Nephew… whatcha thinkin'?"

"Uncle, I think I know how we can beat Mastermind."

Mastermind entered the heart of the pyramid on Sekhmet.

He stood in the center of the innermost room. Glowing alien language encircled him around the floor. Multicolored lights filled the room. He saw his own reflection in the floating sphere.

He grinned.

Where would it take him this time? To his early childhood, with his abusive, alcoholic mother? To his awkward teens, where he was constantly ridiculed and belittled by others? To his loser boss who treated him like worthless garbage all those years?

It didn't matter. He knew how it worked. Some traumatic event would play over and over again – until he summoned the strength to manifest a new power.

What would it be?

Mastermind touched the sphere.

Doctor Troyd stepped outside the meeting room. That went really well. Fortunately the president had already watched Mastermind's video. Things would've been a lot more difficult otherwise.

He and Luke stood in one of the many hallways at the United Nations building. People ran back and forth in a panic, rushing from one room to another. News of Mastermind's planet-wide takeover, the appearance of violent mutants around the world, and the erupting public chaos had government officials and their staffs in a total frenzy.

By now, Doctor Troyd assumed, most of the developed world had seen Mastermind's broadcast. Anyone watching and listening to that recording were now under his mind control. It was probably going viral on the world wide web at this very moment.

Some people, on the other side of the world, might still be sleeping. But as soon as they turned on their morning news, they too would be one of Mastermind's loyal servants.

As for everyone else – all the people who for whatever reason don't catch the video – will undoubtedly get the news from secondary sources and word of mouth.

Friends. Family. Co-workers. Facebook. News like this wouldn't stay quiet for long.

Friends would call each other to see if anyone had mutated near them. Religious leaders would declare Mastermind a false god. Tech-savvy teenagers were probably uploading the video to YouTube right at this very moment.

Of course, not everyone would be enslaved. Not right away, anyway. But the world was rapidly spinning into a state of chaos and disruption.

And when people panic, they don't think.

They're driven by their fears.

In a few minutes, the president would go live on every channel on TV – "we interrupt this program to bring you an important announcement from the President of the United States" – and tell everyone about the so-called "cure". Anyone not already under Mastermind's spell would soon voluntarily inject themselves with the very thing they were trying to avoid.

But Doctor Troyd knew there was one small problem with Mastermind's plan.

This chemical only activated people's cells for transformation. It opened up their DNA and prepared it for integration with new genetic material. But to actually change someone, to actually create a mutant, there needed to be a second injection. People needed to receive donor DNA.

How did Mastermind plan to do that?

Or was he simply leaving that up to random chance? A bee sting here, a mosquito bite there… inhaling a little dog or cat hair from their own pets. What about food? Doctor Troyd wondered… would eating the meat from a hamburger be enough genetic material to turn someone into a mutant cow?

Doctor Troyd was the expert scientist. He should know. He quickly did some calculations in his head. Maybe. It was possible. People could mutate that way. Or mutate from a bite or scratch from another mutant, even.

On the other hand, if they didn't receive any new genetic material, it could, in fact, destabilize the person's entire genetic makeup. Their cells might start to deteriorate and break down. That would leave an awful ugly mess in the end, too.

Maybe Mastermind didn't care. Some people would mutate. The rest would die. Mastermind would still be their god. After all, what more defining trait could there be for a god than choosing who would live and who would die?

Doctor Troyd still held the vial of glowing green chemical in his hand. Mastermind was smart. Mastermind was powerful. But it was this – BioGen X – that *Doctor Troyd* developed, that really made him godlike. So who was really the god? Mastermind – or the doctor?

Luke stared at the chemical. "How come you didn't give that to the president?"

"This?" Doctor Troyd asked. "I gave them the formula. That's all they need to mass produce it. This," he said, "is for you."

"Me?" asked Luke.

Doctor Troyd nodded.

"Mastermind's orders?"

The scientist nodded.

Luke swallowed hard. He was still under Mastermind's control. There was only one thing he could say. "I… I will obey."

"Good boy."

Luke – the other one, back on Eden, with Uncle Charlie and Simeon at the history museum – put on the last component of the space suit. He was covered head to toe, fully encased, protected with a high-tech, super cool-looking, advanced space suit.

"How do I look?" he said through the helmet. His voice came out of a small external speaker, where his mouth would be.

"Like someone from one of your sci-fi movies," said Uncle Charlie. "So what's the plan?"

"First, I need to save Ray, Dawn, and the other me. Then we'll regroup, prepare for Mastermind's arrival, save Ethos, and with the help of this suit, defeat Mastermind and his mutants. If that fails, I'll time travel again… and destroy the pyramid."

"WHAT?!" exclaimed Simeon. "No, no, no. You can't do that! Millions of people throughout the galaxy have visited our temple. You'd cut off every one of their powers! And who do you think they'll blame for that? It'll violate Eden's peace treaty. You can't!"

"There's more than that at stake here, Simeon. You think Mastermind will be satisfied with just Earth? How long before he attacks Eden next? Or some other world? He's got a working crystal. And an army of super powered mutants. We can't let that happen."

"I won't allow it," said Simeon, crossing his arms.

"Hopefully we won't need to."

"Alright," said Uncle Charlie. "But first thing's first. Go save your friends – and your, you know, other self."

"Right," said Luke. He took a step back. It felt so easy and free moving in this suit. He felt lightweight. Fluid, easy motions. It must've used some kind of hydraulics or motorized assistance. This suit probably multiplied his strength ten-fold! Sweet.

He closed his eyes. It had been a while since he last tried to time travel. Surely his energy source was fully recharged by now. He focused. He needed to go back to before Mastermind arrived on Eden. Before any of his mutants showed up. He would save his timeline duplicate copy from dying. He would save Ray from dying. He would save Dawn from dying.

And together, they would stop Mastermind, once and for all!

Chapter 28
THE BEGINNING OF THE END

Time travel was awesome. Luke couldn't believe he was so lucky. He always dreamed of having a power like this. Finally, his life was starting to make sense.

Too bad every time he used it, it took a massive energy drain on the pyramid. He had to go back in time to save his friends. He wished he had enough power left to go further into the future – decades, maybe centuries – and bring back some really cool high-tech, yet-to-be-invented weapons or something. That would surely give them the competitive edge they needed against Mastermind and the mutants.

But it'd be a miracle if he had enough power just to go back and save his friends. Hopefully enough time had passed. He tried.

He closed his eyes and he tried.

Everything around him shifted into a red light, blurring all around him, and then suddenly and instantly returning to normal – sometime in the past. But how far back did he go?

He looked behind him. The suit – the same one he was wearing – still hung on display. Okay. He was definitely in the past. Before they came to get the suit. He needed to get to the garden, to the portal entrance site. He needed to see if he went back far enough – before Mastermind showed up.

Instantly, a white light flashed and he suddenly found himself back at that garden.

He was a little disoriented and confused at first.

Did he just teleport – on his own?

Wait. Simeon said the suit could respond to thoughts. Oh my God. How awesome! This suit could teleport too!

His excitement was short lived. A large shadow passed over him. Luke looked up. It was a gryphon. Dawn. He watched her fly towards Mastermind in the distance.

Damn. He didn't go back far enough. He started running on foot after her.

She swooped down upon Mastermind, flapping her giant wings, knocking him backwards onto the ground.

"What the hell? Stupid bird! Get the hell off me!" Mastermind shouted.

Luke – in the space suit – quickly scanned the area. The heads-up display overlapped his view through his helmet. Data was constantly updated. Temperature, wind speed and direction, power levels within his suit. It tracked Dawn, Mastermind, and the others nearby, reading off vital statistics about each of them.

He saw his other self, still alive. Dawn and Ray too. He felt so glad to see them all alive.

Dawn, in gryphon form, stood on top of Mastermind, talons extended, holding him down. She let out a triumphant and ear-piercing screech. But then Rhino-Man started to charge at her.

His horn pounded into her side with ferocious impact, sending her flying back. But she flapped her wings and quickly regained control, charging back towards him.

Luke – in his space suit, from the near future – watched history repeat itself.

"Slimer, cover the wings!" Mastermind ordered.

Slimer slid across the ground, racing closer, hands extended. Her slimy, sticky goo shot out, splashing through the air, colliding with the Dawn's feathers.

Okay. This was it. Time to do *something*, Luke. Time to change history. "Hey Mastermind!" he shouted from behind.

Everyone stopped to turn and see him. Where did he come from? Who the heck was *he*? All they saw was the armored suit – not the man inside.

"This ends now!" Luke said.

Mastermind chuckled. "Have we met?"

Suddenly Mastermind's Astaria crystal slipped out of his pocket and started drifting upward into the air.

"What the hell?" He reached for it, but the crystal dodged away, floating even higher. Mastermind jumped to grab it a second time – and missed. His crystal moved even higher up into the sky. He looked around. "Who's doing that? Show yourself!"

The crystal drifted towards one of the trees, revealing Ray's hiding spot. "Give that back!" Mastermind commanded.

Dawn shape-shifted back into her human form, shaking off as much of Slimer's goo as possible. She started shape-shifting again, into something new.

"Oh no you don't!" Slimer exclaimed. She doused Dawn with more of her slimy, sticky goo.

So Dawn transformed into a humanoid slime-person too.

"Hey, no fair! That's my power!" exclaimed Slimer.

Luke's HUD had been tracking all persons the entire time. When Dawn shape-shifted both times – from gryphon to human, and from human to slime girl – red warnings appeared over his view screen. Luke quickly read the warning message. Dawn's DNA was breaking down. Her shape-shifting was stressing her cells to dangerous limits.

Ray grabbed Mastermind's crystal. "I got it!"

Arachnus leapt from treetop to treetop, quickly coming down on Ray. Luke saw it coming. His heads-up display tracked all that too.

Luke held his arm out, towards the approaching spider mutant. He sure hoped this worked. The HUD locked in on his target. Luke clenched his fist. The cutting laser fired.

The spider got shot right out of the sky.

Ray turned to see Arachnus, dangerously close, receive a powerful blast from a red laser beam. The wounded mutant fell to the ground and scurried away.

"Um, hey, thanks!" Ray said, waving at the mysterious man in the space suit.

Rhino-Man swung his fist at Dawn, but she skillfully dodged out of the way. Movement in her slime-based body was very fluid and agile. Rhino-Man attacked again. She swerved. He charged horn-first at her, but she gracefully slid out of the way and flicked a little bit of slime on him just for fun.

Luke's HUD alerted him with another warning. Venom snaked her way through the bushes, about to pounce on and attack the other, unprotected Luke.

"Oh no you don't!"

Suddenly something unseen slashed at his armor. And again. And again. Rapidly. Constant scratching and clawing at his battle suit.

"What the—?"

"Why won't you die?" Shadow screamed. Invisible claws struck at him again. "What's this thing made of anyway?"

Oh yeah. Right. The disappearing cat girl. Luke only had to think – and his HUD immediately began scanning other ranges of the light spectrum. Finally, he spotted her. Her body gave off heat. He could see her form. She slashed at him again.

He threw a single punch.

Knocked her out cold.

Wow. This suit must really multiple his strength after all.

The invisible cat girl laid unconscious on the ground.

Luke looked for Venom. Where did she go?

"Stop that!" yelled Rhino-Man. "Play fair!" He snorted through his large nostrils. He swung at Dawn again – and missed! She giggled playfully.

"Luke, look out!" battle-suit Luke shouted at his other self. Venom was right behind him, just waiting for the right second to sink her fangs into his flesh.

White light flashed, and battle-suit Luke teleported closer to his timeline duplicate self. He put his arms around his younger self and immediately activated the force field.

Venom pounced – and crashed into an invisible wall like a bird flying into a window. She even chipped one of her fangs.

"Owww!" she hissed.

Rhino-Man stomped his foot and created another earthquake. Dawn started shape-shifting again.

Warning messages flashed on Luke's HUD.

"No, Dawn, wait, stop!"

She returned to human form. "What?"

"Your cells are breaking down! You can't keep shape-shifting!"

"What?!" she exclaimed. She looked down at herself. She felt fine. Sorta. Oh crap. She was totally naked. Damn shape-shifting. Why couldn't her clothes transform with her body? And now apparently this special ability was killing her too! Sheesh.

She looked around. There was a large bush nearby she could hide behind. She ran there. Now where did she leave her clothes again?

Just then Rhino-Man pounded his horn into Luke's force field. The mutant knocked himself backwards against the invisible wall.

Another warning message flashed. The suit's power reserves were dangerously low. It never occurred to him that it might've been low to begin with, considering it was sitting on display in that museum for who knew how long.

Damn. Okay. Everything would be fine. He changed history. He saved their lives. What they needed to do now was make a quick retreat, regroup with Uncle Charlie, and fully recharge this suit's batteries.

"We gotta get out of here," Luke said.

Rhino-Man charged into the force field again, knocking himself backwards a second time.

Crap. Luke's crystal was in his pocket, inside the suit. No way to get it out without taking off this whole damn thing! How were they going to escape? Maybe the same way they did last time.

Because there was yet *another* Luke – the original one, the earlier version of himself – hiding in the distance with his uncle and Simeon. Gosh, time travel was confusing sometimes. Anyway, *they* had a crystal.

What happened before? The timeline duplicate got killed by Venom. Ray got bit by Arachnus. Dawn started losing control of her shape-shifting. So Uncle Charlie and the first Luke made a hasty retreat.

Rhino-Man crashed into Luke's force field a third time. Geez, this guy didn't give up!

Okay. Luke had an idea. Teleport them all to Charlie's hiding spot, and then they could all escape through a portal.

Just one question… could his new suit do all that?

Rhino-Man pounced his force field again.

Warning messages flashed brighter. Power levels were dropping.

Dammit!

Did he still have enough power to teleport everyone to safety?

Nearby, Dawn finished putting the last of her clothes back on. But as she did, momentarily distracted, Arachnus snuck up behind her and grabbed her with his eight legs. She screamed.

"Dawn!" Ray shouted.

Luke raised his hand again, preparing to fire. The HUD locked onto Arachnus. The cutting laser fired – but instantly diffused the instant it collided with the inside of his own force field. Double-dammit! With a single thought, his force field lowered. He fired again, and with computer-aided precision, he struck Arachnus a second time. It was enough pain to send that spider running away.

Rhino-Man crashed into Luke's back. The suit protected him from the bulk of the impact, but it was still strong enough to throw him off balance. He tripped forward.

The other Luke looked at Dawn and Ray. His facial expression said it all: did either of them have any idea who this armored suit guy was? Dawn and Ray shook their heads, but apparently he was on their side.

Uncle Charlie and the "original" Luke came running from the distance.

As they did, they passed by a small little pond. And Kraken, the sea monster, leapt out of the water, tentacles extended, and grabbed that Luke.

"Whoa—hellllp!" was all anyone heard, before the splash, as Kraken took that Luke under water.

Charlie stopped. "Luke?" Where did he go? "LUKE!"

The timeline duplicate Luke looked in Charlie's direction. What was going on? Too much was happening. Everything was too confusing.

Rhino-Man slammed his fist onto battle-suit Luke's chest. The suit protected him, but suffered some minor damage from the internal earthquake tremors.

Ray stood next to Dawn. He used his power to push away Slimer – not realizing, she was just a distraction.

Venom – *again, on this timeline too* – sank her fangs into Luke's neck. "OWWW!!!" he exclaimed. Her black poison spread into and throughout his exposed body.

Battle-suit Luke was on the ground, thanks to Rhino-Man's relentless pounding.

Warning messages kept flashing on his heads-up display. Systems were receiving too much damage. But then he heard his other self scream. He looked over. And saw his timeline duplicate fall to the ground.

"NOOOO!!!!!" battle-suit Luke exclaimed.

"LUKE!!!!" Charlie called. The old man ran up to the water's edge. He couldn't see them. Where were they?

Bubbles escaped to the surface.

Charlie wanted to jump into the water to save his nephew – but feared the sea monster mutant would just as easily kill him too. He'd be no good if they were *both* dead – but he had to do *something*!

Just then, that Luke's body floated up, lifeless.

Charlie's face filled with agonizing pain.

Rhino-Man pounded on battle-suit Luke again and again. More and more damage. Systems failing. Warning messages practically blinding him from seeing anything.

Charlie fell to his knees.

Somehow, through all the warning messages, the only remaining living Luke – the one still barely protected by the suit – saw Kraken tracking on his HUD. The sea monster's tentacles reached up out of the water, about to snatch Charlie down into a watery grave.

"Nooo!!!" Luke shouted. He had to save his uncle. Instantly he teleported in a flash of white light. He appeared next to the old man. Kraken's tentacle collided into the armor. *Thud.* Luke threw his arms around his uncle. Together they teleported again.

They instantly reappeared next to Ray and Dawn who, thank goodness, at least they were both still alive.

Ray pushed everyone else away with his power. Luke instantly activated a force field large enough to protect them all.

"Hurry Uncle," Luke said. "Get us out of here!"

"Uncle?" Ray remarked, confused.

Uncle Charlie was in tears. "I don't…"

Warning messages flashed in front of Luke's eyes. Power failure was imminent. He couldn't hold these shields up for much longer. Especially with another impact from Rhino-Man.

"He…" said Charlie.

"Take us to Virgo. Or back to Earth. I don't care, just get us out of here!" Luke demanded.

Charlie looked over to the small lake in the distance. Where his nephew floated lifelessly. "He has it…"

"The crystal?"

Charlie nodded.

"We have Mastermind's crystal!" Ray said, holding it up.

Charlie reached for it.

Suddenly, it disappeared. Right of out Ray's fingers. Poof. Vanished. Gone.

"What the—?"

A feline feminine voice giggled.

Shadow appeared in front of them, holding the crystal.

"You!" Dawn shouted.

Ray held his hand out, using his gravity power to pull the crystal out of Shadow's paws. It started to slip out.

"Oh no you don't!" the cat girl screamed.

Why didn't Luke see her? She must've been invisible the whole time, hiding inside their force field, waiting for the right moment to steal back that crystal!

Did he constantly have to be scanning for invisible things to see them on his HUD? Speaking of, a new warning message flashed in front of Luke's eyes.

"Uh oh…" said Luke. "Guys, the shield's about to…"

The other mutants were all gathered around. Able to see and hear everything. Slimer continually threw little balls of slime at them, testing to see if the force field was still there. Venom hissed, waiting to strike the second they were vulnerable.

Rhino-Man snorted and slammed his fist into the invisible shield again. It was the final blow. The shield failed.

Slimer threw another test slime ball. It splashed on the ground next to Dawn's foot.

The mutants charged in.

"Shit!" Ray exclaimed. Shadow barely held onto her crystal with both hands. Ray almost had it. But the other mutants surrounded them, coming down on them. He had to let it go. He immediately spun around, sent one anti-gravity shockwave after another, one by one, quickly blasting away the other mutants. But by the time he turned around back to Shadow, she was gone. Invisible again, and running away with the now-invisible crystal as well. "Dammit!"

Rhino-Man regained his footing and started charging forward again. Ray pushed him back with another blast of anti-gravity.

Dawn wanted to shape-shift. Maybe turn into a powerful dragon or something. But what if what the mysterious armored man said was true? If she kept shape-shifting, would she die?

Luke held out his hand, ready to fire another laser shot. But the power failed.

Nothing happened. Dammit! His suit was too badly damaged and too drained on power. He was suddenly useless. Powerless. They were defenseless.

"Uncle," said Luke. "Help me get this off." Luke pulled off his helmet. For the first time, everyone saw who he really was.

"LUKE!!!" they all shouted.

Venom leaped forward, claws extended, fangs exposed. Ray barely blasted her away in the nick of time.

"Um, yeah, hi. From the future. My crystal's in my pocket, but I can't reach it with the suit on."

Ray pushed back Slimer and Kraken. "Um, hurry up guys – I can't keep this up forever!"

Dawn helped Charlie get Luke's suit off.

Luke stepped out of the suit as fast as possible. As soon as he could reach into his pocket, he grabbed his crystal, quickly drew a large circle on the ground, and marked it with the Virgo symbol. The portal instantly opened.

"How did you—?" asked Charlie.

Arachnus attacked Ray from behind. Dawn sucker punched the spider in its ugly face. "Get off my boyfriend!"

"Thanks Dawn," said Ray, blasting back Rhino-Man.

Charlie jumped through the portal, into the darkness.

"Go!" Ray told Dawn.

She jumped in.

"You next," said Ray.

Luke threw the pieces of his battle suit into the hole and leapt in after.

Ray gave one final gravity blast, pushing the oncoming mutants back. He jumped backwards into the portal. "Geronimo!"

Luke started to X-out the portal. Venom and Arachnus almost made it through the opening. Arachnus reached through with one of his extra arms. The portal closed. It cut the spider's arm off with a clean and instant slice. The black, hairy arm fell to the floor with a soft thud.

Dawn gasped.

Ray held her close.

Luke sighed with relief.

They were safe.

"Everyone okay?" asked Charlie.

"I think so. Where are we?" asked Ray.

"Give it a second," said Luke.

Dim lights began to illuminate along the floor and walls. It was familiar. Just like the pyramid on the desert world.

Dawn looked around. "Are we where I think we are?"

"Not exactly," said Luke.

Uncle Charlie pulled himself together. He caught his breath. "Okay, start talking. Where'd you get that armored suit? And where'd you come from, anyway?"

"I'm from another timeline," Luke said. "A few hours into the future." He sighed. "Ray and Dawn died. I had to save them."

"We what?" remarked Ray.

"That spider mutant poisoned you. We brought you here, tried to save you. But we were too late."

"Where is *here* anyway?" Dawn asked.

"Another pyramid. Floating through space."

Ray shook his head. "This is too much for me."

"Dawn, your shape-shifting… we've got to find a way to stabilize your cells. The more you use your power, the faster they break down. I'm sorry. You can't shape-shift until we figure something out."

She nodded. "Okay." She took him seriously.

"What about your other self," asked Charlie, "from your earlier timelines?"

"I know," said Luke. "On my timeline, the other me died the same way, from Venom. I tried to save him." He lowered his head. He failed.

No one wanted to mention the *other*-other Luke who died a moment ago, either. Two Lukes died back on Eden. Only the one remained. The one from the future. With his high-tech armored suit.

But Luke was all too aware of his other selves' untimely deaths. And it worried him a bit. His *younger* self died. Shouldn't he be fading out of existence now or something? Like Marty McFly in *Back to the Future*, when he accidentally prevented his parents from getting married? Luke created his own paradox. He shouldn't be around anymore. Why was he still here?

Time travel was giving him a headache. It was terrible to think this, but maybe there was some universal principle or something, some special time travel law, that prevented timeline duplicates from surviving for too long. Maybe there was only supposed to be one Luke at any one time. At least this one survived. This one was still alive. The others weren't really dead. A part of them lived on in him.

Poor consolation. But it was the only way they could cope with it. The only way they could make some kind of peace with it.

"Can you go back in time again, and try to save everyone this time?" asked Dawn.

Luke shook his head. "I didn't make it far back enough the first time." He sighed.

"My power takes forever to recharge."

"Hey," said Charlie, trying to keep them positive, "look at the bright side. We're all safe and alive now, thanks to you."

"Yeah," said Ray, "I for one am glad to be alive."

"Me too," soberly said Dawn.

"Time travel sucks," said Luke. "I can't go very far, and when I do, I end up creating timeline copies of myself – who only end up dying. It's not fair, it's not right. I can't keep doing this."

"Luke, don't be so hard on yourself, man," said Ray.

"Yeah," said Dawn. "Your power may be limited, but you're still doing good with it."

"I take it I showed you the Virgo symbol on your alternate timeline," said Uncle Charlie. "But where'd you get your little suit of armor?"

"Back on Eden, actually, at the history museum. Simeon said I could keep it if it'll help us defeat Mastermind."

"Speaking of," said Ray, "we got our asses kicked back there. And we had a time traveler from the future with a high-tech battle suit to help us. Sounds like things went even worse the first time around."

"Yeah," said Dawn. "We're not exactly fighters."

"I know," sighed Luke. "I know…"

"Well," said Charlie, smiling a little. "Maybe it's time you started playing your strong suit."

Luke looked up at him.

"Stop trying to be something you're not," the old man said. "Start being what you are."

"Which is?" Luke asked.

"Smart," said the old man. "Be smart."

Chapter 29

PLAN B

That was, after all, how Mastermind had been playing all along.

"Fascinating," was all the villain said, coming out from behind a large tree. No one even noticed he disappeared during that fight.

Arachnus cried, holding his severed arm. Not to mention several bad wounds from getting hit by the cutting laser. He was in a lot of pain.

"Relax, you'll live," said Mastermind.

The others gathered around. Kraken, Slimer, Rhino-Man, and Venom. Shadow handed the crystal back to Mastermind.

"Good girl."

He focused on the glowing pink crystal. "Amazing piece of technology, don't you think?" He looked back at the ground, where the others had just escaped. "Did anyone see what symbol they used?"

All the mutants shook their heads.

He sighed. "It appears they're going to be more of a nuisance after all. But," he said, "we're out of time. Destiny awaits."

He drew a large circle on the ground. Then he marked the "M1" symbol, the first portal destination he had programmed into the crystal.

The portal opened to reveal the Taj Mahal on the other side. "You," he said to Venom, "Go through, start killing random people. Make sure you're seen doing it. Wake everyone up. Get their attention. Be as public as you can. Your job is to spread fear and chaos. Got it?"

Venom nodded.

"Now go!" Mastermind commanded.

Venom jumped into the portal.

Mastermind repeated history again, exactly as before, with each one of them. He sent Shadow to Japan. Arachnus to Russia. Rhino-Man to Los Angeles. Kraken to Greece. And last but not least, Slimer to the Middle East.

"The desert?" Slimer complained. "I hate the desert."

"Take it out on them, honey." Mastermind looked into her eyes, giving her an order. "Now go. And do your worst."

She sighed and jumped into the portal.

After closing the last portal, Mastermind looked around at Eden one last time. Beautiful place. He'd definitely come to conquer this world next. After all, he was God. And *all* people, throughout the galaxy, would come to worship and obey him.

But Chuck, his nephew Luke, and the others were proving to be a recurring nuisance. Mastermind would not take any chances with them. He couldn't ignore them any longer. He needed to be prepared. Extra insurance. Some kind of guarantee. And he knew just where to get it.

He opened a portal, with the triangle symbol, back to Planet Sekhmet. Across the blazing sand dunes and endless desert awaited the great pyramid, the Temple of the Gods. Where, throughout history, ordinary mortals were given the power to become gods themselves. Mastermind would soon be God among gods.

And his rule over Earth would be eternal and absolute.

"I'm telling you, this won't work," said Luke.

"We have to try," said Dawn, sitting up onto the table inside the medical lab.

"He's right," said Ray. "I'm sure this healing chamber is no different from the one on Eden. If they couldn't help you there, it's not going to work here."

"Geez," said Dawn. "I feel like I'm surrounded by pessimists. It'll work. It has to."

Charlie shrugged. "It's worth a try. Lay down."

Dawn laid across the medical table.

Just like before, lights from above started scanning her. And just like before, it was unable to identify her genome. The computer couldn't recognize her; it didn't know how to repair her deteriorating cells.

After several repeated failing attempts, Dawn finally gave up. "Fine," she said, sitting back up. "But I love shape-shifting. I don't want to give that up. I just got started!"

"I know," said Luke, sighing. Something heavy was weighing on his mind. "Ray, there's something I gotta ask you. You too, Uncle."

"What?" asked Ray.

Luke took a slow breath. "There *is* a way we can defeat Mastermind and his mutants pretty easily. A *smart* way. But," he finally said, "it means we'd have to lose our powers too."

"What are you talking about?" Charlie asked.

"On the other timeline," he said, "I learned something. If we can somehow destroy the pyramid, it'll disable everyone's powers."

"Say what?" Ray remarked.

"Apparently, if I understood it right, the pyramids draw power from the planet, and somehow use that to fuel everyone's abilities, everyone's super powers. If we destroy the pyramid, it'll cut off their energy source, and they won't be able to use their powers anymore."

"But neither will we," said Ray, getting it.

"Right," said Luke.

"You guys can't do that," said Dawn. "We need our powers to defeat them. Okay, so Mastermind's got mind control, and it seems he gave all his mutant lackeys some powers too. But what's to stop Mastermind from finding another pyramid like this one and giving himself the same power all over again? And even if we shut down all the mutants' powers, they're still mutants, and still plenty dangerous without any powers."

"True," said Luke.

"You'd have to destroy two different pyramids too," said Uncle Charlie. "Mastermind got his power from the same temple I did, on Eden. But we saw him with his mutants on Sekhmet, where they likely got all their powers."

"Simeon also mentioned that 'millions' of other people had gotten powers from the pyramid on Eden. I'd be cutting them off too," said Luke. "But I don't have any better ideas."

"Look," said Ray, "whatever we're going to do, we better do it fast. Having powers is cool, but I'd give it up in a heartbeat if it meant saving the world."

Luke slowly nodded. It wasn't as easy for him to say that, but Ray was right. It had been Luke's dream his entire life to have super powers, to be able to time travel, to be a real world super hero. But… not at this cost.

But wait a minute. They were in another pyramid. What if they went into *this* pyramid's inner chamber, touched the floating sphere again, and got a *new* power? They could destroy the other pyramids, cut off Mastermind and his mutants' powers, but still leave them – Luke, Ray, Dawn, and Uncle Charlie – fully powered.

No, wait. That wouldn't work. The pyramids drew power from the core of a planet. And they were nowhere near a planet.

Of course… maybe they could find one.

"Uncle," said Luke, curiously. "We're inside a pyramid, right?"

His uncle nodded.

"Flying through space."

"I believe so," said the old man.

"That means these aren't buildings or temples. They're *space ships.* And space ships can travel to other planets."

"Where are you going with this?" asked Uncle Charlie.

"Exactly!" said Luke, excitedly. "We just need to find the nearest planet, land, power up the pyramid, get ourselves new powers, and then –"

Dawn's eyes lit up. "And then we can disable Mastermind and all his mutants!"

"But we'd still have powers," said Ray. "Because we'll leave this pyramid in one piece."

Charlie shrugged. "That might actually work," he said. "I don't believe Mastermind knows this symbol. He's probably never been here."

"Then it's a plan," said Luke. "All we gotta do is find a planet, and hope it doesn't take too long to get there. I'm assuming these things have warp drives or something, right?"

Charlie laughed. "Beats me!"

Meanwhile back on Earth, history played out the same as it had originally. Luke's little bit of time traveling changed nothing there.

Rhino-Man terrorized Los Angeles. Shadow drew attention in Tokyo. Venom made people run for their lives in India. Arachnus became everyone's worst nightmare in Russia. Kraken made ancient sea monsters from Greek mythology look like amateurs. And Slimer, well, she wasn't so successful. The Middle East had enough conflict and fighting already. Some people actually shot at *her*, believe it or not, but the bullets just passed right through her gooey body.

The world slipped into chaos and fear.

Doctor Troyd met with the president. Gave him the formula for the "cure". More and more people saw Mastermind's video on television and the Internet. More and more people became enslaved to his mind control. And already facilities received instructions on how to mass produce BioGen X.

"My fellow Americans," appeared the president on national television, "a terrorist calling himself 'Mastermind' has infected the world with a plague turning ordinary humans into hideous monsters. He claims to be a god. America is a united nation under *one* God. We will not obey any false gods. I'm pleased to inform you that our top scientists in this great nation have already discovered a cure."

He was, of course, referring to the very thing that would turn people into mutants. But the people trusted their government. They didn't know the president was already under Mastermind's mind control.

"I'm urging all Americans – and all citizens of Planet Earth – to go immediately to your nearest hospital or pharmacy, where vaccines are currently being mass produced and distributed to the public free of charge. If you cannot make it to a distribution center within 24 hours, call the toll-free number at the bottom of your screen, and a representative of the CDC will bring the vaccine to you."

He appeared live on every channel. Interrupting every show. Taking priority over all others. His broadcast was bounced off satellites and sent into homes and businesses around the world. Translated in dozens of languages.

"Please, my fellow Americans and fellow citizens of the world, we cannot allow this plague to spread any farther. Get vaccinated immediately. Have your friends and family members vaccinated. Your co-workers, your neighbors, everyone you know. This is a mandatory worldwide vaccination. If just one person fails to receive the cure, the plague may spread out of control. Act now, and save us all. The mutation plague is highly contagious and extremely dangerous. Don't wait. Get yourself and your loved ones vaccinated immediately."

Phase 5, complete: Get everyone *not* already affected by Mastermind's mind control to voluntarily inject and mutate themselves.

The president continued his speech, mentioning how other world leaders from other nations have been given the formula and financial resources to distribute the so-called "cure" to all their people too.

Sure, not *every* human on Planet Earth would get it. It'd take some time to get it into third world countries. Or people living far away in isolation, out in the wilderness or in remote corners of the globe. But based on how fast information traveled – and fear and panic – Doctor Troyd estimated that 90% of the world's population will be infected with BioGen X by the end of the week. Possibly 40% or more within 48 hours.

It only took a few seconds to inject a needle into someone. A few seconds. That would forever change their lives.

Forever recreate the world… according to Mastermind's vision and design.

After leaving the United Nations building, Doctor Troyd sat in the back of another taxi with Luke. Troyd still had the vial of BioGen X. He still had his instructions to mutate Luke into something. Mastermind left the "into what" part up to the good doctor. Hmm. What should Luke become?

They already had a cat, spider, rhinoceros, snake, sea monster, and slimy-slug thing. Should Luke become a dog? A bird of some kind? No, maybe a turtle. That might be cool.

The taxi dropped them off at their destination.

The Queens Zoo in New York.

The streets were eerily empty. Everyone must've been on the highway, headed for the nearest hospital. Or hiding out at home. Or something. Doctor Troyd wasn't a

New York native or anything, but he imagined the streets would be busier than this. Rush hour was pretty much over. But still. It was practically a ghost town.

But then again, he knew what was going on. Everyone was glued to a television somewhere. Watching the news as Mastermind's grand plan unfolded. The mutant attacks around the world. His "obey me" video playing over and over again on all the major networks. Probably viral on the Internet by now too.

Doctor Troyd made a point not to watch that video. Now that he had his hearing back, he didn't want to lock eyes with that man and hear any commands. So Troyd played along. Mastermind made him a promise – a promise that, so far, he seemed to be holding up. When all this was over, Doctor Troyd would get to see his daughter again. And hear her sing. Her beautiful voice. That was what he focused on.

"Come," said Doctor Troyd.

Luke followed him to the park entrance. The zoo was empty by now.

"Sorry sir," said the only remaining guard. "We're closing."

Doctor Troyd sighed. Again? He pulled out his cell phone, loaded Mastermind's message, and pressed play.

"You will grant this man access to anywhere and anyone," said Mastermind's recording.

The guard looked right at the video.

"Oh, uh, right. Of course. I'm sorry. But you heard about the mutant plague, right? People around the world are turning into monsters. We're closing early."

"We'll be fine," said Doctor Troyd, walking past him. "Oh, and we'll need your keys. We may need access inside some of the animal exhibits."

"No problem," said the guard, handing him the keys.

That little video sure was coming in handy. It helped them get through security at the United Nations building and gain access to the President of United States. It got them into the local park zoo. Hmm. Maybe Troyd should use it for getting into other places too. Like… Area 51? Fort Knox? Celine Dion concerts – hey, he was a fan. Ooh, or skipping all the long lines at theme parks and grocery stores! Yeah. Anything was possible…

They passed various animal exhibits. The aviary. Sea lion pool. Then the "South American Trail" section, where there were deer and bears. Hmm. A bear might be a good fit. Mastermind would appreciate a mutant bear.

But… no. Something else. So they kept walking. Saw some porcupines. That could be interesting. But… nah.

Finally, they came upon a large cage for a familiar winged creature. *Pteropus personatus*, read the display. The fruit bat. "Yes," said Doctor Troyd, smiling as he eyed up Luke. "I think this will do just fine."

Plan B

"This..." said Luke, swallowing hard, "is what Mastermind wishes for me?"

Doctor Troyd nodded.

For a moment, he almost felt sorry for Luke. He was sure Luke didn't actually want to get mutated. When Luke woke up this morning, he probably didn't imagine his day would end like this. Popping out of some mysterious hovering sphere, falling under Mastermind's control, and becoming one of his mutant henchmen.

But, that was life. We don't always get what we want. Or expect. And this was just Luke's fate, his future.

Still, admittedly, Mastermind was a bit crazy. Claiming to be a god, planning to rule the world. Doctor Troyd knew better than to ever cross or challenge him. Mastermind was a force beyond reason. A threat beyond comprehension. Doctor Troyd willingly obeyed, to avoid the consequences.

Oh well. Luke would become a mutant. So what? So would the rest of the world in a matter of days or weeks. And any who resisted, any who somehow avoided the "cure", would be hunted down and undoubtedly killed.

This was the new world order. A new world of mutants. Luke wasn't the first. And he certainly wasn't going to be the last.

Troyd reached into his pocket and pulled out the vial of green liquid. Then, out of his other coat pocket, he retrieved a small hypodermic needle.

"You better take off your clothes," he said. "Your mutations will be a bit unpredictable. Don't want you hurting or choking yourself with your old clothes, depending on how your new form manifests."

Luke nodded. "I understand."

He slowly disrobed as Doctor Troyd filled the needle with the glowing green chemical.

"Now hold out your arm," said the scientist.

Luke stepped out of his pants. Now completely naked. Totally exposed. Completely vulnerable. Luke obeyed and held out his arm.

Doctor Troyd injected him.

"That's done," said the scientist.

"I feel funny," Luke said.

"It hasn't started yet. Relax." Doctor Troyd looked at the bats flying around. Hmm. Catching one might be kinda hard. He saw an entrance to the side. "Now go inside," he said, pointing at the door.

"Oh. Okay," said Luke.

He climbed over the barrier, walked off the path, and went up to the side entrance. "It's locked."

"Here," said Troyd, tossing him the guard's keys.

Luke unlocked the door and stepped inside. He left the keys next to the door.

Doctor Troyd glanced down at Luke's pile of empty clothes on the ground. His glowing pink crystal slid out of a pocket. Hmm. That could be useful later. Doctor Troyd discretely picked it up and tucked it away in his own pocket.

Inside the cage, the bats pretty much ignored Luke. They flew all around him, but none were willing to give him any sample DNA.

"Swat at them," said Doctor Troyd. "Try to get them angry. Get one to bite you!"

"But—"

"Do it!" shouted Doctor Troyd. "Mastermind wants this for you." He hesitated to say it. "Obey his will."

Luke nodded. "Okay. I will obey."

He started swatting. Tried chasing the bats. Finally, after some considerable effort, one finally bit him.

"Ow!" Luke exclaimed. It got his finger. It drew blood.

Both Luke and the doctor knew it was now too late. Luke would begin transforming any second...

And he did.

First his skin turned dark. His ears grew larger. His nose reshaped. And wings – giant black bat wings – spread out from under his armpits, down along the length of his arms, stretching all the way to his hands, connecting from his arms down to the sides of his body.

Brown and black fur spread across his body. His fingers and toes lengthened, becoming more bat-like. Suddenly he could hear more, smell more, sense more.

Despite the myth that all bats were blind, Luke could still see quite well. But now he could also "see" with his hearing. The subtle differences of how the sound echoed around him. He could tell how hard or soft an object was, and how far away it was, just by how the ambient sound around him seemed to bounce off it.

Cool.

"How do you feel?" asked Doctor Troyd.

"I feel... like Mastermind's newest mutant. Ready to worship and obey my god who created me this way."

Troyd nodded slowly. Had they gone too far? Too late for second guessing now. "We need to give you an appropriate name," said the doctor.

"Echo," said Luke. "Call me Echo."

Chapter 30
WHERE NO NERD HAS GONE BEFORE

Luke placed the palm of his hand flat against the wall.

The interactive menu displayed.

"Directions to the bridge," said Luke. Nothing happened. "Um, command center? Control room? Pilot deck? Navigation?"

A map suddenly appeared, identifying their current location and the navigation center, with a dotted red line providing directions from here to there.

"Google would've figured out what I meant sooner," he said.

"That is so cool," said Ray, staring at the interface.

Uncle Charlie looked at the interactive map glowing on the wall. "Hmm," said the old man, "looks like quite a walk from here."

"Then we better get moving," said Luke.

"Or," said Charlie, "we go here," he pointed, "to their teleporter pads. We'll get there a lot faster."

"Teleporter pads?" asked Ray.

Dawn smiled. "Like on *Star Trek*!"

"Right!" said Luke, remembering them from before. "The 'recall' button thingy. How we got away from that alien snake den underground lair cavern."

"Um, right," said Charlie. "Anyway, it's much closer. We'll go there. These pyramids are huge on the inside. We could get lost for days if we're not careful."

"Days?" Dawn remarked skeptically.

"If we're not careful," Charlie repeated. "This way."

He led them to the familiar hexagonal room, where three circular platforms laid side by side along the floor.

Luke stepped up onto one of the pads. "So how do we tell it where to send us? Where's Miles O'Brien when you need him?"

"Who?" asked Dawn.

"Star Trek character," explained Ray.

"Oh," she said. "I guess I should've known that. Is he related to Mr. Spock?"

"What?" remarked Luke. "No. They're not even on the same series. Spock was on the original series, and Chief O'Brien was—"

"It's voice activated," interrupted Uncle Charlie.

"Thank you," said Ray.

Charlie stepped onto one of the open pads. Dawn and Ray stepped onto the remaining third. She held his hand tightly.

"Is this going to hurt?" she asked.

"Won't feel a thing," said Luke.

"Send us to the navigation room," Charlie called out loud.

"Energize!" said Luke.

A circle of white light instantly appeared around each pad, rose up into the air above them, and they all disappeared.

Elsewhere, the same circle of white light appeared on the floor, lifted up, and they reappeared there.

They were on the bridge of this starship. The command center. The navigation room. The place where the pilot – oh my God, there was a pilot.

The room was shaped like a giant dome. With a perfect view of all the stars around them. They appeared to be somewhere near the top of the pyramid. Various computers – at least, they assumed these machines were computers – lined the edges of the dome walls. And in the middle, at the center of it all, was a single chair, a large seat, comfortably positioned in front of several display panels and control pads.

Someone was there.

In the seat. Controlling the pyramid space ship.

They could only see it from behind. But what they saw – a long, thin gray-skinned hand... Could it be? Were they actually in the presence of … an intelligent alien creature?

They were all silent.

Luke looked to his uncle. The old man shrugged, saying nothing. Ray tried to keep his cool, but inside, he was freaking out. Dawn, well, she didn't feel like waiting any longer, so she just started walking right up toward it.

"Dawn!" whispered Ray.

She got closer. "Um… hello?"

The alien turned around.

Mastermind launched out of the sphere inside the pyramid on Sekhmet.

He laid on the floor, curled up in the fetal position, shivering. His eyes stared blankly forward, lost in the psychological trauma of the memory he just relived over and over. But then a faint smile slowly emerged on his face. And his smile got bigger.

Mastermind started to relax. His breathing and heart rate slowed down. He sat up, looked at the palm of his hand, and began laughing.

Perfect.

Meanwhile, back on Earth, the president's message played over and over, in multiple languages, across multiple borders. As did Mastermind's video.

Echo – the bat mutant formerly known as Luke from a slightly different timeline – flapped his new giant bat wings. It took some practice, but with a little effort, he started to lift himself off the ground. "I'm doing it! I'm doing it!" he shouted. "I can fly!"

"I'm thrilled for you," said Doctor Troyd. "I'm not sure where Mastermind wants to send you. I'd guess New York's a good place to start, but I'm not going to take any chances of messing up his 'master plan'."

Echo landed back down on his feet. "What *is* Mastermind's plan? He made us into mutants. But surely he wants more than our obedience and worship. What's his ultimate goal?"

"More than becoming a god?" Troyd laughed. "I don't know any more than you do. He just hired me to help develop the solution for rapid genetic mutation. Frankly, I'm surprised he's still keeping me around."

"Why hasn't he mutated you yet?"

"Because I've got the only real antidote," said the scientist. "I may be a little eccentric, but I'm not crazy!"

"You have the cure? I mean, the *real* cure?" asked Echo.

Doctor Troyd nodded.

"Interesting."

"Um, hello?" Dawn asked, approaching the alien.

It turned around.

"Oh my God," said Ray, seeing it's face.

Luke gasped.

Charlie stood in silence.

Dawn's eyes went wide with disbelief.

"It's one of the Roswell aliens!" Ray exclaimed.

"They're not *from* Roswell," Luke explained. "They just crashed there, allegedly, back in 1947."

It started speaking. In a language they didn't understand. The sounds were hushed and muffled, rapid and unintelligible. Ray couldn't stop staring at its big bulging gray head, those large solid black eyes, and that tiny mouth and nose where its sounds kept coming from.

"I don't suppose you speak English," said Dawn.

It kept uttering in that strange language.

"No, of course not, that'd be too easy," she said.

"We need a universal language," said Luke. "Like math or science or something. Prime numbers. Something we can—"

The tall skinny gray alien lifted its long narrow finger towards Luke, pointing. Then it said a word they all recognized. "Astaria."

Luke looked down at his pocket. The pink crystal partially stuck out of his pocket, still glowing. He pulled it out completely and held it up. "Yes. Astaria." Then he pointed at himself. "Luke." He gestured toward his uncle. "Charlie." And then to his friend. "Ray."

"And Dawn," she said, pointing at herself, standing in front of the tall skinny gray alien.

It shook its head, either not understanding or not caring. It turned back around, focusing on the controls.

"Well that was rude," said Luke.

"Luke," said Charlie, "I've never seen one of… that, before."

Dawn tapped the alien on its narrow shoulder. "Um, excuse me." The alien turned its massive head to look at her. "Hi, sorry. We really need to pilot this ship to the nearest planet, so we can get new powers and stuff, and stop a *really* bad man from taking over our planet. Earth. Do you know where that is? Have you been to Earth?"

The alien shook its head. Did it understand her? The gray creature seemed to sigh, then turned back around to its controls. It made some adjustments, or something, and then looked back at Dawn, waiting for something.

Dawn looked awkwardly back at it. Were they going to a planet now?

The alien started muttering again.

"I'm sorry, I don't understand you."

The alien suddenly got a little more excited. It kept talking.

"What? What are you saying?"

Suddenly Dawn heard her own voice, repeated through the machine in front of the alien, but in the alien's language. Then the alien spoke again, in its own language, and a second later, the same machine repeated the alien's words, in Dawn's language.

"Where do you come from?" it said, apparently.

"Hey guys," Dawn said back to them. "I think he's got some kind of translator."

Her words repeated a second later, in the alien's native words.

Luke and then Charlie approached closer. Not wanting to be left behind or alone, Ray quickly caught up with them.

"Really?" asked Luke. "How cool!"

His words, too, were repeated to the alien in translation.

The alien spoke again, to all of them. "Where do you all come from?"

"Earth," said Luke.

The alien didn't seem to know where that was.

"Um, third planet in the Sol system. Here, do you have star charts somewhere? I can point it out."

"Do you have more Astaria crystals there?" asked the alien.

Luke looked at his crystal. "No, just this one. And, well, I guess the one Mastermind found too."

"And the one your timeline-copy had, before, you know… that squid monster got him," said Ray.

"Oh right. He would've had one too," realized Luke. "Hmm. That makes me wonder. There's got to be another one of me out there somewhere too. From inside the sphere, after the first time I time traveled to save you guys. He'd have a crystal too."

Charlie shook his head. "Time travel makes my head hurt. How can there be three crystals from just the one?"

"It's called temporal stacking," said Luke, referring back to some theory he read somewhere once. "Newton's laws preserve matter and energy, even when the spacetime continuum gets rearranged. Changing history won't force something in the present to cease to exist. That only happens in the movies. You see, the crystal existed on the original timeline, and then future me went back in time, carrying it with me. Now there are two. Unless I return to the future with that crystal, without altering my own timeline somehow, both will continue to exist."

"You're not helping any," said the old man.

"It's the same reason why there's been multiple me's running around too. Every time I change my own past, I run the risk of leaving an extra me on the new timeline." He lowered his head and voice. "But they don't seem to last too long, though. Maybe they don't pop out of existence or fade away… but apparently the universe has some kind of timeline-correcting law the prevents extra copies…" He shook his head. "Time travel is too dangerous. They're dead – I'm dead – because of me."

"Luke," said Ray, putting his arm over his friend's shoulders, "I still don't follow what you're saying. But as for the other you's – it's not like you *tried* to kill them. You were trying to save them! You gotta stop blaming yourself. You did your best, man."

"I know," he said.

"Um, guys," interrupted Dawn. "Am I the only one who still remembers a real live *alien* is right in front of us?!"

Charlie still stared at the alien. Still pretty speechless, too.

"Are there any planets nearby?" Luke asked the alien. A second later, the alien got its translation.

It checked the controls. One of the interactive menus scanned the star maps and finally located one. "No," said the alien. "not for several lightyears."

"Can you take us there?"

"Why?" asked the alien.

"This pyramid," said Luke, "it needs a planet to power the… what'd they call it? The Temple of the Gods?"

The alien paused, confused, but suddenly understood. "Yes, correct, for the human experiment."

"The what?" asked Ray.

"You must be from Ersetu! You speak of the holy sphere, yes?" asked the alien.

"That'd be the one," replied Luke.

"Yeah, I gotta ask," asked Dawn, "what's it for, originally, I mean? Why allow anyone to have powers? Some people just end up misusing and abusing their power, you know. It's why we're in this mess right now."

The alien nodded. "You humans, not long ago, were very primitive. Disorganized, constantly warring with neighboring tribes and communities. We found you, not long ago, seeing you in danger of self-extinction. We thought humans needed leadership. So we began the human experiment."

"I'm afraid to ask," said Ray.

"I'm not. Tell me," said Luke.

"Those proving themselves strong enough or wise enough to face their deepest fears and greatest pains, they received power. Power to lead, to rule, to protect, to prosper," explained the alien. "Our pyramids resided on your planet for thousands of your years. On many continents. Some of your leaders became very powerful and ruled for many generations. Ra, Zeus, Vishnu, Quetzalcatl, Odin, and countless more. But eventually humans became self-sufficient, self-reliant, and began their own technological evolution. We left your planet to study new life on other worlds. But to see your kind here now, using the Astaria gateways, will be very exciting news for the others when they awake."

"Others?" asked Ray.

"Awake?" repeated Dawn.

"Yes. My kind. We are nine thousand in number. Traveling a great distance to discover new life and new civilizations…"

"…to boldly go, where no one has gone before!" Luke chimed in.

The alien looked at him curiously.

"Sorry," said Luke. "So they're all on this ship, inside this pyramid, now?"

"Yes," said the alien.

"Where?" asked Charlie. He finally spoke up. "I've been here a few times. Explored around quite a bit. Never ran into anyone."

"They are… asleep. For lack of a better description," said the alien.

"Suspended animation?" asked Luke.

"Yes, so your people understand localized temporal relativity dynamics?" asked the alien excitedly.

"Um… kinda," said Luke.

Ray interrupted. "Look, not to be a damper on what I'm sure is humanity's greatest moment here, but… we do have a big problem waiting for us back at home. Can we continue with our new plan or what?"

"You seek the holy sphere?" asked the alien.

"Yes," said Luke. "We need new powers, from this pyramid, so when we find a way to destroy the others, we'll still have an advantage over the bad guys."

"Destroy the others?" asked the alien, confused.

"Pyramids. The other pyramids. If we destroy them, it'll cut off the source of everyone's powers, right?"

"Yes," the alien nodded. "But why?"

"It's just something we need to do," said Ray.

"No," said the alien. "If our pyramids are still running, an experiment is still in progress. You are not allowed to interfere."

"But our world's in danger!" exclaimed Dawn.

"Your kind is powerful enough to solve its own problems now," said the alien. "Whatever new problems you face, you are capable of solving them. We do not desire to make any species dependent on us for long. We won't help you. You must find your own answers and fix your own problems."

"What?!" exclaimed Ray.

"But…" said Luke.

"That is our way."

Charlie took a deep breath. He knew a dead end when he saw one. "Come on Luke, let's just go."

"But Uncle!"

"He's not going help us," said the old man. "Don't worry, we'll think of something. Mastermind is our problem."

"No," Dawn said to the alien. "Who do you think Mastermind's going after next, after he's enslaved our whole world? Using and abusing the power *your kind* gave him! Next he'll take Eden, and then, who knows, maybe your home-world too! Then he *will* be your problem."

"Yeah!" said Luke.

Ray seemed lost in thought. "No, he's right," he calmly said. "I can't believe I'm saying this, but I actually agree with the alien. We need to solve this ourselves. Not look to some god-like alien race to save us. If they help us with this, then we'll need them to help us with whatever our next problem is, and the one after that. I don't know about you, but I don't want to be dependent on some alien race to solve all our problems. Like those people back on Eden, helpless to defend themselves while they wait for some Big Daddy in the Sky to come and save them again. We need to learn to depend on ourselves."

"But…" said Luke.

"Thank you," said the alien.

Ray turned to face the alien. "But I do have one request."

The alien listened.

"Dawn's suffering from some kind of genetic breakdown that's way beyond our technological capabilities. Even your healing chamber can't help. And we all know how powerful that is. I don't want her to die. It's not her fault. It's not any of our fault that this happened to her. All I'm asking – not to save our world or anything like that – just save her. Fix her. Please. Just this once."

The alien looked at her.

"The healing chamber cannot repair her?" it asked.

"Says it can't identify her genome," said Charlie.

"But you are human, yes?" the alien asked Dawn.

"Yes," she said.

"Your kind has been in our database since we first discovered Ersetu. There should be no problem."

"Her DNA's breaking down. Thanks to an unstable chemical Mastermind created."

The alien nodded, understanding. "Her core sequences must be too unstable or too few in number. No problem. Return to the healing chamber, and I will override the scanning protocol from here. The automated systems sometimes lack … how would you describe it … common sense?"

Luke smiled. "Yeah."

"Just one question," said Dawn. "Apparently it's my unstable DNA that's been allowing me to shape-shift. Will I still be able to do that, after it 'fixes' me?"

The alien stared at her through its large black almond-shaped eyes. Silence for a moment. And then it spoke. "With your permission, I will program it to upgrade you with quad-helix genetic sequences."

"Quad? As in four?" asked Luke. "Our DNA only has two."

"Correct. Half your DNA will retain its original codes, providing genetic stability and longevity. The other half will be as your current state, allowing you to continue to 'shape-shift' as you call it."

"What? Really?" Dawn asked, excited. She didn't quite follow everything the tall skinny gray alien man – or woman, perhaps – said, but she understood this much: it was going to heal her *and* let her keep her powers! "Thank you!" she jumped up with joy and threw her arms around the alien.

"What… is this… that you are doing?" it asked.

"It's called a hug," she said, smiling.

"But," asked Luke, "I gotta ask. You won't help us get new powers, but you'll do this for her? Why?"

"A continuation of the human experiment," the alien said. "Many of your kind have received special abilities through the sphere. But she will be the first like this. Perhaps she will be prove to be the next step in Ersetu's evolution. I will return to your planet in a few generations to see how this new experiment turns out."

"Um… thanks?" Dawn said.

"It's like a second Eve," Luke said, realizing something. "I bet you tampered with our DNA millennia ago, leading to the current version of human beings. Dawn… you might be the future of humanity!"

"Cool," she shrugged.

"Very cool," said Luke.

"Let's just hope humanity still has a future," said Charlie.

"Right," said Ray. "Let's get her to the chamber."

"Thank you again," Dawn said to the alien.

"Yeah," said Luke. "It was really awesome meeting you. I can't believe I talked with and met an alien face to face! This is *so* going on my blog. Too bad no one's going to believe a word of it."

The alien returned to its seat, facing the controls, and began programming something.

Ray stopped to get one last good look at the dome, seeing all the vast endless stars far outside. Dawn and Charlie stepped onto the circular platforms where they first appeared.

Luke kept babbling. "I mean, wow, can you believe it? I'm on a *space ship*, probably thousands of lightyears from home, talking to a real live alien. I have super powers. We all have super powers. I've got a magic crystal that opens portals to other worlds. Wow. Yeah, my life rocks!"

"Come on, Luke," his uncle said.

Ray stepped onto the pad with Dawn.

"Sure, we gotta defeat a powerful madman bent on world domination, and his little team of super-powered mutants—and I've only died like, what, two or three times already trying to fight them. So no worries there."

"Luke!" Ray called.

"But it's all been so worth it!" he exclaimed. "I met one of the Grays! I actually met a real live alien!"

"LUKE!" they all shouted.

"Sorry, I'm coming!" He hopped onto the teleporter pad.

Charlie pushed the recall button on the wall next to them.

A ring of white light appeared around each pad, lifted up above them, and they instantly disappeared.

The gray alien shook his head. "Humans."

Chapter 31
REGENESIS

"Okay, get on the table," said Luke. "Let's see if this works."

Dawn hopped up onto the medical table. They were inside the healing chamber again. This time, if the alien kept its word, events would play out a little differently.

She laid down. Multi-colored lights scanned her from above. Dawn giggled. "That tickles."

A holographic human doctor appeared by her side. "I've completed my diagnostic and compatibility analysis," he said. "Are you ready to be upgraded?"

"Um, yes, sure," Dawn said.

A slightly yellowish-white light beamed down from overhead, starting from her toes, slowly traveling up her legs, tracing up her torso, down her arms, up her neck, and finally, completing at the crown of her head and tips of her fingers.

The light passed through a second time, moving in the same pattern, this time with a slightly bluish-purple color.

"I feel funny," said Dawn.

Now a third time, a bright green light passed over her body, every part, head to toe.

"Wow," she said. "I feel really… strong."

The lights finally stopped.

The holographic doctor spoke. "All upgrades have been completed. Please wait for final diagnostic."

Different lights scanned her now. It only lasted a second.

"Confirmed. Upgrade complete. Genetic cohesion and dynamic integration stabilized. New genome successfully created. No additional repairs or upgrades needed. You are cleared to go."

The holographic doctor disappeared.

Dawn continued laying on her back. She looked left and then right. "Is it done?" she asked.

"I think so," said Ray.

"How do you feel?" asked the old man.

Dawn sat up. "I feel fine. Really good, actually." She held her hands out in front of her, studying them. "Like a million times better, actually." She tried shape-shifting her hand into something – first a powerful animal claw, then a large steel ball, and finally a webbed mermaid-like hand. It felt so easy, so natural, so effortless. "I think I'm all better," she said.

The holographic doctor reappeared.

"Oh, hello again," she said.

"Additional instructions received," said the doctor. "Fabricating suit according to specifications."

"Come again?" she asked.

"A suit?" Luke repeated.

"What's he talking about?" asked Ray.

Uncle Charlie shrugged.

"Fabrication complete," said the holographic doctor. He opened a panel along the wall and retrieved a folded blue fabric.

Everyone watched him carefully.

The doctor carried it over to Dawn. "This suit will mimic your genome whenever you change into a non-human state. Whenever you return to human form, it will return to the material you see now."

"Huh?" asked Ray.

Dawn took the folded blue fabric out of the doctor's hands. She opened it up. It looked kind of like a solid color one-piece bathing suit. Designed just for her body.

"Wait," said Luke. "Are you saying—" he looked to the holographic doctor, "are you saying that suit will shape-shift with her body?"

The doctor nodded. "Affirmative."

Dawn lit up with excitement. "You mean I won't be naked every time I transform now?"

The doctor nodded. "Affirmative. It will mimic your genome whenever you change into a non-human state. Whenever you return to human form, it will return—"

"Yeah, yeah, I got it," said Dawn. "I so have to try this." She hopped down from the medical table, and paused awkwardly, staring at the guys. "Um, a little privacy, please."

Luke, Ray, and Uncle Charlie all turned away. Ray rolled his eyes. It's not like they hadn't seen her naked before. He'd seen her naked like a half a dozen times already since he met her! Not that he was complaining. She had a great body. Beautiful face.

Amazing personality. He only really just met this girl, but she was something else. Something special.

Dawn quickly took off her old clothes and slipped into the one-piece body suit. It fit her perfectly. Form-fitting, covering all the essentials, but left her arms and legs uncovered. Whatever. This would be fine. Walking around in a leotard was much better than being naked every time she wanted to transform into something other than her normal human form.

If this worked... she could be something small, like a turtle or bird, or something big, like a gorilla or rhino, or anything in between... she could be a gryphon again, or oh – a dragon, or something cool like that... and never have to worry her clothes again!

The suit hugged her skin comfortably. Not the most fashionable thing she ever wore. But it would work. Now – a test. She closed her eyes. And picked something.

A butterfly.

Quickly she shrank down in size. Smaller and smaller. Wings sprouted out from her back. Antenna from her head. Within a little over a second, she went from a five-foot-something grown blonde woman into a tiny, delicate floating, fluttering, beautiful little butterfly.

No pile of clothes on the floor. Aside from her old clothes, that she already took off before, of course. But her new blue suit was nowhere to be seen. It merged with her body. Transformed along with her body.

She floated around. Wow. This was fun. It was like swimming on the air. She felt so free, so relaxed, so uninhibited and free-spirited like this. But, there'd be plenty of time for exploring and experimenting with her new power later. She began shape-shifting back into human form.

It only took about a second. And she fully, completely, and effortlessly returned to her normal human appearance – still wearing the blue one-piece body suit.

"Yes!" she shouted.

Ray turned around, smiling. "All good?"

"Everything's great!" she said.

Luke got an idea. "Hey, I wanna try something. I'll be right back!" He ran out into the corridor.

"Where's he going?" asked Ray.

Uncle Charlie shrugged.

Ray asked Dawn, "So, everything's great. You don't feel sick or weak or anything?"

"I feel fine. Like, for real, honestly fine."

He smiled. "I'm glad."

"My shape-changing seems faster now too," Dawn said. "And takes less effort."

"Must be the upgrades from the… uh, alien."

Uncle Charlie nodded. "He must've anticipated your clothing issue too, and added that as well."

"What makes you so sure it was a he?" Dawn asked. "The alien could've been a woman, you know."

Ray laughed. "I suppose that's true."

Luke came back, lugging all the pieces of his battle suit in his arms. "Ray, a little help here, please…"

Ray helped him.

"On the table," Luke said, carrying it there.

They dumped the pieces onto the table.

"That stuff was heavy," said Luke, exhausted.

The pieces of the broken suit laid on the medical table. A second later, lights began scanning from overhead.

"I wonder," said Luke.

"If this works," said Ray, "you're a freaking genius."

Charlie watched curiously.

The holographic doctor appeared again. "Diagnostic complete. Blueprints for detected model and serial number found. Commencing repairs."

Then this holographic doctor, with lightning-quick speed, began assembling, repairing, and fixing the space suit by hand. He moved so quickly, his hands and arms looked blurry. The others watched, as piece by piece, Luke's new battle suit got repaired good as new – including a smooth polish and sparkling new shine.

Mint condition. Like it had just been rolled off the assembly line.

"Repairs complete. Power cells fully recharged." And the doctor disappeared.

Luke looked at his brand new suit, all fixed up, shiny and new, laid out across the table.

"I *am* a freaking genius!"

Ray shook his head, smiling.

"Remind me to thank our new E.T. friend next time we see him," said Luke.

"What makes you so sure there's going to be a next time?" asked Ray.

"What makes you so sure it's a him?" asked Dawn.

Charlie laughed. "Alright you guys. Let's get back to Earth."

Earth. The third rock from the sun. In an average little star system, traveling along the outer edge of the Milky Way Galaxy. One of a billion stars. One of a trillion planets.

But right now, it was the only planet that mattered.

Because at that very moment, Mastermind – a god – opened a portal inside the LaGuardia Airport in New York City – and in classic god-like super villain style, *floated* into the room for all to see.

Yup. He could fly now. Awesome. A mind-controlling flying madman. Airplanes were temporarily grounded while the mutant plague was getting sorted out. That left a lot of travelers stuck inside the airport. And everyone's luggage held up in inspection for possible contamination.

Which meant a bunch of impatient, tired, stressed-out people waiting in the immediate area.

"Bow down and worship me!" demanded Mastermind.

The crowds turned to face him. Many people screamed or gasped. Some took pictures with their cell phone. A few actually bowed down in worship.

Mastermind shook his head. "Rebellious mortals. Witness my full power!" He floated over to an Italian woman who obviously just came from overseas, and didn't seem to understand any English.

Who she was, why she was here – Mastermind didn't care.

She would serve a new purpose now.

A demonstration of his true power.

He reached out and touched her. Laid his hand flat on her chest. She freaked out, and tried hitting him with her purse. But it was no use. Suddenly – overwhelming pain shot throughout her body, and she fell to her knees, crying out bloody murder.

Her skin started boiling. Her bones started cracking. A hideous tail ripped out from under her clothes. Her face deformed. Scales covered her skin. Her hair fell out.

People started screaming and running away. Except for one brave soul. A kind stranger. Who ran to the poor woman's aid.

Mastermind saw him coming and reached out his hand. The instant the stranger made contact with Mastermind's other hand, he too began crying out in hellish horror.

The Italian woman transformed into some kind of dragon-lizard monster. Kinda Godzilla-esque, but a lot uglier, and somewhat smaller. She still grew several sizes larger, until she had to kink down her neck to fit her head under the ceiling. Her feet alone were bigger than most children. Her tail wrapped around half the baggage claim area. She let out an agonizing roar. Too bad she wasn't Japanese. That would've been poetic irony.

The kind stranger suffered a similar fate. He quickly and painfully transformed into a hairy ape-man. Something similar to Big Foot, but again, much uglier and almost as big as the woman.

Not many stuck around. The giant lizard lady tried to flee – bursting through the exit, smashing through the wall, to the outside world. The massive ape-creature beat his chest and ran outside too.

Mastermind watched the other mortals flee for their lives. "I don't think so," he said. He quickly flew over to them, moving much faster than they could run. First the ones trying to hide or escape inside. Then the people outside. One after another, he touched them – and turned each of them into monsters. Hideous, ugly, horrific, unsightly beasts of all kinds. Some more ugly than others.

They were the first of many.

None escaped Mastermind's touch.

The villain laughed, ascending higher into the air, and looked down upon New York City – *his* city – below.

"People of Earth – your God has returned!"

Back at Stonehenge, a portal suddenly opened across the ground.

Luke jumped through, wearing his armored suit, unskillfully crashing and tumbling onto the grass. "I totally meant to do that," he said, standing up, dusting himself off.

Ray followed behind. His landing was a little smoother, but he could also manipulate gravity, so he had an unfair advantage. Dawn shape-shifted, momentarily, to give herself wings. Her landing was the most graceful. And Charlie, well, he needed a hand getting through. Luke and Ray helped him.

"Thank you," said the old man.

Dawn returned to human form. "We made it. We're finally back on Earth."

"Thank God!" exclaimed Luke.

She looked around at Stonehenge. It was nighttime, but still incredibly beautiful. "Wow…"

Ray looked up at the stars. Some pyramid – where they just came from – was floating around somewhere out there. He'd never look at the stars quite the same again.

"So you think Mastermind's back yet?" she asked.

"Luke," said Uncle Charlie, "you think you can teleport us back to California?"

"Only one way to find out. Everyone, get close."

"Beam us up, Scotty!" said Ray.

They vanished in a flash of light.

Chapter 32

FINAL CONFLICT – PART 1

Another flash of white light and they instantly reappeared inside Luke and Ray's apartment – back in Burbank, CA.

"Oh heck yes!" exclaimed Luke.

"We're back," said Dawn.

"It worked!" said Ray. He looked at all the sand that had blown into their living room. The portal on their wall was gone. But the mess was not. "You know I'm not cleaning this up, right?"

"Eh, I'll just open a tiny portal to the abandoned space ship. The vacuum will suck it all up."

"Wait, the what?" asked Ray.

"Long story," said Charlie.

Luke's cell phone suddenly announced, "You've got mail!" in the classic AOL-sounding voice. "Oh, hey," said Luke, "I got a voice mail from you," he told Ray.

"Oh yeah," said Ray. "You can delete that."

"And three voice mails from my boss," added Luke. "Guess they wondered why I missed work this morning. I don't suppose they'll believe I was trapped on another world."

"Huh," said Charlie, looking at his own phone. "Looks like I got a message too. It's a text message." He had a really strange look on his face. "All it says is, 'we need to talk, I can help, call me' with a number."

"That's weird," said Ray.

"Do you recognize the number?" asked Luke.

"No," said Uncle Charlie.

"You gonna call it?" asked Ray. "Does anyone else know about your powers?"

"No one," said Uncle Charlie. "Just Mastermind."

"Don't call it," said Dawn. "It's gotta be a trap. Mastermind wants you to call him and he's going to brainwash you over the phone or something."

"He needs to make eye contact," Charlie said.

"I know," said Dawn. "But I have a bad feeling about this."

"It's an overseas number," Charlie said, still reading the text message. "44-20. That's the country code for the UK, I believe. London, right?"

"We were *just* there!" exclaimed Luke. "Need me to teleport us back?"

"What? To make a phone call?" remarked Uncle Charlie.

"Right. Sorry. It's fun. That's all." He smiled.

Ray asked, "Luke, where's the remote? I want to see what's on the news. We need to see if Mastermind or his mutants have been spotted yet."

"I'm going to call it," said Charlie, too curious to ignore it. He dialed the number. It rang.

"I don't know," said Luke, helping Ray look for the remote. "I can never seem to find it."

It rang a second time.

And then someone picked up. "Mister Powers."

It was a man's voice.

"Who is this?" Charlie asked.

"A friend," said the voice on the other end. They didn't recognize this voice – but Mastermind would have. And Mastermind would've been furious if he knew this man was talking to Charlie now. "We need to stop Mastermind," said the voice. "Where are you now?"

"How'd you get my number? Who is this?" Charlie demanded.

"Never mind, I'll trace the call. Triangulating… just a few more seconds. Burbank, California. Wow. I was expecting you to still be in the UK. You travel fast, Mister Powers."

"Okay, you better start talking now, son," said Charlie.

"We don't have much time. I'm watching him on the telly now. He's all over the news. Last seen in New York. Turning people into monsters just by touching them!"

"What?" asked the old man. "Say that again?"

"Found it!" said Luke. "My heads-up display located it. God, this space suit is so cool." He dug the TV remote out of the couch cushions. He turned the television on.

"I don't have time to explain," said the voice on the phone. "Mastermind hired me to do a few odds and ends. Erase his public records, set up a meeting with your president, make sure all the major networks got his video…"

"What are you saying?" asked the old man.

"James and Helen. Your brother and sister-in-law," said the voice, "how do you think they knew Mastermind was picking up a shipment in Hawaii?"

"What?"

"I sent them the anonymous e-mail."

"You did?"

"Mastermind's been hiring me for stuff from the beginning. But there's no time. Are you near a computer?"

"No, why?"

"Wait, what's that I hear in the background?" asked the voice.

Luke and Ray were watching the news.

"Is that the news? SWITCH IT OFF! NOW!"

Charlie didn't know what to think. "Luke, Ray, turn that off. Quick!"

"What? Why?" asked Luke.

Ray hit the power button, just as the news started to show Mastermind's "obey me" video again. "What's wrong?"

The voice on the phone said, "Mastermind's got this video he had me send all the major news networks. He's telling everyone to worship him like a god."

"Hold—hold on," said Charlie, interrupting. He put the cell on speaker so everyone could hear. "Go on."

"The networks keep repeating his video. He's controlling everyone through it. Whatever you do, *don't* watch the news!"

"Oh," said Ray.

"It works over TV too?" Dawn asked. "Great."

"It's going viral online too. I'd avoid all media as long as you can," said the voice. "Nation leaders worldwide – including our prime minster and your president – are telling everyone to get some kind of cure too, but it's all part of his plan."

"Why are you telling us all this?" asked Charlie. "If Mastermind really hired you—"

"I know," said the voice. "Why should you trust me? All I can say is—money's worthless if there's no one left around."

"You said you're watching him on TV now?"

"Yes," said the voice. "He's still in New York."

"Hey," said Dawn. "If we can't watch the news, how come you can?"

"I've got it on mute. When he first hired me, he found me online. He was bragging that if we were in person, he could force me to do all his tasks for free. But he'd need to make eye contact for it to work, and I'd have to hear him. Idiot. Ever since, I've been careful to never let that happen. I won't give him that opportunity. And neither should you."

"Then we need to teleport to New York," Luke said.

"You guys can teleport? Damn. That would explain how you got to California so fast. Anyway, you've got your own local problems. There's some rhino-monster attacking Los Angeles as we speak. Not to mention others in Tokyo, Athens, and all around the world. But," he said a little impatiently, "if you can clean up that mess, I may have a way to free everyone from Mastermind's control."

"How?" asked Luke.

"By using his own powers against him."

"Luke," said Uncle Charlie, "remember what I said earlier. Be smart. It sounds like mutants are spread out. You guys can take them one-on-one. You may not ever get a chance like this again."

"Good point," said Ray.

"Okay, Mr. Hacker Dude," said Dawn, "we're gonna need exact locations of all the mutants. Luke – you can get us there?"

"In a flash," he grinned.

Luke and Ray teleported to downtown Los Angeles – what was left of it. Several of the city buildings had crumbled to the ground. The roads were all torn up and destroyed. Freeways collapsed. Dead bodies, fires, overturned cars…

Only a few of LAPD's bravest and finest remained. Firing upon the mutant. Doing whatever they could to slow him down – and buy the escaping civilians more time.

Rhino-Man charged into a police car, launching it several hundred feet up into the air. The cops protected themselves behind barricades, still shooting at the thick-skinned rhinoceros man. But his tough, hard skin and high tolerance for pain made him a difficult beast to slow down.

"You think this is going to work?" asked Ray.

"It has to," said Luke from inside his battle-ready suit. His Astaria crystal was strapped to his left arm. Easy access in case they needed it later.

"Hey dino breath!" Ray called towards Rhino-Man. "Over here, loser!"

Rhino-Man snorted and turned around. "You again!" he growled. He stomped his foot onto the ground. An earthquake tremor advanced in their direction.

Ray quickly lifted himself off the ground, floating above the shockwave. Luke teleported out of sight – reappearing directly behind Rhino-Man.

Still hovering a few feet above the ground, Ray held his hand out at Rhino-Man. "And here we go…"

The large gray monster started to lift off the ground too. He tried to stomp. He tried to smash. But he couldn't touch *anything*.

"Not so tough now, are ya?" Ray mocked.

Luke grabbed him from behind, wrapped his arms around the big beast, and together they instantly teleported away.

They reappeared in the middle of the desert.

But this wasn't the desert planet. This was still very much on Earth. An unforgiving, hot, dry, barren place. Endless sand. No life – save a few dry shrubs and maybe a couple tiny critters. The Mojave Desert. Some one-hundred fifty or so miles away from Los Angeles.

But something was out of place in this barren desert.

An oasis. Or at least it looked like one.

It was a portal. A large hole in the desert sand. Revealing a lush and rich tropical planet. On the other side was a beach, with crystal-clear sparkling water, and a dense green jungle to the side. Clear blue skies, scattered white clouds, chirping birds, jumping fish… A beautiful land. A paradise.

It was the Planet Aquaria.

They reappeared directly above the portal opening. And Luke let Rhino-Man go. Luke teleported away as Rhino-Man fell down into the portal – crashing and sliding into the sand on the other side. "Hey!" shouted the rhino-guy. But then he looked around. He could be in worse places.

But why leave him here? And the portal back to Earth was still open. What were those guys up to?

Luke reappeared back in downtown Los Angeles next to Ray.

"Next stop?" Ray asked.

"Let's see how Dawn's doing," said Luke.

Ray stepped right up to Luke's side. "Ready."

They teleported to New York City.

The streets were eerily empty.

"You see her anywhere?" Ray asked.

"Scanning now." His heads-up display inside his armored helmet scanned the entire area. No signs of life anywhere. This was spooky.

"There she is," said Ray, looking up.

A giant gryphon screeched across the sky, chasing after a little black mutant bat guy.

"Never saw him before," said Ray.

"Get away from me!!!" shouted the bat mutant.

The massive gryphon just screeched louder, talons extended, swooping in to snatch the mutant.

Her claws latched onto him. "Get off me!" He tried pushing against her large talon claws, but it was no use.

Dawn spotted Luke and Ray below. Carrying the trapped mutant – her prey – in her claws. She swooped low, dropped the bat mutant directly at Luke, and flew back up into the sky.

The bat mutant flapped his wings, trying to recover and save himself in mid-air. Luke jumped up, aided by hydraulics in his armored boots and legs, boosting himself up high and fast. He collided with the bat mutant, threw his arms around him, and the two teleported away.

Back in the Mojave Desert, the bat mutant suddenly found himself being thrown down into a portal towards Planet Aquaria.

He flapped his wings furiously. And just as he started passing through the portal opening, he regained control and started flying back up into Earth's atmosphere. Luke landed – the other half of the jump that started in New York City – and turned around to look. He anticipated that a winged mutant might not get thrown into a portal so easily.

Luke lifted his hand, lining up the shot. He aimed the cutting laser directly at the bat mutant. He fired.

And just before the beam struck the bat – the mutant disappeared. The laser beam kept going, zapping nothing.

"What the?" remarked Luke. "Where'd he go?"

He quickly scanned the area. No sign of him anywhere. He wasn't invisible. Not like Shadow. No heat traces or other residuals either. He just disappeared.

Rhino-Man started climbing up through the portal, back to the surface. Luke sighed. He fired the cutting laser at him instead.

"Ouch!" roared the rhino mutant, falling backwards into the tropical planet. Luke quickly teleported away.

Luke reappeared back in New York City.

Dawn was back in human form, still wearing his specially-made blue one-piece body suit. She was kissing Ray when Luke reappeared.

"Any other mutants in the area?" Luke asked.

"No. I lost track of Mastermind when that bat guy came out of nowhere."

"It's okay," said Luke. "We need to take out the other mutants first anyway. You want to stay here and keep tabs on him or help us capture the next one?"

"Um, hello – help you get the next one!" Dawn exclaimed.

"What's our next stop?" asked Ray.

Luke stepped up next to them – and the three teleported.

The Parthenon. Athens, Greece.

Beautiful. Ancient. Magical.

They really needed to come back here when they had more time. And weren't trying to stop super-powered mutants from taking over the world for a mind-controlling madman.

Kraken stood over a dead body. One of several dozen around. All the bodies were twisted and torn. Strangled and mutilated. Kraken showed no mercy.

Neither would they.

Ray waved his hand, lifting Kraken up into the air. But then the sea monster faced them and suddenly *they* were being pulled towards *him*.

"Ray, what are you doing?" Dawn asked.

"I'm not doing this – he is!"

"Shields up!" said Luke. A force field surrounded them.

Kraken dragged them up close and personal – and all back on the ground. Kraken's tentacles lashed at and banged against the invisible force field. Thank God for that. The sea creature hissed and roared, growled and gurgled.

"I take it he's got some kind of telekinetic power too?" Dawn reasoned.

Kraken started laughing. "As if."

Suddenly all three of them got a pounding headache, simultaneously feeling bloated in their chests while parched and dry in their mouths. The pain shot throughout their bodies.

"I control water," said Kraken. "And you've got tons of it inside of you!"

Luke couldn't think straight. He was in so much pain. Like his body was twisting, swelling, and getting ready to explode from the inside out. What was he doing to them? He couldn't breathe. He started coughing. His lungs were filling up with water! They had to act fast. Dawn and Ray started coughing uncontrollably.

They had to get away.

Luke teleported a hundred feet backwards. Dawn and Ray came with him.

Kraken too. The sea monster was still a little too close. The teleporter radius accidentally included him.

No problem. Luke teleported again.

This time they all went to the Mojave Desert.

They fell to their knees, difficulty focusing, choking on their own body fluids. Kraken made a laughing gurgle.

Ray saw the open portal behind them. He reached up, struggling to control his own body, and used his power to suddenly push Kraken backwards into it. The sea monster stumbled, falling down into the hole. He momentarily lost his gripping power over them. Luke, Dawn, and Ray could suddenly breathe again. Their bodies started to relax and return to normal.

"Let's get out of here," Ray said, his throat still a little dry from the displaced body water.

Luke nodded. "I agree," he also struggled to say. "They're not going anywhere."

The three of them teleported out of the desert.

Chapter 33

FINAL CONFLICT – PART 2

Next stop: Jerusalem. Dome of the Rock.

The three of them appeared on top of a hill, overlooking the crowded desert city below. The city was so pretty, even at night. Ray coughed up the last of the water that was still caught in his lungs. "I wasn't expecting that. We gotta be more careful."

"You guys both okay?" asked Luke.

Dawn nodded. "Yeah, I'm okay. My body seems to heal pretty fast now, actually."

"Okay, so remind me who's here again?" asked Ray.

"The slime girl," said Luke. "Scanning for her now."

"Any idea what her power is?" asked Dawn.

"Afraid not," said Luke. "Found her!"

"Where is she?" asked Ray.

"Right over… there," he said, pointing. "In what looks like… a local jail cell?"

"Oh this I gotta see," Ray said.

They teleported in closer. Inside the local jail. Guards armed with semi-automatic weapons stood outside her cell. Slimer sat by herself, leaning on her hand, facing the floor.

As soon as Luke and his friends appeared, the guards started yelling in some other language – probably Arabic. Luke's HUD started translating it immediately, displaying English text along the bottom of his view screen.

"Don't shoot!" shouted Ray, sticking his hands up.

"We just came for the girl," said Dawn.

The guards kept yelling in Arabic.

Luke's translation was not favorable. "Okay, time to go…" He pointed his hand at the jail cell bars and fired the cutting laser. He actually broke Slimer *out* of jail.

She looked up at him. "What the hell are ya doin'?"

Luke ran over to her, grabbed her slimy arm, and dragged her back to Ray and Dawn. Then they all teleported out of there as the guards started waving their guns a little too excitably.

Back in the Mojave Desert, they reappeared.

"Great, *another* desert," Slimer sighed.

Luke pushed her into the open portal.

Rhino-Man had already climbed back out, but hadn't wandered far. Kraken was still on the other side, though, apparently preferring the nice cool ocean waters.

"Back you go," said Ray, using his gravity power to drag Rhino-Man back into the portal hole. Rhino-Man dug his feet hard into the ground, but Ray's power was stronger. The gray mutant fell in again, roaring in protest, but helpless to stop it.

"Keep your eyes out," said Luke. "The bat one disappeared on me. He could be anywhere."

"Will do. Who's next on our list?" said Dawn.

"That would be…" Luke said, reading an on-screen list inside his heads-up display. "Great. The snake lady. In India." He took a deep breath. "You guys ready?"

"Let's do this," said Ray.

A flash of white light and they appeared in front of the Taj Mahal.

Ray checked behind them, Dawn faced the right, and Luke looked to the left. No one in sight.

The place was dead. Vacant. Empty of all people.

And eerily silent.

Sure, it was the middle of the night. Well, probably just before dawn. There was a faint glow on the eastern horizon. But still. Where was everybody?

Luke started scanning for life signs.

Ray stared at the magnificent Taj Mahal behind them. Its massive dome ceilings, elegant architecture, and surrounding towers. Beautiful in pictures. Even more impressive now that he saw it in person.

"You know, I always wanted to come here," Ray said. "Not like this, but hey – we sure saved a lot of airfare!"

"Where is she?" asked Dawn.

"I don't know," said Luke. "I'm scanning. Not picking up any life signs anywhere."

"Could we be too late?" asked Ray. "You sure we can trust this hacker guy? This could be a trap…"

"No way," said Dawn, still looking around. "His intel's been good so far."

"Still," said Luke, "best to stay on our toes. This snake lady killed the other me on the other timeline."

"And this timeline too, you mean?" asked Ray.

"Right." Luke shook his head. "It's tough keeping track of all this."

Dawn shape-shifted herself some wings. "I'm going to get a better perspective." She grew large white feathers. Like massive angel wings. She started flapping them. And elegantly, she lifted herself up into the air. She flew higher… and higher still…

She saw people. Sort of.

Dead people. Everywhere. Hidden away in corners. Laying out in the streets. Some piled on top of each other. It was horrible.

"Oh my God," she said, quickly descending back down. "We *are* too late."

"What? Did you see her?" asked Ray.

"Found her!" Luke shouted, still scanning the entire time. "Over there! Hurry!"

Together, they ran down the open path, around the corner, and into the narrow city streets.

"Jesus!" Ray shouted, almost tripping over a dead body. They saw more around every turn. It was worse than a low-budget horror film.

The look of terror and pain etched every dead face. Fang-like puncture wounds were found on their necks, backs, legs, and anywhere else unlucky enough to feel Venom's deadly strike. The lucky ones died in their sleep. Apparently everyone else started fleeing and panicking – and seemingly no one got out alive.

This mutant was definitely a killer. And she seemed to enjoy it a little too much.

"We're getting close!" shouted Luke as they kept running, weaving through the streets. "Almost there!"

They ran around another corner. Luke stopped abruptly, sliding across the rough ground. Another body fell freshly dead under Venom's fangs. She turned to see them.

She hissed.

"Ray, keep her in the air," said Luke.

"Got it." He held both his hands out, lifting Venom off the ground. The snake lady leaped after them, but Ray's gravity control kept her in place. She was helpless. Couldn't move. It was *so* much easier taking on these mutants one at a time!

Venom hissed again, louder, fiercer, with a look of hatred and intimidation in her snake-like yellow eyes.

Luke prepared to jump. From inside his heads-up display, he charted the exact trajectory and force needed to jump up to her position, grab her, and teleport her back to the Mojave Desert with the rest of the mutant monsters. His suit's mechanical hydraulics gave him the power he needed. He leaped up. Jumped through the air. Opened his arms to grab Venom.

And right at the very instant he was about to nab her – she disappeared. Poof.

Vanished. Gone.

Luke stopped himself from teleporting. He landed on the other side of the street, turned around, and started to panic. "Where'd she go?"

Ray and Dawn looked around. "I don't know!" he said.

"She just disappeared!" Dawn exclaimed. "No wait, up there!" she said, pointing up to the one of the rooftops. Venom crouched on the edge of the roof, looking down at them. The snake lady hissed again and leaped down upon Dawn.

"Look out!" shouted Ray. He used his force blast to push Dawn out of the way, just as Venom's claws narrowly missed her. That was close. Venom hissed at him, then leaped towards Ray, fangs exposed. Ray quickly blasted gravity against the ground, launching himself backwards and up away. Venom narrowly missed him too.

Ray tried to hold himself up in the air. He was still getting the hang of flying. It always looked so much easier in the movies. Venom leaped up to bite at him. "Whoa!" Ray exclaimed, using his power to move himself out of the way. Venom missed. But was undeterred.

Luke held out his hand, lined up the shot, and fired his cutting laser. The red beam shot across the street. Venom turned just in time to see. She disappeared again, avoiding the shot. Damn she was fast.

Luke's heads-up display couldn't track her. She wasn't turning invisible. That could only mean one thing. She was teleporting. She was going to be a little harder to catch than he had hoped.

"Luke, get ready!" Dawn shouted to him.

"Oh-okay!" he replied, not sure what to be ready for.

Dawn shape-shifted into a snake mutant look-alike. Identical in almost every way, except less hideous and a little sexier. Hey, when you can control your own appearance, why not? Dawn exposed her fangs, hissed, and taunted Venom.

"That'sss cheap!" Venom complained.

"Come and get me, you bitch!"

Venom leaped at her.

Dawn leaped at Venom.

Both had fangs out in the open, ready to bite the instant the other was close enough. The two met half-way, locked arms, and rolled and tumbled to the ground. They fought hard. Struggled ferociously. A battle of wills. A battle of strength. Keeping each other's fangs at bay. Desperately trying to get the upper hand.

They struggled. They rolled. Dawn slammed Venom up against the wall. Venom kicked Dawn hard in the stomach. One jumped onto the other's back. They twisted and turned. It was hard to tell which was who. Was Dawn winning? Was Venom winning? The two snake mutants battled it out, hissing and screaming, biting at each other, narrowly missing each time.

A battle of equals. Equally matched. Equally powerful. Equally strong… Or were they?

Dawn shape-shifted a little more. Gave herself bigger, stronger muscles. Made her entire body a little bigger. Even gave herself a nice big cobra hood and fully expanded it. Venom was suddenly overpowered and overwhelmed, quickly terrified by the larger, more deadly snake mutant looming over her. The shadow cast by Dawn's larger snake body washed over Venom. The snake lady cowered.

Luke instantly teleported next to Venom, grabbed her – and they both teleported – but not together.

Luke found himself back in the Mojave Desert empty handed. "Dammit!" he exclaimed. He quickly teleported back to India.

Ray still floated in the air. He searched the rooftops. "I don't see her. Where'd she go?"

Luke reappeared.

Dawn shape-shifted from her powerful super-cobra form back to her angel-like appearance. She flapped those massive white wings and lifted herself up into the air. She hovered next to Ray. "She's gotta be somewhere."

Luke scanned the surrounding area. No life signs. Any surviving people had long since run away. Venom was nowhere to be found. But with all those dead bodies she left in her wake, they couldn't let her escape.

"She's gotta be somewhere," said Luke.

Ray landed on one of the nearby roofs. It was a dense city. And still pretty dark out. She could be hiding anywhere. Assuming she was even still in India. "How far can she teleport?" he asked.

Dawn shrugged. Luke didn't know either.

"I mean," said Ray, "can she teleport as far as you can?"

"Possibly," said Luke.

Dawn said, "So she could be anywhere in the world right now?"

"I guess. I don't know. We barely know the limits of our own powers," said Luke. "I didn't even know she could teleport until a minute ago!"

"Alright," said Ray, still keeping a careful eye out. "We just need to stay cool and think this through. If we were a mind-control killer snake lady, where would we go next?"

Venom appeared directly behind Luke.

"Luke, look out!" Dawn yelled.

Venom grabbed Luke's helmet, trying to pull it off. As long as he wore that armored suit, he was protected from her lethal bite. She intended to fix that.

"Get off me, you scaly monster!" Luke shouted.

She managed to pull it off.

"Hey, give that back!" he demanded, head exposed to the open air.

Venom hissed, fangs exposed, and bit down.

But just as the tips of her fangs started to scrape against Luke's face, something big pummeled Venom from the side, moving fast and hard, knocking the snake mutant away from him!

It was Dawn, transformed into a giant armadillo, rolled into a ball, who then shape-changed back into human form as they rolled away. While Venom was still briefly stunned from the sudden impact, Dawn transformed into a giant eagle – like, a *really* giant eagle – and clutched Venom in her huge talons.

The snake mutant squirmed to get free, but couldn't. Dawn, as the giant eagle, let out an ear-piercing screech of victory. While Venom continued to struggle, Luke ran over to her, threw his arms around Venom, and teleported them together.

Venom got dropped off into the still-open portal in the Mojave Desert, and Luke instantly teleported back to India.

Dawn returned to human form. Ray descended down from the rooftop, softening his landing with his anti-gravity power. Luke picked up his helmet and put it back on.

"That was close," he said.

"You think she can teleport out of the desert?" Dawn asked.

"Let's hope her power doesn't go that far," said Luke.

"Sorry I was a little slow back there," said Ray. "I didn't see her behind you before it was too late."

"She's quick," said Dawn. Then she smiled. "But I'm quicker."

Luke took a breath. "Okay, five mutants down. Two to go."

"That hacker guy said the cat girl was in Tokyo, right?" said Ray. He checked his watch. "Should be morning rush hour over there by now. That our next stop?"

"Okay, the cat girl can turn invisible," said Luke. "So be ready for that. Fortunately, my scanner can still track her."

"And then the spider guy in Russia," said Dawn.

"I hate spiders," said Ray.

Chapter 34

FINAL CONFLICT – PART 3

Apparently the Japanese love cat girls.

Luke, Ray, and Dawn teleported into the heart of Tokyo. A city so busy, so crowded, so lit up with billboards, ads, signs, and lights that it made New York City's Times Square seem dull and boring in comparison. Most of the ads and signs were in Japanese, with some English and other languages mixed in there too. And people. Tons and tons of people. Everywhere.

Venom had killed off and scared away most of the people back in India. But here in Japan, it was just the opposite. There were too many people. No way Luke's scanner could isolate and detect *one* person, even a mutant cat girl, out of this massive crowd. But at least people weren't dying. That was a good thing.

"Um, Luke?" Ray said.

"Wassup?"

"Is that her?" he pointed.

The three looked over to a street corner. People were all gathered around. Posing and getting their picture taken with – could it be? Shadow. The cat mutant. They weren't afraid of her. They thought she was part of some publicity stunt, or marketing campaign, or just a really well-dressed cosplayer.

Luke, Ray, and Dawn moved closer to get a better look.

Unbelievable. Yup. It was her. And she was actually posing with them. Boys and girls, men and women, couples and families… people young and old stopped to get their picture taken with the life-like cat girl.

"Okay, this is officially weird," said Dawn.

"I guess they didn't see Mastermind's video?" Ray asked.

Luke shrugged. "Or maybe something got lost in the translation."

"But why isn't she attacking them?" Dawn asked.

People quickly noticed Luke in his high-tech super space suit. The crowds immediately turned their attention to him too. It seemed they also wanted their picture taken with him!

Ray just shook his head and laughed.

"Hey," said Dawn, approaching Shadow. "What gives?"

"Oh, you," Shadow said.

"What the hell's going on? Not that I'm complaining or anything, but… doesn't Mastermind want you attacking the city or something?"

"That's not what he said," said Shadow. "His exact words were, 'Show them your true nature.' And me, well, I'm cute and cuddly." She smiled. People took more pictures of her.

Dawn seemed a little doubtful.

"Look," said Shadow. "They love me!"

"But… you're a mutant. And you keep attacking us."

Shadow sighed. "Yeah, sorry about that. Mind control. I've got nothing against you guys. I was just your waitress, remember? I'm really an aspiring actress. And now, look at me – I'm famous!"

Dawn smiled. "True nature, eh?"

Shadow nodded. "I hope they blog about me."

Dawn shook her head, laughing.

Meanwhile, people stood around Luke, admiring his tech suit. And Ray, the entrepreneur, got a brilliant idea. "Get your picture taken with a real life super hero. Only five dollars… Or, hmm, what's the exchange rate? Eighty yen! Just eighty yen and you can get your picture taken with—" He leaned over to Luke and whispered, "You have a super hero name yet?"

Luke shrugged.

"—this guy!" Ray said.

"Super hero?" asked a young Japanese guy. "Awesome!" he said with his best American accent.

Dawn asked Shadow, "So you're really not going to hurt these people?"

"Not unless the boss tells me to, like, specifically."

"Right. Mastermind can be… persuasive."

"I don't know why I do it," said Shadow. "It just feels so good, so right, when he tells me to do something. But afterwards… I think about it… and I'm like, did I *really* just do that?"

Dawn nodded.

Maybe these mutants weren't really evil after all. Well, maybe some of them. Dawn knew firsthand how powerful Mastermind's mind control was. Were these mutants just in the wrong place at the wrong time? Like she and Ray were, at that restaurant? What if Ray and the police hadn't gotten there when they did? Dawn could have just as easily been a mutant terrorizing some part of the world right now.

Shadow was the redheaded waitress. Just at the wrong place at the wrong time. An innocent victim in all this.

She wasn't evil. Just controlled by an evil man.

And looking around, it seemed Mastermind's terror hadn't hit Japan the same as other places in the world. She could only guess why. Either way, the people seemed relatively safe here. And Shadow was loving all the fame and attention.

"Stay here," said Dawn.

"What?" asked Shadow, posing for another picture with a couple of teenage girls with pink hair.

"Stay here. Away from Mastermind's influence. Don't watch the news or anything. Avoid Mastermind at all costs."

"You kidding?" Shadow laughed. "He's a million miles away now! I'm finally free! And I can turn invisible, don't you know? I can't help obeying him… but he's gotta find me first!"

Dawn smiled. "You're okay. I can't believe I just said that, but Tiffany, you're alright."

"Call me Shadow."

"Stay out of trouble, Shadow."

Meanwhile, Ray collected some money. And Luke posed. It felt really weird doing this. Dawn rejoined them.

"Come on guys, let's go. She's no threat here."

Luke stopped posing for pictures. "You sure?"

"I'm sure," said Dawn.

"At least one part of the world is safe," said Ray. "No idea why, but I'm not complaining."

"It is a little weird," said Luke. "But time's wasting. Next stop, Saint Petersburg, Russia."

"Great. Spiders," said Ray.

Saint Petersburg, Russia. Another beautiful city on Ray's to-visit-someday list. He planned to travel the world and visit all these famous places one day when his business was bigger, and he could afford first class air tickets everywhere.

He never imagined that he'd be teleporting instantly, with his best friend and his new girlfriend, chasing after mind-controlled evil mutants bent on taking over the world. Wasn't exactly the dream vacation he always planned, but aside from the preventing the end of the world thing, it wasn't too bad either.

Saint Petersburg was beautiful. The gateway to Russia. A famous city. Full of so much history. And art. Canals, bridges, historic buildings, spectacular landscapes, and beautiful cathedrals. Instantly recognizable. Absolutely stunning and beautiful.

Except for… the icky spider webs that stretched and hung from building to building, rooftop to rooftop, tangling up the entire city from overhead. Gross.

Luke immediately scanned for people. Some were dead or slowly dying, undoubtedly from Arachnus's poisonous bite. Others were in hiding. Some were shouting, in Russian, about a "cure" for Mastermind's plague.

"Cure?" Luke repeated, reading the translation on his heads-up display screen inside his helmet. "What cure?"

"As soon as we get the spider guy, we move to Phase Two, right?" asked Ray.

"Right," said Luke.

"I just hope our new hacker 'friend' is good to his word."

"Where are those people going?" asked Dawn, noticing a large group of people lined up and waiting impatiently outside a particular building. "At this hour, too?" It was still very dark out. But all this teleporting around between time zones got her a little jet-lagged. "What time is it, anyway?"

"Late," said Luke. He looked at the building. His heads-up display translated the Russian writing on the building. "It's just a regular hospital."

"Why are they all going there?" asked Ray. None of them appeared to be injured. Arachnus was nowhere to be found. But his webs continued to loom overhead.

Some local man stopped by them, apparently on his way to the hospital. He spoke urgently, pointing to the building. It was in Russian, so no one had any idea what he was saying. But he seemed to be encouraging them to come with him.

Luke's HUD displayed out the translation. "He says they've got the cure ready now," said Luke. "What cure? Against Mastermind's mutation chemical?"

"That was fast," said Dawn.

The Russian man finally threw up his hands and left them behind. He went on to join the gathering crowd outside the hospital.

"Too fast," said Luke. "And what would they need a cure for, anyway? It's not a virus. Mastermind would have to inject them one by one to… wait… you don't think…"

"We've got to stop them!" Dawn said.

They ran up to the crowd. But the language barrier proved to be a problem. They only spoke English; the locals only spoke Russian. Luke's heads-up display translated their words into subtitles, but he hadn't yet figured out if, or how, he could use his suit to translate English into another language.

"Dammit!" Luke exclaimed.

Dawn tried pulling people out of the line. But they thought she was just trying to cut ahead of them!

"Guys," said Ray. "They're obviously under Mastermind's control. We can save them – by completing our mission. We take down Mastermind, they won't want to be injected."

Luke realized he was right. And if people in Russia in the middle of the night were running to the nearest hospital for some "cure" – it was probably happening all over the world right now. The only way to save them – everyone, worldwide – was to defeat Mastermind, once and for all. It was the only way now.

"Alright," said Dawn. But she wasn't about to give up on these people. They couldn't save everyone – but maybe she could help save a few. She transformed into a lion, big furry mane around her head, large jaws – and she roared. She roared loud and clear. Like she had never roared before.

The people freaked out and ran in terror.

Suddenly there was no more line outside the hospital.

Ray was impressed. "Good job, nice thinking!"

"Thank you," she said, blushing as she returned to human.

"Alright," said Luke. "now all we need is lucky number seven. Where is he?" He continued searching and scanning the rooftops and upper buildings.

The spider webs loomed above. "He's definitely been here," said Ray, captain of the obvious. "But he could be anywhere in the city by now."

Luke's scanner searched through buildings, looking for abnormal bio signs. "Come on, come on…" He had to be somewhere.

"Anything?" Ray asked.

"I'm searching!" exclaimed Luke.

Arachnus was actually very close by. But they didn't know it. They were too busy looking up around the webs. Arachnus, the black spider mutant, quietly lurked in the shadows, sneaking up from behind.

He was one arm short. It still hurt like a bitch. Severed from the portal when he reached in after them. He wouldn't make that mistake again. He wouldn't make *any* mistakes with them again.

He knew Ray had some kind of force-push anti-gravity power. And Dawn could shape-shift. And Luke's battle suit had a painful laser beam. So Arachnus had to make his move carefully. Very, very carefully.

The itsy bitsy spider… crawled up the water spout…

They still didn't see him.

"After this," said Ray, "we take down Mastermind, right? Back to New York City?"

"Yeah," said Luke, still scanning. "Without his mutants, he should be a piece of cake. And we'll all wear ear plugs so—"

Arachnus silently jumped from the shadows, landing on Dawn. She screamed. Arachnus clobbered her to the ground, ensnaring her in his seven arms.

"Dawn!" Ray shouted.

Dawn cried out again, this time differently. Like she was short on breath. Like something was being taken from her – painfully. "Ah… ahh… ahhhh!!!"

Ray and Luke surrounded Arachnus.

"Let her go!" demanded Luke.

"Right now!" said Ray, readying his hands to send the hideous spider mutant flying – just as soon as Dawn was out of his icky clutches.

Arachnus tossed Dawn aside. She fell to the ground, short on breath, exhausted and weary. What just happened? Why did she feel so… drained?

He didn't bite her, did he?

The dark spider mutant smiled.

"That's it." Ray flicked his wrist, launching the spider airborne and as far from them as possible. But as the spider went flying backwards, his arms began morphing... morphing into something else.

"You okay, Dawn?" Ray helped her back up.

"Uh, guys…" said Luke, still watching Arachnus.

"I think so," said Dawn.

Arachnus's arms changed, transforming into giant dragon-like wings. A long spiked tail extended from his body. His face reformed too – still had tons of extra eyes, and hideous spider-like fangs – but now he had sharp teeth, big ones, and horns on his head. His skin turned hard and scaly. Suddenly, he was half dragon, half spider, and all terror.

And he flew straight back at them!

"What the fuck?" shouted Ray, staring at the new beast before them. That thing was going to give him nightmares for weeks!

"Stand back," said Luke, stepping forward. He lined up his shot. Aimed. Fired.

The powerful cutting laser shot straight at the dragon-spider monster. It struck him. Arachnus roared out in pain. But kept coming. Fast.

"Alright, I got him!" said Ray, about to blast him back.

But Arachnus was too fast, too strong, too agile. He dodged to the side, swooped down, and pummeled down on top of Ray. Holding his victim in his clutches, he began draining Ray now too.

"Ahh!!! It burns!!!" Ray exclaimed. Something was draining the life force out of him. And it hurt like hell!

Luke fired again and again. Each time hurt Arachnus, but not enough to stop him. Ray gasped for air. Luke dialed up the settings, increasing the laser's power. He fired again. A bigger beam. A brighter blast.

Arachnus tumbled back, screeching out in pain. He let go of Ray.

Dawn ran to her boyfriend's side. "You okay?"

Ray struggled to regain his strength, struggling to catch his breath. "What the hell was that?"

Arachnus transformed back into his normal spider-only mutant form. He stood several feet away. Stared at them through his many eyes. And grinned.

Then he lifted his wounded, severed arm – the one he lost when they closed the portal on him – and let them all watch as he slowly made it reappear, growing out of the severed stump. His eighth arm returned to full size, completely normal, as if he had never lost it. He began laughing.

"That's not good," said Dawn.

"We don't want to kill you," said Luke, charging up another laser shot. "Come peacefully and this will all be over."

Arachnus shook his head. "I don't think so."

Luke sighed. "Fine." And he pointed his hand to fire at Arachnus. But the instant Luke started to move, Arachnus waved all his arms outward, and suddenly Luke, Dawn, and Ray all found themselves flying backwards.

Dawn banged into a street lamp. Ouch, that hurt. Luke collided with a brick wall. And Ray crashed into the front windshield of a parked car. That was going to leave a mark.

Arachnus wasted no time. He flung his arms again, and all three of them launched into the air. Arachnus waved his arms around, manipulating them, keeping them suspended and helpless in mid-air.

Dawn shape-shifted into a bird – but couldn't fly away. Luke teleported behind Arachnus. But the spider turned around, raised another arm, and Luke was suddenly helpless and floating again. Ray pushed back – gravity force against gravity force. Unfortunately, their powers didn't cancel each other out. Dammit. But Ray got another idea. He lifted Arachnus up into the air too.

"Hey, stop that!" the spider monster yelled.

Now they *all* were floating in the air – Arachnus controlling them, and Ray controlling Arachnus.

They began spinning and moving around each other, floating at each other's control and mercy – leaping and lunging at one another, floating forwards and flying backwards, spiraling around each other, never getting too close or too far from each other. Luke fired his laser several times, from several angles. Dawn shape-shifted into various deadly creatures – trying to strike whenever she got close enough.

Arachnus moved in for the kill. But Ray quickly pushed her away, just enough to make Arachnus miss. Arachnus drew Ray closer, but Luke teleported in to save him. Arachnus pushed Luke with a mighty gravity blast, sending him crashing hard into – and through – a nearby building. Thank God he was wearing that armored suit.

Finally Dawn got an idea. They couldn't beat him like this, being tossed around in the air by his multiple arms. But maybe she could trick him into giving up that advantage.

"Hey ugly!" Dawn taunted him. "Bet you can't do this!"

She began changing, rapidly, transforming into a seventy-foot-tall giant. She towered over the buildings, cars, and remaining scattered people below.

"I'm gonna squash you like the little bug you are!" she said. She held onto a building, raised her foot to step on him.

"Ha! I can do anything you can do – and better!" Arachnus snarled. He rapidly started growing too. Ten feet tall. Twenty feet tall. Fifty feet tall. *One hundred feet tall!*

His booming laugh rolled like thunder.

"Uh, Dawn…" said Luke. "What are you doing?"

Luke and Ray fell to the ground. Arachnus's attention dropped off them. He was only focused on giant-sized Dawn now.

"I stole your powers!" Arachnus boasted. "You can't win. I'm unstoppable!"

"Ray," said Luke, "keep him distracted."

"Got it." Ray pushed against the Earth's gravity, levitating himself up. Dawn shape-shifted herself even bigger – matching Arachnus's enormously huge size. The two giants locked arms, struggling to overpower the other in a match of one-on-one brute strength. Ray flew upwards, a small insect in relative comparison, and started hovering annoyingly in front of Arachnus's giant eyes.

Down on the ground, Luke looked at his left arm. His crystal was still strapped there. He tore it off. It was time to use this thing again. He started drawing a long line on the ground. A very, very long line…

"I sure hope this works," Luke said. He drew the line along the far edge of the street, alongside the buildings, around behind Arachnus's enormous spider-like feet, across to the other side, down along the edge of the far side buildings, and finally, eventually back to where it started.

Hardly a circle. But the portal shape shouldn't matter. It just had to be an enclosed and defined space.

Ray continued buzzing around Arachnus's giant face like an annoying pest. "I'm over here. Now I'm over here. Hey, pay attention to me."

Arachnus swatted at him. Ray saw the giant hand coming a mile away, and easily avoided it.

"Missed me, missed me! Ha ha, you suck!"

Arachnus tried to grab Ray with his free hands. Dawn grew additional arms and hands of her own, locking the giant spider monster in an equally-matched struggle.

Well, almost equally matched.

Arachnus was a little bit stronger. Dawn shape-shifted her muscles to be bigger, stronger, more lean and more powerful. She started to feel a bit like the Incredible Hulk, only less green. But Arachnus matched her. And then made himself even stronger.

He might've overpowered her if Ray hadn't kept flying in front of his face. "Stop that!" Arachnus shouted. His voice could be heard for miles.

Luke dashed towards the center of the portal area. He drew a pair of wavy lines. Instantly the ground beneath them disappeared. Luke teleported back to solid ground, near the edge of the portal. But Arachnus started to fall. "Wh-whoa!!!"

Ray used his power to keep Dawn afloat.

Arachnus's giant legs fell through. Then his waist. And some of his arms. But his remaining arms grabbed onto some nearby buildings and street lights. He held himself up. Half way through the portal. He started to pull himself back up.

Luke turned to the wall next to him. He drew a quick small circle. He placed the crystal in the center, ready to draw a symbol. "Arachnus," he shouted, "if I open a new portal, the one you're in will instantly close."

Arachnus knew what that meant. He'd be severed in half. He was too big. He couldn't pull himself up fast enough. Not faster than Luke could draw a symbol. He already lost an arm that way. Could his stolen shape-shifting power re-grow the entire lower half of his body? He didn't want to take that chance.

He peered angrily down at Luke – and let go. He dropped all the way through, shrinking down to normal size at the same time.

The instant his head was through, Luke drew a triangle. A new tiny portal opened on the wall. The previous giant portal spread across the street had vanished.

Luke then X-ed out the new portal.

Dawn shrank back down to normal size too. Ray slowly descended back down to the ground. "Well that was fun," said Ray, dusting off his hands.

"Good teamwork, guys," said Dawn.

Luke agreed. "Now let's make sure they're all tucked away safe and sound, before we take on Mastermind." He looked at them. "Ready?"

"Ready," said Ray.

"Ready," cheered Dawn.

Luke put his arms around both – and they teleported.

Back in the Mojave Desert, one last time.

Rhino-Man and Venom stood alone in the midst of a vast and empty desert. Nothing but miles and miles of endless sand and punishing sun in every direction. Barren mountains in the distance. No sign of civilization anywhere.

Luke, Dawn, and Ray appeared.

"Alright, you've got a choice," said Luke to the two mutants. "Stay here and die in the desert, or relax on the tropical island planet."

Rhino-Man gave him a curious look. "How about I pound your face in?"

Venom hissed.

Luke started drawing a large circle in the sand. The trail of pink light followed wherever the crystal touched. Then in the center he drew the symbol. The portal opened back to the lush jungle and beautiful beach. Paradise. A billion miles away on another planet. Where they couldn't harm a soul.

"Well?" Luke asked.

Rhino-Man sized him up. Could he and Venom take them? Maybe.

Kraken was still on the other side, enjoying himself swimming around in the ocean. Slimer relaxed under a palm tree, drinking out of some kind of coconut. Arachnus, defeated only seconds ago, frowned at Luke and the others when he saw them through the re-opened portal. But he stayed put. Arms (most of them) crossed.

"Time's up," said Ray. He pulled Venom into the portal, dropping her to the other side. Then he moved his hand, about to do the same to Rhino-Man.

"Wait! Fine," said the muscular gray mutant. "At least leave me the dignity to do it myself."

The rhinoceros mutant walked over to the portal, looked in, and saw his fellow mutants on the other side. He sighed. Was this really over?

He stomped his foot on the ground. An earthquake knocked Luke and Dawn off their feet. Ray reacted quickly, waiting for the mutant to try something. Ray lifted himself an inch off the ground, and in one fluid motion, sent the big tough guy tumbling through the portal.

Luke didn't waste another second. Crystal in hand, he didn't even wait to get up and X-out the portal. He just quickly drew a tiny circle, a pyramid in the middle, and instantly closed out the previous portal. Then he closed the new portal. Easy-peasy.

Dawn got up, dusting herself off. "Is that everyone?"

Ray helped Luke up. "I think so," he said.

"The new bat mutant's still missing," said Luke. "And we left the cat girl in Japan. But other than that, yeah. We're good."

"And no way they can get off that planet?" Ray asked.

"Not unless they have a crystal," said Luke.

"Should we look for the bat?" asked Dawn.

"I dunno," said Luke. "He could be anywhere. But he didn't put up much of a fight. I dunno. It's weird. There's something oddly familiar about him. I feel like… like we can trust him. I don't think we need to worry about him."

"You sure?" asked Ray. "You do hear yourself, right?"

"I know. But even if he shows up, one mutant's a lot easier to deal with than five. Besides, he can only turn invisible. Or teleport. I'm not sure. Either way, it's not an offensive power. Still not sure where he came from, though. Whatever. We'll be fine."

"If you say so, man," said Ray. "You're the leader."

"I am?" asked Luke.

Dawn laughed.

"Yeah, well," said Ray, "I figured you know more about this stuff than either of us, with all your comic books and whatnot. So what would Superman do now?"

"Well, save the world, I guess."

"Then let's do it."

"Yeah!" cheered Dawn. "It's about frickin' time!

Chapter 35
SHOWDOWN

First they teleported back to Ray and Luke's apartment, where Charlie was waiting.

He was watching the news, on mute with closed captions. "They just reported that some mysterious heroes took down a giant spider mutant in Saint Petersburg," said the old man with a smile. "Well done."

"That son of a bitch stole our powers!" Ray exclaimed.

"Copied," corrected Luke. "Technically he copied them. If he stole them, we wouldn't have our powers anymore."

"Shut up. He didn't take anything from you," joked Ray.

"Good thing too," said Dawn. "Could you imagine if he had all three of our powers?"

"Yikes," said Luke.

"So what's the plan?" asked Charlie. "Did you get all of them?"

"Mostly," said Luke. "There's a new bat mutant who disappeared on me. And we left Shadow, the cat girl, in Japan."

Charlie noticed a news update. "Looks like other people are randomly starting to mutate. Says there's reports of sightings in Spain, France, England, and… here in the United States."

"It's gotta be that chemical the hospitals are distributing," Dawn said. "We gotta end this, *now*."

"But all his original mutants are taken care of, right?" asked Charlie. "They'd be the only ones with powers. Should I tell our anonymous hacker friend to go ahead with his plan?"

"You sure we can trust this guy?" asked Ray.

"It's worth a shot," said Dawn.

Luke looked to his uncle. "I trust you. Do what you think is best. I mean, he did help mom and dad before, right?"

Charlie nodded softly. "Seems he still believes we have a chance to defeat Mastermind. Ready to finish what your parents started?"

Luke didn't hesitate. "Absolutely."

"Alright," said Uncle Charlie. "Pray this works." He pulled out his cell phone and entered a text message. "Mission accomplished. Proceed with plan." He hit send.

A few seconds later, a reply text message came back. "Confirmed. Uploading now," it read.

Ray looked around. "So what happens now?"

"Now we see if it works," said Charlie. "But either way, you've still got a job to do." He looked to Luke. "Have you made a decision?"

Luke nodded, considering a heavy thought. "As much as I want to kill him, I can't do it. That's a line I'm not willing to cross. But he's too dangerous to let live, either."

"We're behind you, man," said Ray.

"Yeah," said Dawn. "Just tell us what to do."

The easiest thing, of course, was for Luke to open up a portal to the derelict starship. Dawn could distract Mastermind with her shape-shifting. Ray would blast him into the portal. The vacuum would suck Mastermind right in. All Luke would have to do was close the portal – and Mastermind would be gone forever. On the other side, trapped on that abandoned space ship, he'd quickly run out of air – freezing to death at the same time.

That'd be the easiest, fastest, safest way.

But it'd make them all killers too.

And heroes didn't kill. At least, not these heroes. Luke wasn't willing to cross that line.

The alternative, much riskier and far more dangerous option was to somehow disable Mastermind. Make him powerless. And let the police take care of him. Lock him up forever. He'd still be alive, but he wouldn't be able to harm another soul again.

Still, this was the man who killed both of Luke's parents in cold blood. This was the man who came back to LA, possibly to finish off Luke too. This was the man who mind-controlled random strangers, mutated them, and turned them all into super villain henchmen. This was a man who declared himself to be a god – and at this very moment, was actually starting to take over the world.

His mutants were out of the picture. Locked away safe on another world. But it was only a matter of time before Mastermind found new mutants, and larger numbers of mutants, and gave them all powers again.

Luke had considered just dumping Mastermind off on the same planet as his mutants. But that felt too dangerous. What if Mastermind had another secret crystal they didn't know about? What if someone, somewhere else in the universe, unintentionally opened a portal to that planet – and suddenly Mastermind and all his super-powered mutants were suddenly set free?

He didn't know how to destroy the pyramids either, and even if he could, he'd cut off their own powers – and the powers of countless other people throughout the galaxy. That might make a lot more enemies – alien enemies, with high-tech space craft – once they found out someone from Earth was responsible.

Maybe, just this once, he should cross the line. Just kill off Mastermind. Just this once. And be done with it. Fire a cutting laser straight through the center of his head. Suck him through a portal into the vacuum of space. Inject him with his own chemical, without donor DNA, and let his own cells slowly deteriorate and disintegrate him from the inside out.

But would he still be a hero? Did Batman or Superman kill? Captain America? Spider-Man? Sure, sometimes villains died. But the heroes never directly, intentionally, pre-meditatively tried to kill anyone. That was the difference, Luke believed, between heroes and villains. Both had powers. Both, because of those powers, were something more than human. But that being "more than human" part – did it make them above the law? Above ethics? Above morality?

Luke was still a United States citizen. With or without powers. And murder – whether by laser, portal, or deadly chemical – was still murder. Mastermind, no matter how evil, was still a human being. He still, regrettably, had his rights. Luke *knew* he was guilty. But was Luke about to become judge, jury, and executioner for everyone he thought was bad? Did he – a young man with the power of *time travel*, the ability to erase and change history – did he want to cross that line, and single-handedly decide the fate of anyone he so chose?

Yes, Mastermind was bad. Yes, Mastermind was a murderer. And that was the difference between them. Luke had great power now too. But he wouldn't use it to kill. Not now. Not ever. *That* was why he was a hero.

For Luke, there was only one decision when it came to dealing with Mastermind. He just wished it was the easier option.

"We avoid eye contact," he said, answering their question, "and we disable him. We take him down, but we don't kill him. We leave him for the police to take care of – and let the people of world, and all his victims, decide his fate."

Ray nodded. "I never thought for a second you'd say otherwise."

Dawn agreed. "He's vulnerable now without his mutants. Between the three of us, he should be no problem."

"Then let's do this." Luke put his metal-gloved hand out in the center. Dawn placed her hand on top of his. Ray placed his hand on hers.

"Ready when you are, man," said Ray.

"Here we go!" said Luke.

This was it.

A bright flash of white light – and they vanished.

Charlie watched. He stared at the empty space in his nephew's living room, where those young new would-be heroes stood only a second ago. "Good luck, kids," he said proudly.

An instant later, and they found themselves in Times Square, New York City. Still holding hands together as a team.

And then Ray's jaw dropped. Dawn's eyes opened wide with disbelief. "Oh… shit…" said Luke.

Mastermind had been busy.

They should've gotten here *a lot* sooner.

Ray readied his hands. This was going to be a busy day. Dawn prepped herself to start shape-shifting. Luke's heads-up display went haywire trying to track it all.

Mutants. Mutants *everywhere*. Flying mutants. Wall-climbing mutants. Crawling mutants. Mutants crawling out of the sewers. Ugly mutants. Monstrous mutants. Creatures of all types – spiders, scorpions, snakes, frogs, lizards, birds, lions, tigers, and bears, oh my! All that and more. Every animal. And a whole bunch of strange combinations of animals. All mutants. Some still looked somewhat human. But most did not.

Were these all once people? How on Earth had Mastermind transformed so many of them so fast? They were *everywhere!* Hundreds, no, thousands of them! Crawling, climbing, and flying all over the city. Running around in a chaotic rampage. Attacking each other. Tearing apart buildings. Overthrowing vehicles. Roaring, screeching, crying, wailing, laughing, gurgling, hissing… every type of creature, every imaginable hybrid – and then some – were running amuck here.

"Holy nightmare, Batman!" Luke exclaimed.

"You can say that again," Ray said.

"We can't fight them all," said Dawn.

"Everyone, get ready. I'm going to try to send us all back in time. We gotta stop—"

"No!" said Ray. "Save your power. We may need it later at a more critical moment. First we take down Mastermind. Then we find a way to save all these people."

"He's right. If Mastermind gets the upper hand on us again," said Dawn, "we're going to need you to go back in time and save *us*."

"Alright, scanning for him now…" His heads-up display had a hard time processing all the information around him. None of the mutants seemed to display any supernatural powers. They were just … mutants. Scared, confused, angry, out of control mutants.

A few started charging too close. Ray blasted them back with his power. Dawn couldn't figure out what to shape-shift into. Every creature was different. If she made herself too big and strong, a smaller faster mutant could get the jump on her. If she made herself small and agile, the bigger monsters could easily crush her.

Many mutants looked poisonous – was that one a scorpion or a mutant tarantula? It looked like a mix of both. A frog-like mutant hopped on top of one of the billboards, and snatched up another mutant below with its long tongue.

A dragonfly-like mutant with way too many sharp teeth buzzed by, chasing after a female butterfly-like mutant that was holding, what looked like, a lizard baby. Then something with three tails, two heads, and a lion-like body charged out from around the corner, jumped up with a back-flip, and snatched the dragonfly mutant right out of the air with its massive paws! The butterfly woman and her lizard baby flew away to safety.

Some kind of giant ape beast lifted up and smashed two cars together. Some kind of wasp mutant with spider-like legs slowly crawled up a skyscraper. And a squirmy little mole-man hid in the shadows around the corner, watching Dawn and the others cautiously.

"Come on, come on…" said Luke. "He's gotta be here somewhere."

"Anytime now, Luke," said Ray, blasting away a few more dangerous-looking mutants who got a little too close.

"Got him!" Luke exclaimed. "This way!"

"Right behind you," said Dawn.

"Me too," said his best friend, blasting back more mutants.

The three ran forward. The mutants were everywhere. Many ran off in other directions. Several attacked each other. But Luke, Ray, and Dawn stuck out from the crowd – being the only humans in sight. Many mutants spotted them and charged to attack.

Ray blasted the oncoming mutants left and right, and ahead, and above… Oh shit! One popped up from a sewer hole beneath them! "Hang on guys," said Ray. He quickly levitated them all up into the air. Much easier this way. They were out of reach of *most* of the mutants now, anyway. "Where to, captain?"

"He's moving fast!" said Luke. "Wait… he's turning around… he's coming… oh fuck."

"What?" asked Dawn.

Mastermind flew out of nowhere, rushing right past them, as if he didn't even see them.

"What the hell?" yelled Ray.

They all turned around. Mastermind blew past them, racing ahead to his next destination – but he stopped. He hovered in the air – and slowly turned around. He faced them. Made eye contact.

"I was wondering when I'd see you three again."

"Don't look at his eyes!" Dawn shouted.

Mastermind laughed.

"He can fly?!" Ray remarked.

Luke couldn't believe it. "Could he always do that?"

Dawn shook her head.

"Great. What else can he do?" said Ray.

Mastermind grinned. "Glad you asked, boy. Let me show you my true power – the power of your God!"

The super villain looked around. In the distance he spotted a news helicopter, filming the whole scene. He smiled.

He flew straight for it.

"After him!" Luke shouted.

Ray used his anti-gravity power to levitate them in pursuit. Mastermind flew so fast. Quickly escaping. But Ray was starting to get good at using his power. He picked up the pace – and soon they started gaining on him!

Mastermind accelerated right up to the news helicopter. The video camera pointed straight at his face. Mastermind reached inside and placed his hand on the pilot. The pilot started screaming with blood-curdling horror, clawing at his face and chest.

His body began changing. Transforming. Uncontrollably. Into… into… scales… wings… a large tail… the pilot turned into a giant… purple dragon. He screeched with agonizing pain, fiery eyes going wild, as his body quickly grew larger and larger, enormously so, becoming way too big for the limited space inside the helicopter. The front windshield busted out. The frame started to buckle. The helicopter turned sideways, starting to spin out of control. The large dragon-man broke himself free, suddenly finding himself airborne, still completing his radical transformation.

He let out another loud ear-piercing screech as his wings began to flap and he started to fly on his own.

The helicopter, on the other hand, went into a tailspin and crashed into the side of a building. The camera man inside most certainly died. Fiery debris fell to the surface below.

Mastermind floated in front of his latest monster. Making eye contact, he said to the beast, "Kill them." He pointed at Ray and the others.

The purple dragon obeyed.

"Okay…" said Ray, seeing the ridiculously large dragon coming right at them.

"I got this," said Dawn. "Let me free."

Ray released her from his power. She immediately began falling towards the ground. But she quickly transformed – into a powerful green dragon of her own!

The purple one got too close. It inhaled deep, something red lit up behind his nostrils, and suddenly fire spewed out of his mouth in a rushing stream.

"Shields up!" Luke shouted.

The fire instantly spread around his force field, just in the nick of time. For a second, they saw only the inside of the flames, all around them, until it burned off and passed completely over. The force field protected them. Although it did get a little warm for a second or two there.

"Nice one," Ray said.

"Thanks," returned Luke.

Dawn tried breathing fire. Could she do that too? She inhaled deep. Summoned it up. And… blew nothing but slightly warm air. Dammit. Wait, there had to be a way. Fire-breathing wasn't a super power. He was a mutant. Nothing more. There had to be a way to replicate the same ability.

Dawn shape-shifted her insides. She wasn't sure how she did it. But on her second attempt – there was fire. Beautiful, magnificent fire. Blazing out of her mouth like one badass flame-thrower. Oh heck yes. That felt good.

She aimed the fire right at the other dragon. Part of her flames scorched over Luke's shield, but they were fine. The other dragon got burned. It roared aloud again, still ear-piercing, and immediately blew another stream of fire back at her.

"Ray, move us in between!" Luke shouted.

"Already ahead of ya!" he replied.

They moved in front of the fire stream. Luke's force field blocked and deflected the wave of fire. Dawn was left untouched. She laughed, flew above the two guys, and then blasted the dragon with another fire ball of her own.

The purple one spewed another stream of fire. Ray quickly moved them up to block the fire blast.

This was taking too long. "Hold on guys," Luke said. As soon as the other dragon stopped breathing fire, Luke immediately removed the shields, pointed his fist forward, and fired a cutting laser at the dragon's wings.

It sliced off one wing, and then quickly, the other.

"Sorry guy."

The dragon screeched out in unimaginable pain, and without his giant wings to keep him afloat, immediately began tumbling toward the ground.

Dawn dove down, caught the beast with her dragon-like feet claws, and descended slowly, landing them both gently on the ground. Hey, it wasn't his fault he got mutated or mind-controlled. Somewhere behind that monstrous face was a human being.

The dragon still blew fire at her. But Dawn immediately jumped back up into the air and flew away. The newly-mutated dragon shot wave after wave of fire towards her, but he was stuck on the ground – and Dawn and the others quickly flew out of range.

"Good teamwork there guys," said Dawn, flying alongside them still in dragon-form.

"Thanks," said Ray, levitating him and Luke forward.

"I'm tracking Mastermind now. He's headed for the shore."

They weaved through the city buildings as fast as they could. Luke kept Mastermind locked on his heads-up display. Dawn flew up higher above the buildings. From his higher perspective, she could see just how many mutants there were.

It went on for city block after city block, mile after mile, as far as the eye could see. Nearly every person in the streets had been mutated into a monster. No way Mastermind could do all this on his own – could he?

They reached the edge of the city. The Atlantic Ocean greeted them beyond. Mastermind dove into the water.

"Where's he going?" asked Luke.

Ray landed them safely on the ground, at a docking bay along the coast. Some large ships waited to be loaded with the various heavy crates that sat around – but no one was here to work anything. They had either ran away or already been mutated. One mermaid-like person sat along the edge of the dock, in the distance. When the creature spotted them, it quickly dove into the water to escape.

"He trying to hide from us or something?" asked Ray.

Luke shrugged. "Maybe. But I didn't know he could breathe underwater."

"I don't think he can," said Dawn, landing beside them as she returned to human form. "I saw him from above. He's treading water behind that ship over there."

Ray smiled. "Watch this."

He held out both his hands, focused *really* hard, and concentrated on that ship. With all his effort, from across the dock, slowly, he began to levitate that massive ship.

It started rising. Water streamed down its sides. The ship rose higher and higher, little by little – until it was completely out of the water and several feet up into the air. Ray concentrated harder still, struggling with all his might, and lifted it even higher.

Luke and Dawn ran up to the edge of the dock. They looked into the turbulent waters.

Mastermind was nowhere to be seen.

Not in the water, anyway.

As the large ship rose even higher, they saw Mastermind floating in place, behind it, waiting for them, arms crossed.

"Impressive," he said.

Luke aimed his cutting laser directly at the villain. "Give it up, Mastermind. We captured all your mutants. We've got you outnumbered. Surrender peacefully or we'll—"

Mastermind rolled his eyes. Then he glanced down into the murky waters, pointing below. "Say hello to my little children."

A giant shark leaped out of the water and onto the dock. Luke and Dawn dodged out of the way, with it between them. This shark had teeth that would give Jaws an inferiority complex – and, strangely, jellyfish-like tentacles hanging from its gums. And extra eyes across its forehead. Then the shark stood up – on its short little mutant legs – and they knew where this was going.

Ray released the ship. He blasted an anti-gravity shockwave at the shark monster. The creature tumbled backwards. The ship crashed into the water, sending a small tidal wave splashing over them. The shark caught the wave, which carried him forward back towards them – oops – and he crashed right into Dawn. She screamed as the beast chomped at her side, deeply stinging her flesh. She screamed out in unbelievable pain. Blood poured out from her side – that thing bit off her entire arm! The wave subsided, the shark was now behind them. Dawn looked down at her severed arm, in shock. The shark monster turned around, stumbled on his short little legs, flopping back towards her, chomping for another bite.

"Dawn!" Ray shouted.

Luke fired the cutting laser straight through the shark's head. He sure hoped that didn't used to be a person. The monster fell over dead, coming to a loud wet thud as it hit the dock.

Ray ran up to Dawn. She was in terrible shock. She just lost an arm. Her whole body was shivering.

"Dawn! Dawn! Listen to me! Look at me!" He held her face in his hands. "I need you to use your power and re-grow another arm. You can do it, Dawn. I know you can. Hurry!"

She blinked. He got through to her. She concentrated enough. The wound started to close itself up. The massive bleeding stopped. Ray let out a sigh of relief. Slowly a new arm grew in its place. Small at first. Then back to a normal size. Good as new. Just like the old one.

"Dawn, are you okay?"

Dawn slowly lifted her hand to her face. She wiggled her new fingers. She smiled. She was a little light-headed from the loss of blood. But she'd be okay.

"Oh thank God," said Ray.

They embraced in a hug.

Luke looked back at Mastermind, still floating there. The villain shook his head in disappointment.

"Pity," said Mastermind.

"No more of this," said Luke. "You've gone far enough."

"I'm just getting started," replied Mastermind.

"Like hell you are!"

This was going to end – right here, right now. Luke raced forward, activating his armored suit's hydraulics, jumped up into the air, leaping forward with superhuman strength and speed – and collided directly into Mastermind.

Chapter 36

FINAL BREATH

Back at the apartment, Charlie continued watching the news. Still with the volume muted, and closed captioning on.

Mastermind's "obey me" video still repeated. They seemed to replay it every five or ten minutes. It was ridiculous. That damn video was all over the place. Charlie flipped through the channels. It was on that channel. And the next. Oh look, there's a repeat of the president's message, telling everyone to get their so-called "cure". Next channel: more Mastermind. Channel after that: sports. Channel after that, more Mastermind.

Wait, what was this?

Something different. Charlie turned up the volume.

"Lord Mastermind has just released a new video," said the anchor man, "with apparently new information. We're the first network to bring you this breaking news update."

New video? Could that be—?

It switched to the "new" video. It started out just like the old one. Mastermind's face – clear, in focus, and in high-definition – filled the television screen. This was being broadcast in homes across America – and hopefully, soon the world.

"I am Mastermind," he said, smiling. The next words in the video used to be: "Your new god. Bow down and worship me." But that wasn't what he said next. The video abruptly cut back to his first "I am" – and then immediately cut to several seconds ahead – "a disgusting plague on this planet. You" – another rough cut to – "will" – cut – "be so lucky" – cut – "to kill" – and – "ME!"

Nice job, anonymous hacker friend. Not the smoothest editing work ever, but it just might do the trick.

"Kill" – edit – "ME!" – cut – "Do not" – cut – "bow down and worship me". Charlie laughed. Nice touch. Then it repeated, over and over again: "Kill – ME! Kill – ME! Kill – ME! Kill – ME! – NOW!" It showed Mastermind smiling again. And then cut to:

"Share this video with everyone you know."

Charlie suddenly felt an urge to kill Mastermind – right now. And if he saw Mastermind in person, he just might. Charlie had never killed anyone in his life before. He shook his head quickly. Tried to shake it off. The mind control was working. *Against* Mastermind this time.

The TV switched back to the news anchor, who suddenly had a strange and confused look on his face. "Um, apparently Lord Mastermind… I mean, just Mastermind, wants us to kill him now."

Impact!

Luke crashed into Mastermind.

Heavy metal armor suit against mortal flesh. Mastermind felt that. Hard.

The two splashed down into the water.

Mastermind pressed his hand against Luke's armor. He tried transforming Luke into something – perhaps a giant ugly fly, or a disgusting little ant, or some other annoying and bothersome insect mutant. But nothing happened. His power didn't work on technology. It was just armor. Just metal. Not a living thing. Luke's suit remained unchanged and intact.

Luke instantly teleported the two of them away.

A flash of light – a rush of water – and they were gone.

Back in the wide open and barren Mojave Desert, they reappeared with another flash of light. Water splashed down onto the thirsty soil around them.

Luke tossed Mastermind to the ground. The villain crashed hard into the hot and rough sand. Luke, standing tall and proud, stepped over to him. "I have every right to kill you," Luke said. "Not a soul in the galaxy would side with you. You must pay for your crimes, Mastermind. And I'm here to take you down."

Luke held out his hand, aiming his cutting laser directly at Mastermind's head. The laser battery charged up. Yield increased to 150%... 300%... 500%... 1,000%!

"Any last words?"

Mastermind grinned.

"Disarm yourself," Mastermind said, looking directly into Luke's helmet visor. "Lower your weapons, bow down, and worship me." He smiled like the devil. "Now."

Luke lowered his arm. The laser stopped charging. He bent down on one knee.

Mastermind started laughing. He rose up.

Luke lowered his head.

"You will obey me."

Luke looked back up. "Not in a million years!" His metal-armored fist – backed by amplified suit hydraulics – thrust up into Mastermind's stomach with one super-powered mechanical punch.

Blood spit out of Mastermind's mouth. All the wind knocked out of him. The man stumbled backwards, tripped, and fell back to the sandy earth.

Luke rose to his feet. "I can't *hear* a word you're saying, Mastermind. But my heads-up display is translating everything for me to read."

Luke punched him again – hard.

The super villain spun over, falling to the ground again. Mastermind stumbled to his feet a second time – and *bam!* – another punishing impact from Luke's armored fist.

"You killed my parents!"

Another unforgiving pound. Bones cracked.

"You killed Ethos!"

Another pounding thrust. More blood flew out of his mouth.

"You killed countless others!"

One, two, three punishing hits. Mastermind fell to his knees, nursing his injuries.

"You mutated all those people!"

Luke kicked him hard with his mechanical boot. Mastermind spun into the air and landed on some painful rocks – right along his spine.

"You turn good people into killers!"

He laid his boot on Mastermind's neck, ready to crush it with the slightest pressure.

"Tell me why you should live."

Choking, coughing up blood, struggling to breathe – Mastermind whispered, "Please."

"Mercy?" Luke asked. "Like you showed all those people back in New York?"

"You're killing me!" Mastermind struggled to say. He couldn't breathe. He squirmed uselessly, suffering intense pain from several broken bones throughout his body, unable to move or escape out from under Luke's foot.

Luke leaned down – his helmet to Mastermind's face. "Tell me why I should care."

"I… I…" Mastermind gasped for air. He squirmed. He reached into his pocket. His hand gripped his Astaria crystal.

Luke didn't notice. He was all up in Mastermind's face. What should he do with him? Use the cutting laser to slice off Mastermind's tongue? Can't control anyone if he can't speak. Or maybe he'd burn out both eyes. No eye contact, no control either. And neither one of those would kill him. But they definitely would disable him.

Mastermind's trembling hand drew an unevenly-shaped circle along the ground at his side.

Luke's heads-up display flashed a warning message. "Astaria energy detected."

What? Luke looked over. Mastermind finished tracing the circle. Barely two feet wide. More oval than circular. Was he trying to escape?

Luke grabbed Mastermind's wrist. The villain dropped the crystal.

He stepped off of Mastermind, reached down, and grabbed him by the neck. Luke lifted him effortlessly into the air. This suit was awesome. Easily amplified his strength a hundred times. Mastermind's feet dangled in the air as he held onto Luke's arm, trying to break free.

"Going somewhere?" Luke asked.

Mastermind couldn't release himself. His feet kicked and dangled in the air. He tried to pry Luke's hand open from around his neck – but the suit's hydraulics were far too strong. Just then, Mastermind noticed something, up in the sky.

"There you are," he grinned.

Luke's HUD suddenly alerted him to a new presence. A mutant had just appeared in the air – seemingly out of nowhere. Luke looked up behind him.

It was that bat guy again!

"Kill him!" Mastermind ordered.

The bat mutant looked down, seeing an armor-suited man holding his master captive. Echo swooped down.

Luke tossed Mastermind aside like the worthless garbage he was. Luke faced the bat mutant. "I don't want to fight you," he said. "We don't have to be enemies."

Mastermind shook off his disorientation and raced back toward the crystal. It laid there by the still-glowing outline of his new portal.

"Master wants me to kill you," said Echo, "and that's exactly what I'm going to do. Tell me, stranger, when's your birthday?"

What? His birthday?

"I don't have to fight you," declared Echo. "I can make it so you were never born."

Wait… huh?

Oh my God. Luke just realized who the bat mutant really was. Could it be? No. It couldn't be.

"Luke?" Luke asked.

Echo stopped in his tracks. The other guy's voice did sound a little familiar. "Luke?" he asked back.

"You popped out of the sphere," battle-suit Luke said. "Didn't you? But Uncle Charlie and the others weren't there, were they?"

"No… hey, how did you know that?" Echo asked.

"Luke… I'm you! From another timeline."

"What? No way."

"Yeah," he said. "I didn't know I'd create a timeline duplicate by changing my own history. But it happens, every time."

"What? Really? Well, I guess that makes sense," said Echo. "Temporal stacking, right?"

"Right!"

Mastermind, kneeling over his now-larger portal outline, shook his head. What *were* they talking about? Whatever. It didn't matter. He placed his crystal in the center of this bigger pink circle.

"So there's two of us now?" Echo asked.

"Well, kinda. Sorry you got mutated, buddy."

Echo shrugged. "Whatever. I kinda like it."

"I know. You're—"

"Batman!" Echo exclaimed. He laughed. "Just kidding. I go by 'Echo' now. Cool, right?"

"Totally."

Mastermind rolled his eyes. He marked an upside-down "U" with two smaller circles on each end. The portal instantly opened as Mastermind scurried backwards as quickly as possible.

The open portal immediately began sucking in a lot of air. The abandoned starship – and a lot of icy cold darkness -- waited on the other side.

Luke's HUD started flashing all kinds of warnings: "New portal opened. Danger! Danger! Massive vacuum!"

"What the?" Luke turned around. He saw Mastermind flying away to safety. And a whole lot of air and sand rushing towards the portal. Tumbleweed rolled in. Wind started blowing from all directions – all draining down into that hole.

He needed to close that portal – fast. He reached over for his arm – wait, where'd his crystal go?

High above, Mastermind started laughing. "Looking for this?" He held Luke's crystal in his other hand. He must've grabbed it when Luke was holding him up, and got distracted when Echo appeared! Mastermind dropped it over the portal. "Whoopsie! My bad."

A small tornado of dusty, sandy air had begun swirling around the mouth of the portal. Like all the water swirling down the bathtub drain – except it was all of Earth's atmosphere, draining out into deep space!

The crystal fell straight into it.

Luke jumped after it. But he was too far away. He reached for it – and missed! The crystal went down the drain, disappearing somewhere on the other side, somewhere in that abandoned, exposed-to-empty-space starship.

And now the swirling vortex had caught him, pulling him down, rapidly sucking him to the same doom. He saw the blackness of space beneath him. He had only a split second to react. He disappeared in a flash – and teleported to safety several hundred feet away.

The winds still blew, growing stronger, all moving down towards that hole. But he was far enough away to hold his ground.

"If I can't have Earth," shouted Mastermind from the distance, "then no one shall!"

He flew away.

Luke looked back at that growing tornado as more and more of the Earth's atmosphere rapidly drained out into deep space. He had to do something. He had to do it fast. He looked back at Echo. They'd have to finish this another time.

Mastermind was almost out of view. But not entirely. Especially with Luke's HUD tracking and zoom vision.

A flash of white light.

Luke teleported directly in front of Mastermind, all the way in the distance, high up in the sky. Mastermind abruptly collided into his armored suit.

"Goddamit! That's *really* getting annoying!" he exclaimed.

"Give me your crystal!" Luke demanded, holding out his hand. He wasn't playing around. This was urgent. Every lost second meant more and more of the Earth's atmosphere gone.

"What for?"

"We need to close that portal, Mastermind!"

"In your dreams, space man."

"You'll die too!"

He grinned. "No I won't. I hear Aquaria's nice this time of year."

"But…" Wait. That was perfect. As soon as Mastermind opened up a new portal, it'd automatically close the old one. Luke smiled inside his helmet. "Go ahead."

"Oh, and if you're thinking my escape will close that portal, guess again space cadet. That rule only applies to individual crystals, not portals in general."

"What?"

"You heard me. The only way to close that portal is with the crystal that created it. And it's lost somewhere in deep space right about now."

"You son of a bitch!" Luke threw another punch at him. Mastermind dodged out of the way. Luke attacked again, but Mastermind was clearly much more agile in the air. The villain started laughing.

Oh yeah? You think that's funny?

He was close enough. Luke teleported again.

Mastermind vanished with him.

They reappeared *dangerously* close to the mouth of the portal. Sand and dirt swirled violently in the air. The tornado of dust and debris escaping down the portal made it difficult to breath and nearly impossible to see. Well, for those whose faces weren't protected by a high-tech space suit, anyway. Luke immediately shoved Mastermind to the ground, leaned on top of him, and pushed his head back over the open, sucking portal.

"Get off me!" Mastermind demanded.

Luke pushed Mastermind's head deeper into the portal. The relentless vacuum pressure and icy coldness of deep space gave him a splitting headache. His eyes started icing over.

He screamed out loud.

"Your crystal, Mastermind."

"Never!"

Echo watched fearfully from a distance.

"…Master?" the bat-mutant muttered.

"Save me!" his master commanded.

But Echo was afraid. He knew what that portal was capable of. It sucked down a giant alien snake creature, and all its deadly little babies. He wanted to save his master – but his instinct for self-preservation was just a little bit stronger.

Mastermind yelled, "Damn you, save me!" He started slipping. The sand beneath him started sliding, draining down into the portal too. Luke stayed on top of him. There'd be no escape this time. But the strong winds and sliding sands drew them both closer and closer to a mutually dark fate.

Mastermind stared into Luke's visor. "Damn you – I'm taking you with me!"

Mastermind shifted his weight, kicking his legs up into the air – and using his new power of flight – flipped them *both* backwards, down together into the dark portal. He clutched tightly onto Luke's arms – the sucking force was too strong – they both went in.

"Master!" Echo cried out.

There was a flash of white light from the other side.

And suddenly, both Mastermind and Luke appeared a hundred feet away, on the desert surface, safe from the swirling and growing vortex. For now.

"I knew you wouldn't let me die," mocked Mastermind. "You would've killed me by now. You had your chance."

Luke sucker-punched Mastermind right in the face.

"Oww!!!" His nose started bleeding.

Mastermind started to scurry away. As soon as he was free, he launched into the air, quickly flying away.

Luke held up his hand. Aimed the shot. Fired.

The red cutting laser struck Mastermind hard in the back. Sliced right through him. A few inches to the right, and Luke might've shot him straight through the heart.

But this was only a flesh wound. But it was enough to ground Mastermind. The villain fell and crashed hard to the sandy surface, sliding forward several feet on his face.

Echo ran over to his master.

"I SAID KILL HIM!" Mastermind shouted at his mutant servant. "KILL HIM NOW!"

"But Master…" Echo pleaded.

Mastermind held his hand over the open hole in his chest. The laser cauterized his wound – no blood. Just a dark hole. Suffering in pain, and realizing he was quickly losing this battle, he looked up at his bat mutant, rage filling his eyes, and demanded, "Go back in time and prevent him from ever being born! I don't care. Just kill him now – or I'll kill *you* like I did your parents!"

Echo's first impulse was to move. Mastermind gave him a direct order. An explicit command.

The instinct, the impulse, the overwhelming desire to obey swelled up from within him. But… something else started to swell up from with Echo's mutant bat body too. Anger.

Mastermind murdered his parents.

And he saw it happen over and over again inside that sphere. It was how he got his power of time travel. And he still couldn't save them. Echo's fists clenched. He wanted to obey his master. He *had* to obey his master – but he *refused* to obey the man who killed his parents in cold blood!

Mastermind was the reason his life was a mess. Mastermind took away his family. Mastermind took away his dreams. Mastermind took away his very life. Turned him into a mutant. He'd never love again. Never live a normal life again.

Mastermind was evil… and Mastermind must die!

"N…no," Echo struggled to say.

"WHAT DID YOU SAY TO ME?" Mastermind growled.

Echo fought the greatest internal battle of his life. His body wanted to move. His body felt like it was on autopilot. If he just let go for one fraction of a second – he'd instantly travel back in time and murder his younger self. But no. He held on. Barely. Struggling. Losing his grip. But he summoned all his might, all his will, all his strength – and mustered up the courage to say the words, "I said no."

Luke smiled.

"Stupid bat!" Mastermind shouted. He grabbed Echo's arm, spun him around, and tossed his straight toward the swirling vortex. The gusts of winds rushing down that portal caught his wings, rushing him even faster to his doom!

The sand and dirt flew everywhere in his face. The wind carried him uncontrollably, faster, into the spiraling death. But Echo wasn't about to give up. Not like this. His master betrayed him – and he wasn't about to let him get away with that.

Seconds before Echo disappeared down the swirling vortex, he closed his eyes, concentrated – and everything around him shifted into a red blur of light.

He reappeared three seconds earlier – right behind Mastermind. Mastermind had just tossed Echo towards the portal. This Echo – from three seconds in the future – shoved Mastermind from behind, as damn hard as he could, launching the villain uncontrollably towards the portal. The same winds caught him too. The villain dropped to the ground, clawing his fingers into the sand, but the suction force continued to draw him in – closer and closer – and closer – "Help me!!!!" he shouted, until finally, Mastermind fell over and vanished inside the pitch-black portal.

At the same time, Echo watched his slightly-younger self get sucked towards the portal, and at the last second, disappear. He saw himself time travel, back to this current moment. And since he didn't change his own history – just his future – there was no new timeline duplicate.

Awesome.

Luke saw the whole thing.

"Oh my God," he said. "You just killed him."

Echo turned to look at Luke. But said nothing.

"I…"

Echo stopped him. "Mastermind's dead. I don't have to obey his orders anymore."

Luke let out a sigh of relief.

"Go live your life," the bat mutant said. "I can't."

Luke felt sorry for his timeline duplicate. "I…" There was one part of this plan he still hadn't figured out. What was to happen to all the mutants, after Mastermind was gone? They couldn't just live normal lives in society anymore. Where would they live at all? "Come with me," he said. "Stay with me."

"And live like a human?" Echo asked, doubtful.

"Yeah. Or, you know."

"No thanks." Echo looked at the vortex over the portal, still growing, still sucking in Earth's air, still getting worse. "Besides, you have something more important to take care of right now."

Damn. How was he supposed to close that portal now? Mastermind had the only other crystal. Both crystals were now lost somewhere on the other side of that portal. Lost somewhere in deep space, for all he knew. He needed a crystal, fast, to close this portal – while there was still enough air left on Earth to breathe!

What about on Eden? His other-other self – the one Kraken killed – did he still have a crystal too? Oh, it didn't matter. The Edenites would've ejected his body into space by now. That crystal was gone for sure.

No, there was only one option.

Luke had to go for it.

"I sure hope this suit is air-tight."

What was he saying? Of course it was. It was a *space* suit!

Luke ran towards the portal.

He jumped into the sandy tornado. Got sucked into the vortex – and vanished into the darkness on the other side.

Chapter 37

HERO'S DESTINY

Total darkness – except for the light and debris rushing in from the Earthside.

Luke's HUD immediately began scanning the area. He couldn't see much with his naked eyes. But his visor screen overlaid an image of what he would see, if he could.

He saw the interior of an alien space ship. Nothing like the designs or architecture he saw on Eden, or the pyramids for that matter. His HUD identified and displayed what were probably control panels, power relays, and life support systems. As his HUD analyzed the ship's structural data, it was clear this vessel had received some major damage. Several cracks. A major rupture up ahead. Probably where all the air was going.

Oh gross. He saw the remains of the multi-eyed alien snake wedged up in the corner, blocking a large part of the wall rupture. Its body was all mangled and twisted. Its teeth broken and chipped. Based on the teeth marks along the nearby wall, it apparently tried chewing its way out of the ship.

And there, inside its mouth, a dim pink glow.

Luke was weightless, floating in zero gravity. But all he had to do was think about getting closer, and built-in propulsion on his boots and backside slowly thrust him forward.

And so far, he could breathe. The suit automatically detected a lack of oxygen, and switched to an internal air reserve. According to the read-out on his HUD screen, he had about twelve hours of breathable air left in his suit. Plenty of time.

He slowly glided up to the dead alien snake's carcass. He nervously reached inside its mouth. Felt around. It was slimy and cold. This thing was dead, right?

He pushed open its mouth a little more. Reached in a little deeper. He saw it. That crystal. His beautiful crystal. Lodged in the back of its mouth, behind some teeth.

The snake's lifeless eyes blankly stared back at him.

Luke reached in deeper.

Almost got it…

He felt the crystal in his hand.

"Yes!"

He broke it free. Pulled it out.

Nothing looked so beautiful.

Even if it was covered in frozen alien saliva.

Luke turned around.

MASTERMIND – ice-covered, boiling skin, bloated, and lifeless – floated in front of him.

It nearly gave Luke a heart attack.

He gently pushed Mastermind's body aside.

It was going to be hard to X-out a portal this big with such a strong vacuum. The easiest and safest way to close it would be to open a new portal somewhere safe, like to Eden or something. All he needed to do was teleport back to Earth, stay away from the tornado, and quickly open a new portal.

Piece of cake.

Mastermind's left eye, partially covered in ice, slowly turned and looked at Luke.

A flash of light. Luke disappeared, teleporting out of the space ship. Mastermind disappeared too.

Back on Earth, Luke reappeared several hundred feet away from the portal. The tornado surrounding the hole had grown even larger, reaching even higher up into the sky. Hurricane force winds blew from all directions, rushing towards that portal.

Mastermind's cold, bloated body crashed down onto the hot sand beside him.

Gross. Why did his suit teleport a dead body with him?

No time to worry about that now. Crystal in hand, Luke knelt down, and quickly drew a small circle in the sand. The trail of pink light glowed as he traced the outline. Then in the middle, he marked the symbol for Eden.

The previous portal instantly closed. Luke looked over his shoulder. The winds quickly settled down and dispersed. The tornado consumed itself – and disappeared. The still-flying sand scattered out as the tornado died, raining down onto solid dry land.

Earth was saved.

Luke let out a sigh of relief. Then he moved the crystal over the small portal to Eden, crossing it out, closing it too.

He stood up. One problem solved. Now… where did Echo go?

He scanned around. There was no trace of him anywhere. Did he time travel somewhere? Where – or when – would he go? If he went back in time to fulfill Mastermind's orders – and prevent Luke from being born – would Luke still be here? Wouldn't that create a paradox, and prevent Echo from doing it in the first place?

Just then, something grabbed Luke's leg.

Or some*one* rather. Luke looked down. Mastermind was still alive. And quickly thawing. The madman clutched Luke's leg, pulling on it to help himself up.

"Mastermind!" Luke exclaimed.

Eyes still frosty, face half frozen, he began to chuckle.

"You… can't… kill me," he said. "I am… God!"

"You're not dead?"

He began laughing maniacally. "You can't kill me," he smirked. "I really am God!"

Mastermind immediately placed his hand over his heart, touching his chest. And in his next heartbeat, Mastermind began crying out in unspeakable agony. The pain. It was overwhelming. Unbearable. Impossible. He screamed louder. Oh – make it stop! Make the pain stop! He… couldn't… take it… anymore!!!

Luke stepped back.

Mastermind began transforming.

His skin turned red.

His arms and legs grew larger, vastly more muscular.

His eyes burned with a fiery rage.

His whole body grew larger… and larger…

He tore through his clothes.

His Rolex watch snapped off, falling broken to the sandy ground below.

He burst through his shoes. His hands turned into animalistic claws. He tore into and shred apart what little remaining clothes still hung on his ever-enlarging body.

Luke took another step back.

Larger. Larger.

Ten feet tall. Fifteen feet tall. Twenty feet tall. And still growing.

Horns ripped through his skin and spawned out of his head. The nails on his hands and feet turned nightmare black. A long tail struck out from his lower back. More and more muscles, bigger and bigger, throughout his entire massive red-skinned body.

The horns on his head grew bigger and bigger, curling like ram's horns. His feet became monstrous claws that dug into the Earth. His hands grew bigger and bigger, fingers cracking and bending in inhuman and unnatural ways. He still grew taller and taller. Bigger and bigger. It didn't stop.

Fifty feet tall.

One hundred feet tall.

Two hundred feet tall.

And still growing…

Luke took another step back, staring upwards at the rising monster. What did Mastermind do to himself?

Nearly two-hundred and fifty feet tall.

The beast roared – and it boomed and echoed like thunder across the desert. He beat on his massive chest. It shook the Earth.

And as his transformation slowed to a halt, Luke saw what this "god" had become – a towering monster demon.

And that demon looked down at the tiny speck known as Luke, the little armored space suit boy who dared to defy him. Mastermind lifted his enormous foot to squash this annoying pest once and for all.

"Oh shit!" said Luke. He didn't know what to do. The massive foot came down. The shadow covered over Luke and all around him. He did the only thing he could think to do – teleport – just as Mastermind's gargantuan foot slammed into the Earth, creating a giant crater and massive earthquake in the process.

Ray and Dawn were kissing.

Luke reappeared next to them, right where he left them at the shipping dock.

"There you are!" Ray exclaimed. "Where'd you go?"

"Oh, well, you know…"

"Where's Mastermind?" asked Dawn.

"Funny you should ask that," said Luke.

The three of them teleported back to the desert.

Mastermind was gone.

Ray looked around at the vast wide open desert. "You sure this was where you left him?"

"Positive," said Luke.

"He couldn't have gotten far," said Dawn.

"Something that big won't take long to show up on the news," said Ray. "Back to our place?"

"Done."

They disappeared in a flash.

"Luke!" exclaimed his uncle, back at the apartment. "Ray, Dawn… Glad to see you're all okay."

Dawn checked her newly replaced arm. "You have no idea."

"What's happening? Is it over?" asked his uncle.

"Not quite," said Luke.

"Anything on the news?" asked Ray.

"Our hacker friend stuck to his word," said Uncle Charlie. "He released the edited video. Anyone who sees it will want to kill Mastermind on sight."

"That may be easier said than done," said Luke.

"Most of the networks are showing the new version now," said Charlie. "But his old video is still running on some other channels too. The Internet, I imagine, is flooded with both."

"Great," said Luke. "So half the people will want to obey Mastermind, the other half will want to kill him."

"There was a major mutant outbreak in New York," said Charlie, "but it doesn't seem to be spreading any longer."

"Yeah… apparently Mastermind can transform people just by touching them now," said Ray.

Charlie nodded solemnly. "I saw him turn a pilot into a dragon… Anyway, aside from a few isolated cases around the world, most people seem to be staying human for now."

Just then Ray noticed something on the TV. Some major breaking news in Los Angeles. Going live to their on-location reporter. "Hey, turn it up. I think we found Mastermind."

Charlie quickly turned up the volume. "I'm Alex Alvarado reporting live for NBS News," said the news reporter. "A new mutant – bigger and more terrifying than all the others – has just been spotted near Griffith Park. No other mutants have been witnessed in the area since my last report. And, I'm happy to report, the rhinoceros mutant that was terrorizing downtown Los Angeles has been neutralized by a mysterious duo of, what this reporter is calling, the world's first real life super heroes."

"Wait, what?" remarked Ray.

"Kathy, would you show our viewers that footage again, please?" said the reporter.

Luke and Ray leaned in closer. Was the reporter actually talking about them? Were they caught on camera?

Kathy, the news anchor back at the studio, began narrating. The TV cut to a video of Rhino-Man smashing through walls and tearing up city streets with his stomping-earthquakes. "This is earlier footage from when the rhinoceros mutant started destroying downtown Los Angeles – but pay attention to the back left corner of your screen." There was a flash of white light. Luke and Ray suddenly appeared. "The identity of these two individuals is as yet unknown, but they seem to possess classified military technology being employed to neutralize and capture the powerful mutant."

"It's not classified," said Luke.

"I'm not military!" exclaimed Ray.

They watched themselves, on TV, defeat and escape with Rhino-Man. Pretty impressive stuff. They almost looked like they knew what they were doing!

"Similar sightings of these two individuals have been reported all over the world, wherever super-powered mutants were attacking civilians," continued the reporter.

"Hey!" said Dawn. "What about me?"

"How they manage to travel around the planet so fast is also unknown, but experts speculate they may be using some kind of 'teleporting' technology, previously believed to be only hypothetical. We'll provide updates on this mysterious duo as we learn more. Back to you, Alex."

"Trio!" exclaimed Dawn. "We're the dynamic *trio!*"

"Thanks Kathy," said Alex. The TV switched back to his live, on-the-scene location. The camera zoomed in to the famous Hollywood sign behind them in the distance. Mastermind – the giant that he was – began crawling up the mountain. Helicopters and military jets swarmed around him. He swatted one out of the sky, sending it crashing into the mountainside. He crawled even higher up the mountain – to him, it was just a big hill. He smashed and squashed through the famous Hollywood sign in the process.

More helicopters surrounded him. Trained snipers on board fired upon him. It hurt. A little. Like a tiny little insect bites. Nothing more. He roared. He reached out, clutched one of the helicopters, and threw it spiraling into another one. They both exploded upon impact.

"Both the military and local law enforcement are working together to take down this unbelievably larger-than-life mutant," continued the reporter. "But so far—"

Mastermind began speaking. His voice boomed for all to hear for miles and miles on both sides of the mountain – across the LA Basin and the San Fernando Valley. "Here me, my children! I am your God! I am Mastermind, ruler over all the Earth! You will worship me! You will obey me!"

Alex seemed confused. He returned to face the camera, microphone in hand. "The giant demon-like mutant claims to be Mastermind."

Mastermind slammed his fist down on another jet rushing by, knocking it hard and fast to the ground.

Boom. Another fiery explosion on impact.

Alex paused for a moment, listening to an update in his earpiece. "I've just been informed that riots have begun breaking out near hospitals and other cure distribution centers around the world. People are claiming that the vaccine is, in fact, the very source of Mastermind's plague. Previously unexposed people soon began mutating after receiving the vaccine. And independent lab tests are now showing the chemical to be extremely mutagenic. Officials are now warning citizens *not* to receive their cure until after further tests can be verified."

"Well that's good news," said Charlie.

"Officials are urging citizens around the world to stay in their homes, let local law enforcement contain any existing mutants, and to please keep the roadways clear and telephone lines free for emergency and official use. All mutants will be detained humanely until a real cure can be found. Local law enforcement and military divisions are working in cooperation around the world to keep the public safe and regain control of our cities. But if you ask me" – he looked at the giant demon behind him – "we sure could use a helping hand from those mysterious heroes here in Los Angeles again right about now."

Luke turned to Dawn. "You think you can shape-shift as big as him?"

"Probably. Maybe. I dunno," she said.

"Do your best." Luke turned to Ray. "What about lifting him? You think you can levitate him and hold him in one spot?"

Ray shrugged. "I'll try."

"What are you going to do?" asked Uncle Charlie.

Luke said, "Something I wish I didn't have to do."

Chapter 38
FINAL ACT

A flash of white light – and the three heroes arrived in Hollywood, not far from where Mastermind continued to keep the police and military quite busy.

The cops were also still busy evacuating people out of the area. Tanks rolled up and began firing upon the giant beast. Jets fired missiles. And Mastermind laughed.

"Whatever you do, don't let him touch you," said Luke.

"Or look at you," said Dawn.

"Or talk to you," said Ray. "I really wish we had a better plan."

"I need you guys to keep him busy. Our mission now is to save as many lives as possible," said Luke.

"You sure this is the only way?" asked Dawn.

"If I can't time travel back far enough – then yeah, I'm afraid this is our only option."

"Good luck, man," said Ray.

Mastermind stepped on a tank, crushing the metal under his massive weight.

"Go, hurry!" said Ray.

He and Dawn charged towards Mastermind.

Luke closed his eyes. He concentrated hard.

Backwards. As far back in time as he could go. He knew this wouldn't work. But he had to try.

24 hours. 48 hours. One week. One month. One year…

Could he go back in time far enough to stop Mastermind from killing his parents? From getting his power of mind control? From ever overhearing Uncle Charlie talking about the crystal in the first place?

Come on… dammit!

Everything shifted into a brilliant red blur.

Luke jumped back in time – as far as his power would let him.

The City of Los Angeles transformed around him. The sun moved backwards across the sky. People returned to their cars, their homes, their jobs. Luke reappeared. Found himself standing in the middle of the city streets. He almost got hit by a car. Luke quickly jumped out of the way, onto the sidewalk.

How far back did he go?

Newspaper. He needed a newspaper.

Suddenly he felt an earthquake. Someone screamed. Then more screams. He looked. People pointed at a skyscraper in downtown Los Angeles. The building started to collapse.

Uh oh.

Another small earthquake. Then another building shook. All downtown.

Shit. Rhino-Man was there. He barely went back in time at all! Just a few hours. Maybe. If that!

He had a choice. He could teleport to downtown and help stop Rhino-Man, but he knew his other self and Ray would be there soon enough anyway and take out Rhino-Man by themselves. And helping them would alter his own timeline, and likely create another duplicate – who would only somehow die anyway, and Luke just didn't want to risk that.

And that worried him. The longer he stayed in the past, the greater the chance he'd knowingly or unknowingly change his own history. And since he now knew *another* copy of him existed – the mutant Echo – he worried that at any moment, either one of them could die. That whole anti-duplicate timeline preserving law of the universe thing. Luke didn't think it really mattered if the last survivor was a mutant or not. He could die just as easily as Echo.

And right now, in the past, there were now *three* of him – himself, his other self fighting alongside Ray, and the mutant Echo. He didn't want to tempt fate too long. He couldn't change much at this point anyway. He couldn't go back far enough. So he closed his eyes, concentrated, and used what little power he had left to jump forward. Light around him shifted into a blue hue. Time fast-forwarded. And suddenly Luke was back in the present, the instant after he left.

Ray and Dawn charged towards Mastermind. Ray levitated himself up off the ground, sending himself flying higher. Dawn shape-shifted into some kind of mythological bird – beautiful multi-colored feathers, massive wings, and talons any mortal would fear.

"It didn't work," said Luke. "Guys? Oh."

He sighed.

"Good luck, guys. Don't die."

He said it for himself, too.

Hmm. Maybe there was another option. Maybe he didn't need to go that far back in time. He wanted to save all those people – prevent all those deaths and random mutations around the world. But that wasn't an option any more. But maybe… maybe he could stop things from getting any worse.

If he went back to the desert, several minutes ago, he could stop himself from accidentally teleporting Mastermind's frozen body out of that abandoned starship. He could leave Mastermind trapped on the other side, a million miles away in space, where he couldn't harm anyone!

No giant demon.

No additional deaths or hideous transformations.

It involved some risk. He'd be directly altering his own timeline again. Would he create another duplicate him? Sheesh, time travel was a mess. Whatever. It was worth the risk. Countless more lives were still at stake.

Okay. It was a plan. Just a few minutes back in time. That was all he needed. And then he'd teleport back to the Mojave Desert. He'd warn his younger self, or immediately toss Mastermind back into the portal, or something. He closed his eyes. Concentrated.

And…

Red shift of light.

"It didn't work," Luke saw himself say. "Guys? Oh."

Dammit! Only a few seconds? That was it? His power took way too long to recharge!

Before the other Luke saw him, this Luke immediately time-traveled a few seconds ahead – back to his own time, the instant he left. He sighed.

"Well, that didn't work either."

Fuck.

That left only one thing…

Luke held his crystal in his metal-gloved hand. He took a slow breath. He really didn't want to do this.

But he was out of options.

He knelt down and started tracing a circle on the sidewalk. He drew the symbol for Eden.

And the portal opened.

He looked back at the giant Mastermind demon in the distance – and jumped in.

"Hi, welcome to Eden! I'm Tristina—"

"No time," said Luke. "I need to get to your temple."

"Of course," she said. "Would you like me to teleport you there now?"

"Please."

And he was gone.

He greeted the guards at the door. "Hiya, fellas." If only they knew.

Luke vaguely remembered how to get to the innermost chamber now. The Temple of the Gods. The Altar of Destiny.

This was where his parents got their powers. Where Uncle Charlie got his super vision. Where Mastermind got his ability for mind control.

Hopefully, this was also where Mastermind got his latest and greatest new super powers too. One explosion should do the trick. Completely disable Mastermind. Make him normal. Make him mortal again. The police should have no problem handling a regular human. They weren't prepared for someone with powers. No one was.

Of course, even if Mastermind's powers were completely cut off – would everyone who got mutated by his touch return back to normal? Or would they be stuck in their new form forever? Either way, Luke had to do this. Had to stop Mastermind from mutating any more power. Had to prevent Mastermind from controlling anyone else – ever again.

It, unfortunately, came at a very high price. His uncle would lose his powers too. But it didn't stop there. There were the millions of other people throughout the galaxy who had acquired powers through this pyramid too. Luke really didn't want to think of the fallout after he completed what he came here to do.

He arrived at the innermost chamber.

He walked in. The alien writing along the floor illuminated. The spotlight from above centered over the mysterious pedestal. A floating sphere emerged.

He stood close to the pedestal. He took a deep breath. "Okay. You do can do this." He glanced back over his shoulder, at the entrance to the chamber. No one was around. No one would see him. He raised his arm – pointed his hand at the pedestal – and fired.

Meanwhile, back on Earth, Dawn and Ray had their hands full.

Dawn clawed at Mastermind's eyes. He grabbed her and started squeezing her to death. She morphed into liquid form, leaking through his fingers. Then, while falling like a human-sized raindrop to the pavement below, she transformed again – into an even larger dragon than before. And thanks to their encounter in New York, she knew how to breathe fire now.

Ray assisted the police in escorting people to safety. When Mastermind almost stepped on a fleeing family, Ray quickly blasted them out of the way. The giant demon's foot slammed onto empty ground. Then when Mastermind kicked a police car into the air, spinning it out of control towards defenseless civilians, Ray caught the spinning car in mid-air with his powers, regained control, and gently placed it back down on the ground.

Luke's cutting laser wasn't even making a scratch.

"What the hell is this thing made of?"

He needed to increase the yield.

200%.

The cutting laser fired brighter and hotter.

Still nothing.

300%.

The beam actually cut off a tiny chip.

400%.

Starting to bore through.

500%!

The pedestal started to crack.

Dammit – 1000%!

"Warning," flashed across his HUD. "Power reserves rapidly draining."

"Do it!" Luke exclaimed.

The pedestal cracked and split all over. It glowed red from inside. Luke held the laser focused on it, penetrating deeper and deeper. Blasting it harder and harder. It cracked a little more. And more. Chunks began breaking off…

"Danger! Limit exceeded!" flashed across his HUD.

"Almost there. Just a few more seconds…"

The cutting laser suddenly powered off. It was dead. Luke tried firing again. Nothing.

"What gives?" he demanded.

His heads-up display read: "Laser overheated."

"Dammit!" he exclaimed, punching his metal-gloved fist into the badly damaged pedestal.

It was just enough. The finishing blow.

The cracks within the pedestal glowed brighter and brighter. The floating sphere disappeared. Large chunks and pieces of the pillar broke off, falling apart faster and faster. And behind those pieces, inside the core of the pedestal, Luke saw its glowing power source.

His HUD read: "EXTREME DANGER! EXPLOSIVE CHAIN REACTION DETECTED."

Luke saw the glowing core get blindingly bright.

"MASSIVE EXPLOSION IMMINENT!"

Luke instantly teleported out of there, disappearing with a flash of light – only to reappear back in the garden near the portal entrance. He looked in the distance, past the beautiful city, and suddenly saw the most brilliant flash of light. It was so bright, it instantly turned everything in front of him into a black silhouette and completely white-washed everything else out. It made even the sun seem insignificantly dim for that instant. And then daylight returned to normal – revealing a radioactive mushroom cloud in the distance larger and more massive than anything ever dreamed of on Earth.

Warning sirens blared throughout the nearby city.

Luke stepped into his still-open portal, but stopped, and looked back at the giant looming radioactive cloud. "I'm sorry," he whispered. And then he walked completely through, closing the portal behind him.

Back in Los Angeles, he looked up to see Mastermind in the distance, with Ray and Dawn still fighting him – along with more uniformed officers and military personnel than he could count. But the death toll continued to rise. Mastermind, the giant that he was, smashed his fist through nearby buildings, instantly killing anyone still in them.

Then he reached down onto the ground, scooping up a handful of terrified, fleeing people – men, women, children, officers, soldiers – who were too slow to escape.

As he clutched them in his hands, they began screaming and transforming, turning all into demons – small, human-sized ones – at his mere touch.

Driven mad by their transformation – or perhaps as part of his power – they became evil, rampaging throughout the streets, killing innocent civilians, attacking other police officers, violently digging their claws into soldiers and tearing them limb from limb. Bullets fired. But their wounds instantly healed. These newly-created demons were unstoppable.

Dawn and Ray had their hands full.

Ray tried levitating as many as he could at once, keeping them from harming anyone else. But Mastermind reached into a building, smashing his fist through the walls, transforming more people inside into even more demon spawn. The new monsters jumped down into the streets and joined the fray.

Some demons centered around two small orphaned children. Dawn jumped into the middle, grabbed the two kids, threw them onto her back as she transformed into a unicorn, and then charged forward, rushing them to safety as she poked and tossed demons aside with her horn along the way. The kids rode to safety – but for how long?

Dawn shape-shifted back into human form. Looked around. More and more demons everywhere. Killing fleeing civilians and fighting officers left and right. There were just too many of them.

"Help!" shouted Ray, blasting demon after demon as more and more surrounded him. Dawn ran after him.

Luke saw it all. Dammit. Mastermind was still turning people. He probably only lost his mind control, which no longer seemed all that important. He was still a giant, still transforming people, still very much taking over the world.

A world that, if Luke didn't do something soon, would be populated with nothing but mutants, monsters, and demons. And the countless bodies of all the slain innocent victims. A world recreated in Mastermind's image.

Dammit! He destroyed that pyramid on Eden for nothing! Only one option remained. He knew the mutants all got their powers from the pyramid on Sekhmet. It looked like Mastermind got his new powers from the same one.

Only one small problem. Destroying that pyramid would make Luke and Ray lose their powers too.

But then he watched Mastermind scoop up more people, turn them into demons and monsters: raging hellhounds, multi-headed ogres, hideous trolls, scaly beasts, and more male and female demons – all sorts of terrors from the darkest of nightmares.

He saw the military unleash all their firepower and fury upon Mastermind, and the growing numbers of hellspawn, but their demonic bodies instantly healed and repaired themselves. More people died. Mastermind smashed through more buildings, and all who touched his red skin rapidly began transforming. There was no way to stop this. No way to take Mastermind down.

Not while he still had powers.

Luke took a heavy breath. He knew what he had to do. He wasn't sure how they could defeat Mastermind or save the world without any powers – but if he didn't act now, there'd be no world left to save.

He took his crystal and began drawing a new portal.

The massive pyramid on Sekhmet waited in the distance. Blazing heat, scorching winds, burning sands. The desert planet's two suns sizzled from above.

Luke's suit automatically kicked in some kind of internal air conditioning system. That was cool. Literally. He teleported up to the pyramid entrance.

He pushed the blue button at the door control panel.

He really wished he didn't have to do this.

All his life, he wanted to be a time traveler. And now he finally had it. He finally had his dream. But… at what cost? As limited as his power was, it was still his dream. It gave him the chance to live the life he always wanted.

Maybe, if he waited long enough, his power would recharge enough to let him go back and save his parents. Maybe, if he waited long enough, he could go back and prevent Mastermind from ever rising to power.

No mutants. Ever. No mind control. No deaths. Life would be… normal.

He'd still have a family.

But could he take that risk? Even if he waited a year for his power to recharge, would it still be enough? What if he could never go back that far? History would remain unchanged. And worse, Luke would have allowed the present horrors to continue.

Mastermind might eventually be taken down. Somehow. But after how many lives were killed or transformed? After how many mutants? After how many monsters? After how many demons? And what if Mastermind succeeded? What if Ray and Dawn died – permanently – this time?

All because Luke waited too long to do what he *knew* would end Mastermind's reign *right now*. All because Luke wanted to hold onto some childhood dream, some fantasy, of being a time-traveling super hero.

It wasn't worth it.

They would have to figure out a way to defeat Mastermind without any powers. They would have to be normal and powerless – so Mastermind would be normal and powerless.

He entered the innermost chamber.

He didn't like this. But he had to do it.

In one swift move, in one final act, he'd permanently destroy all of Mastermind's powers.

He stepped up to the pedestal.

Wait.

He had a thought.

Maybe he didn't have to do this.

Well, not exactly.

He didn't have to destroy the whole pyramid. He didn't have to blow up the Altar of Destiny.

He just needed to cut off its power source.

Simeon said the temples drew their power from deep within the planet. It was the very reason why he couldn't travel that far back in time. The pyramid only had so much energy available. What if the pyramid, temporarily, lost all its energy? That would cut off everyone's powers – but once the energy was recharged, they'd get their powers back. Good as new. But by then, they'll have defeated Mastermind.

He hoped.

Okay. So if he just wanted to disable the pyramid, just temporarily drain and cut off its power source – where and how would he do that?

Destroying the Altar would blow the whole thing up. Couldn't do that. Hmm. Luke remembered how they got inside this pyramid the first time. He and his uncle were underground. In that snake den. They came up to a glowing mechanical cylinder of some kind. With a recall button that teleported them inside.

Could that cylinder be how the pyramid drew its energy?

It was worth the chance.

Luke immediately ran out of the chamber, down the long corridor, and eventually back outside under the blazing suns. Okay. Where was that damn pit again? Where did he slip and fall before?

He ran up the sand dunes. Tried to retrace his steps. Ah-hah! Found it! Over there. He ran down the slippery sand dune, started sliding uncontrollably, and then jumped into the deep, dark pit. Down he went. He fell. And fell.

And *splash!* He sank deep into the underground aquifer. Deeper and deeper. Finally his metal boots hit rock bottom. Solid ground. Deep underwater. His suit's heads-up display immediately displayed a scan of the area. Nothing but wide open vast space. A small ocean underground. Apparently his suit wasn't very buoyant. Like at all. And it was a long ways back up to the surface.

But he could still breathe. His heads-up display kept track of how much breathable air he still have left in reserves. Hmm. Okay. Now what?

Scanning through the pitch black waters, his view screen outlined all the underwater boulders and sloping terrain. The ground seemed to drift up towards a cliff in the distance. That was *probably* the way he and his uncle went the first time.

He teleported. A flash of white light in the midst of the perfect darkness. He landed on the ledge, near the surface of the water. He could see the tunnel ahead. It had to be the one they passed through before. He traveled onward.

It was completely dark, except for the pink glow given off by his crystal still attached to his arm. Fortunately, the heads-up display outlined everything for him, allowing him to walk "blindly" through the dark. Still, having a pair of headlights or something would've been better.

Just then, a single beam of light projected off the top of his helmet. Oh. That was nice. Why didn't that come on before? At least now he could see where he was going with his naked eyes. He traveled up the tunnel – and entered into the den where they almost became that alien snake's lunch.

Deeper in. Up the last tunnel. Finally, he came into the small square cavern, where the large cylinder still hummed with its red lights still glowing. It gave off a lot of heat too. This definitely had to have something to do with the pyramid's energy source. What else would it be?

And look at that – a control panel! Luke looked at it carefully. He found the recall button they used earlier. But what about these other buttons? Could it be as easy as simply hitting an "off" switch?

The control panel had a small interactive video screen. Luke pulled off his metal glove and placed his palm flat against it. The screen lit up.

"Input command," it read.

Okay. This was promising. "How do I temporarily shut off all powers?" Luke asked aloud.

No reaction.

"Um, disable experiment. How do I temporarily disable the active experiment?"

"Authorization required," the screen read.

Luke sighed. This was taking too long. Whoever these aliens were, and whatever "experiment" they were up to on Sekhmet, sooner or later they'd notice their pyramid was down. Let them fix the damn thing.

Luke put his glove back on and aimed at the control panel. "I've got your authorization right here." And he fired.

Mastermind suddenly felt weak.

Dawn was exhausted. Ray too. They attacked Mastermind when and as they could, but spend most of their time saving the innocents and fighting back all the demons and monsters. The military and police continued firing upon this giant, seemingly in futility, until one jet's missile – soaring through the sky – struck Mastermind in the back with a powerful explosion.

His flesh burned. He roared out in pain.

The wound did *not* heal.

Everyone noticed.

Suddenly, all the tanks, jets, and countless other military vehicles spontaneously unleashed all their remaining firepower at once. Mastermind was bombarded. More and more wounds covered his massive body. He fell backwards, creating an earthquake upon landing.

Ray and Dawn looked over. This was their chance. Dawn shape-shifted some wings and started flying. Ray pushed against the Earth's gravity to begin moving – but nothing happened. Ray tried again, concentrating harder. Nothing.

Why wasn't he flying?

He quickly looked around. He spotted a small piece of debris that used to be part of a truck or building or something. Too mangled to tell. He held his hand at it, channeling all his strength to levitate it off the ground.

Nothing happened.

"Dawn!" he shouted after her.

She turned to look back.

"My power's gone!"

That might explain why Mastermind was suddenly vulnerable. More bullets, rockets, missiles, and more bombarded him. He roared out in pain through all the fire and smoke.

Dawn still had her power. She didn't get it from the sphere. She transformed into the one thing demons fear the most – an even bigger and stronger archangel. Her blue body suit morphed and expanded with her. She stayed human, grew giant angel wings, and rose to fifty... eighty... one hundred... two hundred... finally three hundred feet tall!

About a dozen news reporters caught it all on camera.

She tried carefully not to step on anyone or anything. Of course half the city was already in ruins anyway. The military ceased firing. Mastermind's giant demon body laid bruised, battered, and broken across the mountainside.

Dawn – the mighty and powerful archangel – stood over him. She reached down, grabbed Mastermind, and kneed him hard in the balls. If only she had a giant sword right about now...

Luke stepped through a portal, back into Los Angeles. Did it work? Was he successful?

His view screen identified two giants – Dawn and Mastermind. The villain had fallen. But he wasn't dead yet. Dawn held him down. He struggled against her. He fought hard. But he was weak from his many bad injuries. His body wasn't healing any more. The relentless assault from the police and military had nearly destroyed him. And now Dawn was personally going to finish the job.

Chapter 39

JUSTICE AT LAST

Luke looked back through his portal at the pyramid in the desert. No explosion. No mushroom cloud. But apparently it worked. Mastermind lost his powers.

Of course, so did they. Well, Dawn still had her powers. Lucky girl. But would it be enough? Mastermind may be powerless now, but he still was a giant demon with rapid healing and incredible strength. If they were going to defeat him, they were going to need some help.

And he had an idea who might suddenly be willing to do just that.

He quickly crossed out the portal to Sekhmet – and started drawing a new one. The symbol in the middle: two wavy lines. The portal opened to the tropical beach planet of Aquaria.

Rhino-Man, Venom, Arachnus, Kraken, and Slimer were still there, not far from the portal's entrance. They all turned to look at Luke through the newly opened portal.

"Hey guys. Guess who's no longer your master…"

Mastermind struggled to get up. But Dawn's strength far outmatched his own. Both news helicopters and military choppers swarmed overhead. And by now, they knew Dawn was one of the good guys. Thanks to her and her super-powered friends, many lives were saved today. They were indeed heroes. And now she had Mastermind right where she wanted him.

"Get off me, you stupid girl!"

Dawn shook her head, holding him down tight.

"I said get off me!" Mastermind yelled, looking directly into her eyes.

Nothing. Not a single damn impulse. Dawn smiled. "What'd you say?"

"I SAID LET ME GO!"

Total eye contact. And she heard every word.

Dawn giggled. "I don't think so."

Ahh, that felt good.

Suddenly, Mastermind started shrinking. "Hey, what are you doing to me?" he asked. His red skin started to look a little pale. His body got smaller and smaller. His demonic claws started shifting back to human form. His horns withered away. He was transforming back to normal! "Stop that!" he demanded. "Stop changing me!"

But it wasn't her. This was happening on its own. She watched his face and body shrink smaller and smaller, morphing uncontrollably back to his pathetic and powerless human form. No more horns. His tail shriveled up. His muscles deteriorated.

He kept shrinking. Against his will. Dawn picked him up, holding him in her giant hand. He got smaller and smaller. "Stop this, now!" he pleaded.

Almost back to normal human size. He yelled at her. "Why can't I control you?!?"

She smiled.

"Because you're powerless, Mastermind," she said to the little man trapped in her grasp. "It's over. We beat you."

He tried to push himself free from her giant fingers. No use. He tried touching his chest. Nothing happened. He looked up at her. How could they have beaten him? How did they— Suddenly, he had a realization. "You… no, impossible. Impossible!" he screamed, trying to break free. "You couldn't have destroyed the temples!"

"Guess we did," she said.

"But… my master plan! I… I was to be your god!"

She laughed, looking at the little powerless man in her hand. "Plan's changed, Mastermind. The world won't be yours anymore." She looked down, seeing several police officers and armed soldiers at her feet. She squeezed him a little tighter, just so he knew she could crush him any time she wanted.

"Wh-what are you going to do to me?"

She pulled him close to her face. "I should give you a taste of your own medicine. Force you to become a hideous mutant like you did to so many others…"

Fear filled his eyes.

"But I won't," she said. She crouched down and lowered him to the ground. She released him – into police custody.

They immediately tackled him, slamming his face to the broken pavement. They cuffed him, gagged him, and blind-folded him. They weren't taking *any* chances. Countless other armed officers and soldiers surrounded him, weapons all trained on him, ready to fire the instant he flinched the wrong way.

Mastermind was naked, powerless, and bound. They shoved him into the back of a police car – one of the few nearby vehicles not smashed or destroyed. They slammed the door on his face.

Dawn shape-shifted back down to normal size. But she kept the wings on just for good measure.

"Thank you, Angel Girl," said one of the officers. "The world will not forget what you and your friend did today."

Angel Girl? "Actually, my name's—"

Ray approached. "People are changing back," he said. "The ones he touched. They're returning to normal."

He and Dawn made eye contact. Nothing was said between them, but they both knew he had lost his powers. But it was worth it. Mastermind was finally defeated.

Luke teleported to join them. He saw the police car carry Mastermind off, surrounded by a small caravan of other cop cars and military escorts.

"Everyone okay?" Luke asked.

"We did it!" exclaimed Dawn.

Ray nodded and smiled. "It's over."

Luke looked around. Los Angeles was devastated. But the day was saved. Several of Mastermind's latest mutants still ran amok, but slowly, one by one, they started changing back into human form. Every last soul, every last man, woman, and child who had been transformed by Mastermind's touch – began to find their humanity once again.

"Thank God," said Luke.

"What do you think will happen to him?" Dawn asked.

"I dunno," said Luke.

People began coming out of hiding. Children. Their parents. Business executives. Unemployed actors. Everybody. People hiding behind cars. People hiding behind building rubble. People who had been transformed by Mastermind, but now had miraculously returned to normal.

A crowd gathered around Luke, Ray, and Dawn. They all knew who took Mastermind down. The ones who saved them all from the horrible fate.

News reporters began pushing their way to the front of the crowds. "Alex Alvarado, NBS News," said one of them, shoving his microphone in Dawn's face. "Tell me, are you the world's new protectors? Are you, in fact, the world's first super heroes?"

"I, well…" said Dawn.

"No comment," said Ray.

Another news reporter burst in. "How did you defeat Mastermind? How were you immune to his powers?"

A different one asked, "Where did you get your powers?"

"Please," said Ray, "we're just here to help. We couldn't have done it without all the uniformed—"

"Are you military? What government organization do you work under?"

"What? No!" exclaimed Ray.

"Can we expect to see your battle suit on marines on battlefields overseas?" asked another reporter.

"Huh?" asked Luke.

"Look," said Ray, "we're just regular people, like you, who… well… had super powers."

"So you *are* super heroes!" Alex Alvarado exclaimed. "What are your names?"

He shoved the microphone in front of Luke first. "Um," he said, looking around. He still hadn't thought of one. He searched the crowd. There was a little boy, maybe five years old, wearing a t-shirt with Captain America's shield on it. "Captain…" said Luke.

Captain what? Captain Space Explorer Man? Lame! Captain Powers? No way. Captain… He could time travel. At least, he used to. Maybe, hopefully, he would be able to again. Someday, in the future. "Future," he finished. That'll have to work. "Captain Future," he repeated.

Actually, on second thought, it sounded kinda dumb. But the name already took. Reporters started calling him by that name. The little five-year-old boy jumped up and down with excitement.

"And you?" asked Alex, moving the microphone in front of Ray's face.

"Um," he said. He really had no idea. Comic books and super heroes were Luke's thing. "Actually, we're not looking for any public fame or recognition—"

"Speak for yourself," said Dawn. "I'm Dawn Stein, I'm an actress, and I have the power to shape-shift." The reporters went crazy with questions. Dawn looked directly into one of the cameras. "So casting directors, I can play *any* part."

Luke was loving this attention too.

"This suit is one of a kind," said Luke. Technically, not really. But on Earth, it was an original. "With it, I can teleport, raise shields, see in the dark, blast things with my laser…"

Ray shook his head.

Dawn smiled brightly. She impressed some of the little kids by shape-shifting into some fun, cute humanoid animal forms. First, she made herself look like a bunny girl, then a kitten girl, and a puppy person with long flappy ears.

"Are you guys a team?" Alex asked Ray. "Do you have a team name? Will you always be there to protect Earth from super villains like Mastermind in the future?"

Ray leaned over to Luke. "Get us out of here, buddy."

Luke laughed. "Right. No problem."

In a flash, they disappeared.

The crowd went silent – and then started clapping and cheering. The day was saved. Mastermind had been defeated. People celebrated. They danced. They cheered. They grabbed the cute person standing next to them and kissed them passionately.

"You heard it here first folks," said Alex Alvarado back into his camera. "Mastermind has been defeated. Mutants everywhere are returning to normal. The day, my friends, has been saved. All thanks to our very own super heroes. Whoever you are, wherever you may be – thank you, dear heroes, for saving the world today."

But the day wasn't quite over.

Mastermind sat in the back of a police car, blind-folded, gagged, and handcuffed. They were undoubtedly taking him to some maximum security prison. Probably post around-the-clock armed guards. But it wouldn't matter. Mastermind was destined to be their god. One day his mutants would return to free him. Or his powers would manifest again and he'd break himself free. Turn every guard and fellow prisoner in that jail cell into powerful mutants slaves again.

He grinned. This was perfect. They were taking him to the very place where he'd find the most dangerous of all criminals. They'd become his ultimate mutants.

Suddenly – *bam!* – something hard crashed into the side of the police car. The vehicle spun over, crashing upside down, sliding several feet away.

"Holy shit!" one of the officers exclaimed, staring at several black spider-like mutant legs crawled up on top of the car.

The two officers escaped out from under the car, grabbed their guns, and found defensive positions behind large rubble and smashed cars from the earlier conflicts. Arachnus climbed on top of their upside-down police car. Slimer covered the windshields of other cars in their caravan, forcing some to drive off the road and crash. Rhino-Man charged into and flipped over the other vehicles.

"Damn! We need backup!" the other officer yelled into his radio. He gave their location. "I count *five* mutants attacking us."

The first officer fired at them.

Venom turned and hissed at them. "Thisss isn't about you," she said. "Leave usss alone."

"Um, dispatch – please hurry."

Kraken tore off the door of the car holding Mastermind.

Venom slithered up to him, reached inside, and with a flick of her sharp nails, sliced loose his blind-fold and mouth gag.

She stepped back.

Mastermind was still upside down. But when he saw his mutant, he smiled. "Venom! You've come to sav—"

Arachnus's arms reached in from above, pulling Mastermind out and on top of the car.

"Arach—" he said.

Arachnus quickly spun a web around Mastermind, tangling him up, trapping and ensnaring him before the villain even fully grasped what was going on.

The other officers watched. What were they doing?

Arachnus snarled at Mastermind. "You stole my life. You turned me… you turned me into this!"

Rhino-Man finished rolling over the last car. He snorted, stomping his foot. "You turned us all into killers," he shouted from across the street. "I never killed nobody until you took control of me!" He growled loudly. The people in the overturned cars were alive. But wisely, staying out of his way.

Venom jumped up on top of the car. Her scaly green skin and yellow piercing eyes came face to face with him. She hissed with her long forked tongue. "You think I want to be a ssssnake?" She exposed her fangs.

"You think we should do something?" asked one officer to the other.

The other just shook his head. "This is justice."

Slimer climbed up on top of the overturned car too. Venom stepped aside to let the gooey girl get close. She stood face to face with her creator. He couldn't move. He couldn't budge. Arachnus's web made sure of that. Venom hissed, fangs exposed. "Any final words, 'boss'?" the slime girl asked.

He looked at her fiercely. "Let me go and I won't punish you for your insol—"

Kraken's squid-like tentacles stretched up from behind him, wrapped around his head – and twisted, hard and fast.

They all heard a crack.

Venom could hold back no longer. She lunged forward and sank her fangs into his chest, filling his heart with her deadly black poison. Arachnus tossed the web-ensnared villain to the ground.

Mastermind, still barely alive, wailed silently in agonizing pain. Rhino-Man snorted furiously and stomped his foot – into Mastermind's chest. "I hate what you've made me – what you've made us all into!"

Mastermind couldn't breathe. He coughed up blood. His eyes filled with intense, sharp, unspeakable pain. The black venom spread throughout his body. Everything quickly grew dark.

Slimer leaned down. Her face was the last thing he saw.

"*You* are worthless scum. I hate you. We all hate you. You don't deserve to live."

That was the last thing he saw or heard. The pain overtook him. His frail body could survive no more.

"But I…" he struggled to say. "I'm better than…"

And Mastermind's last and final breath escaped him.

The villain laid dead in the street.

Arachnus jumped down off the police car. He still wasn't satisfied. He ripped open the web around his prisoner, grabbed Mastermind's limbs with his multiple spider-like arms – and in one swift move, tore Mastermind apart limb from limb.

"Damn…" said one of the police officers.

Venom looked back and hissed at them.

The officers held the guns at the ready. "Don't move any closer!" one of them ordered.

Rhino-Man turned to the cops. He snorted. "Leave us be," he said. "We have no issue with you… yet."

Considering all the toppled buildings, damaged roads, and major losses they suffered today, it was going to take backup a while to get to them. Maybe it was best to leave these mutants alone for now. They weren't attacking civilians. They weren't really targeting the officers either. They just wanted – and perhaps deserved – a little personal time with the man responsible for their fate.

Should Mastermind have gone through "due process" and receive a fair trial? Of course. But sometimes, it was better to let nature take its course.

The mutants looked down on their mutilated former master. He blinked no more. He breathed no more. He moved no more.

Mastermind was no more.

Rhino-Man snorted.

"So now what?" gurgled Kraken.

"Now," said Venom, "we go our separate waysss."

Police sirens came from up ahead. The sound of an approaching helicopter. The mutants scattered.

Chapter 40
CONCLUSION

"Oh God," said Ray, collapsing on his living room couch. "I'm *exhausted!*"

"Me too!" exclaimed Dawn, landing next to him.

"Me three," said Luke, removing his space suit.

Charlie helped him. "You guys did good today."

"Good?" remarked Ray. "We did freaking awesome!"

Dawn smiled.

"I'm really proud of you Luke," he said, looking at his nephew. He looked at Ray and Dawn too. "All of you."

"I wonder if we're still on the news," said Dawn. "Where's the remote?"

Luke stepped out of the last of his suit. His uncle embraced him with a big hug. He whispered to him, "Your parents would be really proud."

Luke smiled. It was bittersweet.

The news seemed to be repeating the facts they already knew. Mastermind's mutants were returning to normal in New York and Los Angeles. Facilities around the planet had stopped producing or distributing the mutation vaccine. And Mastermind, the false god, had been overpowered by three courageous heroes – "Woohoo! That's us!" shouted Dawn – and was now in police custody, where he awaited an international trial for his countless crimes against humanity.

Of course, Mastermind was dead. But the public didn't know that yet.

Dawn flipped through the channels. She found one showing footage of their awesome heroics earlier. And their impromptu interview after defeating Mastermind. "Um. Captain… Future," a recording of Luke said on the TV.

"Nice name," Dawn said.

"Yeah, thanks," said Luke.

"You really dig this super hero thing, huh?" asked Ray.

Luke nodded. "Too bad we didn't get to keep our powers."

"What?" asked the old man.

"Hey, speak for yourself! I still have my powers!" Dawn cheerfully declared.

"Hey, you're right," said Uncle Charlie. "I can't access my super vision anymore either." He turned to Luke. "You destroyed both pyramids?"

Luke nodded. "I'm sorry. It had to be done. It was the only way we could stop him. But don't worry, I didn't destroy the second one, on the desert planet."

"Oh?"

"Just the thingy that draws power up from inside the planet. With any luck," said Luke, "the aliens will return to their pyramid and fix it. And one morning, hopefully soon, we'll have our powers back."

"He hopes," Ray chuckled playfully. "Personally, having powers was fun, but I wouldn't mind a little peace and quiet and just relax at home for a while too. Portals, aliens, mutants, time travel... Not what I was expecting when I got up in the morning."

"I know, some date, huh?" said Dawn.

He smiled. "Yeah, that's true. Bet no guy's ever done anything like that with you before."

Dawn shook her head. She smiled warmly. Gently held his hand. "I think, after all we've done and been through, we deserve a little R & R…" She gave him a seductive look. "And you played your cards right, mister."

"My cards?"

Wait… the car ride back, after he rescued her from Mastermind and Doctor Troyd at that abandoned warehouse… she said if he played his cards right, he'd get to see her naked again.

Suddenly Ray had a burst of energy. He sprung up from the couch, still holding Dawn's hand. "We're gonna… be in my room… if you need us," he said to Luke and Charlie. "Please don't need us."

The young couple disappeared into his room.

Luke shook his head and smiled.

It was going to take some time before the world got back to normal. Cities around the world – especially New York and Los Angeles – suffered a lot of damage.

Although Mastermind's "cure" – the BioGen X chemical – had ceased production, many people were still infected. Those he had touched to transform all returned back to normal. But those who changed because of the mutagenic chemical would never be the same again.

Unless…

"Here," said Doctor Troyd, handing a compact disc to one of the president's science advisors. "This is the real cure," he said.

The science advisor seemed skeptical.

"I don't blame you. Go ahead. Test it. Do whatever you need to do. I saved it in case Mastermind ever tried to turn me or my daughter. It should restore those who've already mutated, if we don't wait too long to treat them."

The scientist still had doubts, but took the disc just in case.

"Now if you'll excuse me, I need to catch a plane back to Los Angeles. Here's my card if you ever need to hire my services."

Doctor Troyd opened the door to his apartment in Los Angeles. It was quiet. He threw his keys on the table. Walked into the living room. And there he saw her.

There, on the couch, was his teenage daughter, still watching the news. He stood there. She was alive. She was okay.

She thought she heard something. She turned around and saw him. "Daddy!" she exclaimed, running up to him. She hugged him. *"Daddy,"* she signed, *"Are you okay? I saw the news."*

He stopped her. "I can hear again," he said.

"What?" she asked aloud, still signing. "...Really?"

He nodded. "He kept his promise."

They hugged again. "I'm just glad you're safe," she said.

"Me too," he replied, holding her tighter.

"I was so worried about you, Daddy."

"I know. I'm sorry," said the eccentric doctor. "You're safe now. We're both safe now."

"So," asked Charlie, looking at the pieces of Luke's armored space suit on the floor, "think you'll ever need this thing again?"

"You kidding?" asked Luke. "Simeon said the crystals can open up portals all over the galaxy! I can't wait to go exploring!"

His uncle chuckled. "That's my nephew."

"But if you're asking if I'll ever need it to fight a super villain again... let's hope not. But," he said, "if I do, I'll be glad to do it. I mean, I know you feel bad for dragging me into all this. And I know Mom and Dad wanted to keep me out of this world... But, I gotta say, it felt *great* being a super hero."

"Some people are just born to do great things," his uncle said.

"I mean, like, for the first time ever, I feel like my life finally makes sense. Like I belong. Like I finally know who I am. I mean, most of the time, I had no idea what I was doing. But it felt good trying to figure it out."

"Wanna know a secret?" Uncle Charlie asked. "Most of us don't know what we're doing half the time. We're just doing the best we can, with what we've got. And Luke, you did really good, with what you had."

"Thanks Uncle."

"You really believe you'll get your powers back someday?"

"I hope so. I think so." Luke held his glowing pink crystal in his hand. "But even if they never fix that pyramid on Sekhmet, chances are, there's another pyramid out there somewhere. And if there is, I'm going to find it."

Charlie nodded. "It's a big universe out there. Anything's possible."

"We got lucky, you know," said Luke.

"I know it feels that way."

"No, seriously. That hacker guy, from London. If he hadn't edited Mastermind's video and uploaded it to all the news stations, it would've been a *lot* harder fighting Mastermind. We got the advantage when the cops and troops jumped in. They might've been fighting *us* instead of Mastermind, if it wasn't for that video."

"I suppose you're right," said Uncle Charlie. "I wonder who he was – or if we'll ever hear from him again."

Luke wondered that about all the original mutants, too. Would he ever see them again? Hopefully they wouldn't cause much trouble, because Luke and Ray didn't have their powers anymore. But Dawn still did. And Luke had his armored battle suit. That was a definite advantage. It was a start.

It was amazing how one bitter old janitor nearly destroyed and took over the world, with nothing more than an Astaria crystal. Maybe there was a reason these crystals were hidden and buried. Maybe there was a reason only five symbols were recorded on the Tablet of Ningishzida. Maybe there was a reason the aliens removed their special pyramids from Planet Earth a long time ago.

Maybe humans weren't ready for such power.

But if any new would-be villains should rise again, Luke was ready. With or without powers, he'd be there. And he had a feeling Dawn and Ray would be ready too.

Hopefully that would never happen though. Hopefully the world would stay safe – or at least, manageable with normal means and powers. Not super powers. Because right now, he didn't have any super powers. Okay, a super suit, yes, but he missed his ability to travel through time.

He really hoped he'd get that back one day.

He held the glowing pink crystal in his hand. Maybe one day could get here a lot sooner. "Uncle," he asked, "are there any other pyramids you know about?"

Luke's adventure was just beginning.

And his wasn't the only one…

A little over a hundred miles away, in the middle of the Mojave Desert, Mastermind's glowing crystal sat lodged in the dirt, half buried. The man's torn clothes laid in the sand around it, a fading reminder of how close the Earth came to annihilation.

But just then, a bat mutant appeared.

Echo looked around, finding the portal closed and Mastermind gone. Then he noticed something in the sand. The crystal. He used to have one of these. Before Mastermind took control of his mind. Before he became a mutant.

He walked over to it.

The black mutant picked up that crystal and held it in his bat-like hand. He knew just how to use this…

End of Book One

For more *Adventures of Captain Future*
and other stories by David Michaels

www.superpowersunlimited.com

Thanks for Reading

DAVID MICHAELS is the author of the Adventures of Captain Future series. He began his writing career many years ago by self-publishing sci-fi/fantasy short stories online. He now writes for both the written page and the silver screen. And if you catch him in person, he'll tell you he's actually a time-traveling super hero himself. We're pretty sure he's just kidding, though.

He currently resides in Burbank, CA. In an apartment. With thirty-two roommates. Because that's the only way to afford rent in California.

Thanks for reading this book. If you'd like to send fan mail or just say "hey", you can reach him at david@superpowersunlimited.com.

17108974R00210

Made in the USA
Charleston, SC
27 January 2013